PURSUED

SHILO CREED

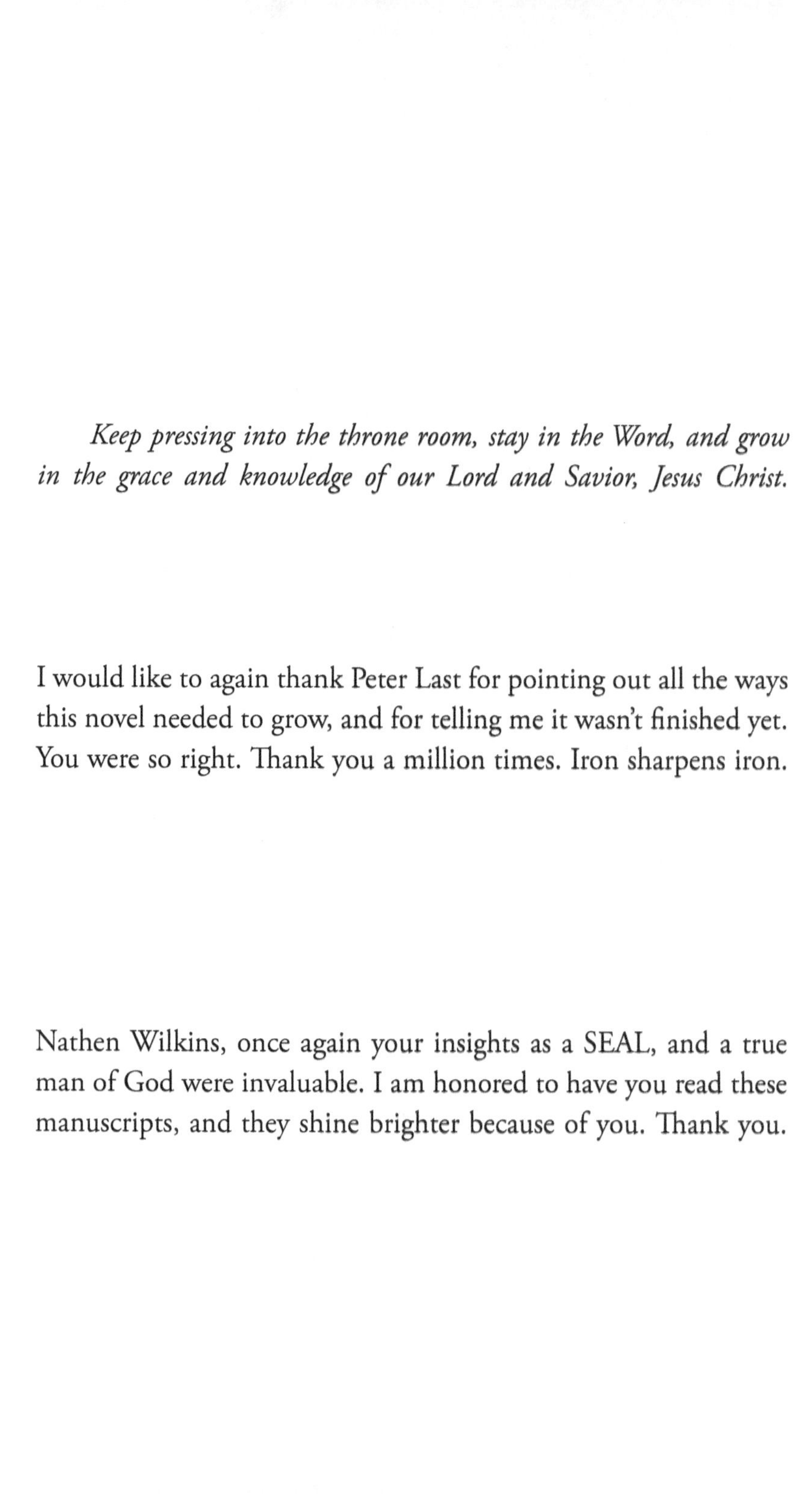

Keep pressing into the throne room, stay in the Word, and grow in the grace and knowledge of our Lord and Savior, Jesus Christ.

I would like to again thank Peter Last for pointing out all the ways this novel needed to grow, and for telling me it wasn't finished yet. You were so right. Thank you a million times. Iron sharpens iron.

Nathen Wilkins, once again your insights as a SEAL, and a true man of God were invaluable. I am honored to have you read these manuscripts, and they shine brighter because of you. Thank you.

1
SAGE

DESTITUTE OF THE FIRE OF GOD, NOTHING ELSE COUNTS; POSSESSING THE FIRE, NOTHING ELSE MATTERS.~ SAMUEL CHADWICK ~ 1934

Battle is a heartbeat away. The air screams it, growing so still that it steals my breath in the midnight and congeals on my skin like frost. City lights glint off abandoned cars in a shadowed Wilmington alley, out of gas like all the others. Ahead, Jacob drops one fist, stopping me in the shadows, spring-loaded from his SEAL training and in full control.

My heart rate spikes, making me long for the safety of a sterile exam room, where rules and outcomes are predictable. A faint scuff on the rooftop means we're not safe here. They want Jacob most of all, so they can tear him apart to discover what makes him so powerful. A single shot is all it would take. The thought burns until stepping out between Jacob and the forces pursuing us is my only option.

Every molecule inside zeros in on him, my entire universe condensed into human form. Project 157 bound us together, entwining our futures, and now all the New World Order's power is seeking to bring us in. If they kill him, will I cease to exist too?

Darkness blurs his motion, using cover as he pulls me down next to a delivery van with two flat tires.

"What are you doing?" he asks.

Words won't come as Jacob holds up three fingers. Eyes glinting, he scans the roof lines behind, lifting two more. At least five agents.

Every camera, satellite and operative are searching for us. An acidic taste fills my mouth as the starlight frames Jacob's face. But the past is inescapable: He's shackled to the wall, growling against the pain Dr. Sutton inflicts, and watching for me over his shoulder while under heavy guard. The cold cell they locked me in is a cage that's impossible to escape, deep inside.

The uncontrollable energy of a jump shrieks through me, forcing my muscles to contract. It's the same force that made Jacob's strong heart flatline multiple times after enduring Project 157.

"No," I whisper, resisting it.

Not now.

Jacob shows no signs that the green haze is taking him; he's still scanning the rooftops with complete focus. My vision tunnels as the voltage climbs, my breath too fast. I'll never survive, not when that world almost killed him. If you smell something dead, run. The scars on his forearm and shoulder match a lion's bite to perfection.

Covering the faint haze seeping from my center with my hands is useless. Like that will stop it. The telltale color is a guarantee that a jump is imminent.

Jacob was unconscious for days after the experiment, while surviving what he called the spirit. The chances of my dying in either place are so much higher. My body isn't like his, conditioned and resilient.

Jacob turns, so close and alive in the midnight, mouthing a word. *One.*

I stifle a moan as K-60 spikes inside every cell.

Two.

His wide shoulders bunch, contracting. He points to the left, the movement slight, at a tight opening between two buildings.

Three.

Chaos erupts, shifting the night. He takes my hand, pulling me forward, the devastating current sizzling.

The van's window implodes. Gun rounds strike a metal ladder straight ahead, sparking in the gloom. My stomach dry heaves, green fog filling my vision as I stumble. Please, no. Just stay here with Jacob. The terror of how Rivera died makes me trip—a warrior sacrificed at Admiral Ash's command.

A shadow flits, weapon firing as a soldier descends a second-story ladder. Jacob explodes into action, and the crushing grip of energy expands without his touch. He meets the enemy with a high kick, ripping him down and laying the man out with in three swift moves.

Years of medical training catalog the injuries Jacob inflicts. Broken rib, internal bleeding, severe concussion, crushed windpipe.

Shards of concrete slice my cheek, and the hot rivulet of blood pushes down the impending jump. Another round pings to the left. I shriek, covering my head, running from the potassium's power as much as the men hunting us.

The air turns to sludge as haze flows from my core. Jacob spins, pushing me aside and slashing a soldier behind with a swift knife strike. He slams the man's sternum with his shoulder, the movement blurred by speed.

"Run!"

His command hits me, repelling the otherworldly sensation, losing me from the energy spike. My legs churn as fear strangles me. Isn't one world's terror enough? A sound above reveals another form descending. Jacob snatches me backward, a pistol upraised, then obliterates the lock on the doorway with the gun's handle.

He dashes through the door, scanning, weapon steady. Inside, the darkness is complete. I cling to the back of his shirt as he moves fast, veering toward a set of stairs; we freeze at the top, listening. Cubicles fill the room.

"Breathe, Sage," Jacob whispers, and I force a slow inhale, trying to match his calm. "They're in the front entrance. When I tap you, run for the far door. Stay low."

The moments creep by as too much oxygen makes me lightheaded. My vision adjusts as I lean against Jacob's solid chest, absorbing his control, letting the touch wash away the last vestiges of haze.

A shadow deepens to our right. Jacob's firm grip alone keeps me from bolting. Two more figures enter the opposing door, silent and sweeping with rifles.

Jacob's hand clamps harder. What is he waiting for? They'll be on us in a second, weaving through the room. He releases my arm, bumps my back, and we surge straight toward them. My arms go up, hip catching a desk, stumbling hard.

A man roars, the wall shudders. Jacob drives the soldier's weapon upward as they collide. My shoulder slams into the doorframe, rolling past as something crashes behind. Jacob shoves a soldier against the wall as I scramble away. Crouching in the hallway, everything has fallen silent, I refuse breath, as every sense hones in, desperate for him to come.

Please, Jacob. Please come through that door.

Deep grunts echo through the opening, then eerie quiet. Counting makes it worse. He should be here by now. Movement causes me to flinch. He kneels so close, his knee touching mine. "Put these on."

A still-warm Kevlar vest and helmet almost drown my slim frame. Jacob's already wearing a set. He puts an earbud in and listens as he sets a rifle in my hands.

His fingers run over the one he kept. "A .300 Blackout. My favorite."

"Hope you're not planning on me using this." The heavy weapon strains my arms.

"Well, don't point it at me, for starters. Did you miss basic or something?" He pushes the barrel toward the ground as his eyes glint with a teasing light. "I left your safety on."

"Thanks," I whisper, longing to be an asset, like I was on the Olympia as Ash and Dr. Sutton experimented on him. Out here, it's me who needs protecting.

He presses the radio further into his ear. "South window exit is our best bet." His deep voice settles my nausea. "Next time we see operatives, turn and check behind like you own the place. We're just two more of the boys now, and with so many teams searching, they won't recognize everyone."

My mouth is as dry as cotton, but Jacob's at home with the rifle and night vision goggles he snaps down over his eyes. The weapon in my hands proves I'm not cut out for this world. Boot camp almost killed me. I'm a medic who loves well-ordered labs and data.

"It'll be a long run, but we've got to get out of their search pattern. You good with that?"

His concern galvanizes me. "Sure."

He nods, then clicks my goggles down. The room lights up in shades of black and white instead of the green I expected. The horrid color turns my stomach. At least I didn't jump. Maybe I won't.

A heavy sense of doom pushes in at the uncontrollable nature of the K-60 that seeped into me from Jacob after the experiment. It was worth it to protect him from them. Jacob stands, and we pass the men on the floor.

He crouches below the south window and eases one eye over the sill.

"It's clear." He listens for a moment. "Basic parachute landing fall."

"What?"

He flips his goggles up and frowns at me. "You didn't go to jump school?"

"No."

"Keep your arms crossed in front of you. Land on your toes with your knees bent, then absorb the fall by crumpling to the side. Each joint gets a little of your weight. I'll go first." He takes my rifle, tucking it under one arm, and rolls out the second-story window without another word. I stretch forward, stifling a shout. He lands like a cat, rolling to flip over his shoulder, then to his feet.

Before thought can stop me, I climb the sill, easing onto my stomach, dangling by my fingertips. Eyes squeezed shut, I let go, and the rough brick sears my palms. Too fast!

Jacob's arms catch mine and he pulls us backward, absorbing the impact. He has me up with the rifle in my hands before I get a breath. Two soldiers rush around the building. Jacob spins away from them, scanning the perimeter. He barks over his shoulder, "Cover the east side."

They jog forward and disappear past the corner.

Jacob turns to me. "Great job following directions."

His amusement at my frozen stance makes me huff, then he sets off down the dark road at a punishing pace that I can't keep for long.

"Jacob."

He slows, not even winded, as we hug the deepest shadows.

"Here." He takes the rifle. "We have to push it." He squeezes my hand as I gasp for air. "The city is going to be crawling now that they've sighted us. There's no time."

The heavy chop of a helicopter thrums in the night. It's scanning for us. Fear crashes in. "What chance do we have?"

"There's always a chance, Sage. Everything is possible to one who believes."

He pulls a small box from his Kevlar vest and dips his finger into a black paste. "This will confuse the face recognition cameras, plus it's got infrared blockers."

He applies the paste in large random blocks on my face. The gentle touch is a far cry from what his hands can deal out. His eyes soften as he avoids the cut on my cheek, and soon, we're both like modern art, but it's too thin a shield against the all-seeing eyes.

"Is it just me, or does Wilmington seem like a third world country?" I ask, glaring at the littered streets and run-down buildings.

He glances around. "Been a long time since I was off duty. When was the last time you were?"

"Almost a year."

"That was before global leadership took over," he scowls as two men slink past, hoods pulled low. "I'm less than impressed with the results. But step one for us is the old rail station. There's an emergency cache in a locker there." He scans the dim sidewalk.

"Who does it belong to?"

He sighs, frowning at the rifles. "Team Three keeps four or five at different locations for emergencies. There are some traceless cards, a clean phone, duct tape, the essentials. We're gonna have to ditch these, which is a shame." He sets the .300 Blackout in a dark alley, then takes off the vest, keeping two pistols. It's a relief to take off the extra weight as I scan the road, knowing anyone breaking curfew like us has a reason to.

"Won't Ash be watching the locker?" I ask as we set out at a brisk walk. A few street lights work here and expose too much, so I keep my head down and a desperate grip on Jacob's hand. There isn't a moving car in sight, not since the N.W.O. outlawed personal vehicles. Welcome to freedom.

"Can't watch what you don't know about. They're not official. Still, we surfaced here, so Wilmington is ground zero." The spark in his eye clarifies that he's on his A-game, putting his vast skills to use.

My tongue is so dry the words stick. "Did you feel that jump coming?"

He stops, his mouth flat. "When?"

A shrug downplays my dismay that he didn't. "When they found us."

I grit my teeth and pick up the pace, unwilling to let him see the fear shimmering. He snatches my hand again, engulfing it in his. Jumping would leave us limp and exposed, in need of resuscitation. How could I shield him now if he were lying comatose in the street?

"Sage."

My stomach churns. We need a code or something, or a way to stop this from happening, but a lab's necessary for that, with all the specialized equipment we'd run from on the Olympia.

"Sage." He stops, swinging me to face him in the dim streetlight. "We'll be all right."

He's so sure in the face of this chaos.

"What if you jumped in the middle of that fight?" Anxiety rears up, too strong to contain, knowing what Ash would do if he caught him. What he would do to both of us, but Jacob's clear blue eyes don't flinch.

"But I didn't," he grimaces. "It's been four days since the last one." The regret in his voice is the polar opposite of my thoughts. "Maybe…" He has to force himself to say the words. "Maybe, away from the Engage, I can't."

It burns me that he wants it, when I can still feel his cold body twitch under the defibrillators, or see his glassy eyes and the hours of watching him lie in a coma, guarding him from Sutton's plans for brain implants. Still, the thought has merit. If distance from the ship and Project 157 keeps him here, all the better.

"We need a plan. You've got to give me all the warning you can when it's coming. I don't have my medical equipment or a safe place to hide you."

He studies me; then his eyes soften. "All right, but it's possible the effects are wearing off."

The pummeling weight of worst-case scenarios makes me grasp the idea, but the haze that flowed from my stomach says I better stay on my toes. He draws me closer, sensing I'm on the far edge of okay. "We're going to stick together, Sage, you and me. Getting over the border into Central America is mission one. We can do this."

"Sure, we can outrun the entire New World Order and The Collective. Easy."

"Right. You up for hitting the locker tonight? Hostiles are only going to get thicker around here. Give them enough time and they'll find us on the cameras."

A fluttery feeling pulses in my hands. "Yeah, I've got too much adrenaline to rest."

We weave down the dark streets, hand in hand, like any other couple, out after curfew, faces painted. Jacob and Sage, the strangest pair ever. His grip tightens, and he's got that faraway vibe in his eye, as if remembering the world he goes to when he jumps.

We veer around a few people standing on the sidewalk. Everyone has something to hide, and no one stays still for long, because every time the camera picks them up, they lose citizen points. Without them, they won't get toilet paper or food. Turns out tracking everything isn't as fun as they said it would be. We keep our faces toward the pavement, hugging the shadows.

Jacob's square jaw is a far better study than the decaying city. He impressed me before I met him. Just reading his file from a medical standpoint was enough. Jacob Carter is two levels past the top, and that's why Ash chose him for the experiment. He needed someone strong enough to survive the punishment of light and sound that killed everyone else on board the ship. The same thing that's coming to kill me.

There's no way to know what the experiment's strange form of potassium will do to us. K-60 facilitates the jumps, but it also lends increased energy and wound healing. Getting through tonight without the extra mental clarity would be next to impossible. Especially now, pushed past my limits.

Jacob stops beside me. "Here's the plan."

Foot traffic is heavier here. After the last pandemic, with cities starving during lockdowns, the night has taken on another life. People are desperate for the essentials, but trying to slip under the government's thumb is dangerous beyond compare. Distant gunshots make everyone flinch.

"The locker is in the top row at the old rail station. Number 504. You get the bag while I cover you." I scowl as he relays the combination. "Be sure to use your knuckle on the keypad, grab the pack and exit to the south."

My lip draws up, struggling to orient compass points.

"That's straight past the lockers, then down the steps. There's a grove of trees where we'll reconnect."

Air hisses through my tight lips. "What if they find me?"

"Curl up into a ball and stay still. I'll come for you." His eyes glitter in the night, confident.

"Promise?" My laugh can't cover my desperation.

His eyes hold mine. "I owe you, remember? It's not something I take lightly."

It's easier to pretend things will be all right when he's in front of me. "When do I go?"

"Should be another three minutes' walk." Our shoulders brush as we close the distance, cutting around a man whose dark eyes don't leave my figure. Jacob's glare makes him turn away. My heart pounds when we stop at a corner, studying the station.

"Cross the open area fast." He studies the silhouettes of the buildings. Just a shred of his confidence would be amazing. "I'll move first. Count to sixty, then go." Catching my expression, he adds, "I'm watching over you, Sage."

He leaps high to reach a fire ladder's lowest rung, pulling himself hand over hand, then disappearing into the night.

Sixty comes way too fast.

I imagine bullets and crumpling to the ground. With a moan, I start forward, legs trembling, tugging my hood lower to shield my short, blonde hair. A screen on the rail station shows a news report. World peace. The New World Order has ushered in a perfect era; there is no war. An empty laugh escapes. Because they already killed the resistance.

Locker 504 is under a light, whose glare reveals me mis-typing the combination number, waiting an eternity for the screen to clear, heart slamming, before trying again. To get it right, I have to expose my face to the camera, but the door clicks, swinging open. The backpack inside is heavy, and I don't bother shutting the locker as I rush toward the stairs, struggling to get the straps over my shoulders.

Two figures move up the far edge of the steps, watching my hurried flight, but my skin crawls on reaching the park. Jacob is nowhere in sight. I shrink against a trunk, heart twisting.

They've taken him.

Splitting up was stupid. The bark is rough on my palms as an unnatural stillness descends, with only the Spanish moss wavering in the light breeze.

They're here.

The knowledge is rock solid, though the path ahead is empty. A faint whisper of sound behind, then a harsh gloved hand covers my mouth and I thrash against the sudden pressure.

There's a whoosh of leaves and the attacker crumples under a shadowed figure. Jacob. Motion converges from both sides as two more dark forms rush in. Jacob's silhouette is clear cut as he pops off four shots, plunging the park into starlight. A writhing mass of men takes him, the pistol winging into the night.

In the dim moonlight, he rises from the mob as his flashing hands and boots create a barrier around him. A third figure snakes behind Jacob, leaping for his neck. Jacob reaches over and clamps the man's neck in an iron grip. When he bends forward to flip his opponent, the others spring on him.

I draw the pistol, but can't be certain to miss Jacob. A shadow rushes my way, and I grimace, pulling the trigger. But he's there, with heavy arms crushing my ribs. He shoves my gun-hand down, twisting it up behind my back. Jacob throws off two of his attackers, but the others don't let up as the man hikes my arm higher.

Jacob goes down and I buck with every ounce of strength, growling. They roll closer, locked in battle, into the deep dark under the trees. The man gripping me lets out a strangled sound. Then, somehow, it's Jacob towing me forward. "Run!"

In mid-stride, a black cord descends over his face, then constricts on his exposed neck. His veins bulge. Snarling, he slams backward into the man who's choking him. Jacob's hand flies to a knife on his opponent's belt. It flashes in the moonlight as he severs the cord, drawing a heavy stream of blood from the attacker.

"Sage!" he shouts, before he's locked again in hand-to-hand combat. I'm no threat, and they all converge on Jacob, forcing the knife from his hand as they pin him against the ground.

One turns toward me, terrifying, his face cloaked in goggles and a mask. I make it two strides before he crushes me and throws me down next to Jacob. The men struggle to keep Jacob pinned, then one of them nods and all six turn switches off on their vests.

"Communications off." The largest of them stands, pulling up his night vision, revealing a chiseled face as he glares down.

"Carter. Dishonorable discharge was the last thing I expected from you. Criminal." He spits the last word as a curse. There's a tenor in his voice that catches me off guard, like it's a personal injury. He nods, and another man eases his hold on Jacob's neck.

"Jones, you know that's a lie," Jacob snarls.

Does he know these men? They'd been waiting here, banking on his coming for the locker, the only ones who knew about it. Team three. My chest constricts as time's uncaring march drags us toward disaster.

Jones steps in, sets his heavy boot on Jacob's exposed neck, killing me. "You murdered a teammate."

Jacob glares up at Jones, gaze unwavering under the pressure.

"Ash killed Rivera." Jacob's voice grates with a note of pain at the memory.

"Ash?" Jones questions, his eyes dropping for a heartbeat. "Why should I believe you?" Still, his boot eases up a hair.

"The bullet I took for you in the desert ought to be enough."

They glare at each other, warlords, supreme operatives. I can't breathe. One of them swears and Jones withdraws his boot.

"You shut your communications off because you know I didn't do it. You know me. All of you. Rivera and I…" the words choke Jacob worse than the fight, and the agony in his voice makes me cringe. "Admiral Ash forced us into an experiment. Rivera didn't make it. I was re-classified as government property."

Jones hisses and the rest of the team flip their goggles up, more human in an instant. Jacob bucks hard, gaining his feet, and the air snaps with an electric tension as they eye each other.

"I don't want a fight," he says, his hands spread. "But I won't be Ash's guinea pig. He doesn't own me." Jacob glares at the men.

A look of dread passes among them. With the N.W.O. takeover, the thought of slavery isn't far off. Jones flicks the radio on his shoulder. "Wrong target. I repeat, incorrect target."

Breath returns as Jacob nods at him, and Jones throws the pack near his feet. "Got bad news for you. Ash is being inaugurated by The Collective as High Chancellor of the U.S. this week. Word is, they're rolling out mandatory chip implants next month. You won't be able to buy peanuts without one. The noose will only get tighter." He turns to the men. "Boys, this cover-up's gotta be immaculate or we'll all become science experiments."

My stomach heaves as Jacob tugs me up. Ash, ruling the U.S.? Everything's spinning out of control. He'll have every weapon at his disposal to catch us.

"Run hard, Carter."

Jacob clasps Jones's hand with a nod; then the team fades into the night as if they never existed. Jacob's hand slides back into mine, and he tows me forward, letting out a disgusted sigh.

"Are you hurt?" I ask, longing for my medical equipment.

He strides into the deepest shadows. "I should have known they were here."

"The way you did with Tex?" His abilities are a mystery entwined with K-60 somehow. "When you saw in the dark?"

He gives an empty laugh. "That's what Ash thinks, Sage, but I didn't see with these eyes."

Jacob tugs me behind the corner of a building, motioning for silence, then three soldiers trot past, scanning the park with weapons ready. The way you saw them coming? It's tough to tell what flows from his training and what comes from… the spirit, as he calls it.

"When the lights went off on the Olympia, it was as if something settled onto my shoulders. An ability I don't have all the time."

We jog down a dark alley. How long will it be until they find my face from the locker footage? I'm struggling to keep up in more ways than one. "So, sometimes you have this… ability, and sometimes not?"

"It isn't ability, it's more like... anointing."

The air gets clearer for a second, sending goosebumps down my arms. What was that? The word pleases him, but the power in it shocks me. Did that come from the spirit, too? Is that what's making my hair stand on end?

"When I saw Team Three closing in back there, I went in. Just me. I didn't wait for that quiet voice inside, or any direction from the spirit. See where all my skills got me? With a boot to my throat. If I don't learn to pay attention..." He hisses through his teeth. "It was stupid, that's all."

We jog through the night, but I can't sort out his meaning. Does God speak to him? He stops, easing one eye around a building, then draws us further into the shadows.

"So, you're not a superhero?" I ask, while his arm stays wrapped around my waist. "Bummer."

It makes him laugh, like I knew it would. "Superheroes don't slip up, do they? I didn't pay enough attention to my spirit, and I'm as fallible as anyone on my own."

The helicopters are thrumming, searching in an expanding circle from our first appearance.

"If I don't stay sharp..." He lets out a harsh breath, and his eyes glint. "They took me down. That could have been it for both of us. That's too high a cost."

I want to tell him he's wrong, but he won't hear me. He didn't become a SEAL by giving in, and losing is his worst-case scenario, no matter what world he's fighting in.

"It took your entire team to do it," is all I say.

He frowns. "The more time that passes, the harder it is to pay attention to that inner knowledge. My training and instincts aren't enough to get us out. I need the Almighty's leading."

His words send a chill to my core. Can he know God like that? It's the K-60 that causes his episodes, but I can't erase how he'd fought Tex on the Olympia, or that he knows things he shouldn't. The thoughts pile up like an avalanche, far too heavy, so I veer away from them.

"What are we going to do about Ash?" It's not a better subject, that's for sure.

His jaw clenches as we slip through the ruins of the affluent city. "First, we gain some breathing room. Take things one step at a time." He sighs as we avoid the cameras. "Physical skill and training are where anyone can fail. But the spirit—that's where victory is." He pulls me forward while the helicopters pound closer. "It's time to go underground."

I manage a grunt as my legs burn from the jog. Jacob tugs his hood over his face, leaving his square jaw showing, and grips my hand tighter. My lifeline.

We stop under the ancient trees lining Fifth Ave, where a wrought-iron fence protects a historical building. The stone sign reads Burgwin Wright House, but there's also a small metal one pushed into the grass. Permanently closed. Gatherings prohibited for public safety.

"At least there won't be any staff for us to deal with," Jacob says.

"You mean for you to deal with?" I counter.

Half of Jacob's mouth curls into a familiar grin. "Right."

The light in his eyes eases the tension in my shoulders.

"Two cameras. One on the porch, the other on the sign." He drops the pack, taking out two small, bright pen lights. It takes a lot of adjusting, but we get them set up, pointed at the cameras to confuse the image.

"We're clear. Move out." He boosts me over the fence, and my jeans catch, so I flop onto the lawn. He leaps over, the motion as smooth as glass.

The double locks on the wooden door slow him for a few seconds, then he crouches within, like a teenager pulling shenanigans. "Came in here with my cousin when we were fourteen. Used the tunnel for a lot of things back then." One brow arches, making my heart catch. "But you're better company."

We move along the hallway lined with black and white photos of Wilmington in the 1800s, the floor creaking. He has history here, and picturing him as a boy twists me inside. There's so much more to him than what I know about. Who was he before Project 157? The thought sparks a desire that grips like thirst. Jacob crouches at a door that's half my height, and one swift strike from his boot swings it inward with an eerie creak.

"How long will we be down there?" I ask, veins constricting near the dark hole.

"Less than a mile. Ready?" He bends a clear tube, and it casts a green glow into the narrow, wet down shaft. Sweat breaks out at the color; it's all too familiar. I'd rather go without light than see that horrid tint, but he's staring with rapt attention as it bathes his face. I can read it there, the intense longing. It terrifies me, remembering how the Engage disappeared when he stared at it.

I snatch the stick out of his hand, hiding it behind my back. "Jacob, I need you here."

His eyes snap to mine, present again, and a rueful smile lifts one corner of his mouth. "It's…" His expression falls, jaw clenching. "I'd give about anything to go back."

His words are like a gut punch. "Well, you'll have to wait until we're further from Ash's shackles."

"Doesn't seem like I have a choice, anyway." He tilts his head toward the tunnel. "Ladies first."

The glow stick makes the narrow tunnel even more sinister. "You're sure about this, right?"

"It's the only place we won't be dodging cameras. Doesn't it look relaxing in there?" His bantering tone eases the coil of stress. That's Jacob, hard as steel, with a glint of mischief in his eye.

The ancient ladder creaks as it takes my weight, and the pressure expands as I teeter there. This is a bad idea, with all of Wilmington waiting to crush us.

"The tunnels are sturdy, they'll hold together another hundred years," he says. My skin pricks. Can he read my thoughts? Must be the cool air wafting up from the darkness. Right.

He crouches by the entrance, his blue eyes level with mine, too close. Too alive. So far inside my guard, just like he's always been. I soak up his confidence, then descend into the dank, cramped tunnel, watching for snakes. Aren't there venomous ones in North Carolina?

The roof of the tunnel keeps the entire city of Wilmington at bay. Cringing, I shield the light as much as possible as we creep along. Time slows without orientation, blending with the musky air until the sound of rushing water turns my muscles to mush. "We won't swim out of here, will we?"

I rub my arms as Jacob studies the rotting edges of a wooden grate above his head. "Did that to you once already, figure that's enough."

With a violent slam, he forces the dented grate from its connection to the ceiling. "We should be east of the Cape Fear River."

Hating to let Jacob near the light, I shine it up the opening. He frowns. "Ladder's rotted out on this shaft. Stand back a minute. This is going to get messy."

Algae on the damp wall clings to my shirt. Muscles bunching, he presses his elbows into the opening above his head, surging upward, inching higher in short bursts, grunting as earth and rocks rain down around him. The choking dust makes me turn, then he's gone.

"Jacob!" My voice is a squeak, as every nightmare I had as a kid rushes down the tunnel. Wasps and snakes. I can't move.

"Sage, take my hand."

The pile of loose dirt shifts as I scramble up. His scarred hand reaches for mine, imprinting forever. He hauls me out of the tight opening and into the embrace of a bush. Thorns catch as I brush sand off his shoulders, the tension fading at his nearness.

"About a mile south, we'll drop into the industrial area. It's more open there."

We keep to the shadows, avoiding a footpath next to the river. For Jacob, everything is simple. Conquer one objective after another; for me, walking a straight line is tough enough right now.

A tangled mass of worry and what-ifs swirl around the green energy, but Jacob's silhouette centers me; this is his world. Extract hostages, overcome unthinkable odds. I'm a Navy medic, a radiation nerd, with anxiety that's eating me alive.

The wind carries a snatch of a human voice, and I shrink back as a gang cuts through the trees toward us. Jacob steps out, chin high. They spread out, menacing, as he snatches a knife and gives it to me. "Put your back against a tree and use this if you need to."

I reverse directions, my mouth dry, wishing the irritating glow stick was gone—should've ditched it long ago. Three figures leap forward, but Jacob is like a machine. They crawl away without landing a blow.

My hands tingle as I scowl at the large knife that reflects the awful color. Wait. I lost the stick in the tunnel. Green haze sinks from my stomach to float around my feet like a ghost. The first crazed shriek of energy rams through my chest as my muscles go rigid. Just like before a jump.

"No!" I shout, contorting in the iron fist of a jump.

The thugs have regrouped, uneasy in the face of Jacob's skill. One of them points at me, tortured in my own supernatural glow, and a round of swearing echoes. They turn and run into the darkness.

Jacob spins as I grimace, bathed in the haze.

"Sage!" He's there, wrenching the knife from my frozen grip, then touching my face. "Here, stay with me!"

His lungs heave as he steps close, body pressed against mine. I cry out as the energy breaks off, fading. Trembling sets in hard as I crumple into him.

"Remember what I told you?"

My voice wavers like my heartbeat. "Look for a man named Demyen."

"Don't jump without me, Sage. It's a wild place." Now he knows how I feel whenever the K-60 takes him. "Come on, keep moving."

He doesn't let go of my hand until we creep up a decrepit ladder on the side of a three-story abandoned steel plant about a mile to the north. The inky sky seems closer on the flat roof. It feels too close, as if the universe is pressing in. Does the spirit lie just beyond?

A chill snatches my remaining energy as I settle in, hugging my knees. Jacob takes a monocular from the pack, scanning the quiet road. "Trucks will start running near five, before sunrise. The right thing will come."

We split our last bottle of water, but I can't contain my thoughts any longer. "What will we do, Jacob? I mean," my voice catches hard, "can we hide forever? They call it unity, but it's a coup of the globe, and their eyes are everywhere."

"The U.S. is the epicenter, the bullseye. But Central America? We can disappear there for a while, if we're careful. Then I'll implement step two."

My eyes drop from the stars to Jacob, crouched near the roof's edge. A sliver of light glints on his tense jaw as he scans through his monocular, and I struggle to breathe in the sharp wind. "What's step two?"

His fingers clench and my nerves swerve out of control. "I disable Ash and Sutton."

His words suck the oxygen from the atmosphere. "What?"

He gives a slow nod that terrifies me. "I won't let them hunt us forever, Sage. They worship science, and we aren't their only experiments."

"You can't protect the entire world!" I say, throat burning. "How could you stop them?"

His eyes glitter in the starlight as he studies the sky. "Something will come up."

Jacob doesn't play by the same rules, and so much of him is untouchable, and forcing him to change course is like harnessing the wind. Dread and longing emulsify into an elixir that tells my future. My universe condenses into this man, the one determined to dive into the fire.

He settles beside me, my heart rate easing when he blocks the breeze. His voice rumbles straight into my ear. "I'm sorry you got dragged into all of this."

The scruff on his jaw is perfect, catching the starlight. Blinking back tears, breathing in the scent of him, the truth implodes in my soul. Jacob will always be a part of me, no matter how much time we get. I hate step two, but I love him for it, too.

What if he had a different nurse on the Olympia? Even now, with everything that's happened, I'd never change our past. "I'm not."

He studies me, reaching for the stray lock of hair the wind tugs, but pulling back. "You could have stayed normal."

"Normal is boring." I shrug, sniffing. "Maybe a little boring would be nice."

His gaze draws me in, as deep as the ocean. I lean closer, letting the future go, because there's only this moment with him so close.

"I belong here with you, Jacob."

The semi-truck rumbles over a rough road after hours of heat that build under the rippling tarp. Its full load of corn has been a soft ride since we snuck in. The kernels rattle all around, and silky dust coats my skin. Jacob singled this one out in Wilmington, the only freight they didn't inspect at the state line because of its broken tarp mechanism. How did he know? The grain leaving the starving city feels like a coffin surrounding me. The perfect logic of the N.W.O.

"Hurry, Sage," Jacob says, but the words sag inside my dehydrated brain without effect.

I stopped sweating in the intense heat hours ago, and my thoughts and muscles feel like syrup. Falling is probable as the road zips past near the rear of the truck. But Jacob's there, towing me through the corn toward the ladder.

We're slowing, and it takes an age to realize it's late afternoon. My vision blurs, everything too dry in the hot dust. Jacob lifts the tarp, peering out. "We're in Florida, near Ocala. This is our stop."

He cradles me from behind as I stumble down the metal ladder. We hit the ground as the truck approaches a stop sign, and I lose my balance. Jacob carries me through a ditch into an orchard, out of sight. It feels safer under the leaves, but that's foolish; satellites are searching for us, and even the sky is our enemy. Are they using thermal imaging? Worry ripples higher, growing into a hurricane.

"Open your mouth," Jacob squeezes half an orange, holding it above me. Its sweet juice makes me shiver as it hits my tongue.

"Oh, that's good." Energy spreads to the rest of my body as he scoops up two more from the ground, brushing them off. When they're gone, my brain is back at full speed.

I cross my arms with a sigh. "Florida, huh? I was hoping for Texas."

"Why?"

He swings the bulging pack over one shoulder. "Because Florida means another boat in order to reach Central America."

"You're a Navy medic and you've got something against boats?"

If only that teasing expression could stay in his eyes. "Yes, sir. Boats are overrated. The last two were traumatic."

"They're better than swimming. You don't like sharks, if I remember right." He puts a section of orange in his mouth, one brow arching.

Watching him is way too enjoyable. On board the Olympia, our roles were clear: nurse and patient. But out here? I turn, scanning the grove, knowing the chances of losing him are too high. Suppressing nerves, I wipe my palms on my pants. "Where to now?"

"I know a guy. He's a… transporter."

"And that means?" I ask.

"Paco moves things, anything, for the right price. He's also… questionable."

"Ah." What sort of man would Jacob label that way?

"He picks up this time of year around Bonita Springs. Which is a lot of miles to cover on foot. We'll have to figure out a ride."

His knowing where we are is just another perk of hanging out with an elite operative. We down some more oranges and set off down a long row of citrus.

Walking provides too much time to think. Too much time to worry. I swat a fly, glad to be sweating again, as the insects and a question pester me. "How did you know that truck had a broken tarp? That it would slip through, uninspected?"

"That's the thing about the spirit. Being there, knowing that it exists, changed everything. It's real, and it's the code this world runs on." He taps his chest, eyes shifting to mine, hesitating. "I think man was created with six senses."

"Six?"

"Yeah, except we lost one when Adam ate the fruit. It was our spiritual sense and the knowledge that it brings."

"But you got it back," I whisper, stepping over roots. On board the Olympia, Jacob knew what to do and when. There is no physical explanation for his ability. I shiver in the wafting heat, swallowing hard.

He nods, and the sheen of tears in his eyes is shocking. "It's like the most incredible treasure. I…"

That place is calling him, like a siren luring him away. Only two hearts on Earth are full of K-60, the mysterious potassium so invaluable to Ash, and my single aim is to keep them together, but doing that when he's longing for a jump doesn't make things easier.

Above the short trees, the corner of a building rises, and a huge silver funnel belches white steam from the distant roof. Jacob's strides lengthen until I'm trotting to keep up. I scan the orchard as he outpaces me. What's making him rush? Goosebumps race up my arms, but there's nothing out of place, no helicopters or pursuit. Cortisol spikes, knowing he's not wrong.

"Jacob," I whisper, needing to know.

He stops, turns toward me. Green haze wafts from his stomach.

"No!"

He looks down, eyes full of ecstasy. A sound makes me flinch. "What is that?"

Jacob's hands can't stop the haze any more than mine could as he scans the sky. "Drones."

The buzz grows by the second, turning my gut sour. They sound like a million giant bees bearing down. My worst nightmare. Throw in a snake, and I'll faint.

"Lots of them," Jacob grimaces. "In a search pattern. They'll have cooled thermal imaging." He curls forward as the glow thickens. "Run."

The word sends a jolt of adrenaline straight into my heart as we sprint toward the building. How much longer until he falls limp? I don't have any water! Without it, Jacob will sink through the ground, and the probability of recovering him then is zero. I've got to find some, stat, or this jump will kill him.

Thoughts pound like ocean waves breaking on shore. I don't have a defibrillator or an IV, nothing at all to keep his body alive if things go haywire. Jacob skids to a stop, scanning the yard between the orchard and the factory. The drones' whir grows, turning my blood cold. They're right here.

"Ten seconds!" Jacob points to the factory wall. A huge propane tank sits beside a set of pipes running into the building with an ethereal growth of ice perched on top of the regulator like stalactites in a cave, forming a shelter of sorts. "There."

Jacob jerks, muscles rigid. There's no time!

"Not here," my cry makes him growl, fending off the intense energy. He stumbles toward the tank as I sling his heavy arm over my shoulder.

I've never touched him while he's jumping, and it rends a cry from my mouth as voltage slams my ribs. So much for my theory that touch will stop it. The shock spreads through my body until breathing becomes impossible. We stagger in the open, exposed.

"The c… cold…" Jacob's jaw locks up, but it's enough. The ice will shield us from the heat sensors.

His rock-hard muscles squeeze as I lurch the last few feet. Wincing, I take the bruising as he locks up, body rigid. I've got to get him beyond the ice before he breaks my neck.

The persistent buzz threatens, closer by the second. Swirling fear and haze mash my thoughts into a tangle. Jacob falls, one boot sticking out past the ice. I dive on top of him in the tight space, jagged ice ripping at my back as the formation of drones sweeps over the trees straight toward us.

Twisting, I jerk on his boot, but his leg won't bend! Maybe the thick sole will shield his body heat. I freeze as the drones scan the yard, keeping my back to them, covering Jacob, finding his eyes frozen on the sky.

He bucks under me as my hair whips in the drones' prop wash. There are so many, and they fail to pass like I hoped.

His hands are going translucent, sinking into the dirt. I need water now! The terror of him disintegrating into the earth forces action. There'd be no recovering his body like this; it was always on the water before. I press against the ice, but my skin freezes to it; there isn't enough time to force it to melt.

The drones move on, their tight grid pattern darkening the sky. I risk a glance over the frozen pipes; twenty yards down the building, a faucet's blue handle beckons. Jacob's muscles jerk; there's no time. Tucking my head, I sprint behind the drones into the open.

I skid on one knee as if I'm stealing a base and crank the handle. Cold water sprays onto my ribs, the sensation like bees' stings. There's a pool of green at my feet!

Wait.

The buzz is back. I whip around, drenched, as one drone splits from the well-organized pack.

It flies straight to Jacob.

Rage boils, as uncontrollable as the haze. I yank the pistol with a growl and launch for the wicked drone that's flying low, flipping the weapon so its barrel is in my hand.

Two strides away, I throw it, letting all the hatred inside push it forward. Rotors spin off in all directions and the drone crashes into the ice. Plastic shards ping as it hits the ground, its camera pointing at the sky near Jacob's feet. I kick it away and leap, squeezing the water onto his stomach.

"Ah!" At the water's touch, Jacob goes limp. His arms are underground! I snatch his shirt, trying to roll him over, but my own muscles go rigid.

With a growl, I fight the K-60 with everything inside. "No!"

Jacob needs my attention, but I'm sopping wet, and the water makes it too easy to jump. I whimper, knowing the drone might have identified him. The thought forces the clamping power of the haze to loosen as I focus hard on Jacob. His arms come free of the earth before he solidifies, avoiding the dangerous middle ground when his body tries to die. My trembling fingers find a steady pulse in his neck.

I glare at the drone, imagining Ash and Dr. Sutton watching footage of a military issue boot behind a juice factory. I scoop up the pistol and hit it again, sand and plastic shards spitting everywhere. "Not today, Ash."

After a careful scan of the area, I gather what's left of the drone and run deep into the trees. The pieces fling wide and I rush back to Jacob.

How long will he be out? Will he remain stable? His leg is easy to move now, so I rummage through the pack. A black hoodie will do. I slice it open with a combat knife. The fabric keeps off the fast-setting dew as I tuck my body close to Jacob's, his heartbeat my only comfort.

I breathe in his nearness, listening hard for drones or footsteps, trying to slow my wild pulse.

2
JACOB

AN EXTRA ORDINARY PERSON IS SOMEONE WHO CONSISTENTLY DOES THE THINGS ORDINARY PEOPLE CAN'T OR WON'T DO.
~ Nido Qubein

A drop of liquid hits my stomach and the incredible freedom of a jump takes me. Everything else is gone; there's only intense speed and the glorious lightness of being outside my body.

Surging faster, the six-dimensional life of the spirit floods in as light solidifies me and water sprays up at my impact in a broad river. Its crystalline flow sends life into every fiber at the liquid embrace. The current sweeps me forward with my arms outstretched. Landing in the river elevates my desire for its voice, and I swim deeper.

A… And they… overcame him by the blood of the Lamb and by the word of their testimony and they loved not their lives unto death.

The words mix with the current that tugs me closer to shore, where my glimmering, golden path lies embedded in the riverbed. Still underwater, a dark shadow spreads as a huge form wavers above. It makes a slippery, gray sort of word rise: *airplane*, but that's wrong; nothing like that exists here. It's gone as fast as it appeared and I stroke hard when my path takes a sharp curve up the bank. The eerie feeling lingers, cold somehow.

At the surface, the light tastes like honey, with a warm yellow sound. One deep breath cleans the shadow from my mind. *I was away too long.* A laugh escapes on the rocky shore, recalling my first time in the spirit. Pitiful was my definition, so desperate for the knowledge and strength of the Almighty. Muscle flexes now, and my scars glow.

"Hadena."

My whisper makes the twin blades snap open, and the solid hilts bring a grin. *It's good to be back.* Pebbles shift as I stride up the bank, following my path into the forest. The hush under the canopy is like my own breath.

One tree looms in the distance, twice as tall as the others, drawing me like a beacon. I lean into a jog, yearning to uncover the mysteries of the Tree's levels.

The air changes within the Tree's canopy, tingling on my skin. The physical realm is like a dream at the edges of consciousness. But the looming threat of failure there lingers, a chilling possibility where I feel the boot on my neck even now. It raises questions that only the spirit can answer.

But near the Tree, all things seem possible, and possible becomes probable with certain knowledge. I trot up the knobby living wood steps, where my glittering golden path leads straight to the third level. A sense of satisfaction wells up, because the simple act of standing here, at the right place and time, is a victory all its own.

"Mara?" I call.

The door swings open of its own accord, but the room is empty, and every sense sharpens as I peer inside.

"Come in!" Her voice is like a bird's song.

Passing the couch makes me shudder; pain once consumed me there, so close to death.

"Jacob!" Mara's ancient face lights up with her long white hair braided and draped over one shoulder.

When I lean down to hug her, she takes my face with both hands, studying my soul.

"Ah! You've been baptized with power! Now, you are ready for true work."

"Yes. It's good to see you."

"Come, come, sit with me for a while." She shuffles to a small table, where I ease into a creaking chair made of sticks and twigs, thankful when it holds.

"Demyen had the same expression when he sat there yesterday," she says, suppressing a smile. "I've been weaving chairs since before you were born, and the both of you together couldn't crush one."

A tiny bird hops to the window, flits to her shoulder, then nestles into her neck. She laughs, her wrinkles crinkling. A sigh escapes me as I taste the colors and hear the scents.

"Haven't seen Demyen for a while," I say, relaxing into the chair.

Mara's eyes gleam as she gazes at me. "There is a strong link between you and Demyen. Your calling it is *one.*"

Demyen's Watcher, Jaden, had said the same.

"It is good that his ancient strength and your youthful vigor serve together. The Almighty's ways are perfect."

"Ancient?" I ask. "He's not much older than me."

"So you think." She raises one brilliant white brow. "He's older than me, *by far.*"

I squint, trying to believe her. She waves a hand, brushing aside the thought.

"We've more important things to cover today." She gazes at the empty room. "Raeual!"

My Watcher materializes from thin air, his massive frame taking up most of the room, right where she's looking. Light flows from his skin as he grins at us.

"We're going to the Brink," Mara says.

Raeual's expression falls and his hands spread before him. "W… why?"

My gaze bounces between them as Raeual's reaction makes my breath come faster.

"Because it is there that seen and unseen mix," she says, making me wonder. "Adriel!" she calls, and another Watcher appears.

Raeual frowns at him, crossing his muscular arms. "We're going to the Brink."

Adriel's brows rise, then he sighs, swiping one hand through short blond hair.

"I'll give you a few moments to prepare," Mara says to the Watchers, taking my elbow and guiding me to a small pitcher of water. "Drink now, Jacob, it will do you good."

She drinks twice as much as me, then lets out a satisfied sigh and stretches her shoulders.

"Are we heading off to battle?" I ask, unnerved.

She chuckles, wrapping her wrists in long strips of cloth. "No. The Brink is… well, you'll see. I mean that too. You'll *see*, Jacob. It will be very loud and quite an arduous task for Raeual and Adriel, dangerous even, but well worth the knowledge you'll gain. Take my hand. If we lose that connection, you won't hear me until we return. Ready?"

"Um…"

"Perfect, let's go." The jaunty look in her eyes makes my skin tingle.

We find Raeual and Adriel stuffing their mouths with scroll. They look up, like children caught with a candy jar.

"Now?" Raeual asks around a mouthful.

"It is time." Mara nods, an ancient queen, so frail, yet so powerful.

She takes my hand. "Do not lose me, Jacob. Squeeze my hand as hard as you can; you'll not hurt me."

Her slender hand slips into mine, palm to palm, fingers entwined, and her grip is far stronger than I counted on. Raeual steps behind me with a sigh.

"I cannot believe we're doing this," he says as he wraps his arms under my arms.

I flinch as his bear hug tightens. "Um."

He's so much taller that my head doesn't reach his shoulders. Adriel does the same to Mara, dwarfing her. I grunt, eyes wide, frozen in the odd embrace.

"You have no idea," Raeual grumbles, locking a hand onto his other wrist against my chest as if I'll try to escape.

Mara closes her eyes, and words flow from her mouth. Their meaning eludes me, but they wrap around us, infiltrating cells and vibrating the air, making energy shriek through my frame, and a faint green tinge fills the room. It's softer, somehow; not a jump, but close.

The current leaps higher and the entire room wavers the way Raeual does before he disappears. I blink, and a flare of vermilion explodes, disintegrating everything into open space that rips us forward. I grasp Mara's hand, worried her bones will snap, as Raeual squeezes harder, the speed tearing at every molecule.

Mara's staring straight ahead, focus complete, eyes bright.

Almost there.

I flinch at her voice, right inside my head.

Yes, I can hear you as well.

I try not to think, not of anything.

You're amusing, Jacob. Hold tighter to my hand.

The glint of stars appears, rushing past at the frantic pace of a jump. An expanse of blue light hovers at the horizon that's familiar, but it normally lasts a millisecond. We race toward the blue fog, and Raeual moans, resisting, slowing us by sheer strength in the hurricane-force solar wind. His crushing grip is like a vise, but here at the Brink where realities mix, there is no air.

Now!

At Mara's command, the Watchers haul back, pulling our speed to a crawl. I grimace, doubling down on Mara's hand, desperate to maintain the connection in the ripping wind, here where the worlds reach out to each other. It lacerates as we slow, struggling against the innate power. It vacuums my legs and free hand forward, like hanging over a cliff's edge, and Raeual strains to keep us in place.

The surrounding blue disintegrates into a billion pieces. Individual molecules are visible as we hang in time and space, but they expand until atoms with their electrons in orbit clarify, floating all around. A gust shrieks, and I know we'll shatter if we stay here too long.

Yes, we must hurry. Look and see.

As our speed zeroes out, the atoms slow further, revealing quarks and neutrinos in orderly orbits. But here, seeing the invisible exposes the fabric of the universe. At the core of every particle is a spectrum of light and color that determines its shape, size, and function.

Everything has light and sound, or a vibration, if you will.

The thought explodes, reaching forever in all directions.

Yes, light is the basis of the physical order, Mara responds.

At the Brink that separates the physical from the spirit, even now, thousands of years later, the Almighty's Word rules. *Let there be light.* And there, in that first command, all the raw building blocks *are.*

Now, look further into the light, Mara urges.

I squint; the compression of Raeual's grip trembles in the tearing atmosphere. Mara squeezes my hand.

Light is both a wave and a particle.

I flinch. *Like Yeshua. Fully God, and fully man.*

Yes. Go forward now.

Raeual and Adriel ease up and the wind draws us fast enough to see the atoms and electrons again.

See these two electrons? Mara asks, pointing to two orbiting packets of energy. *They are alike in every way. The same frequency, the same sound wave. Moving as one in time and space.* Her arm trembles as she reaches out against the flow to flick one into the raging solar storm, where it resettles, far to the right.

Now, we warm this one. She breathes on it until it glows red. Far off, the linked electron gleams with the new color.

This is quantum entanglement. No matter how great the separation is in time or space, the particles mirror each other.

Raeual groans; his arms shiver, fending off the intense suction of the Brink.

We haven't time. There is so much to see, yet seeing affects all things.

My hand slips on hers until just her fingertips remain in mine. Adriel cries out as he strains toward the spirit.

It's time.

Raeual roars in my ear at Mara's release, straining backward against the flow. The punishment of sound and wind grows as he fights the eternal current. His arms shift, and I jerk forward, stifling a shout, knowing the Brink would tear me apart alone.

Come... on!

Raeual's silent cry lends strength, and we gain speed, the atoms fading back into a sheen of blue. Then the gale dies out and we streak past bright stars. In reverse, Mara's room re-materializes. Raeual and Adriel fall back, hitting the floor and panting hard.

Mara stumbles as she turns, and I catch her elbow. She smiles, then claps her hands and the little bird alights on her shoulder, its tiny head cocked. She whispers and it takes off, returning with two small green twigs. Mara gives them to the Watchers, still sprawled on the floor, hauling in air.

"Thank you, the journey was perfect."

They chew the twigs, and color returns to their faces.

"Easy for you to say," Raeual mutters.

"Come." She pats my arm, still leaning on me, but recovers her strength near the pitcher. She pours water into the basin, and the sound ripples into me. Hunger burns, and this scroll is the sweetest ever as the words echo.

Truly I say to you, whosoever would say to this mountain, be removed, and be cast into the sea, and does not doubt in his heart, but believes that what he says comes to pass, he will have whatsoever he says.

"Wait. Quantum entanglement proves that verse. Change things in the spirit, and the physical will transform too."

"Yes, science is discovering that the Almighty's Word is true. But understanding the *source* cannot be overstated. When unobserved, every physical particle exists in a cloud of possibilities. Wrap your mind around *that*. Solid things like rock and wood, at the atomic level, are moving, *vibrating*. But when observed, when *seen*, they..." She searches for words. "...solidify. The physical order *is* reacting to us." Mara nods, urging me to reach further into my hobby study of quantum physics.

"Each particle exhibits differently, depending on who is looking. That's hard science."

She dips her head. "Which means..."

"What you focus on, believe, and speak shapes the world around you."

"Yeshua said that our words, believed, can move mountains, but there's a catch."

I raise my brows.

"He said you must *believe* what you say. It's easy to believe things will go wrong, get worse, fail. It's our default setting. Very few will dare to believe the New Covenant. Instead, they speak doubt and fear, then hope the opposite will happen. It is foolish to plant weeds yet pray for a crop of wheat." She hands me more scroll, which has a wild flavor to it, like an exotic herb.

And God said, L… Let us make man in our image, after our likeness: and let them have dominion over the fish of the sea, and over the fowl of the air, and over the cattle, and over all the earth, and over every creeping thing that creeps upon the earth.

"*Dominion* means to rule. The Almighty's purpose for you is to rule. But rule what?"

"Fish, birds, cattle, all earth and creeps."

Her eyes crinkle as she laughs. "Yes, and what is missing from the list?"

"Other humans," I say.

She pats my arm. "But rulership is not going well for most, is it? Evil spreads in a fallen state. Yet, you are called to make Earth like Heaven is. How? *Believe* that what you *say* comes to pass."

"But we can't tell God what to do."

"Ah. This point is a poison to faith, and paralyzing. You must understand the Kingdom and the covenant. A covenant is an agreement between two parties, outlining the responsibilities and actions allowed. Let's say you had a legal document of ownership of a horse."

Memories of Haseleph make suspicion stir in my mind. "Okay."

"According to law, it belongs to you, correct?"

"No, I mean, yes?"

A chuckle brightens her eyes. "Yes, but what if you were ignorant of the ownership?"

My stomach clenches as the vision from long ago slams into full reality within. I'm destitute, hungry, and cold, but all the time, everything I need is available.

"My people perish for lack of knowledge. If you don't know what's yours in the covenant, you can die a beggar, though the Almighty called you a royal priest. Using the things given in your covenant is *not* commanding the Almighty, it is being obedient. If He gave you a horse, then you'll need it, but if you never get on its back, the failure is yours alone. He won't force you to ride, Jacob; that's your responsibility."

She hands me another scroll with a familiar flavor.

M.. most assuredly, I say to you, he who believes in Me, the works that I do he will do also; and greater works than these he will do, because I go to My Father. And whatever you ask in My name, that I will do, that the Father may be glorified in the Son. If you ask anything in My name, I will do it.

"Can you complete the work He has for you sick? No. Poverty stricken? No. The covenant does not serve you, it's what makes you *able* to serve Him. We were all born into a slave mentality, but believers are *a chosen people, the Almighty's special possession.* Think like He does and understand the Kingdom, or failure crouches at your door."

Kingdom. The word stays inside like a splinter.

Mara scowls, eyes far off, as if listening to something. But her voice isn't hushed any longer, now it's forceful, driving me back a step. The hair on my arms stands on end.

"The enemy seeks to kill you. The time is at hand for the great battle."

A chill races across my skin as she shudders, looking around as if unsure of where she is. But I'm not ready. Life depends on concepts as deep as space and time, and the test is coming. *Almighty, help me.*

I stalk, low and quiet, through the old forest, dropping into a valley with steep cliffs on three sides. Memories of the lion's attack set my nerves on fire as my scars glow brighter, searching for a whiff of rotten flesh. Pity the lion who crosses my path after Mara's warning.

A slim whisper of sound makes adrenaline surge. Something leaps from the cliff above and I spin with Hadena's twin blades before me. A figure lands, standing to brush off his pants.

"Demyen?"

"Aye, Boy!"

Hadena snaps shut and we eye each other. He's the same as ever, a mountain of a man with a dark curling beard and brilliant emerald eyes. Half my mouth tips up as I slap his meaty shoulder. "Where you been?"

He shrugs. "It's a strange time. I've been chopping wood, and more wood, and still more."

He's got more bulk than before. "It's done you good."

I stuff a wad of scroll into my mouth so he doesn't beat me to it.

A grin splits his beard as he takes some from his own pouch. "Aye."

The glint of pleasure in his eye brings a deep sense of satisfaction. Long ago, I would have survived about three minutes without him. Mara's comment stirs curiosity though. Older than she is? His skin is smooth and not one hair shows a hint of white. Still, the question feels too personal to voice. We set off, chewing scroll in the serene silence, and its words echo straight into my soul.

We look not at the things which are seen but at the things which are not seen: for the things which are seen are temporal: but the things which are not seen are eternal.

Just like this world once was to me, and words aren't visible either, but they're the source, the code on which everything runs, the frequency of life or death. The unseen ruling over the seen.

The forest before me warps, giving way to a rippling gray image of a boot at my throat.

"You alright, Boy?" Demyen questions.

"There's something I don't understand."

"Only one?" A smirk accompanies his words.

"Okay, here's *a* thing I don't understand: What can I count on, and what can't I?"

Demyen frowns. "The child of El Shaddi can always count on salvation, healing and provision. This is written."

"Yeah, but…"

"Ah, *but.* The most dangerous of words."

His frown can't stop my question. "Once, I could see without light, but not always. Sometimes, knowledge comes, things I shouldn't know, but not always. Am I missing something? Shouldn't I have those results all the time?"

"Hmm. You're talking more about gifts than covenant rights."

"Gifts?"

"Aye Boy, keep up. Let's say…" he plucks a twig from above. "This twig is pure gold. Let's say Mara gave it to me."

"I'm tracking."

"It's mine, so I can do whatever I want with it," he says.

"I thought we were going somewhere with this," I say.

He squints at me, then lashes out with the stick. "I could hit you with it."

I duck, spinning away. "Not a chance!"

He laughs, running his fingers over the wood. "Or I could give it to you." But he pitches it into the forest where it melds with the undergrowth. "Or I can toss it out. That's like a covenant right. Something that belongs to you, but you choose how, when, and *if* you use it."

"Okay."

"Spiritual gifts aren't like normal gifts. You don't own them the way you can a shirt or a sword, nor does the covenant promise that. Spiritual gifts are *for* believers, and they work *in* you as the spirit wills, not as you will, *for* the body of Christ."

A grunt escapes, "That's what happened on the ship, it came over me, like a cloak."

"Aye. So, like certain organs digest food, or pump blood, so too in the body of Christ, people are suited to a gift, though they don't choose when it's in action. You can, however, miss moving in the gifts altogether."

A branch snaps off to our right. Demyen and I freeze as Raeual and Jaden appear, standing at attention, staring beyond us. The air changes and every nerve pricks as it grows heavier and sweeter. Demyen grunts as the forest disappears, the ground becoming brighter with every heartbeat until a pool of shimmering golden light expands before us.

I've felt it before; the way the fabric of the world vibrates, rising to a higher frequency when survival is questionable. My knees hit the ground as the glow reflects off the Almighty Himself. It's impossible to tell if His form is that of the Lion of Judah, or the blueprint of man, maybe both, but everything is here; all life and knowledge, shivering within until nothing else matters.

"You are My chosen." The ground rumbles at the words. *"My two olive trees that pour out My oil upon the earth in the last days."*

It's my oldest memory that never existed before.

"Yes, Lord," Demyen and I respond together.

"The work is great, My chosen." His voice is an elixir of life that prevents the weight of His words from crushing me. *"It is not by might, nor by power, but by My Spirit. Be faithful unto the end."*

He steps closer, then, as thick as honey, a stream of oil pours onto my head, running down my jaw, filling the air with a new fragrance that stabs straight into my heart. Demyen moans, and a cry stifles in my throat as my fingers dig into the molten ground. Every thought grows quiet, filled with a single purpose: *Worship Him.*

The intensity peaks as a vivid vision forms all around. It's the flat gray of the physical, the bleak tone heartbreaking after the magnitude of His presence. Searing heat rises off the hard-baked earth, the sky above the color of steel. There is no water, nothing green in sight. The physical realm is dying, now on its last breath, and grief floods my being. Choking dust swirls between me and an angry crowd of hollow-eyed people. Then a figure rises, enveloped in a dark cloud, with murky flames flaring at his side. The sight makes my blood turn ice-cold. Evil flows from the midnight form, with wicked tendrils of black fire searching for me, then lashing out at my neck as darkness rushes in.

I gasp, shaking my head, flat out on the golden floor again, with one thought reverberating.

"Ask," He says, knowing my inmost being.

"Can… what will happen to Sage?"

"There is a place of hiding she may enter, to be shielded from the coming storms." Relief floods me, and He draws closer until the light peaks to an intensity that overcomes all else.

A shadow filters through my eyelids, and a groan escapes. Demyen stands there, brows knit as he studies me, but his hair and beard glisten with anointing oil. The scent fills the air, brimming with the high notes of the call and the deep, sweeping sorrow of the vision. It's heavy, even mixed together.

Demyen clasps my hand and pulls me to my feet. He doesn't let go, staring hard into my eyes as his own shimmer. He knows something I'm missing. "Aye, Boy, it's good to stand to the end with you."

Questions pile up as my dry mouth and clammy hands prove that the oil is part of me now, infiltrating to my core.

"It's bitter in your belly, isn't it?" Demyen asks, gazing into the forest with burning eyes as he swallows hard.

"Yeah." My heart pounds as my stomach heaves. "What did He mean, *olive trees*?"

Demyen's face is solemn as he searches through his pouch. He lofts a fragment of scroll, inspects it through narrowed eyes, and holds it out. Then he takes it back and rips it in half, rubbing the second piece between his fingers.

"There, that's enough for now," he says, wincing as he eats the smaller piece. "Brace yourself."

The scroll is like any other, soft and fragrant, but dangerous too, with an electric shock that sends a ripple of dread into my bones.

And I will give power unto my two witnesses, and… and they shall prophesy a thousand two hundred and threescore days, clothed in sackcloth.

The words drive me back until my heel catches; only Demyen's solid grip prevents a fall. "Aye, hit me the same the first time."

The scroll smolders inside, and heat blooms outward, gathering speed until it hits my mouth and both palms like a freight train. Demyen adds his other hand to my shoulder as I crumple forward.

"What, exactly, did we agree to?" I ask, heaving air in the hushed forest.

Demyen sighs, then lets me go. "To whom much is given, much is required."

"That's not an answer."

"Power and sackcloth." Demyen arches one brow, mischief igniting in his gaze. "Sounds itchy."

A flit of motion to our right reveals Ian stepping onto our path, hands on hips. "Party out here today?"

He's more muscular than before, though still trim as he pushes his sandy hair back. Demyen shakes his hands out, then strides up to him, clasping him on the shoulder. "The question is, what for?"

Ian's gaze doesn't waiver as he juts his chin at me. "What's wrong with him?"

Demyen's emerald eyes tighten at the corners as I teeter with hands on my knees. "Not a thing. Looks like our paths align for a bit."

Ian sniffs, eyes darting between Demyen and me. "Smells like oil, which is never early nor late."

"Aye," Demyen says, pointing to the ground that still glows with a waning light. "Times are changing. Stay sharp. We should move, fast. The thief is never far from fresh anointing."

"Of course," Ian adds, "but slow is smooth and smooth is fast."

His comment hits hard, so familiar from that gray reality where it was Rivera's favorite phrase. Sorrow wells up, knowing he's still lost in the flames. It adds to the weight that's pressing me into the ground. I wasn't much of a witness to him. What hope is there for filling the call with that track record?

"Smell it?" Demyen asks, keeping his voice hushed, one hand on his sword. "The best time to steal a seed is before it takes root. Hear me, Boy? Be on your guard. Hurry now."

Exhaustion keeps me grounded to the spot. He turns when I don't follow and slaps one firm hand onto my shoulder. "'Omets."

The word unlocks the air and breaks the tension away. With it, balance returns as the wind stirs, bringing a hint of stench. "Thank you."

He nods, but his eyes scan the trees, driving home how serious he is. Flexing my hands, knowing Hadena is ready, we set off, finding that our paths spread out, then travel parallel. Ian's comment makes physical knowledge hover closer than normal, and each footfall is careful and soft, stalking forward as the heaviness falls behind.

The trees thin here with a meadow stretching away. My path takes a sharp turn to the right, further from Demyen and Ian, running over a dry, rocky stream bed. My eyes tighten; it's too quiet as an odd wisp of scent reaches me. Still, my path is there, beckoning me forward. The stones shift under my weight, but stay silent as dappled light plays over the rocky section.

Unease brings me to a full stop, testing the air and scanning. My head tilts, studying the area. Something's off about the stream bed. It's too short, without the gradual drop of a waterway. Through the trees, Demyen pauses as well, his stance sinking lower.

The rocks are so sharp that it's painful to stay still, and two more steps bring me to the center of the area. Slow breaths keep thoughts clear as every sense strains for anomalies. *Wait.* My path glistens in a patch of bright light, then peters out to nothing. Scowling, I look back. A golden thread in the trees to the left makes me flinch. *Two paths?*

The stones heave, all at once, flexing upward with a chaotic eruption. I stagger forward, then smash chest-first into the pile of stones that hurls me skyward. The sharp rocks change color under my hands even as my legs scramble, sliding down black... *scales?*

"Oomph." The mass under me bucks hard, flinging me high, where I flail with arms and legs pinwheeling. The black bulk chases so fast that the concussion stuns my lungs and makes stars swirl.

Whomp.

The air sucks hard, then smacks my face as I slide down... a dragon's back.

"What in tarnation?" Demyen's shout echoes from far off.

The leathery wings beat again, revealing a glimpse of the forest far below before my hand finds a good grip on a horn. The beast shakes like a dog, flinging me off into the sky. Super-heated air rushes past, the wings turning air pressure into a weapon. Then I'm airborne until the long serpentine tail whips up, whipping me square in the back.

The air leaves my lungs in a rush as sky and forest flip past. Momentum runs out, and the inevitable plummet makes my stomach drop until a whoosh of wind makes me curl up. Searing pain slices down my back, and the abrupt change of direction disorients every sense. The beast has my belt in a sharp claw, and the land below is a blur, then a white veil envelops everything. The belt cuts my stomach, then a sharp pop releases me as it snaps.

Free falling, I burst from the cloud cover with arms and legs wide. The belt slithers away, toward the fast-approaching ground. A shadow cuts over the forest, its strange shape burning into my mind—a dark triangle with an ellipse centered on top. But there isn't enough time to react before a massive set of claws close around my ribs and burning sulfur acidifies my lungs.

Scales scrape my skin, and another blast of air draws me upward. I rip at the heavy paw as treetops swoosh past and branches catch my legs. The claws tighten, my veins bulging at the pressure, and leathery wings pump.

A vile stench deadens the air, the atmosphere far too thin as the beast gains altitude with its snout pointed skyward. *No air.* Spatial orientation evaporates as useless struggle depletes my last reserve of oxygen. My heart slams with an erratic beat as clouds zip past and we surge straight up.

One thought solidifies as my eyes roll back. *Hadena.* The blades snap out, but the darkness emanating from the beast is like fetters. Despair coils inside, tighter than the claws. *Resistance is useless.* Everything goes blurry, and my head lolls against the sharp scales. But deep down, the sensation of the oil running over my head pushes back. Life is still there, in my core, with eternal energy. Refusing the disorientation brings a grimace as I condense, determined to see life instead.

Hadena scrapes over the scales. *Pathetic.* But the oil promises more, with an essence that's not my own. Scales and sky blur together, but one last flare of energy funnels into a command.

Strike!

Sparks sizzle as the blades glance off. *Pointless.* All it has to do is drop me. Still, the vision of *Him* rises, stirring one word.

"No."

Nothing changes, except the tunnel vision narrows further as the thin air wails past. Then a jet stream rocks the beast hard, and the leathered wings billow. It readjusts, its grip loosening for a half second. *Air.* It forces the darkness back. The dragon wheels hard, and the glittering gray face of a mountain flashes far too close. The beast twists as the stone zips past.

We land hard, the other rear leg taking most of the creature's weight, and the whisper-like sound of wings folding echoes off the cold rock that's smashing my face. The beast shifts, I suck in air, then it throws me hard against the cliff. I bounce off, then sprawl on the ledge.

I crab-crawl backward, the lean, hot atmosphere squeezing harder. The super-heated temperature fills the space between us with malignancy as blood trickles from my mouth. The dragon snarls, crimson-stained teeth showing as it looms above, its raw power mesmerizing. Scales flash like gems, shimmering a million colors in succession, before settling into a reflective black. Razor-edged horns wreath its head, narrowing toward a square snout. Here, in its strange pyramid-shaped shadow, nothing else exists; there's only the beast with its consuming, intelligent gaze that pins me to the rock. The wings double as front legs, with sharp claws at the middle joint. One slams down next to me, quaking the mountain.

"Trying to change things, usurper? Don't you know God is sovereign?" The smooth baritone is a shock. Claws spray shards of stone as they slam down, far too close. I skitter back against the cliff, my back exploding with pain. "From the beginning, fate determines every action. Every…" It leans in until its huge dripping jaws are inches away. "Last breath."

The dragon's flashing gaze radiates an unnerving capacity. Ripping my gaze from its spell requires a shout, but this scenery isn't any better. Sheer cliffs shoot straight up behind, and nothing but sky shows beyond our narrow perch.

It hisses, noxious breath making me gag. "Physics proves sovereignty with a mathematical equation for all matter that defines the future. There is no free will. This equation is inescapable: I am your fate, written before the ages. Everything will happen exactly as God wills." The well-armored neck shoots out as I leap away. My skin constricts, anticipating the searing pain of a last bite, but it rams me instead, driving me against the cliff. Stars fill my vision as I pile up against the rock with stunning numbness, but it's the statement that weighs me down, hampering movement. How could I resist eternal will? The beast rears high, gloating.

My hand comes away brilliant red from the gash on my back.

"I am Baal Bismillah, and your life ends *now*." It spears the rock with one front claw, coating me in its dark, pyramid-shaped shadow.

The shimmering line of my path runs under the rear claws, then, slow enough to make my blood run cold, the dragon pulls its three-toed foot away. My path ends there. *Right there.* My eyes snap up to its flaring red orbs, meeting an expression of demonic glee.

"You can't escape."

My lungs burn as the furnace of its body heat turns the rock into an oven. Staying here means death. Memories flash, pulsing images that shiver up from the past, until it's Demyen before me, emerald eyes blazing. "The path *never* terminates."

The second my gaze breaks from its burning eyes, the dragon reacts. Rage flashes as its chest expands, releasing a bellow so loud it makes blood trickle from my ear. I crumple, hands over my head as the sound breaks me apart, rising to an electric crackle that quakes the rock and ignites the wound on my back into agony.

Miniature bolts of electricity streak down my limbs, centering on the wound, hammering there until blood flows afresh. My stomach revolts at the scent of burning flesh, but the voltage still rattles inside my mind. The golden shimmer of my path is visible when the beast slams me against the stones with a brutal claw.

The path never terminates.

The truth alone rises inside, past the pain with Hadena locked in my grip. The burning air, the sheer power of the dragon, and the *end* of my path battle hard against the slender threads of knowledge. The snake-like neck coils, jaws wide open. I dive forward as if to prove its point, landing right where my path ends. The harsh rock rips at my stomach as I skid over the last golden thread, expression twisting. Claws rake my legs, drawing a cry. The lungful of air billows dust ahead of my slide, and there, hidden underneath, is my path.

It ignites inside, and I low crawl past the pounding legs. That beloved shimmer runs right over the edge of the cliff, revealing a simple fact. *I can't stay here.* Claws make the rock explode next to my head, but my fingertips find the ledge, and with a battle cry, I haul myself into thin air.

My arms flail until I reach terminal velocity, with tears streaming from the speed in the ice-cold air. Clamping down the innate fear clears my mind and makes the skin on my neck tingle, so I twist hard in time to kick the dragon's snout. The motion rockets me into a dense cloud. The fall feels slower inside it until I burst out to find the dragon inches behind. Diving away, my hands pierce the air like a swimmer, surging down, but I can't outrace his weight.

Raeual emerges from a flash of light, his face contorted in a war cry. The dragon speeds closer, but the Watcher's brutal right hook turns its vile snout. The teeth snap shut, far too close. I twist and shove the gappig jaws that slam me like a train. The move plasters me on the wreath of uneven horns above his eyes. Gripping one, the heat sears my hand, but my priority is exiting his business end. Letting the wind slide me higher, I cling to the dragon's neck as our flight levels out.

Raeual is there, windshear tearing at his dark hair. "Dive!"

A gust makes my grip slip. Behind, leathery wings beat, then fold tight, rolling to the right, and I sling off, free falling again. A wicked tail whip almost breaks my leg, creating a spin that gains speed.

"Raa…!" Raeual's bear hug stops me so fast that my head lolls.

More clouds obscure the sky, and blacking out is imminent, but the beast could grab us from any direction. Heartbeats pass, each one more sinister than the last as the current rips at our clothes. Then the clouds are gone, and the beast is there, surging at full speed. Raeual hauls upward and I buck hard to avoid the snap of six-inch teeth. The impact of its head makes stars dance as I'm plastered between Raeual and dragon scales.

There are no rules in the sky, so I slash at the burning red eye with Hadena, but the blade glances off a clear scale. The dragon shakes like a wet dog, flinging us upward and ripping me from

Raeual's grip. With a roar, my fingertips find the longest horn and I swing astride the wide neck again. This time I'm ready for its dive, and Hadena pummels the scales hard.

Sparks fly from its mouth as trees appear far below. Deep anger flares, and I twist the twin blades in together, forcing them under the tight seal of two scales. A savage grin comes at the beast's shriek of pain that makes the fast-approaching trees shudder. The dragon shakes its head, but Hadena bites deeper, and the dive turns into a barrel roll.

Momentum frees me with a yelp, then thin pine branches whip me; the ground is *right there.* Spreading out only gives me another heartbeat to say goodbye. Trees turn to matchsticks beside me as the dragon dives, its iron stomach shearing off the forest. I tuck and somersault, with both blades hammering, pushing me away. One rear claw snatches my shirt inches before impact and the wings beat hard, compressing the air like a blast zone. Straight ahead, one sturdy pine doesn't give way as the beast's chest catches the trunk.

The world spins into chaos as momentum flips the long tail up and over, and I crash hard into Raeual, who deflects me into a stream, rocks and water spraying. The wound in my back ignites to agony at the water's touch.

Green haze flares up all around and irresistible speed draws me forward, as if I never stopped falling. Far off now, Raeual frowns at me until the Brink flashes past, and thoughts of the flat gray physical surface.

Truth is obscured in this realm, but at least there's no dragon on my tail. My body draws my spirit in like a magnet as frosted pipes and a vast building materialize. The tight embrace of my body brings a grimace, resisting convulsions because Sage lies next to me with one delicate hand on my neck. It takes a breath to lock in, the spirit once more concealed.

The fight and the fall stay clear for another second, but the physical past rushes in like ocean breakers; we're lying under dark fabric, and evening is falling. Sage moans, her brows knitting as she sleeps. Adrenaline responds to my chaotic thoughts, and I switch to box breathing to bring it down.

"No!" she struggles, movements sluggish in sleep. "Get away!"

A wisp of lion stench reaches me, making my skin prick. Before my first jump, the worlds started mixing for me, too. Sage will jump soon. The thought hits me like a gut punch.

"Get back! No!" Her slurred cry makes me groan. Can she survive? What if we're not together?

A growl forces clarity, but when I blink, the dragon's strange shadow is all I see. The pyramid outline, with the eye in the center, makes the sick, dead scent grow. *Here, in this realm?*

"Sage!" Everything's there in that one broken whisper. She risked everything to protect me on the *Engage,* but there's every chance in both worlds that I can't help her when she jumps. I brush the hair from her cheek. "Sage, wake up!"

Her brown eyes snap open, fear shining there. "Jacob!"

"Shh… It's all right." My jaw clenches, knowing I dare not tell her about dragons when lions are stalking her dreams.

"You're back." Relief floods her voice.

"We need to move. Now." I shake free of the strange symbol, wishing the water's touch would linger instead. Lion stench still hangs in the air, a rank, dead scent where it shouldn't be. There's no time. Senses on fire, I pull her to her feet, the torn hoodie falling away. Headlights cut through the falling night, then sweep across the orchard and stay there.

"That's where I threw the drone," Sage whispers, pointing at the short trees.

There is no time to clarify. We duck behind the propane tank as two uniformed agents appear, striding into the orchard.

"My fingerprints!" Sage is breathing hard, hands clenched. Reality is no better than her nightmare.

"They'll never see them. Stay here."

Moving fast and low, I sprint to the car. It's unmarked, with two radios and a laptop inside. The fuel tank is full, equaling a free ride to Key West. The factory is closed for the day, and the rest of the lot is deserted, increasing our chances. I pop the hood and force one battery cable off just in case, then ease it shut. Seconds later, I crouch next to Sage.

"They'll have chest cams. Got to take them out together." I hand Sage another pistol. "Keep them facing away from each other and us."

"Um…"

"Might work out so I can take them both. Do whatever you need to keep the cams looking at the trees. Move." I can't give fear time to lock her down.

The men are still in the orchard. On autopilot, my breath slows down, deepening, triggering a hyper- alert awareness that's kept me alive more times than I can count. But I can't let it rule; it must be tempered with the unseen, with the perfect knowledge the spirit brings, where life is.

I duck the scrubby tree branches, sprinting, sensing Sage close behind. Both agents kneel, putting pieces of the drone into plastic bags with nitril-gloved hands.

We slip from tree to tree until the chest cams are visible; that live feed is our worst enemy. I twist a still-green orange from a tree and whip it far to the right.

They both stand, searching for the source of the sound as I explode into combat mode. Two heartbeats carry me into the first agent. I plow into his back at full speed, forcing him into the other and they go down hard. I pistol whip the first. He doesn't rise, face in the sand.

The other lurches forward. Before he can turn, my right arm locks around his neck. He grabs my forearm, struggling as I clamp down the hold and lock it with my other arm. I keep him aimed at the trees, then search behind for Sage. Securing both agents is top priority.

She's behind me, dragging the first one back, but a pulsing urgency deep in my gut prevents me from knocking this one out. Years of training pressing in, pinching me to act. *Incapacitate him. Now.* Everything in my head screams it, but I hone past my intellect, listening to that sense deep inside.

I ease my grip, allowing the man one sip of air. The veins in his neck swell with fresh blood rushing to his brain. He kicks like wild, but I'm caught by what I can't see: that still, quiet voice.

Why wait? One smooth motion brings the pistol to his head. He goes still, hands in the air.

My breathing is slow and steady, sensing. *Secure both agents and clear the area.* One simple objective I can't obey.

Mara's words are so clear: unseen over the seen. Minutes slip past; Sage creeps up, out of camera range, a question on her face in the dusk.

I shake my head and wait.

A radio on the man's vest crackles. "Timmons, report."

My eyes slide closed. If I dropped him like I *should* have, we'd already be in the car and our trail would be hot within minutes.

The pistol digs harder into his temple. Squeaking, he fumbles for the radio. My grip on his neck increases, he flinches, trying to nod as sweat rolls down his neck. I ease up and he squeezes the button.

"Ah… Timmons clear."

"Did you find Drone 1121?"

I clamp down on his throat again, hissing in his ear. "It's a typical malfunction."

When allowed air, he relays my message.

"Got another, Number 2107, went down 30 miles south."

I increase the pressure of the pistol, but give him air.

"On it, boss."

The radio falls silent and the check inside clears. Training takes over, and he falls limp. I drag him back toward a tree.

"Tape."

Sage slaps the roll into my palm. "You are so terrifying when you do that. How'd you know the radio would go off?"

I twist, finding her eyes, gauging how much she can handle. "There's another world, Sage, but it doesn't run off this one like you'd expect." I rip the tape and wrap Timmons's arms around a tree in the moonlight. "The spirit is the source."

She sighs as I secure the other agent. "So that's why you can't wait to jump, because you learn things there?"

"It's like accessing pure life." I rip two more squares of tape and slap them over the cams. It might buy us extra time. I pull Timmons's phone and scroll through texts. The top one is his orders on this drone collection. I type a reply.

Optics and guidance system malfunction for drone 1121. En route to 2107.

The phone vibrates.

Proceed, will fix at base.

I press the bag of drone parts into Sage's hands. "You sure smashed this thing."

She takes the bag with two fingers as if it's a snake. "It was looking at your boot. Made me angry."

The moonlight plays on the curve of her cheek, and my breath catches. Every op requires teamwork, and it forms a deep bond of trust, but Sage risked everything on the *Olympia* to save me. What if she dies in a jump? I turn so she won't see it in my eyes.

"I'll be sure not to make you angry, then." The tease makes her frown at me.

With a smirk, I grab a knife and slice the top of Timmons's hand. Blood runs in a rivulet down his wrist.

"Jacob!"

"He'll be fine. Much better without this." The minute tracking chip is slimy, but the blood on the sand rearranges, forming the shadow, an ellipse with a triangle behind it.

"Ah," I groan, heart pounding at the image. What *is* the point of trying to change things? If the future is set in stone, then everything is following an unchangeable course.

Questions swirl until I look away, needing to be present. "Regular soldiers have trackers. Except us. SEALs can't risk being identified on ops. Besides, we'd cut them out, but I figured a guy like this would have one."

"I refused mine," Sage says, rubbing her arms in the damp air.

"Why?"

She shakes her head. "It never sat right, letting them pinpoint my life. Plus, we radiation nerds had an exemption since the chips fry under certain conditions."

"That's one of the many things I like about you," I say, moving to the other man and placing both chips into a bag. "Let's move. We've got thirty miles without suspicion."

Seconds later, the battery cable is back on, and we slide into the car.

"And after that?" Sage asks.

I pull out of the lot, veering away from the subject and Bismillah's lurking thoughts. "Then things will get interesting. Hey, is that a lunch bag?"

She takes an insulated bag from the floor. The usual hunger after a jump grips me, but I convince her to eat a protein bar before I inhale the rest.

A display on the dash jumps to life. The words *Breaking News* scroll across the screen. The footage of a desolate city littered with bodies is gripping. Sage covers her mouth at a young child's blank stare, his broken back sprawled over a destroyed wall.

"The Collective quells brutal unrest in South Africa. Rebels responsible for the genocide are now in custody. The N.W.O. is pleased to announce that the planet is once again war-free. Peace and safety to all."

My brain freezes on a single frame, where a strong-bodied man lies twisted, his limbs at odd angles. His mangled neck makes my gut clench. Dark bruises reveal a handprint that snapped his neck. I glance at Sage, flicking the power button.

The image stays with me; only pure hatred could have fueled that brutal murder. My skin crawls, and a sharp pain in my side brings a grimace along with the dragon's words. Are we all taking inevitable steps like robots? The strangled man had no power to change his fate. Heat flushes up my neck, unwilling to give in. "They have to be stopped."

Sage turns to me, her eyes burning. "The Collective? It's not you, Jacob. You don't have to save everybody."

I keep my gaze on the road, jaw tight. It's what I've always done, protected the weak, brought down the enemy. Why can't she see that?

By mile twenty-nine, the heaviness lessens on a long bridge over a glittering swamp. We haven't passed another car yet, which is a tribute to the N.W.O.'s strict curfew. I stop and dial Paco.

"Need a ride."

"No rides!" he barks in a Hispanic accent.

"Bermuda," is the only thing I say.

The line is silent for a moment.

"When?" Paco asks.

"Tonight."

He hisses, but I don't respond. He sighs. "Boat's full."

"You'll have to make room then."

He's highly creative with his swearing, but when he wears out, he adds, "Gordon's Pass, Naples. 3 A.M."

The phone goes silent. I get out, grabbing the drone in the embrace of the tropical night. The drone pieces splat far below where gator eyes glitter in the water. The phone flies further, landing with a plop. Sage watches out her open window with an arched brow.

"Paco does *not* like loose threads," I say, scanning the horizon.

"I see."

I slide back in the car. "He's a rough character."

She stares at me, one side of her mouth pulled tight. "I've met a few of those."

A hollow laugh escapes at the thought of putting a pretty blonde on his boat. "Just stick close. Real close."

A rueful smile plays on her mouth. "That's my plan."

Her words strike deeper than expected and my heart twists. What if she jumps alone and I can't protect her? The only thing worse would be if I jumped while onboard with Paco, leaving Sage to fend for herself. It's a wasted thought; jumping is uncontrollable, and focusing on it will solidify a bad outcome.

"You're going to bend the steering wheel," she says, her features soft in the dim dash lights.

I loosen my fists, forcing another laugh to cover my thoughts.

She clears her throat, her face pale. "So, when you jump, what's it like?"

Out of the vast sea of information, what's the most important? "The energy increases until you're moving so fast, *so far*. When you get there, it's doubtful you'll remember anything from here."

A shuddering sigh escapes her. "So, there's no way to prep."

"All you need is the light, Sage."

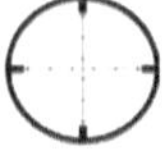

Wires dangle from the car's laptop and radio power cord, which I tore out an hour ago, but who knows what other trackers the car has. Time presses in from both sides. Every minute we spend in this car is one closer to them zeroing in on Timmons's strange behavior. Still, he's a small fry in a sea of bigger fish as long as the drone didn't get a clear shot of my boot. Plus, Paco waits for no man, and three o'clock is fast approaching.

The barren roads are testament to the N.W.O.'s "superior" form of freedom: Save the planet first. Eat meat once a month if you have high citizen points for good behavior, use public transit, and own nothing. An honest grin forms. What would my score be? Negative ten thousand.

Lights flash ahead, and my left eye tightens. I stop on the back side of a curve, taking the monocular from the bag.

Sage shifts out of from an uneasy sleep in the seat. "What's wrong?"

"Roadblock. Stay here a minute."

A small patch of scrubby forest shields us from the lights. Stalking through the trees in the deep night shifts me into hunter mode. The monocular reveals a vehicle scanning station with bright floodlights. *Timmons's chip will come in handy after all.*

A police car idles beyond the blockade, blue light from a screen bathing an officer's face inside; he's paying no attention. Calculations surge through my mind. The car is almost out of gas, and we're three miles from the pickup location.

Humid air coats my skin and swampland glints on both sides of the road; it's not terrain Sage can handle. I stalk back to the car, using every scrap of cover. We're so close, and there's no other option.

Back inside, I take out Timmons's chip. "There were two agents; there's got to be another bag of food in here somewhere," I say, eyeing the pallor of Sage's skin. Her energy is running far too low.

She finds it in the rear seat and peers inside. "We've got standard government issue. A protein bar, a nutrient shake and a fiber supplement."

I grunt. "I need plastic wrap."

She digs further. "Well, well, what have we here?"

She takes out an item and my mouth falls open.

"A cookie?" I whisper.

"Chocolate chip." Her voice is full of reverent awe.

As if it were made of fairy dust, she unwraps it and inhales its scent, her eyes fluttering shut. Is her skin as soft as it looks? I soak in her enjoyment, wishing this was her normal. She rips it in half and holds it out.

"No, you eat it. I'll take the wrap." I say, enjoying how the dash lights play over her face.

"No way, we're splitting it." She shoves half toward me. When I make no move to take it, she adds, "Do *not* make me force you."

She stares at me, her sober expression giving way to a grin that I can't help matching.

Our fingers brush as I take it, tingling clear up to my elbow. Does she know how she affects me? "After seeing the drone's condition, I'd better listen up."

She takes a bite and her head falls back against the seat with a groan. How long has it been since either of us ate something homemade?

"Maybe I shouldn't have knocked Timmons so hard. His baking skills might be irreplaceable."

"Nope, he did not make these," she says.

"No?" I question, eyes locked on her mouth as I take a bite. With the looming security check, each second is precious, so worth spending together, breathing the same free air.

"Have I deduced something that you missed?" Her delight ramps up a notch. "A grandmother baked this; look how crispy it is on the outside and gooey on the inside. This took years to master, like a rare work of art."

I stuff the rest in, nodding. But deeper hunger stirs: to get her to a safe place, away from Ash's grip, to feed her cookies.

I take the wrap, muttering, "How many layers would simulate human skin?"

"Four," she says without hesitation. I side-eye her. "Yeah, I'm on a roll here. Do four. It'll be perfect."

The sugar and her sudden optimism give her skin a pink flush that makes me want to stare. I lay the ID chip on the back of my hand, but Sage takes the wrap. Her motions are smooth as she works. Her fingers are so delicate next to mine, which are crisscrossed with scars.

The chip stays put when I make a fist. "All right, you'd better lie on the back floor."

She scrambles over as I put the car in gear, running scenarios and visualizing. I stretch, then set the heavy duffel on her back and speed up to fifty-five, the engine whining. Got to make everything look normal, I'm just a federal agent out after curfew without clearance. *If they've flagged this car…*

Box breathing takes over as we approach the station with its swinging arm blocking the road. I flip down the visor, lessening their view as we stop under the searing lights. I open the window just far enough to run my hand under the beam. The machine's steady red light has me cataloging weapons.

It turns green.

The barrier creeps up at a snail's pace. I pull away and watch for lights in the rearview.

"Stay there, stay there," Sage says, peeking over the back seat.

"You saying that for our sake or his?" I ask as the distance grows.

"His."

But the drone footage, along with Timmons's location, combine in my stomach to form a tension I can't dispel. A sharp hiss from the back seat makes me glance in the rearview. The officer's lights are on, and he's coming.

I jam the accelerator to the floor. The gas gauge is not friendly, hovering on empty. Can I change anything? The dragon's burning eyes seem so close, too real.

"Jacob?" Sage grips my seat, watching the pursuing headlights and pulling me from the memory.

We careen around a corner, tires squealing. We ticked too many red flags in a row, and training demands we assume that all forces are centering on us. Risk assessment makes things clear. "We've got to ditch the car," I say, eyeing the rearview as the headlights appear around the turn. "You up for a run?"

She groans as we approach a neighborhood without a single light on. Details lock in on autopilot. The layout is two elongated ovals, one set within the other. The houses are tightly packed, with unkempt pools that glitter in the moonlight.

"Rolling blackouts. Perfect. There isn't much time to reach Naples; if we... get separated, head south, to the beach. Don't wait for me—Paco's men will meet you at the furthest point of Gordon's Pass."

"I can't..."

But the quiet street curves hard, offering a few seconds shielded from the officer's view. I crank the wheel, forcing the car into a slide, ensuring the rear fender catches a light pole. I reach back to steady Sage as the car crumples around it. Glass implodes, Sage shrieks, and we lurch to a halt. I snatch the duffle. "Go."

We sprint past the closest house. The officer will have to inspect the car, buying precious seconds, but it won't be long until N.W.O. agents cram every inch of this county. We run into the dark, weaving past houses, dead center in the development, and skid to a halt behind a house.

"Listen," Sage pants, clinging to my arm.

A line of vehicles snakes into the development, zeroing in, cutting our chances further. The teams fan out, forming an ever-tightening net.

"Hurry," I tug her forward, struggling under the odds stacked against us. If we miss that boat…

Sage stifles a whimper as headlights illuminate the street behind; it's a BearCat SWAT four-door, with a ten-soldier capacity. I leap a wood fence, then snatch Sage's shirt and yank her over. We crouch, cataloging assets. Preventing engagement is paramount.

Headlights glint, enclosing the neighborhood as they converge. Sage's lungs are heaving and worry gleams in her eyes as swift footsteps spread down the street on the far side of the fence. They'll start a systematic sweep, going house to house. The hill to the south leads to the boat, but the agents are thickest there. I'll have to lead them north to create an opening.

More SWAT vehicles pour in as the first front door gets kicked in, the sound making Sage flinch. This place is like an ant's nest and soon, it'll be a roiling mess of agents and civilians, which is the first bit of hope I've seen. "It'll take them a while to clear this neighborhood. Stay low and follow me from ten feet behind."

She nods, but can't tear her eyes from the lights. The next cover is a pool that smells like a swamp, where I weigh escape routes against Sage's ability. A shed sits next to the pool, the door hanging off square, and the floor creaks under my weight.

"They're so close," Sage whispers, both hands clenching my shirt.

A woman screams, then a child joins in. *Let the chaos begin.* White plastic catches my eye, sticking out from under a box. Pool shock. I tuck it into the pack and exit the shed, rushing to the next hide site—an old car parked near the chain-link fence.

Shadows flit over us as a team smashes a door one house away. A civilian takes off down the street; he doesn't make it three strides before they taser him. Sage groans as another BearCat parks on the road. The noose is too tight. I risk a glance into the car's back seat; a yellow jug of brake fluid is lying there.

The door squeals as I force it open and Sage hisses through her teeth. I stash the brake fluid and pull her around the hood of the car as a team rushes into this yard. We need knowledge that doesn't originate here. A flicker of peace is enough. There is a way out, and we have to find it.

Lights flood the yard as a civilian bursts through a back door. He makes it to the fence, but a taser brings him down and officers drag him away.

Ten seconds.

One corner of my mouth turns up; the still, small voice inside is enough. I take Sage's hand and count down. The entire place is crawling with agents who leave no opening, but I only see the wide-open gate, and that in five seconds, we'll move.

"Go," I say, sprinting forward, towing Sage as searchlights flow around us, dancing away as if choreographed so we can pass through the gate and dive behind bushes alongside the next house. The clamor grows as agents corral people on the street.

I'm drawn to a brick house across the street where an old man's face appears in the window, staring straight at us. His white hair catches the glimmer of searchlights as he nods, then beckons us.

"How can he even *see* us?" Sage whispers, peering through the bushes.

A green light inside is more concrete than the curb. Without a shred of hesitation, I plot our path into the house. Three doors down, a team preps to enter another home, and when they hit the door, we sprint across the yard onto the small porch. The door opens before we stop moving; we slip into the hot interior.

"Hurry, I've got a place you can hide," the old man says, pointing.

"How did you know they're looking for us?" I ask.

The man laughs. "Dreamed it. Two nights in a row. I was a preacher before they made it illegal, and I'm still a preacher after. You're a brother, in more ways than one." He gives a crisp salute as he opens a pantry door. The space is tiny, with a sparse smattering of dry goods on the shelves.

"Take whatever you need. There's a trapdoor in the floor that leads to a crawl space." He hands me a small, worn Bible. "Take this."

Someone pounds on the front door as I grip the book and step in. "Thank you."

He laughs again. "Whatever Yahweh says, I do."

I pull Sage into the tiny, dark room.

"I'm coming! No need to bust anything!" he shouts, his voice wavering with age. Just before he shuts us away, he whispers, "Southwest. No idea if that means anything to you, but I'm supposed to tell you."

The door clicks shut, leaving me to wonder.

"What now?" Sage has my forearm in a white-knuckled grip.

I click on a penlight. "We stock up, then move." Checking my watch is like a punch in the gut. "Forty minutes until pickup."

The pantry is pitiful, but it's not food I'm after. Baking soda, vinegar, sandwich bags, and water bottles should do. I yank the trapdoor and jump down. "Gonna have to crawl, sorry."

But Sage is there beside me in the dank crawl space and we scurry to the nearest exit, pushing through cobwebs until I rip off the screen cover. "Got a job for you: Empty all these bottles." I reach over and smash a spider before it reaches her. "Fill them a quarter full of vinegar, then cut the corners out of the bags and fill them with baking soda. Suspend one bag of soda over the rim, then screw the lid on to secure it. Don't let them tip. I'll be back in two minutes."

"*What?* No, we have to stay together."

"Got to create an opening. I'll be back. Have some soda bombs ready, will you?" I don't give her time to resist by moving through the narrow opening with more empty bottles and chemicals, then crouch behind a shed and plan my route.

Southwest. What does it mean?

Further on, there's a quiet spot behind a shed where the pool shock and brake fluid release a sharp, pungent odor, making me hyper aware of the ticking clock: 90 seconds until detonation. Two sprints through the humid shadows, and I tuck the last bottle in a gutter, then double back toward Sage. A pop precedes a stream of fire shooting skyward far to my right.

One. The shadows are like home, creating cover as I stay low. Pop.

Two.

Screams echo as the third bottle shoots flames, drawing agents like moths. I skid up to the crawl space and take Sage's hand. Our eyes lock as a shiver runs up my arm, a shriek of energy unique to us alone.

"Bombs?" I ask, ignoring it.

She hands me three.

"One street to cross. Stay low." The agents are taking the bait, rushing toward the fires and leaving a gap to the south.

I shake the first soda bottle as we sprint, waiting until it gets rock-hard in my hand. At the corner of a house whose front door hangs at an odd angle, I study the street. Headlights are the enemy. The water bottle crinkles in my hand, telling me its time has come. I pitch it at the house, towing Sage away. It goes off with a loud pop that draw shouts, but we're far ahead.

We sprint past the last house; an agent steps from the tree line, so I sling Sage to the side and roll. His shots flare wide, and my swift uppercut slings him aside. I snatch his pistol, bashing it into his neck. He falls back, limp, and we drag him beyond the tree line.

I check my watch and hiss through my teeth. Eighteen minutes would be plenty if I were alone. Sage's blonde hair glints in the moonlight. Thank goodness I'm not.

"Let's go for a run."

Gordon's Pass is the last spit of sand in Naples, Florida, and Sage is still exhausted as I scan for Paco's men. Not far off, the beach ends in a high barrier of large rock. The steady rhythm of waves takes me back to BUDs: beating my body far past breaking, finding another level. My journey in the spirit was so similar. Dying to find life.

Sage steps closer as the dark beach and wild wind press in. "Where's the boat?"

Starlight glints off a dinghy where two men struggle to load a heavy crate.

"There." Relief floods me at the sight.

She stops. "We're taking *that* across the gulf?"

"Paco's a careful man; he'll be waiting a mile or so offshore with the real boat."

"What's in the crate?"

"I'm sure we *don't* want to know." I grin down at her, hoping to fend off her nerves.

The click of a rifle's safety going off makes me freeze. In Spanish, I drop Paco's name, then wait for a response.

"Si, rapido."

We wade through the waves and I help Sage in, but the crate takes up most of the space. Her skin is icy cold even after the run. She was hypothermic the last time we were in the water together, and all the ways this could go sideways press in. I force them away, visualizing our safe arrival in Central America.

The dinghy tilts in the waves with the steady dip of oars and a small electric motor. Sage presses against my side as the cutting wind strips her body heat.

A dark smudge appears in the distance. Paco's got a new boat that bristles fore and aft with weapons. It's a dull black, with almost zero reflection. Knowing Paco, it's radar-absorbing as well. Three similar vessels float a few yards out.

"Is he expecting trouble?" Sage whispers.

"Yeah, we just arrived."

She snorts as the dingy bumps against the hull and hands reach for her. I pull myself into the thirty-eight-foot cruiser, a half second behind. She's already squirming in a man's embrace, twisting away from his advance.

My elbow slams his jugular, without thought, and my other arm snakes around his neck. The fluid motion forces him into a solid headlock. He lets her go, but my anger flares, too hot for control.

Click. Click. Click. Click.

Every rifle on board levels at me.

"Paco. It's been too long," I growl into his ear, loosening my grasp a bit. "The girl's off-limits."

"Si, si."

"Tell them to stand down."

Paco squeaks out the command in Spanish as I let him go, stepping between Sage and the rest, ready.

Paco rubs his throat, his black hair glinting. He's got an eye patch, which is new. A long scar runs beneath it, from his forehead to his ear. His men glare, the air crackling as a massive figure rises from the bow. He's got to be six foot five, and well-armed. My stomach clenches; bringing Sage here was a *bad* idea.

"Figured she payment, Carter," Paco says, rubbing his neck.

"You owe *me,* remember?" I say, nerves on fire.

"Border patrol doubled. Word is, they looking for a couple." He crosses his arms, glaring with one eye.

I shift as the rifles hold steady aim. Good thing he doesn't know what's breathing down our necks. "Back 'em off, Paco."

He nods, the men stand down, and the big guy stops next to Paco. I dig in my pack, unzipping a small compartment, and offer one of the small storage devices from the *Olympia,* knowing his weakness for barter. "Names and numbers. Military. That's payment enough for the extra trouble."

His eye flares before he covers it. "Near lost my boat last time. They got birds now. Maybe you worth more as a prisoner."

My eyes narrow. "I saved your neck once; should I break it now?"

Sage presses against my back as Paco grins, showing one gold tooth. He's as wild as a typhoon and just as unpredictable.

"That no necessary. You be on duty, though." He snatches the device, slapping me on the shoulder. "Margie! Bring the Browning .30."

The giant shifts, turning aside.

"Margie?" Sage whispers behind me.

He returns, shouldering a thirty-caliber machine gun with a two-hundred-round belt. I take the heavy automatic weapon, nodding as I slide the bolt, finding the action smooth. Margie towers over me, wearing a vest lined with grenades. The men struggle to load the crate from the dinghy, but Margie moves in, hefting it over the gunwale as Paco takes the helm.

"One mile, then the gauntlet," he says, forcing the throttle forward. The boat leaps ahead, its engines well-muffled. It's an impressive setup that cuts through the water like a shadow, and the other boats follow suit, slicing through the night.

"Sage," I say over my shoulder, "hole up over there." I point to the curved console near Paco that won't provide a shred of cover in the face of heavy fire. Still, it's better than the open deck.

The Browning's weight will be an asset when balanced on the platform at the bow. I settle in behind the weapon, and pull tension from my shoulders. The ocean waves have been home to me for years, and they lend comfort now.

"Sánchez, load Carter up," Paco shouts, and a wiry Hispanic man sets a heavy box at my feet, ready to load a long string of thirty-caliber rounds.

The gulf is quiet with the swell at three feet. Hundreds of calculations settle—the wind shear, how the heat over the water will affect the Browning's performance. The men take up positions along the rail, weapons ready. Margie crouches a few feet in front of Sage. Paco's never one to underestimate an enemy, and he's prepped for all-out war. There's no turning back now, only this last chance to slip past the gaping maw of the N.W.O.

A searchlight reflects off the water and I lock down a cortisol spike. This is it.

"Approaching vessel, prepare to be boarded," a loudspeaker ripples out of the dark.

Paco jams the throttle forward, and the boat surges toward the line of border patrol. The others in our fleet spread out, making a run for it.

"Stop for inspection!" The lights are blinding as they focus on us.

Seven patrol boats float before us, then bright muzzle flash punctuates the light.

Pop. Pop. Pop.

The man beside me leans forward, returning fire on the closest patrol vessel, then jerks hard to one side, falling to the deck. I swing the machine gun, motion smooth, laying down gaping holes along the waterline. The boat slows, swallowing the ocean, listing hard as men jump off its side. It won't be on the water long… That leaves six.

I turn to the next, refusing to flinch as rounds blast Paco's boat, fiberglass shards bursting skyward. This target surges in a zigzag pattern, preventing me from leveling the Browning's worst damage.

Fire rains down and I tuck the weapon closer. There's only this moment, this shot. Three men on our starboard yelp, then disappear into the gulf, but the patrol boat rears over a wave, offering a broadside shot the Browning ensures they'll never recover from. Paco whips our boat hard to starboard, and I lock my boots in the bow, firing at the next vessel.

The heavy thump of a helicopter pounds the air. I grimace; our chances of survival just dropped.

"We got company!" Paco screams, as another patrol ship roils in flames far to our left.

The helicopter's cannon flashes. One of our fleet explodes into a bright ball of flames. Paco cranks the wheel, maxing out straight toward the helo. "Carter!"

I center in, blowing its cannon with the first burst. The bird rocks hard, and I swing up to the rotors' base as a fresh spray of bullets hits our deck. Focus tight, I hold until the rotor blows off and the helo drops fast, its rotor screaming until it cuts deep into the ocean, frothing white water.

Our boat rocks and Sage screams. "Jacob!"

Paco is sprawled across the deck, a pool of blood expanding beneath him.

At the rear, only one gunner remains. I twist, finding Margie laying down heavy fire, still in front of Sage.

"Take the helm!" I bellow, firing off another set of rounds, taking on the closest patrol.

She's frozen, staring at Paco as the boat settles into the swell.

"NOW!" I roar. We're sitting ducks for the remaining border vessels. She leaps for the helm, grimacing as she slides through the slick. I chop one hand toward the south. "Full throttle!"

The boat strains hard, veering as she over-corrects, but the heavy thump of another bird makes me growl. A quick check of my ammo reveals fewer than twenty rounds.

"Jacob!" Sage shouts, on a collision course with another cruiser.

"Hold!" I dive for the gunner crumpled on the deck. It's Sanchez, whose glassy eyes stare at the black sky. He's got three grenades hooked to his vest. I yank them, pulling the clips.

Sage screams as we bear down at fifty knots at the oncoming boat. Margie and I lob grenades as we close in, timing with the waves. The water explodes with heavy fire from the helo.

I point right. "NOW!"

Sage cranks the wheel and I slam against the hull as the patrol boat veers just inches away. It bucks as the first grenade goes off, then careens sideways, ramming us halfway down the starboard side.

The second grenade blows the rear of the boat and its nose tilts skyward, ripping off a chunk of our gunwale. The helicopter sweeps around, waiting for distance from the dying boat to fire.

They won't get it.

I center the Browning on the rotor as the last two grenades blow. Their blast combines with the helo's as its fuel tanks detonates. The concussion sends Sage sprawling my way through the slick of soot and blood. Forcing consciousness through the high-pitched buzz and pressure, I scoop her up and leap for the wheel. The rear gun is empty, and the sea seethes through the ruined gunwale.

The motors scream, their mufflers peppered with holes, as we race into open water. *Southwest.* The words fill my mind. The flaming chaos all around is a magnet drawing reinforcements. I grip the wheel; everything's quiet directly south, but deep inside I'm certain those words are for right now. I set a southwest course and we fade into the deep night. The disorientation from the blast dissipates, and I re-grip Sage when she sags in my arms. She shakes her head, swallowing hard, face streaked with soot, eyes wild.

The night air rips past, the scent of salt and gunpowder as familiar as rain. Nothing on this boat reflects light, not even when the fresh helo's search lights sweep straight to the south where logic told me to go. Southwest is right where we need to be.

Sage grips my arm, scanning the deck, her eyes finding focus. Only Paco and Margie remain; the others must have washed overboard. Margie slides on his knees, pressing one soot-covered hand over a wound on Paco's left shoulder that's pumping blood. He pulls Paco onto his lap, uttering an eerie wail that entwines with the engine's scream.

Sage leans forward, and I let her go. Margie throws his head back, the veins on his massive neck standing out with another cry. The cubbies along the gunwale are peppered with holes, and one door is swinging with the waves, but Sage takes a shredded first-aid kit from it, and they do what they can for Paco as I run the boat full speed for miles until we're a speck in the vast dark. I throttle down, and the vessel settles into the ocean. A surge of water flows through the massive hole.

"We'd best not sit too long." My voice is gruff from the thick smoke as I kneel to find Paco's face pasty white. "She'll last longer up on plane."

The ocean is claiming the boat, so I check the bilge, finding the wiring blown in half. Reconnecting the red wires takes seconds, restarting the pump's steady hum.

"*Mi hermano!*" Margie cries, staring at his bloody hand, keeping pressure on the wound with the other.

Brother?

"Paco!" Margie's shoulders tremble as he presses on the wound.

I pull Sage up, checking her for injuries.

"I'm all right." Her voice wavers as I take water bottles from the cubby and insist she drain one. I chug three, then turn to Paco with pain sizzling from a hundred minor injuries.

"His axillary artery is wide open. Without surgery, he'll die." She shrugs, eyes sliding down, trying to run from the truth. "But blood loss will take him long before then."

Waves lap over the deck, washing away the red. Paco flinches, his face contorting in an unconscious struggle. Margie cradles him, but it's Paco's expression that carries me back to the *Olympia*, where Rivera fought the same battle. Sage clutches my tattered shirt, because the deep sensation of fear flowing from Paco isn't imaginary.

My heart pounds as I kneel. The eyepatch is long gone, and the empty socket gives a heavy impression of death already. Rivera's screams as he died echo too loud in my head, and terror fills the boat. Paco is teetering over the same abyss. *Forever.*

A breath of wind stirs the fresh salt air. Margie's moan pricks at my skin in the night. Soot and lacerations cover my battle-scarred hands.

Seen and unseen.

I draw on eternal words. *God… who calls the things that be not as though they were.*

He called for light when there was darkness.

This is life or death to you, Jacob.

It's life or death for Paco, too. How far do words reach? From the spirit into this world? Straight from here to hell? Can they stretch that far? But faith isn't bound by space, and neither is God's Word.

The breeze stirs again, igniting memories. I longed to be strong in both worlds, and it's this one where I feel weak now. But I need to reach further, to the divine nature of the Almighty, taking on His thoughts, His ways, and His work.

Deep-seated hatred rises for the vile grip of hell that's tightening by the second. Lion stench fills my lungs—whether real or imagined, I can't tell, but it makes my blood boil nonetheless. Had he ever heard the truth? Did he reject it?

A keening cry builds in my lungs until it can't be contained; I throw back my head and bellow into the night. I'm on my feet without knowing how, my skin tingling with energy, and still, the outcry won't end, as if I'm knee-deep in the spirit's water. One thought reverberates as my hand shoots skyward.

Call things that are not...

"Paco." But my hand feels so powerless as it falls to his shoulder. Words tangle, at war with doubt and his wounds, so obvious, so *real.* So permanent. I clench my eyes, searching for true sight. The water washed away my pain before, and the scars on my forearm are real too.

Paco's face contorts into a silent scream.

"He's going," Sage whispers.

Let there be light.

Long ago at the hut, Peter poured out the oil onto Solomon's brow. I can do the same.

"Paco, be healed." The words feel far too small to fend off the iron grip of death as the ocean air steals them away. "Wounds, seal up."

A heartbeat passes, and even the wind falls flat. I blink, every sensation of the spirit gone, empty and feeling a fool.

Margie flinches, pulling his hand from the wound as if singed. Sage is there, inspecting the ragged injury. Her wild gaze flicks to mine. "The bleeding stopped." Her fingers press hard against his jugular. "He's still alive."

"We've got to keep moving; try to keep him steady."

Paco's grimace sears itself into my mind. *Lions and flames.* I glance at Sage as the boat surges onto plane.

Morning creeps up the horizon as the ocean swells gather strength. I brace against the helm and the wind that's determined to steal moisture from my eyes. Margie's still holding Paco propped against the haul. Sage slumps against his muscular arm in an exhausted sleep. What a circus we are.

Paco flinches, and Margie draws him closer, inspecting the shoulder wound. With a moan, Paco wakes, staring up at the red-blushed sky. I recoil, hands frozen on the wheel. *Both* his eyes are open. Margie stares down at him, then strains backward.

Sage comes awake, blurry sleep washed away as Paco grabs his chest, fingers trembling at the wound's edge. His fingers explore his face, his eyes, and his guttural cry makes Sage flinch.

"How…how this be?" Margie asks, his face ashen as his gaze locks on mine.

I throttle down and kneel next to them, looking into Paco's two perfect, blazing brown eyes.

Sage's hands clamp over her mouth, staring. "Jacob Carter, so help me, how did that happen?"

Swirling emotion tightens my throat. The breeze tugs at my whisper, "The spirit overcame the flesh."

"That is *not* an answer."

"It's the only one that exists."

"Please!" Paco cuts in, his perfect eyes wild. "Tell me! Where is God? How do I come to him?"

The words well up from my childhood in a hot church basement. "If you confess with your mouth to the Lord Jesus, and believe in your heart that God has raised Him from the dead, you will be saved."

The terror of the flames still burns in his eyes. He cries out, his hands still covering the wound. "I believe, Lord Jesus! I believe!"

He makes the sign of the cross, muttering; then he glances from Sage to me. "You..." He licks his lips, breath heaving. "You know what I saw?"

I nod, my mouth a firm line as Rivera's fate bites into me.

"You sure this work? This believing in Jesus?"

"Positive."

Margie is trembling as he stares at me with fearful awe. Paco lets out a long breath, wincing at the movement.

"Gloria a Dios."

The coast of Belize is within sight, and we're listing far to starboard. The deserted beach is a mix of creamy sand and mosquito-infested mangroves. Monkey River will be the perfect place to hide, with an expanse of untouched rainforest where we can disappear. The boat held up, but it's tattered and struggling as we pass Placencia.

Sage grips the bullet-ridden railing. The deep circles under her eyes and the dull fear brewing there demand a rest. We'll fade into the jungle and recover from everything before planning the next move.

Paco hunches, gripping his shoulder in the light swell as we cruise past beach houses, but he's on his feet, which is something, considering Sage was sure he'd need blood. The turquoise Caribbean sweeps past as he presses a phone to his ear; the boat creaks as Margie's shadow covers me.

"Paco, my half-brother. He save me from the slaver. I owe him everything." His nose flares as Paco stumbles on the swell, his shoulder wrapped in his torn shirt. "Now, I owe you."

Paco hisses through his teeth, slamming the phone against his leg. Margie steps beside him, bracing him as another wave tosses the listing boat.

"The Pretoria job went south," Paco says, frowning up at his little brother. "You got to fix it."

Margie nods, but Sage is staring at me with fear shining in her eyes. She drops her gaze and turns to the crystal water, but not fast enough to hide the truth. The effects of Project 157 are still breathing down her neck, looming like a hurricane, poised to swallow her.

Is it possible to protect her from it? I should have warned Demyen to watch out for her. Pressure builds as the dangers of both worlds collide. Losing her during a jump is unacceptable, but there's no plan of action, no way to prevent it.

Monkey Village is straight ahead, with dilapidated shacks perched on the mouth of the river. Already, people are gathering at the tiny wooden dock that's lined with small watercraft. I reach forward, looping a rope around the piling. A row of armed guards files onto the dock, eyeing us, very out of place in the poverty that surrounds.

"Those yours?" I ask Paco, easing toward the Browning.

"Si, si! For the package." Paco points to the crate, which has two boards blown off. "This will pay for the new fleet, plus some." His gold tooth glints in the sun as he greets the guards in English, the official language of Belize.

I take Sage's hand and move toward the pier, eager to escape their gaze. The boat bumps the doc and Paco stumbles again. Margie grips his elbow, but Paco shakes him off and stands straighter. A smile curves Margie's broad lips, then he steps in front of us before I leap for the dock.

His eyes shine as he nods at us with a deep reverence. "A life for life; whatever you need, you call. I know war, Paco should be dead. You save him." His gaze flicks to my hands as he dips his head. "You need me, I be there."

His hand engulfs mine, then we leap out of the boat, inching past the squad of guards, keeping our faces low. One of them turns, glaring as we step into the crowd of locals. They're dark-skinned and on foot, in threadbare clothes. A few worn bikes cruise past, loaded with bananas and coconuts. I step behind a crooked wooden building, tucking Sage behind me, then ease one eye around the corner. It reveals what I figured.

The guard takes out a phone, studying its screen, then he scans the street, searching. For us.

"Does he know?" Sage asks, her voice raw.

I lean back. "We have a bounty. He'll be wanting to collect it."

Her fingers bite into my arm. *Never mind about that rest.*

We ease behind the building, the bare dirt glistening with broken glass and rusty bottle caps. "We've got to cover your hair; you stand out like a beacon around here."

She runs a hand over it, frowning. The gaunt look she's been working on is unsettling, demanding care.

A little girl skips between two huts, skidding to a stop upon seeing us. I smile and squat, fishing a flashlight from my pack, and hold it out, pointing to the handkerchief covering her wild black hair.

"Trade?"

She puts one finger in her mouth, so I drop my eyes, and she flits closer, looking at the light. We swap, then she takes off, her bare feet spraying sand, piling it up in an ellipse, with a triangle behind it. The air tingles across my skin. Why is something from the spirit following me here? What is the symbol? But there's no time to deal with it, not now.

Sage ties the bandana on and soon we trade a pocket knife for a bunch of bananas and coconuts. We take a slim foot trail that cuts into the jungle, using the enormous trees for cover, while I watch the trailhead. All quiet.

We follow the twisting path for a while, finding that it dives near the murky water of the Monkey River at intervals. Sage gives an empty laugh, watching the fruit swinging from my pack.

"Jacob Carter, the walking positron factory with his mini positron emitters."

I turn with a grin. "Both of us have something in common with bananas now."

But she's looking past me at the river, her eyes wild.

"Is that an alligator?" she asks, pointing.

I turn, studying the murky water. "Croc; it's got to be a fifteen-footer."

She shudders as a blue jungle crab skitters into its hole next to my boots. I unsheathe a bowie knife, wishing it was a machete because we have to leave the path and let the jungle swallow us. She's slapping mosquitoes and dripping sweat as I step in, pressing for higher ground, careful to leave no broken leaves near the trail.

"Stay back about fifteen feet and stay sharp." Training takes over, using cover, and reading everything. Risking it with snakes is far better than leaving a trail by chopping.

We cross a path about six inches wide and three inches deep that winds deep into the jungle's heart. I crouch and beckon Sage.

"Is that from a snake?" Her voice is full of fearful awe.

"No. It's a leaf cutter ant trail. It's going to rain."

She swats her neck. "I don't see any ants."

"Right, trail's empty; it'll rain soon."

We scale a steep rocky cliff where the canopy rises higher behind the ledge, so our silhouettes won't be sky-lined. The perfect hide site.

"We'll rest here for a while."

She sinks to the rock outcropping with a sea of rainforest spreading below and rips a banana from the bunch. "Oh, man. That is *the best.*"

"Nothing like fresh off the tree, is there?" I pinch off large, smooth leaves and build a bed of sorts, and the overhanging branches come together well for a roof. The first fat drops splat down, staining the rock in a disturbing form. Heavier rain obliterates the pyramid and ellipse, but they don't leave my mind.

"You were right about the rain," she says, pulling me into the present, as she gazes over the jungle, hugging her knees.

"The ants are never wrong."

"Neither are you."

I grunt, hacking a coconut open. "I'm wrong plenty when I don't listen to my spirit." Clear juice flows from the fruit. "Drink up."

The mosquitoes form a cloud around her. A tree nearby has a tube of mud twisting up its trunk, so I pinch it and small termites flow out. A few crawl onto my fingers, where I lick them up.

"Ugh!" her disgust is priceless.

"Come on, they're minty fresh. You want bloodsuckers or mint-flavored protein? The choice is yours."

She swats her face. "Are you serious? Eating those will repel mosquitoes?"

"Of course, what do you think we do jungle training for? Plus, they don't bite."

I hold out my hand and she picks a few off, her nose wrinkled. Her touch sends a shiver up my arm, but she doesn't notice, too focused on the termites. She grimaces and shoves them in her pretty mouth, then surprise fills her eyes. "They *are* minty."

I crush a few more and rub them on her arms. The mosquitoes dissipate as I tuck stray hair behind her ear. Our eyes lock.

"Rest now." My voice comes out husky.

She takes my hand and presses it against her cheek. Her trembling fingers bring a frown. There are no words for everything that's between us. I run my thumb under the cut on her cheekbone, then pull my hand away, the surge of emotion too strong.

She sinks down onto the leaves as the rain pours in true jungle style. I sit before her, watching clouds gather above the canopy, tracing the symbol in the puddle before me.

She stirs, her voice soft. "So."

Maybe that's all she'll say, too exhausted to go on.

She sighs, forcing the words. "With Paco…you bent the rules? I know wounds. He should have died."

I look out over the lush jungle canopy, rain softening the edges of everything. A quiver runs up my spine, and her question swirls with Mara's words, clarifying into truth.

"No. I didn't bend anything," I say, searching for a way to express it.

"But you did. That shot was deadly. I've seen it plenty; even a transfusion wouldn't have brought him back. People don't get up from that. You did *something.*" Her voice trembles, and I twist to find her rubbing her neck.

"Think of it this way: Laws were established at the dawn of the world, but people forgot them. I didn't bend a rule; I *used* one. It's not a common one, but that doesn't change its power. It's just as sure as gravity. More sure, in both realms."

Power. Samson spoke of power and authority. That's what makes the law function: authority, words, and faith mixed together. But the dragon's silky voice wraps around the thought. Maybe authority is an illusion, and God's sovereignty is forcing everything to happen. The thought feels like standing on an oil slick.

Frustration is clear on her face, so I go on. "Electricity existed since the first dawn, Sage. But humanity didn't know about it; they couldn't use it, but it was there with the ability to prevent thousands of people from freezing to death or starving. But without *knowledge*, it couldn't affect a single life. The spirit is the same once you learn how it works. You can't see it, can't break it, or damage it, ever. All I did was plug in to it. The power was there, waiting for someone to figure out how to use its infinite supply. Yet most don't know it exists."

She groans, stretching out. "Someday, I want actual answers."

I felt the same once, but Project 157 allowed me to make the leap into genuine life. The further I go, the more there is to learn. I take the Bible from my pack and flip to Romans, chapter eight.

"For the law of the spirit of life in Christ Jesus, has made me free from the law of sin and death." The words make goosebumps race across my skin, striking straight into my heart.

Sage sags into sleep as I sit, chewing on the deep things, circling around the questions that strike like lightning. God *is* sovereign. Does that leave me any choices in life? Hours pass as more questions press in, along with the burning image of the dragon's strange shadow that pursues me through realms.

Then, toward the village, a flock of green parrots flushes from the treetops. Tense heartbeats pass, and another flock takes wing. *Closer.* Right where we cut up the mountain. The deep call of a howler monkey echoes, and the treetops shiver as the troop flees. My senses pique; every jungle noise is like gunfire.

I ease the pack on, checking the pistols on each hip and the one in the shoulder holster. Two brilliant macaw parrots flush right below us, like forest jewels.

"Sage." I pull her up before she's awake. "Run!"

She stumbles, snapping out of deep sleep. I leap down a jumble of boulders, cutting a fresh path to the river. Something flings away. The Bible! There's no time to turn back for it now. I grimace at the loss, plunging downward.

"Jacob."

Green haze swirls around her hips. I look at my hands. It's flowing from my palms too.

"Hurry." My heart slams, dangers converging. Did he already alert the N.W.O.? Training demands I treat it like a worst-case scenario. Energy jolts between us as I grip her hand, and we leap through the slick jungle, dropping fast and reckless.

"Make it to the river…" I grimace, throwing one forearm up, smashing through low-hanging thorns.

Shouts rise behind. They found our nest. Sage shudders, running pell-mell, sobbing, "Don't let me go!"

I'm already crushing her hand. A rifle goes off as we burst onto the main trail far beyond where we left it. Sage cries out, one hand covering her shoulder. Blood runs between her fingers.

The river's right there, its banks steep and tangled with undergrowth. Sage goes stiff as the veins in her neck strain in the green swirl.

She's jumping.

She'll die without the water.

My own muscles turn to stone, and haze fills my vision. Seconds. That's all I have to save her before we disintegrate.

I slam my shoulder into her ribs, momentum driving us over the bank as more shots echo. She cries out and I wrap my arms and legs around her like on the *Olympia*.

The sound of a boat motor roaring makes me cringe as we plummet toward the muddy water where crocs rule, with bullets zinging past. My grip is so tight, it's leaving bruises.

Except, I'm not trying to hold on to her body. I'm trying to hold on to her spirit.

3
SAGE

To really achieve anything, you have to be able to tolerate and enjoy risk. It has to become a challenge you look forward to. In all fields, to make exceptional discoveries you need risk— you're just never going to have a breakthrough without it. ~ Steven Kotler

Green lightning streaks through my body, ripping apart each molecule. Jacob's crushing me, but my breath is gone anyway, as pressure builds inside. My hands melt into his chest as we fall.

We hit the river, sending a seizure up my spine. The chaos ramps higher as we plunge. I'm torn apart, far inside, in places I didn't know existed. Jacob jerks, the water bubbles, something snaps loud and we fall, plummeting a million miles per hour. I claw at him, terror driving me.

The speed rips us apart; he's reaching for me, re-gripping a hundred times, but I'm a shadow now and impossible to seize. Darkness wraps around my feet, up my legs until it slithers into my nose, filling my lungs with acrid sludge. It's alive, injected into every crevice, infecting me. So heavy.

"Sage!" Jacob's scream echoes from another world. An orange flicker grows into wafting flames that lick across my skin as I surge ahead. It singes my eyes and blisters my lips, but there's no light inside the writhing flames. Their roar is worse than the heat, striking a chord of terror, as I fall further into the vise of hell, then slam onto a sticky surface coated in fire.

Creatures move inside the smoke. *Lions.* The flames blacken my skin as the first beast approaches. It's gaunt, with a hide that's rotting and a sparse mane that kindles with dark flames.

"Raeual!" a voice screams, but it's so far away, and the gaping maw and yellow teeth fill my vision. "Get her back!"

My hair catches; the awful scent entwines with knowing this is eternal.

"Raaa!" A voice rips the air above me, but I'm dead, *forever dead.* If only death were a quiet, endless darkness, like I pictured.

The lion leaps for me, flames crackling in the intense darkness; its dripping jaws descend.

An explosion of light makes me cringe.

"Sage!" The desperate voice is familiar, somehow. A bolt of light strikes the lion; it rolls, still clawing toward me with dead eyes locked on me. The darkness clamps so hard there's no room to struggle.

Sparks shoot off a round shield; voices shout, rending the torrid air. The brilliant outline of an immense man appears, reaching for me.

I cry, longing for the outstretched hand, but my arms won't move as my ruined eyes water in the war between dark and light.

He touches me, and I suck in the first breath.

"Help… me!" I gasp.

Another figure appears, pulling, but the darkness inside won't let me go. It's too heavy inside my lungs, eating me. Being torn apart would be mercy compared to the flames. I force my eyes to lock on the blinding light, taking the injury. *I won't stay here.*

Arms wrap around me, but the touch is painful, too bright, too warm. The intense speed picks up again, stripping even more of me away. I slam into something, and the concussion flings me far from the warm embrace. Stone and dirt bring me to a sudden stop, listless arms collapsing as my cheek grinds into rocky soil.

Where is this? I grope around, trying to recall anything other than dark flames that still burn in my thoughts. *They're part of me.* Everything is so dim, a land made of shadows. Wiping my eyes changes nothing as my heart pounds with a desperate, erratic rhythm.

My legs won't hold my weight, leaving me to crawl, scraping my hands, searching through the fog as the raucous cry of a raven grates my ears. The sky is an iron curtain as I search for the creature.

The harsh flap of wings makes me crouch, then a sharp beak pecks my leg.

"No! Get away!" I shout, but the glistening black bird won't leave, studying me with one dull eye. A stench on the breeze brings a wave of queasiness, and the greasy smell of a rotting carcass fills my burned lungs. I twist, searching for the source, and the bird rips at my exposed leg. A low growl makes my hair stand on end, sparking a distant memory.

If you smell something dead, run.

Whimpering, I lurch away; the raven flogs my back with claws and beak. Its wings pump hard, wafting my burned hair as it soars away. Terror flows as the sickening scent increases. My legs give way, and I tumble, my palms slicing open on the sharp, unforgiving gravel.

It's close.

I roll, and a lion looms over me, saliva dripping from yellow teeth. One ear flaps, almost cut through, and the flames leap in his eyes. One paw crushes my chest. He shifts, the pressure increasing. *Can't breathe.*

He doesn't speak, but his thoughts are inside me: an intrinsic connection that links us.

You're mine.

I whimper as his claws slide out, crusted points piercing my skin. He growls, jaws inching closer. The claws sink deeper.

"Ah!" My cry is useless.

I own you.

It's truer than anything. I belong to him, heart and soul, with no escape. One more blink and he'll send me back... I shiver, terror rising.

"You!" a voice rips through the terror.

The lion whips toward it, the ground quaking with his roar. A figure flashes in and something glints, lofted high. I roll, trying to crawl away as the battle shudders the ground.

The lion's snarl pitches up, pain etched into the sound. Heavy footsteps make me scramble faster. "No!"

"Sage! *Sage!*" The voice is so broken that I turn, shielding my eyes, blinking in the painful blur of light that streaks into my brain. It's a man, but my watering eyes can't stand the sight.

"Sage…"

Something brushes my face, and I scramble back.

"This… this can be…." The deep voice is choked with tears.

"Don't hurt me," but he already is. Being so close to the light makes pain pulse through my head.

"No…"

Eyes adjusting, I crack one open. Tears course down a handsome face with a square jaw and clear blue eyes. Pain spikes as I turn away.

"Come on, I'll get you to the hut." He shifts even closer.

Clenching my eyes doesn't block out the piercing light, and I cry, the pain swirling as he lifts me to my feet. Blood oozes in a hot river down my stomach. Every nerve screams at his touch.

"Here, I'll carry you." His voice trembles, rumbling in my ear as he scoops me up. There's no energy to resist.

He strides forward, passing into deeper shadows and dead trees. This entire world is dark and frightening, and the air burns like sulfur.

I'm lost.

There is no home, no safe, no hope. A cry lacerates my parched throat. Existence is torture, making me long for darkness.

"Shh… you need water." He sets me down, and I hug my knees, skin sagging over bones. The tinkling sound of water makes my throat swell with thirst.

"Here." The man's arm glows as he brings a palmful of water to my cracked lips. The liquid's touch makes me recoil, retching as it stings.

"No," he groans, "this can't… I was sure you had the light."

I can't stay here, near the water, or his shimmering skin. My calf shrieks as I crawl past dead tree trunks and collapse into a slime of rotting leaves. Breathing is too much. Then, soft footsteps crunch, drawing closer from deep within the trees.

"Demyen!" the man behind calls out.

"Aye, Boy. You're alright, the Almighty be praised. Never seen the like!" Demyen's voice is even deeper, and it grates like sandpaper.

"Raeual had a good bit to do with my survival."

"Your hurt, aren't you?"

"It's nothing, just a scrape."

"Who's this?" the other man asks.

I blink hard, cheek pressed into the ground as their words puncture my midnight.

"I… it's Sage…" His voice is agony. "What do we do?"

For a second, the desire to comfort him surges, but I can't. Can't even comfort myself.

"Aye. She's bad off."

"But… how do we get the light into her?"

"We don't."

"What?"

"Only she can do that."

The words are meaningless. All I want is a place to hide. A dim place where the light won't stab my brain, but movement is agony.

"Then I've got to get her to the hut before nightfall."

"She won't stay there. I've seen it before, Boy; she won't abide the light, and when darkness falls, her energy will return and she'll break out. Best thing to do is watch over her here."

The first man growls, frustration brimming.

"She's the one you were all in a dither about last time?" Demyen asks.

There's only a moan in response. Quiet moments pass as I clench my eyes, longing for sleep.

"Demyen? How is it possible that I didn't know she was…"

He sighs. "So much hides in the physical order. People can look right, talk like they know the truth, but the spirit exposes the roots."

"I've got to make her see."

"Not possible, Boy. All you can do is plant the seed."

The light intensifies, burning in and making me crinkle up inside. The image of two giant figures etches into my retina.

Retina. The word comes from far away, wrapped in a green fuzz. I concentrate on it, desperate to escape the glowing figures.

"Raeual..." The first voice hesitates. "What's going on?"

"It's time to go back, Jacob. It won't be easy. Galel took the brunt of it last time."

Jacob. The name strikes me, familiar yet so far away, with a green tinge wrapped around each letter.

The color grows, pleasant compared to this hateful light, so I strain toward it. Jacob grabs me, and I thrash at his touch.

Green haze grips me even tighter, pulling me forward. The first journey's vivid reality slams hard, drawing a scream. The haze sucks me forward, but on the horizon, the bloom of dark flames spreads.

"No!"

Desperate, I maul Jacob's neck as Raeual and Galel brace behind shields. Speed rips apart every cell, and dark flames reach out into my soul, but Jacob twists, covering me.

Covering me. Images flash: He's got a man with an eye patch in a headlock, then lightning flashes on a deck of a ship as Jacob fights off Tex in the rain, protecting me. The darkness sucks me in, severing the memories. Hot wind roars as Jacob strains against it. I'm slipping right through him, disintegrating into hell.

"No, stay with me, Sage!"

Exhaustion saps every drop of energy and will. Raeual and Galel roar, sparks spitting from their shields. Then a lion roars, and it rattles straight into my bones.

"Save me!"

It's like holding on in a hurricane. Jacob bellows, right in the beast's face, and the wind swirls harder, changing direction as we pick up speed, enveloped in green. The melting heat fades, but I'm still connected to it, no matter what world I run to.

Then my body's there, far beyond, like a beacon in the infinite expanse of time. Inside a damp, hot hut in the jungle, my shell is pale and frail, a reflection of me. I crash into it at terminal velocity. It pinches *so tight*. I suck in a breath, shivering and jerking, the seizure uncontrollable.

A child in the corner screams and runs out as I buck off the low pallet. Jacob twitches and rolls to his feet, lofting me in a heartbeat. My empty arms make it around his neck, pressing against his warm skin, but the truth can't be erased. Hell owns me.

"Jacob…" I sob as terminal weakness drains my body.

A dark-skinned man rushes through the doorless entry wearing a long-sleeved shirt and shorts, a bandana around his neck. "Ja, man, Percy go fishing, my biggest catch be awake."

Jacob scans the man, his sharp eyes catching everything. "Where are we?"

"Near Monkey Village, man. This be my palace, I build it for wife thirteen!" he cackles, showing crooked white teeth, slapping his knee.

My heart slams, then falls quiet—a shock of emptiness that will sever me from my body. *Please no.* It hammers again, erratic and dangerous, shaking me to my core as an icy sensation rushes down my nerves.

"Where's my pack?" Jacob's so strong, cradling me in his arms.

I watch the steady pulse in his neck, mine like a washing machine inside.

"Here, I dry everything out." Percy watches Jacob like he's a new species.

"Thank you." Jacob lays me down, but there isn't enough energy to shift positions. His ocean eyes darken as he presses his fingers against my jugular. He flinches; my volatile pulse is an enemy I can't fight. His warm hand settles against my throat as he murmurs something that's not English; the warmth of the strange words spreads, flowing into my veins.

He brushes a lock of my hair aside, then his jaw clenches. He turns, packing weapons with clinical precision. Percy runs a finger over one pistol.

"This a fine weapon."

Jacob points to a small table in the corner. "If you'll trade for that Bible, it's yours."

Percy's brilliant teeth flash as a wicked bite of pain emanates from my shoulder. I inch my fingers toward it, finding a bandana tied over a wound. Gunshot. The memory is murky, as if it happened to someone else. Maybe it did, to a girl who was ignorant of the dark.

Jacob takes the small leather-bound book from Percy. His eyes slide shut as he rubs the cover, as if it's solid gold. He stashes it, then lashes down the heavy pack. "Why did you help us?"

"It not good for the crocs to taste people, man!" Percy cackles again, then grows serious, his eyes darker than ever. "I know who after you. He obey... *them.*"

The way he spits the word leaves no room to wonder who *them* is. Some people still want to live free of the New World order; thank God one of them found us.

"Does he know about this place?" Jacob asks, turning to inspect my shoulder.

"He find my boat sooner or later. Hopefully later. That bullet graze her shoulder. I make her wife fourteen, man, if you don't want her."

Jacob frowns at me, but my heart keeps pace with the tortoise and the hare chasing each other, and my limbs, ice-cold.

A flock of birds sweeps past the open door. Percy spins, hand going to the pistol. "That be sooner, man!"

Percy sticks his head out, the weapon held low. Jacob hisses through his teeth and presses his fingers against my neck as his eyes burn into mine. "There's no time. Stay with me, Sage. Don't go where I can't follow."

Tears prick my eyes. I'd give anything to obey him, but I'm teetering on a knife's edge.

He picks me up and eases to the door. My legs flop, struggling to fend off the lions a little longer.

"Come on, I show you the way." Percy beckons from the jungle's edge. Jacob sprints after him, the rainforest flashing past. My mouth sticks together, hands numb in the tropical heat.

Percy's a shadow in the jungle, and Jacob races after him like he's not carrying an extra two hundred pounds between me and the pack. A bullet bites into a tree, the white wood exposed. My lips won't move, won't obey, won't cry out to protect him.

Percy ducks, eyes like saucers. "Hurry, man, we hole up behind the falls!"

"Sage!" Jacob dodges a branch, splashing into a stream, sensing that I'm fading. The water mushrooms right next to us, and the sound makes my heart leap to life. "You know the truth," he cries, lungs like bellows. "Jesus died to take your place and your sin. You've got to trust Him with your life, His for yours. Do it now, Sage!"

His words pierce through the crazy pattern of my heart and scare me to death. The stories from Sunday school made me certain I'd never measure up. The numbness spreads along with the truth. God would never keep me. Not when He knows the failure I am.

The truth strikes like Jacob's dagger, deadly and solid. *I could never live up to His expectation.*

The thunder of a waterfall fills the air, muffling more shots behind. Jacob curls forward, surging through the cool, waist-deep water, and straight into the white falls that dive from high above.

The water pummels me, twisting my head under its punishment and filling my nose. Then we're within the hush of a shallow cave behind the veil. Jacob forces me into Percy's arms.

"Sage, please!" His voice cracks as he takes weapons from the pack. "Take Jesus as Lord!" He groans, torn; then he turns, water spraying as he rushes out to war.

I reach after him, fingers trembling. *Don't go!* The veil of wavering water is steady, and willing him to reappear has zero result. Tears make a warm course in the wild jungle water on my face. A twinge of green issues from my stomach, and Percy's white-rimmed eyes stare as the energy builds.

He wades to a rock outcropping, laying me down inches above the water, watching like I'm an alien. Digging in a small pack at his hip, he holds out a section of red-stained root, hesitating. "Chew this, it help the heart."

He presses it into my mouth, then backs up against the far wall, eyeing the haze flowing from me. The bitterness spreads as I chew the wood. Anything to stay out of hell.

Really?

My treacherous heartbeat produces a brutal honesty. Unworthy is my singular definition, the very reason Heaven isn't mine. The bitter juice stings my throat as I stare at the falls, the water like the veil that separates the worlds. A crimson stain dives over the edge and mars the flow. Blood.

Please, no.

The image blurs. Blood. Jacob says it will save me. Thoughts swirl, erratic in the increasing green glow. Did Jacob just give his to protect me? I curl forward, a cry collapsing my lungs. Percy's pistol takes steady aim at the water, but the haze grows around me. *Not without Jacob!* I condense, willing it away, but it's an unstoppable force.

Percy's eyes go wide as the cave fills with the K-60's glow, his gaze shifting from me to the falls.

My muscles hammer, body jerking as I disconnect. "Don't... sh... shoot... Jacob."

Percy backs away as my hand falls into the pool of water and I sweep forward, light as a feather, the biting weakness of my body left behind. *But the darkness is so close.* I spread out, desperate to slow my descent.

"NO!" The hot wind rips at me, but I'm alone with no one to rescue me. Through the rushing wind, dark flames leap high, calling me home.

"Help!" The intense speed slows, so I scream again, louder, the name sticking in my throat. "Help me!"

The lions are coming! Skeletal, three of them stalk forward. *Hunting.*

"Release her." A voice reverberates above, its infinite power reaching even here in the pit.

The lions cringe at the words, their heads dipping low. The voice breaks my connection to the heat and the air grows lighter as I rise, sweeping past a blue-tinged cloud, until everything is shadows again.

Something slaps my skin, there's one breath, and I crash into dry sand, spewing it upward. Crumpled there, a quiet tread fills me with terror. Forcing up to a sitting position, I squeeze my eyes shut against the brightness. *Not a lion.* It's easier to look at the man's shadow as he towers above.

Then he crouches and pierces me to the core. "Hard to choose, eh?"

I squint up at him, taking in his curling beard and burning emerald eyes that make me turn away.

"There's a cave over yonder. You'd be more comfortable in the shade." The hatred I expect is nonexistent. I wipe my eyes, squinting. The shadows *are* deeper over there. He helps me limp over and settle in the cool dark, where the pain of his touch fades.

"It takes dying to live," he says, standing at the mouth of the cave, staring out over the forest.

The flames are still here, before my waking eyes, searing me. My sardonic laugh echoes off the rocks. "Death would be a mercy."

"Aye." He crosses his arms until the silence forces me to continue.

"I mean, both ways are death, right? One way I face a God I can never please, and when I fail, get sent back to pure torment. There's no choice there."

"What if you're wrong?" Demyen asks, then steps into the glaring light of day.

The question is like a festering wound that itches deep inside as the day wanes. Each breath is agony, tinged with sulfur, as if it's coming from inside me. When night settles, the dark eases my pain. I stand, wavering, bracing hands on my knees. Outside the cave's mouth, a lion's roar rattles straight into my heart. A shiver of dread knocks me to my knees, but the rattling doesn't lessen.

Green haze.

I look up; the man's sitting on a rock, a sword across his knees. His emerald eyes never stray from mine as the haze multiplies. There's an entire world between us: He emits light, while I'm enveloped in darkness; he's strength to my atrophied weakness.

The tearing speed draws me, but something powerful shields me from the flames this time. A whisper echoes all around in the solar wind: *"The prayers of my saints."*

My body is there, limp on the stone ledge. Jacob is crouched in the water beside it, head bowed. I jerk and shudder, trapped inside, one elbow cracking against the stone, pain exploding. Jacob's gentle hands pin me down until the jump lets me go, exhausted and weaker, with a heart that's no longer trustworthy.

He brushes my cheek; everything is there in his eyes: the gulf between us, and his longing. "You made it."

The relief in his voice makes tears overflow, no matter how hard I blink. He opens his mouth to speak, but the falls steady rhythm pauses behind him. Jacob spins in the waist-deep water, a pistol steady. Percy's hands go up with the falls beating his back. Jacob has a knife wound on his upper arm, blood crusted around it.

"I clean up… out there."

Jacob nods, lowering the weapon.

"Thank you."

Then he turns to me; but I'm the most pitiful thing in two universes, and I can't hold his gaze. He goes on like he doesn't see it. "I don't think he called Ash. It was a group of local mercenaries hoping to nab the entire bounty."

"I say good riddance," Percy says. "The jungle always suffer under men like them." He wipes his brow. "You two, you not from Earth, are you?"

What will Jacob say?

"We're human, same as you," Jacob replies, tucking the pistol into the small of his back.

"That green light say udderwise." Percy licks his lips, eyes darting between us.

"Just don't let the N.W.O. degauss you; it comes with some strange side effects." Jacob slides the pack onto his shoulder.

Percy spits to one side, the current sweeping it away. "We never serve the Order." His eyes have the same glimmer of awe that Margie's did as he nods at me. "I bring more blood vine for you."

It steadies my heartbeat within seconds. "I'd love to test this stuff in a lab."

"That might be awhile." Jacob takes me into his arms. "We need to move."

"Where?" Percy asks.

"Somewhere there's food and no people. She has to rest."

"I get you there." He strides under the falls.

Jacob scoops me up, and I press my face against his chest as the water beats down. The beauty of this place is overwhelming. Leaves brush my skin as Jacob's heartbeat soaks into my ear, teaching mine. He strides toward a boat tied near the hut.

"Hold up." Jacob's voice is low. Percy freezes two steps from his vessel. "Take her."

"No, I can stand," I insist, since life is flowing again, regenerating cell by cell as goosebumps race down my arms. *Thank you, K-60.*

Jacob eases up to the bow, studying a thin, almost invisible wire running from the sand into the boat.

Percy whistles. A useless urge to protect Jacob surges up as he studies a small mound of fresh-dug sand and pulls a knife, hesitating. A few seconds later, the tension goes out of his shoulders.

He takes a gray brick from inside the boat. "You never know when three pounds of C4 will be of use."

He removes something from the top and tucks the pieces into the pack. Stepping into the boat makes me shiver. The tripwire was invisible to me. Percy motors a few miles down the coast where mangroves grow thick and wild, a maze he knows like his own pulse. We skim over a slick of mud, and I screech as the boat rocks.

Percy laughs. "This boat go where water *was!*"

I grip the rail as we plunge back into the salty water where a manatee makes a slow escape. Percy stops in a sheltered cove and the boat bumps on the narrow spit of sandy shore, far within the mangrove's embrace. "Take these too."

Jacob takes a bunch of fruit tied onto a wire with three fish dangling from the bottom. Percy presses a machete into Jacob's other hand, then he pats the pistol, his gaze reverent. "Many thanks."

"Same to you," Jacob says.

We stride into the rainforest as the buzz of Percy's motor fades and jungle sounds fill the air. This is about the furthest you can get from the Collective.

Jacob raises one brow. "Ready?"

My fingers cover the bullet graze at my shoulder. "I guess. I need to clean up your knife wound soon."

Jacob sweeps with the machete, muscles bunching, his pace set extra slow for me. "Let's get a little farther into cover first."

The wet heat of the jungle presses in and sweat pours under the endless barrage of mosquitoes. Every step makes my legs burn, longing for time to recover. We make a quick termite detour and the bugs dissipate.

Jacob's neck glistens, reminding me of the *Olympia*, under heavy guard, as he ran the obstacle course like a machine. Tears fill my eyes for all the times he's taken the hard side of a fall, shielding me.

"Jacob," I whisper.

He turns, expression sharp, then softening as a smirk appears on his firm mouth. His eyes match the sky as he studies me. "I was expecting haze."

"You're..." Embarrassment flares as I struggle for words. "Thank you for *everything.*"

He steps close and tucks my hair behind my ear, his grin growing. "I was thinking the same thing. Without you, Sutton would have had a brain chip to control me with." One brow goes up, a teasing light in his eye. "Sage and Jacob, positron factories forever."

I laugh, looking down, unable to handle the life flowing from him. "I need to clean that wound."

He rolls back his sleeve, and I set to work, glad for something familiar. "Sure wish I had a stitching kit. It could use three or four at least."

"I'll do you one better," he says without flinching as I wash away the dried blood. "There's another Leaf Cutter trail."

This one has ants on it, thousands of them, most carrying a section of green leaf above their heads. He selects one, and it drops its leaf, straining with wide mandibles. "Pinch the wound shut, will you?"

"Why?" I ask, doing as he says.

He aims the ant at the wound, and it bites hard. One quick twist, and just the ant's head is left. He repeats the procedure with three more until they hold the wound shut.

"That is so gross."

He laughs. "I thought my ingenuity would impress you. Rivera loved that trick."

His eyes soften, but terror makes sweat break out. It's too real, too close. Looking down reveals that the ant trail is empty. Jacob drags the toe of his boot through the dirt, forming a familiar shape, it's the same one he'd etched on the wet rock. I shiver, staring at it.

The sky breaks open, rain falling in sheets. Jacob tilts his head back, letting it run over his face in rivulets. Mesmerized, my eyes trace the water's path down his muscular neck.

His firm mouth tilts up with a laugh. "It rained once *there.*"

His eyes stay closed and his skin seems lit of its own accord. Everything he doesn't say is clear. All the mysteries, the knowledge he's gained, are intoxicating to him. What did he do to earn it? Is it even possible for me? He finds life there, but the rotten stench of that place finds me even now. That world remains a nightmare of ways to die, but after seeing him there, it's clear why he longs for it. He catches me staring.

"Come on." He pulls huge leaves together. I inch closer under the shelter, skin on fire as it touches his. "Did you?" He swallows hard. "Did you come to the light?"

I drop my eyes, horrified that he'd seen me, so dark and skeletal. "I can't talk about it, Jacob."

He leans back as if I slapped him. Emotions play across his face, but the coil of tension in my stomach won't let up. The rain patters down, and he turns, studying the jungle. "And I can't lose you, Sage. What's so hard about receiving life? You know the alternative."

Rivera's screams are my own, deep inside. "I can't live up to God's expectations, Jacob. Especially now," I turn, wishing I could hide, "knowing what I am."

Jacob reaches out and brushes my arm. "That's the thing, Sage, it's not about you. It's about Him, and all He gave you."

My dad's anger always terrified me; I could never live up to his expectations. God would end up sending me back to hell, and that would be unbearable. Jacob must see it on my face because he sighs, tugging at my heart.

"Ever had a jungle marshmallow?"

"Nope."

He splits open a huge green seed pod, pulling out a fluffy white filling.

It melts in my mouth with a sweet softness. I'm hungry for so much more than food. For safety. For life. *For Jacob.* I push it down, huddled in the mud, lost in the wilds of the world as my knuckles brush his, worlds apart.

4
JACOB

Sage is stronger; two days have done her good with the pace set at easy. The jungle's life seeps in—everything here is growing. Still, it can't compare to the spirit, where the essence, the source of life, pulses, but I can sense it now, all around.

The oil is a constant companion too, a scene that replays a million times in my deepest parts. It soaks into the fabric of this world as well, solidifying the pounding desire to stop Ash and Sutton. It's my calling.

Sage pokes the low fire, trying to dry out after the persistent rain. She hates the idea. Her shoulder wound is only a scab, which she attributes to the K-60. The dark circles under her eyes are almost gone, too, but she can't cover the haunted look in her eyes. My fists clench, longing to force her into the light. What if the seed doesn't grow in time? Is my inability to convince her proof that the dragon was right? Is she forever destined for darkness? My stomach twists at the thought, and I turn away, praying.

The chorus of birds' cries fall silent. I scan the tight perimeter of our third hide site. The boy, Artan, from Percy's hut, has come each day with fish and fruit.

Yesterday, a jaguar stalked past, almost invisible in the shadows. Watching it with Sage and Artan was like a piece of heaven. Then, I showed Artan how to move through heavy cover, like the cat, catching Sage watching. Her face showed the same longing I feel deep inside, but scripture burns between us. What fellowship does light have with darkness? A sharp pain stabs in my back as I study the jungle.

A branch snaps, pulling me from the agony of separation from her. Artan never makes so much noise. I draw the Glock, its familiar weight like an extension of my arm. Sage is on her feet, face pale. Silent, I point at the trees. We ease behind wide trunks as I shift into box breathing, keeping adrenaline in check.

Dead silence fills the jungle. Then, like a wisp of fog, Artan steps into the clearing, his expression bright. A slow breath releases the hyper-focus. Today, he's got jackfruit, mango and star fruit tied to a pole over his shoulder. He turns, searching the area with a scowl.

Sage sets one hand over her heart, sighing. Artan doesn't miss the sound and turns our way. He's a part of this place, at one with the jungle, but I scan the forest before stepping out, tucking the Glock at the small of my back.

"More mangos? Yum." Sage grins, ruffling Artan's hair. She comes alive every time he visits, lighting up at his presence. Her love for kids makes me wonder if she'll ever have the chance to hold her own. *Our own.* The thought is like a kick in the gut, so strong that I turn to study the gigantic ferns. An entire world separates us, and I can't bear it.

"Yes, ma'am." Artan's English is perfect, with little of the Caribbean lilt Percy has. "I climbed high to get them for you. Do you like Keneps?"

"Ken-what's?" Sage laughs, and part of me wishes we could hover here, away from everything.

"I'll get you some." He turns to me. "Then you can show me how to fight!" He holds up both fists, bouncing on his toes.

Sage watches me, and the war inside is in her eyes too. The haze will take her again, and it stabs like daggers, knowing she might not return. My failure to reach her sears like hot coals.

Soon, Artan is back, and we discover keneps might be the best food this side of the spirit, like a key lime pie straight off the tree. Sparring with him is enjoyable; he's a quick study, and his eager heart makes me smile. Letting him inside my guard builds his confidence, then I unleash speed, tapping him in quick succession. His mouth hangs open as he steps back and I squat in front of him, grinning.

"You know there's a fight that's even more important?"

"What kind?" he asks, stepping closer.

I touch his chest with one finger. "The one in here, the battle for your soul. There's another world all around you."

His eyes are like saucers. "Percy is right—you *are* aliens."

An empty laugh escapes. "No, I'm a man, like you." His thin frame puffs out at the compliment. "But *you* have to choose life or death. Every person is born into sin that separates us from God, but Jesus—" I take a breath, seeing the electrons at the Brink, both wave and particle at once, a mirror image of Jesus in the flesh. "He died to pay the price for every sin."

He nods. "My Mamaw says so."

"The question is, what have you done about it? All my skills wouldn't do any good if I didn't use them," I say, tapping him three times, lightning fast. He jumps away with a giggle, but turns back with solemn eyes.

"What's the catch?" he asks.

I smile at his perception. "It's the gift that will cost you everything. You lay down your life, your will, your plans, and you get *His* instead. Death for Life. Good deal, if you ask me."

My eyes swerve to Sage. She's hugging herself and staring hard at the ground. I will the words to reach her as her face tightens. More than anything, I long to wipe away whatever image she has of God, to show her the consuming love that flows from Him.

"How?" he asks.

"Believe in your heart and say with your mouth that Yeshua is Lord." It's so simple. Is it pride that's holding Sage back?

"Yeshua is my Lord." A shiver runs down his spine and his eyes question with both hands over his heart. "What is that?"

My hand engulfs his slim shoulder. "That's *real* life. His in place of yours. Now, you're a new creature, and you must follow His ways."

"So now *we* are aliens!" he says with a grin.

"Sort of. We are strangers here, and our true home is with Him." I cover a grimace, knowing I'm as much a stranger to Sage. It's a sharper pain than a bullet wound.

"What if I mess up?" he asks.

"God, Yahweh, He doesn't expect you to be perfect, but He expects you to grow. See the trees?" I wave my hand at the dense jungle, crouching at his level, knowing it's something he'll understand. "Could a sprout hold this fruit?" I loft a mango as big as his head.

"No."

"So your job is to grow, and the fruit will come in time. Get a Bible and read it every day— it's your basic instructions for life."

Artan rushes in, his arms wrapping around my neck, the touch somehow so healing. I hug him, throat tight, praying Sage will hear. Soon, Artan fades into the jungle, combining his natural skill with my instructions so he doesn't leave a trace.

I keep my back to Sage for a long time until the frustration boiling inside is manageable. *You can only plant the seed.* Oh God, may it germinate fast. Night is wrapping its embrace over us, and I dare not light a fire in the dark, not even when the jungle comes alive with night sounds.

"Jacob?" Sage's voice is so soft I almost miss it.

I turn, longing sweeping through me to wash away the fear that shows at the corners of her eyes. There's no one here to notice how close we get. My breath comes faster, filled with the thought of her soft skin, as the entire universe condenses into her and me.

Then the breeze stirs, and I catch the faintest whiff of lion stench, and the now familiar stab in my back.

I flinch, breaking away from the desire that lies so heavy in the air. That was close, so close I half expect to see tawny fur in the jungle. But here, the fight is far more veiled, the enemy concealed, his bite so subtle.

Sage and I couldn't be more separate, worlds apart, and it's the anointing oil that fills my mind now. I can feel its warm tingle running down my face, and it reveals the weight of responsibility and a cost I'm paying right now.

The complete commitment is right and good, but I never dreamed the one thing I want in this world would be so out of reach. *Sage Emerson.*

"Do you believe that?" she asks.

I swallow hard, wondering if I'd spoken aloud. "What?"

Her face pinches as if in pain. "That God doesn't expect us to be perfect?"

I look up at the stars, knowing I'll have her in my arms, oil or no, if I keep looking at her. "Failure is a part of learning. When you come to Him, your spirit, the eternal part of you, becomes like Him. It's your mind and body that need renewing, until they look like Him too. That doesn't surprise Him."

"It seemed so simple for Artan."

Pushing her won't help and the right words take a while to surface. "It *is* simple, for everyone."

She shrugs, inspecting the ground for the enormous insects that emerge with the night.

"I'll watch over you," I say, wishing I could in the spirit. The long hours of night creep by as I watch her sleeping face and pray with fervor.

I wake her before dawn; it's time to move to a new hide site. Even a novice would see the flattened vegetation here, and there's another rock ledge a hundred yards to the south. We should move further, but I'm drawn to it, as if that green light is there, but red everywhere else.

There isn't much to do at the new site other than set my pack down and pull some branches together. It's eating at me as much as everything else, the inactivity. I can't stay here much longer, hiding out. The urge to hunt Ash down is too strong; besides, it's my calling, my job on this side.

Sage's color is better this morning, and her heart has been solid for two full days. Could she stay here with Percy and Artan? *I build it for wife thirteen, man!* That's a negative. But I'm torn between moving on Ash and knowing Sage needs me. The thought of her next jump makes sweat bead.

A flock of birds takes off, and every sense sharpens. From this height, it's easy to watch the path of something heading straight toward us. *Be Artan.* Sage steps next to me, her brows knit as we crouch low. Far below, Artan steps into our old clearing with a stick over one shoulder loaded with fish and fruit.

He turns a full circle, searching. Sage draws a breath to shout, then a splat of red explodes from Artan's thigh, and he goes down hard, clutching his leg, refusing to cry out. I twist, clamping a hand over Sage's mouth, blocking her cry.

They're here.

I hiss through my teeth, draw the pistol from Sage's hip holster and press it into her hands. "Stay quiet and shoot anything that approaches."

"But…" She's leans toward Artan, curled on his side.

"If they catch us, he's dead anyway." I hate the pain on her face, but she has to focus. Everything hinges on it.

I spin, calculating the bullet's trajectory, pistol low. It's probable that the shooter moved downhill. Taking on the jaguar's stealth, I drop toward them, circling with senses on fire.

A small square of pitch black shows through the foliage. Silence coats the world as I ease behind the operative, fending off the variable of when Sage will go for Artan. Two swift moves drop the operative without a sound.

I take his earpiece and rifle, then stalk along the invisible perimeter. Another figure crouches in the dense growth, turning around a heartbeat before I'm on him. Dodging the sharp uppercut of his rifle, I roll into his legs, twisting the weapon down. He falls back, and I slam the butt of the rifle into his face.

Sweat is pouring by the time I drop the eighth one, back where I started. Artan is in view, just below. He's curled up in a ball and there's a tourniquet above the wound. Sage is on one knee next to him, pistol steady, eyes blazing.

The earpiece clicks. There's no response. At least one more operative lurks, testing with the radio; now he knows he's alone, with no one clicking back.

A fierce determination rises. *They'll never touch her.* Scenarios run through my mind. No helicopters are pounding, meaning it's one small team with no calls for backup coming through the earpiece.

What is going on?

A man steps into the clearing, hands clasped behind his head, elbows spread wide, staring straight at Sage. "Carter!"

Sage flinches, rage darkening her face. *Rear Admiral Adam Brooks.* She shakes her head, jaw clenched, the past piling up on her as the tip of her pistol tremors. The weapon in my hand keeps steady aim on his forehead.

"I came to talk, Carter."

Sage tucks Artan close with one arm, and the demolished drone comes to mind. Across the distance, our eyes meet and I shake my head.

"You know I'm the only man standing. I didn't come here to bring you in, or this would be long over," Brooks says, his voice loud in the unnatural hush.

The pressure increases; it's possible he's telling the truth. Why *is* Brooks here? He could have had us right then, with an easy shot. My lip curls as Artan moans, but Brooks just stands there, exposed.

Stay there, I mouth to Sage.

She looks down at Artan, his face a mask of pain. We can't run and save him, too. Besides, there's no recoil inside urging me to run. Maybe this is part of my path.

I fade into the jungle, knowing Sage is losing it. Sniper school training enables me to circle behind him, using every scrap of cover. The bird sounds are coming back, adding cover. Sure hope Sage doesn't shoot me, aiming for Brooks.

A fallen cluster of palm fruit lies next to my boot: small, hairy coconuts that are perfect. I pick a handful up, every motion syrup-slow. We had a literal blast with them during jungle training.

"A conversation, Carter, that's what I came for. I'm not bringing you in." Sweat rolls down Brooks's neck, betraying his bold stance as he stares down the barrel of Sage's pistol.

Careful stalking brings me right behind him at the edge of the clearing. If he was lying, we'd be in full combat with troops pressing in. A toucan's call reverberates at a steady interval, high above.

The situation doesn't add up, but there's no other action than the one before me. I slip a lighter from my chest pack, waiting for the bird to cry again, then roll the striker in time, lighting the first nut, counting down. Flames lick up the dry husk, spreading to the others and burning deeper until the fibrous tops catch. I whip them at Brooks, the extra oxygen flaring the burn. He ducks the flames, and they go off one by one, nature's mini grenades.

Pop. Pop. Pop.

My strides keep time until we collide. He's a good fighter, but it takes just four swift moves to lock him down.

I drag him by the neck into the trees, scanning for movement. There's nothing, just the smoldering husks. Brooks's face is darkening, blood pooling under my grip, so I ease up.

"What are you doing here, shooting kids?" I can't keep from gripping harder; he doesn't deserve that sip of air.

"Ack…" He gurgles, lifting his hands.

I pull a pistol and bowie knife from his side and relieve him of four more weapons before dragging him further into the brush, out of Sage's sight.

"I didn't shoot him." He wheezes. "I told my men not to."

"Right now, you're my problem, Brooks," I growl in his ear.

"You… deserve to know." He's choking, but Artan is suffering because of him.

His motives must be untangled. *Is he bait?* There's no movement in Sage's direction, so I take his radio and check the frequency. It's not typical military, but that's far from a conclusion. There is no click back. Nothing.

"Only brought eight. Knew they'd be no problem for you." He doesn't struggle, keeping his hands up, eyes bulging.

I clamp a zip tie from my chest pack in my teeth. With a seamless movement, the tie tightens around his wrists without a struggle, which makes my skin prick. The entire N.W.O. could hover just out of range.

I step before him, leaving him on the ground. "Say it fast."

He frowns, rolling to his knees. "Tex went AWOL."

My stomach lurches, but my face betrays nothing. "Told you that was coming."

His eyes flicker before returning my gaze. "Genocide, South Africa, over a thousand bodies."

The video clips in Florida, and everything I didn't want to believe, rush in. It was Tex who strangled that man, enjoying the life slipping from him. I should've known. Part of me did.

A leaf moves, and I lock down the urge to swing the Glock. One of Sage's brown eyes shows, glittering with anger, the barrel of her pistol trained on Brooks.

She heard.

"You're the only one who can stop him, Carter," Brooks pleads.

"So you came to beg for help cleaning up your mess?"

Sage is shaking, hiding inside the cover behind Brooks, but the image of the man's mangled neck on the TV screen won't leave me. How many more will Tex murder for a sick thrill? It *is* my job to stop him.

"Left chest pocket," is all Brooks says.

I unzip it and pull out a slip of paper with a number on it.

"Where is he now?" I ask, mouth tight.

Brooks sighs. "That's the problem. I don't know. He's gone dark. We believe he's still in Africa, the west coast."

I laugh. "You don't know? The man's got more hardware than a tank. How could you lose him?"

"Listen," he hisses, shaking his head. "Ash didn't send me. I'm here on my own, because you and I both know the bloodbath won't stop. Sutton's the only one who might have a handle on Tex's exact location."

"Why don't you ask her then?"

"Sutton and I are no longer working together. She and I have different visions for the program." He frowns, seeking balance as his knees sink into the mud. "We both know that no one else can take him, and Sutton has better things to do, apparently."

There are too many loose ends and anomalies to stay here. I drag Brooks back to a tree and tie his hands to it. Then, with a stern look at Sage, I fade into the jungle.

We meet near Artan. The boy's cold, his leg purple from the tourniquet. Sage's hands are busy inspecting the wound; the bullet went clean through the muscle. She's trembling, and my anger boils too close to the surface as well.

Why the boy?

I clench my fists at my stupidity, and a shriek of electric energy burns my palms as if they're in the spirit's water.

"Jacob, you can't go after Tex. It's a trap, you know that," she says, without looking up.

Her harsh whisper deflects the strange sensation in my hands. Then the memory of the pool and my healing comes so strong, where my wounds sizzled shut. The spirit's here, beyond the veil. *Seen and unseen.* But one is so much more powerful than the other.

Artan grimaces; he's so tough, without a sound like a jungle creature. I kneel next to him, scooping him into my arms, words welling up that I've never heard, never spoken, yet they flow like a river.

I stride into the jungle away from Brooks, setting one hand on Artan's forehead, the words still coming. There's no sensation now, no fresh scent of the spirit, but the truth is still there. The memory of my own wounds closing sharpens; the pain falls away like fetters.

Then the dragon's words swirl, too. Can anything change this? Was Paco's healing prearranged, a path I had to take? My stomach knots, pushing away, needing laser focus. The sweet aroma of allspice reminds me of the spirit's life, and a sense of internal balance returns.

Strange words cascade out as I picture Artan stepping into the pool, seeing his knit brow smooth out, his head tilting up in relief as his leg wound seals shut.

Artan's face relaxes before me in real time as we brush through the jungle. Sage glares in Brooks's direction. "You're going to leave him there?"

"There's more to his part of the story than I can pick out. We might need him later."

I keep a sharp eye for snakes, scorpions, and men as we cut through the jungle.

"You're not even *thinking* about going after Tex, right?" Her voice is tight.

Artan shifts in my arms, his eyes clear, the way I saw inside. He pats my chest with one small hand as if to comfort me. How many children has Tex killed? How many more await the same fate? I can't do nothing.

"Who else will, Sage?"

"It's not your problem."

"It wasn't, but now I know about it. A deranged super soldier is out there, hunting. How many more will he kill? It shouldn't be their problem either."

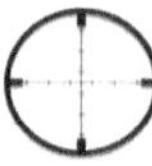

"Jacob, you know this is a trap." Sage hasn't eaten for two days, and she wrings her hands together, studying our current position—a few miles from Etretat, France.

"That's the funny thing." I pursue the sheer white chalk cliffs with a monocular, where the Atlantic Ocean beats a narrow strip of beach at their base. "We're gonna turn the tables. Sutton has no clue she's about to become a hostage."

Sage moans, shaking her head. "Nothing is right about this. We shouldn't be here; they're playing us."

Brooks provided everything we needed to travel: false IDs, complete with contacts that will fool any iris scanner, and N.W.O. bank cards loaded with currency. Now, we're two law-abiding citizens of a corrupt government. I watched our six the entire time; but for now, Brooks isn't interested in pulling us in, and my plans are shaping up.

"I thought you'd like France, or European 29, or whatever they're calling it now." The darker her mood grows, the farther I lean the other way. It's not my best plan ever. Maybe none of this is, but Tex is out there, with one thing on his mind.

"Jacob, please!" Her hands slam onto the old French military Jeep's gray hood. "This is crazy! Brooks knows where we are. *Brooks*, the same man who subjected you to Project 157 just to see if you'd survive."

"He let us go. Remember? Sometimes people regret things. They need a chance to right their wrongs."

An empty laugh escapes her. "His list is too long."

I sigh, looking down the pebbled beach. It's the perfect ambush spot: remote, quiet, gorgeous. The sky over the ocean is dark. Sutton's ship is in the gloom, running ahead of the storm.

"Listen." I lock eyes with her, needing her to be with me and wishing we could be. "When you're downrange under heavy fire and things are at a standoff, you've got to change your cards. Make something happen. Reset the odds. Change the rules. I'm not a runner, Sage. Spending the rest of my life hiding won't float it for me. This is our chance to trade in for a new hand. We have to push back. Who knows what we'll find?"

She swallows hard, crossing her arms, jaw tight. "That's the problem: I *do* know."

"I can find a place for you to hole up," I offer, but I'd be half crazy not knowing if she was safe.

"No. I'm not leaving you." I know she's thinking of how long it's been since we jumped, and the terror waiting there.

"What's keeping you from giving your life to Him?" I ask, knowing it's the greater risk than what we'll face in a few minutes.

She sighs, deciding. "I… I'd never make the cut. I'm not like you, Jacob. All that's inside me is… unworthy." Her eyes shimmer.

"The things that give you peace are my chaos. I'm not righteous enough to come to Him."

I step around the hood and pull her into my arms. It's more than she's said before, and every word is poison. Her cheek rests against my chest, but her trembling makes me cringe. "I wish you didn't have to face war in two worlds, but there's no changing it. We've got to fight strenuously, but we need God's strength to do that. The first step is to see Him for who He really is."

"I keep thinking of Artan." The words catch in her throat. "The leg wound should've been debilitating, but he acted like he didn't have any pain when we left him with Percy." She looks up at me. "How did you change it for him? You don't play by the rules, Jacob."

"Is that an accusation or a compliment?" I ask, letting a half smile cover the gut-wrenching worry.

"Both." She frowns.

"You're right, I'm not playing by *those* rules—the normal ones we've always lived by." The right words are imperative. "But it's not about me, it's about the Almighty's will coming to pass. Saving you was His work, and you have to accept it."

"That makes no sense," she sniffs, standing up straighter.

"You can't *become* the light on your own; none of us can. It's His righteousness, given to you."

She flinches, pulling away. I check my watch, forcing down how right Demyen was.

"Twenty minutes until go time. You remember what to do?" I step back to the flight map spread on the hood.

"I help you on the cliff, then drive the Jeep down to the beach and pick you up. Next, I drive like mad for that cave." She points north around a sharp bend in the 335-foot sheer chalk cliffs.

"Perfect." I slide the pressured air bottle out of the REBS compact grapple launcher Brooks had been so kind to supply me with. The grapple will hook into about anything, and the powered rope ascender is already on my vest. "It's time."

"Sutton is everything we've been running from. This is like diving straight into the fire." She shudders when she says it.

"I guess we're both determined to do it, just in different worlds." The words are out before I think better of it.

Her mouth flattens into a grim line, and her eyes narrow. Both my hands go in the air, changing tactics.

"Come on, it'll be fun." The Jeep crunches over the two-inch gravel of the beach as we cruise up the winding road. Cold air rips at the ocean and a heavy bank of fog hovers over the turquoise Atlantic far below, ensuring seclusion and a low, close flight for the helicopter. *Perfect.*

The Jeep gains the clifftop; the view is stunning. I can't smell the beauty, or taste it, since this flat 3D world is where war is now.

A protruding boulder makes the perfect anchor for the rope.

"This is your end. Don't drop me." I hand it to her with a smirk, the knife wound on my arm pinching.

Her face goes pale. "Wait a minute. 'Help me up there' means dangle you over the cliff?"

"You got this. Just keep it tight until I tell you to let go."

"Eh…" Her squeak forces me to turn away, shielding a grin.

I press the earpiece in tighter, "Check."

"I can hear you." Her voice is flat.

"Eight minutes." I step to the very edge, wind buffeting as it surges up. There's nothing but 300 feet of air. The Eurocopter Dauphuin ferrying Sutton should lift off the *HMS Defender* right now. That fog bank will only tighten up their planned flight path even closer to the shelter of these cliffs.

My thick Kevlar vest and magazine pouch with the climbing harness keep the rope in place, and the light ACU camo pattern blends in well. "I need twelve feet, then we wait for their arrival. When I say, let go."

"Let…" She winces. "Let go? As in, drop you? I can't believe this."

"Yeah, move to the side when you do so the rope doesn't catch your leg."

She steps around the rock, locking the rope around her hips, her face a mask of worry.

"See you in a few minutes."

Her eyes glaze over as the bass of a helicopter beats the air, right on time. I lean out over the chalk cliff, relishing the adrenaline rush. "Give me some length."

The wind snatches my words, but Sage lowers me face first, straight down. "Hold!"

I work my light-colored boots into the white rock, lifting the launcher to my shoulder. A thin bush has a tenuous outpost a few feet to the right. The steady thrum of the chopper roars closer, but there's time. I surge against the rope over to the bush, straining to rebalance in its cover.

"JACOB!" Sage shrieks into the earpiece. It's nothing like being out with the guys.

"Keep steady."

She growls in response, and the helo materializes out of the fog, barreling toward me. A slow breath through my nose provides smooth action, locking the launcher at my shoulder.

Pushing the pressure away, I visualize the grapple wrapping around the landing gear as time ticks past. *Ten seconds.*

Inside the bird, figures start to take shape. Pilot, copilot, three guards, Sutton in the center. My lip curls as my finger tenses on the trigger. I let out a breath and fire.

"What's happening?" Sage cries in my earpiece.

"Hold!" The grapple cable snakes through the sharp wind, but the hook strikes true, doubling around the landing gear with a sharp clack.

I feed the rope's end through the ascender, the far end zinging away too fast as the helo sweeps past. Snarling as the tool jambs, I yank it out and restart. Three seconds, and the helicopter will pull the grapple cable away.

"Let go!" I shout; the ascender's still jammed, the slack gone.

There's no change in the tension at my chest. If the helo rips the grapple cable away and then she drops me, I'm dead.

"Let me *go!*" I thunder as the slack runs out. With the cable in a vise grip, I pitch the jammed ascender away into the abyss.

"AHHH!" Sage screams; the chopper pulls, and the rope lets loose. "Jaaaacooooob Caaarteeer!" Sage shrieks as I free fall.

It lasts for a heartbeat; then the surge of my weight makes my grip on the grapple cord far too tenuous. The chopper sags as the pilot corrects for my sudden appearance. Hand over hand in the wind shear is too slow, drawing me toward the bird at a snail's pace. The chopper door slides open and a guard scowls at me, shouting in French. The powered ascender would've had me there in 2.2 seconds, snatching him from the bird.

A current of rough air pitches me into a spin as I draw a pistol from my hip. My first shot goes wide, but the second knocks him back as I dangle from one arm.

I'm target practice now, holstering the pistol to focus on the climb. My arms burn in the prop wash, the wind shear adding pounds of dead weight. Shots flare as the fog closes in, consuming the bird, then me. It's so dense that the landing gear is nothing but a shadow.

Pop. Pop.

Grimacing helps me climb the last thirty feet like a sprint. I'm late, without a single shred of the necessary surprise—never a good position. Shaking it off, my hand closes on the long tube of the landing gear. I draw the pistol, look up, and take a bullet to the sternum. My ribs convulse, airless. The Kevlar held. Have to trust that. I swing the weapon up, ignoring the pain and fire.

A guard pitches from the bird, arms flailing. I kick violently, out of breath, and swing one knee toward the pipe. Blackness creeps in at the edges of my vision while I hang from the pipe by one knee. The fog is a disorienting blanket.

Air!

My ribs cramp, then haul in oxygen. A jubilant shout echoes above.

Don't get too excited yet, boys. I'm still here.

The wind rips as soaking fog slickens the metal. Visibility is less than two feet. My lungs loosen, getting a full breath, and my vision clears as I crouch on the slippery pipe. The door above swings open. My boots slam the landing gear, launching me into the bird to bear hug the guard. Momentum carries us clean through the other door.

Letting him go, I twist sharply as we fly through, snatching the far landing gear.

"Jacob! Where are you?" The Jeep's motor screams behind Sage's voice.

"Having some trouble," I grunt, slamming my other hand onto the pipe. With a roar, I pull up, snatching a boot in the doorway. His shot is wild as I yank him out. He flails for the pipe, but the pistol is already in my grip, taking out the third guard.

The second soldier gets one elbow locked on the landing gear and his arm snakes around my neck. We dangle in the chop and I buck back, smashing his face with my head. We dangle from the pipe, fog swirling as the bird tilts. I throw one elbow into his neck. His grip on the pipe fails, but his weight pulls me back until the wind sucks us away.

My arms thrash at nothing but air, then my knee strikes the pipe, hooking there, upside down. A desperate twist kicks my other boot high, locking it in. I cross my arms over my chest, hanging in the wind.

The slick pipe is an enemy, stealing time until I straddle it and ease toward the door. There's no movement inside the bird. The pilot's outline shows through the fog. *Where's the copilot?*

A shot pings off the pipe. I leap forward, rolling into the helo. Movement to the left snaps me into hunter mode, landing blows, one after another. The soldier crumples; the pilot turns, releasing the sticks, a pistol in his hand.

I dodge fast and somersault behind his seat. The bird teeters, the auto HOV button lighting up. Double blows to his carotid arteries make his eyes roll back as he sags to the side. A scrape behind makes anger flare.

Sutton.

Roaring, my spin kick slings her pistol away. It wings into the fog as I yank her from behind the seat.

A briefcase is handcuffed to one wrist, and her high cheekbones and hard mouth twist in her typical show of disdain. She struggles as the helo fights the rolling fog on its own.

"Just as nasty as ever, I see," I hiss, cranking her arm high and pulling the taser that I tweaked for her.

Its twin prongs bite her neck, then her eyes roll white as she goes rigid, while I handcuff her arms in front of her, the case dangling. It takes precious seconds to clip a life vest on her and hit the button, inflating it.

Leaning over the slumped pilot, I ease the left stick forward. The guidance system handles the pitch and yaw, and the altimeter drops to twenty-five feet. Sutton staggers, the unique electrical frequency still messing with her brain as we reach the door. She's struggling as the rotors whip inches from our heads. I leap out; she slithers after me, the briefcase clanking. I cross my legs and grip my chest with one hand. Sutton won't fare very well on impact, but the vest will protect her organs.

The cold water almost rips her away before we surface, riding a swell. Shore is farther than planned. Sutton floats limp, then gasps, thrashing, her dark eyes wild as she sucks in salt water. She clutches at me, spewing, cuffs clanking, but I rip her hands away, the vest keeping her face aimed up.

"Help!" Her yelp holds true terror as another wave smacks her in the mouth.

I snarl, tugging her through the sea. "The way you helped me? Shackled to the wall?"

She goes still, her eyes flicking side to side before locking on my face. No recognition flashes there yet, still addled by the taser. Water feels like cement from that height too, and the opportunity to ramp up her fear while she's disorientated is not to be missed.

"What is it, Sutton, you don't like sharks?" On cue, a sharp fin cuts the surface. There's not much space between the dorsal and tailfins, but it's enough for Sutton, making her recoil. The fins sink, then reappear on our far side.

"He's circling, Sutton, it's feeding time. Ladies first."

She rolls so hard that her face goes under, but I yank her up by the hair, straining for control, thinking of all the lives Tex has ended because of her. Stroking firmly keeps her pointed toward the dark fin and the ripple it leaves behind. The sleek blue shark cuts closer, outpacing my efforts for shore.

"Keep splashing; that's a fine dinner call."

She locks down, rigid and trembling.

"You know, your eyes, they're like a shark's: dead." The lion's eyes, full of wicked light, are so similar, but this reality is enough for now.

Waves lift us, making it harder to track the shark as we near shore. I click the radio. "Twenty seconds."

"I see you!" The relief in Sage's voice is warmth against the icy sensation spreading from Sutton.

Smooth rocks greet my knees; I heave Sutton through the battering surf as the Jeep careens toward us, sliding to a stop.

Sage hops out, her face flushed.

"How'd it go?" I ask.

She rolls her eyes, opening the Jeep door. I shove Sutton in, easing next to her on the seat, soaking everything.

"Personally, I experienced a lot of technical difficulties," I add as Sage grips the wheel, speeding toward the cave.

A box on the floorboard contains a contraption with wires, probes, and a heavy lithium-ion battery I spent a good bit of time building. Sutton's eyes fix on it, then her gaze rises to my face. Her skin goes a shade whiter; now she knows me.

I jab the probes into the back of her right hand, fighting revulsion at her proximity. She flinches, but can't pull free of my grip. I flip the switch with my boot and her arm jerks as the electricity fries the N.W.O. chip.

I move the probes to her forehead, and she struggles. Grabbing a fistful of her hair forces her still as the mini EPM fires a second time. Her eyes roll back, making me worry that the voltage is too high. The probes fall away as her pupils dilate.

"You degaussed me; now I've returned the favor."

She yanks away and I'm glad for the inches between us. Scanning her head and hands ensures she's no longer emitting any signals. *Thank you, Brooks, for the equipment.*

"Ah, your brain chip is no longer sending messages, either. That extra voltage was perfect."

Her neck twitches at the words.

"Your disappearance at this location will look like that shark did his worst. Won't Ash be sad?" I fight for control, the past pushing me. She built a super weapon, then set him loose on the innocent. "What's it like, knowing you can't escape?" I ask, eyes burning with all she did to Sage and me. "How many others were before us? How many have you killed in the name of science?"

She turns her face to the window, so I lift the briefcase, the double cuffs cutting her wrist.

Sage aims for the thin strip of beach where waves slam the wheels; the cave is a half-mile ahead. I jimmy the cuff; this case has a complex locking system—quite advanced. That digital readout may have a tracker of its own that's still functioning, even with the saltwater beading up inside. Have to fix that.

The window slides down with the push of a button, such a normal action, set at odds with my life. Gripping the case by its side, I shoot the digital face at a steep angle.

Sage shouts, the Jeep swerves suddenly, and Sutton screams, "Stop it!"

I glare at her, pulling it back inside. "What's so important, Sutton?"

The case may be more valuable than she is. Darkness sweeps over the Jeep as we slide to a stop on the algae-coated floor of the cave.

"Time for your interview," I quip, dragging her out. "Maybe a few mental aptitude tests afterwards?"

Sage gets out, glaring at Sutton.

"I feel the same way, Sage. Keep your cool."

Our eyes lock and I nod. We have to stick to the schedule.

Sage shakes her head, snatching the case, clinging to control. She throws it down, pulling the pistol from her hip. Double-fisted, she fires five rounds at the case. I duck as shards ping into the Jeep.

Sutton falls to her knees in the slime, reaching out. "Stop, you fools!"

"Shoot it again, Sage." The case is nearly indestructible; my first shot revealed that much. Sutton wouldn't trust anything less. Besides, watching Sage unleash her fury is satisfying.

"I'll open it, just stop!" Sutton shouts, slipping on the algae.

"Now we're getting somewhere," I say.

"If you haven't ruined everything." Sutton crawls toward the case, and I pull Sage's gun hand down.

She's trembling, glaring hard at Sutton kneeling in the thick slime. Pitiful, yet so proud.

"Shh," I breathe in Sage's ear, willing her to gain control. She growls, shoving the pistol into its holster as Sutton works at the case.

"You ruined it," Sutton mutters, her fingers caressing the destroyed leather. A soft click echoes and the dented lid sighs open, revealing a dry interior.

I scoop it up and Sutton follows with cuffed hands outstretched. "Be careful…"

Her entire world is right there. Digital storage, circuit boards, diagrams, and one small vial are secured inside.

The vial draws me like a magnet; I loft it to the light at the cave's entrance. It's tiny between my thumb and finger, and a thrill runs up my arm. The clear fluid inside is mesmerizing. Sutton can't take her eyes off it either as her cuffed hands hover underneath it, as if I'll fumble it. Her sigh of awe seals my suspicions.

"Is this what I think it is?" I ask.

Her eyes flash to mine, shining with fear now. She was so bold on the *Olympia,* so smug, but when I reconnected with my body in the shackles, breathing out the water of the spirit before I drew my body back through the wall, that same fear glistened in her eyes.

My fist closes around the vial, energy surging. *It's the spirit's water… here.*

Tears prick as I turn away, overwhelmed as I zip it into a deep pocket in my vest.

She's right; it is more important than anything she's had before. She curses, then glares at me. "Tell me what it is, Carter. It's no substance known to man."

I turn, hating that she's been testing it, *handling it.*

"It's nothing you'd believe." I grip the chain between her hands and tow her through the slime, further into the cave, aiming for an eye-bolt drilled into the rock. She's rattled now, alone with people she's tortured, but she still presses for info.

"The liquid is extremely caustic. It eats through everything except glass."

She's prying, desperate to know.

"Sutton." She flinches as I snarl her name. "Where is he?"

She lifts her chin, framing her usual disdain. "You'll never reach Ash. You don't know what he'll accomplish."

"Ash?" I ask, willing to let things play out for a bit.

Her eyes flash, realizing she's given the wrong answer.

I play my cards, laying them down one by one. "I've gotten what I came for: all your research, a lifetime of sacrificing people on the altar of science so you can have power. It's a competitive field, and a conniving woman like you would keep your best far from cloud storage—from the Collective, even." Her eyes cut to the case, laid open on the Jeep's hood, as if to confirm it. "That's the way you play the game. Keep things hidden so you can use them when they turn on you." The vial tingles straight through the Kevlar. "But it's all safe with me now."

Her lip twitches, so I lean on the raw nerve. "Wonder what I should do with it?"

"You won't escape Europe 29. Not now. They'll make you pay."

My brows go up. "I'm not the one who needs to worry about escape. *You are.*"

The words hang there as my eyes move extra slow up to the roof. "See those watermarks?"

Her eyes travel up the slick walls in the dim light. A foot or so from the high ceiling, the algae stops.

"It's low tide. *Now.*"

I say nothing more, just take a single step back.

Her chin puckers, staring up at the waterline. "Who…" Her jaws clench. "Who are you looking for, then?"

"Tex."

She gives an empty laugh. "Who cares about a deranged pet? Let him run himself to the ground."

"Pretty sure the thousands of people who are dying care about him," I whisper, my gut turning at her callousness.

"Tex has three main security codes. He's blown through two of them already," she remarks, as if that's answer enough.

"Not your best programing then. And the third?" I prod.

"The third has a virus attached; if he tries an override, it will release into his brain and kill him."

"Then why haven't you activated it?" Heat surges up my neck.

"He may be crazy, but he's not stupid. He's got some type of signal blocker preventing it."

"So, you knew the chances of his going AWOL were so high that you installed a virus?" I turn toward the sea, clamping down red-hot anger, knowing she wanted the same for me. "So much for control. You've got science experiments running amok everywhere… hunting you down, even." I sneer at the irony.

She covers a jolt of fear.

"It could've been Tex after you today, then you'd be ice-cold already, or worse." The thought rattles her, but she lifts her chin to cover it. "It's good to remember you're mortal, and the power you're messing with will bite back one day. You and Ash will pay."

She snorts, but a glance at the cave opening betrays her fear. Water is lapping at its edge already. "Ash is untouchable. You don't know who he is, or what he controls…"

"He doesn't control me, or Tex, apparently. Your team doesn't have an outstanding track record."

"I don't need a team."

"No? Maybe not, but you *do* need a way out."

She yanks on the cuffs, drawing blood. "Near as I can tell, he's working his way toward Durban. Dense population, highest death toll. Tex is nothing more than an animal; his time will soon be up."

"Yet you can't stop him."

She sniffs, "He's a ticking bomb, and I'll add a fourth layer of safeguards next time. Besides, Ash will come out on top like always. Tex is a tool, one Ash will use to his full advantage."

Her words crawl into my mind and lodge there, far too personal, as she tilts her chin.

"The expendables in Africa are worthless, but science is perfect. Any price is worth its advancement. Anomalies like you advance our knowledge, but every experiment can be lost without setback. You, Tex, all the others, are the servants of science."

Sage growls, launching for Sutton's back. I snatch her in midair with one arm. She swings, snarling, but I restrain her, whispering in her ear. "You're the better person, Sage, stay that way."

She groans as I set her down, but her words spew out. "You, Ash, and Brooks, you're all sick, completely deranged."

"Oh, please." Sutton's dripping disdain is back in force. "Don't lump us in with the likes of Brooks. He's a complete failure. An imbecile. Ash gave him a dishonorable discharge after watching the tapes. He let you go on the *Olympia*. He should've been... decommissioned."

Her words hit me like a fifty-caliber round. Sage sags in my arms, breath leaving her in a rush. Sutton turns and I school my features before she can see my shock, but she raises one brow.

"Didn't know that, did you?" Her condescending gaze makes my skin crawl. "He's got to be the reason you got this far, but you've accomplished nothing. I've got copies of all my research. This is only a setback."

My gaze runs up the wall to the waterline. "We'll see, Sutton; have fun with your setback."

Then I take out the intoxicating vial so she can get one last look.

"Good thing you didn't lose anything *important.*"

Her nose flares.

Sage grabs my arm. "Jacob, the water!"

The tide is coming in, lapping at the Jeep's bumper.

Sutton yanks at the cuffs, but the zip tie will be impossible to break like that. I take out a small knife and set it on the ground a few feet from her, then let Sage pull me toward the entrance. She snatches Sutton's case off the hood and the Jeep throws turquoise seawater high as we jet onto the beach.

"Why did you leave her the knife?" Sage asks as a wave rocks the Jeep, making me rev it higher.

"Because I am not like her," I reply, cradling the vial in my fist.

We step off the tiny prop plane into the African night. Miles of wilderness surround, but with eighty percent of its iconic species now extinct, it's not as dangerous as it once was.

"African air is always so thick," I say, taking Sage's bag as the plane's engines rev, aiming down the long-abandoned runway with vines entangling the narrow airstrip. A half-moon gives a silvery tint to the plants closing around a hanger with one end collapsed.

A sudden jolt of energy makes my muscles clench. I don't need to look; the haze is building, and a shiver of delight spreads even as I search for a safe place for Sage. My movement grows jerky as the jump takes me. She gasps, but finds no haze flowing from her own stomach.

"Hurry!" She tows me toward a dilapidated hangar, digging with one hand in her pack. "Jacob, I don't have any water!"

The terror in her voice makes me grimace.

"How could I be so stupid?" she hisses as we skid under the roof, dry leaves crinkling as she darts about, searching.

My jaw locks up, keeping me from telling her to watch for snakes; the black mamba is a grumpy species. Then my arms clench in the intense green grip. The haze gathers like a physical force, tearing apart every cell.

"S… SSSS," I can't even say her name as she sprints back to me.

"No, no, NO!" she shouts as my boots sink into the earth.

My tongue's caught between my teeth, and blood trickles, while I fumble for the chest zipper. It's the only water left; the only way to prevent disintegration. The energy shrieks higher and my eyes roll back in my head. I hit the ground, but it won't hold me.

My stiff fingers refuse to find the vial. With a cry of relief, she rips open the pocket, withdrawing the vial. It's so small between her fingers. Will it be enough? I'm sinking into the heart of Africa.

"Jacob!" Her free hand finds a rock under the leaves; with a grimace, she shatters the vial above my face.

Glass, and a few precious drips of life, splash around my mouth; a convulsion forces one hand to my face, palm wet. The liquid burns against my lips, then drips inside. "Ahh."

I relax, disconnecting, but I look back as the speed carries me away. Sage repositions my body, pulling it out of the earth as it re-solidifies. She strokes my brow, checking my pulse, engrossed.

But the distance steals her from me and everything on Earth fades away. My lips and palm tingle where the water touched them. A jolt of searing pain there fades to a fantastic sensation unlike any before, one that spreads into my mouth until its taste fills me. *Raw power.*

I plummet right next to The Tree, leaving a divot in its shade. A scan of the sky makes the tension fall away; there are no fast-moving shadows bearing down. Dusting off makes the sensation in my palm increase until I grip my wrist with a wince. Everywhere the water touched feels like fire.

Racing for the stairs, and avoiding Watchers and people, the power builds on my tongue. The emerald pool at the top beckons as the heat spreads down my throat. Taking the uneven stairs three at a time, I make a desperate sprint. The air is thinner as I skid through the highest door with the heat reaching a furnace pitch on my lips.

No one's here, just the life-giving water and me. I dive in, arms tight, fingers cutting in without a splash. The wound on my back flares with pain that almost drives me from the pool. Then relief floods at the blessed coolness, and I stay under until the water speaks, entering the depths of me.

A…and I will give power to My two witnesses, and they will prophesy one thousand two hundred and sixty days, clothed in sackcloth. Th… these are the two olive trees and the two lamp stands standing before the God of the earth.

There are more words, but a spasm in my back steals them from me. Grimacing, I reach for the wound, finding it now just a scratch that the water is healing up. Concentration returns as the water's voice fills me again.

These have power to shut heaven, so that no rain falls in the days of their prophecy; and they have power over waters to turn them to blood, and to strike the earth with all plagues, as often as they desire.

The Almighty's words about me. The meaning swirls as I surface, propping my back and elbows on the wooden edge, a chill racing down my spine. Those words define me, *are me,* and yet, they're thousands of years old. I'm there, in the scroll. The words have always defined me, even when unknown, but what do they mean?

Moments pass as communion with the water washes the Earth-worry away. The emerald pool settles my future within the mysterious words. That, and the strange tingling in my lips. It's not disturbing like it was, but it is persistent. The heat builds in my mouth even now. Opening it, a cloud of green haze escapes.

Thoughts fly, watching it flow; I'm not jumping, and there is no drawing sensation, no inescapable speed. The haze curls away, dissipating above the water. The tingling moves to my right hand when my mouth is shut.

My palm appears normal as heat builds again on my tongue, increasing to an unbearable level. My lips part and haze streaks straight to my palm, rolling there like a miniature hurricane; my fingers tremble as a strange scent fills the room, and the water responds.

And I will give power to my two witnesses, and they will prophecy one thousand two hundred and sixty days, clothed in sackcloth.

The words bring peace as time slides past, watching the haze ebb and flow from my mouth to my hand, desperate for knowledge.

Bolder now, I blow it into my palm. It crackles like fire, swirling in a perfect sphere in my hand. Soft footsteps make me look up.

The doorway shows Mara's silhouette, holding a tray. She gasps, her warm smile fading to wide-eyed horror. She drops the tray, cups scattering, as her eyes rivet on the tendrils of haze flowing from my nose and the green fire in my palm. Guilt hits like a tidal wave, making a hot sensation creep up my neck. With a cry, she covers her mouth; her long white braid swings as she spins, nimble as a doe, to disappear through the doorway.

I stand, shedding water, shaking the fire from my hands as a heavy cloak of shame descends. It's wrong somehow; else why would she react so? I scowl, willing the heat away, out of my mouth. The tingle fades, though it doesn't disappear. A shiver takes me.

What have I done?

Bending my mind to the physical order, I search for the answer, and see Sage break the vial, the water dripping onto my lips. The spirit's water, *there.* Have I desecrated some law, or broken some covenant between the worlds? What if going back is impossible now? The thought swirls as one finger runs over my lip, longing to change the past.

All the wishing in the world can't do that. Striding from the pool, I pace the living wood floor, looking over the forest and seeing nothing. My hands tremble as my feet hover on the steps, embarrassment flooding. My exit will be the same as my entry—fast and quiet.

Trotting down the levels, footsteps warn me to duck into an alcove as a Watcher ascends. Only two levels to go, then the forest will surround me.

"Jacob." Mara's soft voice behind makes me freeze.

Her previous expression of repulsion prevents me from turning now.

"Jacob," she pleads, her tone so soft it could have been a sigh.

Shoulders drooping, I turn, struggling to raise my eyes. Tears prick her own, her weathered face softening into a smile.

"Forgive me. I…" She blinks and shakes her head, but her hands are trembling, too.

Holding a half breath, I hope the haze will remain at bay. She squints as though pain grips her.

"*My Jacob*… it can't be you…" She bites her quivering lip.

"I'm sorry, I don't know what's happening."

She runs to me, arms outstretched, and I bend, enfolding her. She pats my back as if I'm a boy crying from a skinned knee, then leans back, studying my face, concern gripping her.

"When I saw you," she shakes her head, one tear escaping to trace her ancient cheek, "with *the fire*, it was a shock. That's all. You've nothing to be sorry for. It surprised me is all, I didn't know…" She winces, biting back more words.

"It seems I know nothing," I say with a rueful grin, thankful that she knows of it, though getting that knowledge out of her might be a battle.

"All will be revealed. Such things arrive precisely on time." Her confidence seeps into me, easing the shame.

"Mara, what is it?" Even my whisper is too loud.

She smiles, but her eyes pierce me with sorrow. "The fire is a prophecy. An ancient word, now manifest for the end of days." Her hand cradles my face. "*Jacob*, wield it well."

Light outside draws our gaze. Through the dappled shade, a streak like lightning zaps into the woods to the east.

"Ah!" The light in Mara's eyes returns. "Go bring that one to me."

"What?"

"Hurry, Jacob." A Mona Lisa smile appears. "I know much that knowing never knew. You'll have to run!"

It's a relief to unleash the coil of tension inside on a sprint, and at some point, her directive takes on meaning. *Sage!* She meant Sage is here. My heart twists. What if I don't reach her, and the lions take her? A distant shout makes me skid to a halt, denying my straining lungs air to locate the sound. It's her!

"Sage!" The shout is useless as I burst into full speed, and soon thin scrubby trees hinder motion. "Come on!"

It's like swimming through a forest of thorns, knowing she needs me *now*. A cry of frustration explodes as I burst through the thickest patch, then my feet slip toward a cliff's edge. Arms flailing, I almost go over, but the stiff wind blasting up the rock keeps me from falling. Across the misty valley below, another mountain rises, and Sage's scream is closer now. My heart leaps; her voice sounds strong and different from last time… but she's in trouble. "Sage!"

She's on the far mountain, and a lion's snarl makes me bare my teeth. I'll never reach her in time! With desperate motion, I sprint along the cliff's edge as the thorns rip at my shoulder, making me waver on the slimy ledge. The valley is wide, uncrossable before the lion does its worst.

"Get away!" Sage's shout echoes and the stone beneath me breaks off.

"No!" I inch right, but the shale gives way and landing hard on one knee doesn't prevent a fall. Rough stone grinds my skin, body sliding down a wider section. "Reau…" The hard landing cuts off my cry as momentum forces me over the next ledge. Dangling by my fingertips, I have a single aim: to reach her. I kick one knee over the edge and roll onto a narrow path along the steep mountainside.

Any mountain goat would be at home here, and soon its hoof beats pound along with my stride. A glimpse of a pure white coat keeping pace one level higher brings hope to life.

"Haseleph!" I shout, as the magnificent horse leaps down, his hoofs spraying stone shards into my face. An inviting whinny floods me with relief as he shakes his glorious mane, then bends one front knee, bowing so I can swing aboard.

As soon as my legs clamp onto his sides, Haseleph leaps forward, his sheer speed makes my eyes water. His hooves strike sparks as he traverses the treacherous path with ease. "Run hard, boy!"

His ears prick forward, and his strides lengthen, but the narrow trail ends, fading into nothing.

"Stop!" I shout. "Halt!" But he doesn't. Muscles bunching, he gathers for a leap with no possible landing and I yank on his long white mane. "No!"

The reasons we don't get along come rushing back. "Haseleph, NO!"

We soar into thin air, and sickening silence floods my ears while time morphs into slow motion. The arc of his leap angles toward the treetops below. The long whipping strands of his mane burn my hands, and horror spreads from the sensation as the brilliant white transforms into black scales.

"Clever dragon," I whisper as the beast reveals its true form, a steep dive exposing its terrifying bulk. The leathery wings snap open.

"Eh!" Letting go, I curl to avoid the tail's wicked slash, and freefall in a spin.

Air spews from my lungs as Raeual hits me like a linebacker, then a wave of super-heated air blasts my face and the dragon makes a second pass, its jaws snapping closed where we were a heartbeat ago.

"Have we…" Raeual grunts as he strains further, avoiding one wing's downstroke. "Learned nothing from last time? Go for…" Air currents shred his shout as the massive rear leg strikes out, blasting Raeual away and yanking me upward.

This time, the beast doesn't have a solid grip, and a violent twist frees me to drop through the fog above the valley. Wind shrieks, but every sense is bent to the feel of the air as it rushes past.

Heat builds, so I kick into a somersault, slamming violently onto a snout that matches the mist to perfection.

Wing. Raeual meant *go for its wing.*

Hadena flashes out as I swan dive off the beast's forehead, then twist into a strike position. The air turns to concrete, telling me an upstroke is coming, but the beast is invisible, its scales rippling with a perfect mimic of the backdrop. Hadena falls a breath too late, and the leathery wing chops me so hard that blackness creeps in.

But it's Sage, somewhere far below, that makes me shake it off and drive Hadena's dual blades through the leather. Air blasts through the holes, almost ripping me away. I flatten out and keep the blades deep, grinning when the color morphs to black around the wound. The dragon's shriek rends the atmosphere as its flight tilts sharply to starboard.

A poof of fresh pine needles explodes over the wing's leading edge, confusing the scales' cloaking ability further as Hadena lengthens the slices and the beast lists even more. The wing shreds a tree, and the beast careens hard. The collision knocks me off, and two branches rake my ribs before the next forces a full stop. "Oomph."

I dangle there, lungs fighting for breath, as my first arrival to the spirit comes back in a rush. Except now, the enemy lurks above. The dragon struggles, crashing through the trees, with air gushing through the twin openings. Another shriek pitches higher, until I cover my ears, desperate to escape the sound. It builds to an electric crackle, and the bolts strike straight into my back; pain makes me arc in agony.

5
SAGE

My gut churns in the African heat, smoothing Jacob's t-shirt and wishing he'd open his eyes, because this jump is coming on too strong; I'm staring down the gauntlet of hell.

Water. I've got to find some. I push off Jacob's chest and stumble outside the hangar as the haze builds. The stench of rotten liquid makes me lurch left, yanking back a section of bent sheet metal to stare at a dark, leaf-filled puddle. My muscles seize, clamping tight, and I fall in.

Speed drags me backward as I fight to stay in my body, but it's so fast there's no time to scream. Heat singes, and no amount of effort slows me.

What if you're wrong? Demyen's words fill my mind as eternal night closes around me.

Dark flames consume my feet and wafting heat billows my hair, sending the stench of death straight to my core. Will the voice save me again? There's no sound besides the entwined roar of the flames and lions.

"Please!" I scream as one name forms within. *Jesus.*

"No," a lion growls, striding forward with its singed coat smoking. "You're as far from perfect as a human can get. Call out, He'll toss you back the second your filth shows. You're mine, and you know it."

There's no air to drag over my blackened lungs. It's true; I could never measure up.

What if you're wrong?

The molten wind steals all moisture as a constant dying takes over, forever on the verge of suffocation. The lion steps closer. Will his bite last forever too? My head lolls, ruined eyes straining to focus on the dark at my feet. Terror wells inside; an army of worms writhes toward me. They'll get in my skin… *inside.* I buck hard, but the lurid midnight clamps harder.

Only a whisper will come. "Jesus."

The universe screeches to a halt as everything goes blank; still and empty. There's no air, no temperature, no light, no lions. The coolness of space is disorienting, floating in nothing.

The emptiness exposes my heart, every doubt and fear, and all that my selfishness can't hide. The darkness in me goes so much deeper than thoughts or actions. Death codes every scrap of DNA, a mutated pattern separate from life at its most primal depth. It's *my* darkness. The knowledge strikes like a war hammer—there isn't any light in me. Death rules, and no number of good actions can rewrite my baseline code. My face contorts, sorrow burning.

Then everything changes, and space morphs into a massive room, gold-plated and intricate, with pure beauty in every crevice. A table with loaves of bread and an ornate seven-pronged lamp stand before a heavy veil of gold, purple, and blue that separates this room from another.

I've no right to be here where everything is holy, holy, *holy*. The purity expels my foreign code and tears spill over.

A rugged wooden cross appears before the veil, blood flowing from the Man nailed to it. His eyes find mine as He twists in the torture, His entire body ruined, abdomen flayed open, His jaw bleeding.

"I'm sorry," I whimper; but words can't stop his suffering. Crushing anxiety presses in, because I can't save Him, or me, or all the soldiers who bled out under my care. I'm not enough; never will be.

"I AM."

The words knock me to my knees, and He exhales, a long sigh, body going still, eyes glazing over. My sob breaks the sacred silence, and the temple quakes until the veil rips from the top to the bottom and a scent floods out, strong incense that carries knowledge straight into my core. It takes dying to live, because my code can't be rewritten.

The room beyond is a pure warm light that beckons me. My hands cover my face, shielding my weak eyes, as the light draws me in. It feels like… *home.* I lean forward, letting it touch me, knowing that crossing the threshold will destroy everything that defines me. The light's too strong, too pure for my code to survive.

The wrathful judgment waiting to strike doesn't exist. His eyes were pure love that pulses forever in the fabric of time and space.

I AM.

The words pierce past all my doubts and fear. It's true. *He is.*

He is worth my life. I stagger up and step forward, right foot passing the entrance; dying to get even one heartbeat next to Him. "Jesus, You are Lord."

The light hits me full force and I crumple, stricken by the glory. My head slams into the floor, an empty husk, but in the same instant, the light surges in. *Takes my place.* No longer me, but *Him,* alive in me. Bursting outward, the code of life breaks the darkness and builds a new blueprint. It lifts me to my feet, and I step into the holy of holies.

"You are," I whisper.

It's not about me, or my failures, it's all about Him. The cloud of light envelops, but no, it *is* inside every fiber.

For you died, now, Christ lives.

Everything changes in that instant, the temple fading, and a forest materializes far below with a deep woody scent of pine that's so strong I taste it and hear its warm hum. A thousand sensations pummel as leaves thwap like whips. I slam into the soft loam, and breath in the smell of brown with its low vibrating sound.

Alive!

My hands, sunk into the warm dirt, have a hint of light emanating outward. Tears brim with a gratitude unlike any before. He is *All in All*. Vague memories swirl of dead trees and harsh light, but they're a nightmare that doesn't own me anymore.

"Thank you." My whisper echoes louder until it bursts into a shout. "Thank you!" I bellow, the words uncontrollable.

The light has translated me, no longer of the flames and darkness, and time is meaningless as I drop to my knees, weeping for joy. A leaf brushes my cheek, and I hear its color.

I stagger to my feet, weak but full of wonder, my fists full of dirt that sings a soft harmony with the blue sky. *So alive!* Containing a shout of pure joy is useless, and it ripples away over the mountain's foot where a bank of fog gathers. My air runs out, and another sound startles me—the snap of a twig close behind.

I whirl, face to face with a lion. Heartbeats pass, frozen in time as pure hatred flows from its low growl.

Heat builds inside. There's no way I'm dying after living for 2.5 seconds. The dry soil in my fists and the light breeze on the back of my neck might buy time. The lion sinks, coiling for the strike, and I pitch the dust into his gaping mouth, ducking hard, one knee slamming down.

A bestial shriek rends the air, and the sky dims, distracting the lion for a breath. My wavering legs pump, leaping for a low-hanging branch. Claws catch my thin-soled shoe, drawing a scream that wastes energy. With desperate force, my calf locks over a branch, but the lion rushes to the trunk.

A fog bank snakes around me with a chill twinge of rot. "Go!"

Hand over hand, I scramble upward through the thinning outer branches, but the enemy keeps pace, nearer the trunk. A branch snaps, and I plummet as the lion leaps, claws raking air. My elbow hooks a lower branch, tearing my shoulder. Another metallic shriek threatens to implode my eardrums, and it rises to a crescendo that snaps like lightning. The lion lands below and stays crouched, its wild eyes scanning the sky.

I use his hesitation to gain altitude, my lungs heaving as an enormous shadow darkens the fog. The lion creeps closer to the trunk, his belly dragging the ground. Open wounds and flies cover his hide, and the longer I study him, the more fear churns.

The air pressure changes, pressing down as everything gets darker and the shadow takes shape. Something immense is coming, careening over the trees. I cling to the branches as the treetops shear off nearby, and branches pepper me.

Oomph.

The odd sound mixes with a crash as more sticks pelt me. All at once, the air gets easier to breathe and the full light returns. It doesn't take long to spot the lion, and his burning yellow eyes find mine. The glee there makes me shrink against the trunk, far too exposed.

Something heavy smashes the tree beyond the lion, causing him to spin and hiss. The branch under my foot snaps, and I fall with a yelp to the lowest branch.

"Sage!"

Wait, that's *my* name. Looking within, it surfaces, Sage Emerson, *El Shaddai's child.* The thought brings a shiver as I search for the source of the voice.

"J… Jacob?" He's familiar, like a dream that's returned a thousand times, except now he's dangling from one hand on a branch. The lion hesitates, unsure who to take first. He lets go, landing on his feet with primal grace, even more muscular than I remember him. His skin has its own sort of glow, as if light lives inside. "There's a lion!"

Two blades snap out into his palms, pointing downward, ready to strike. He locks eyes with the lion and smiles. My stomach drops, but the beast sinks to its belly, snarling.

"Get!" Jacob swipes at the lion, whose claws scramble, spitting dirt in his haste. The blades disappear with a soft sound, and Jacob strides to the base of my tree, rubbing his lower back.

"Um, did you… fall out of the sky?" I ask.

He studies me with desperate eyes, then the air leaves him in a rush. "You… the light! You have the light about you!"

I hold out one hand. It certainly lacks the radiance his skin has, but just thinking of the new code makes me grin as I undertake a very humbling exit from the tree. "Yes!"

I brush off my pants, unable to meet his eyes. Next to him I'm skin and bones. He laughs and clutches me in a full-on hug. His scent fills my lungs with six-dimensional perfection.

He steps back in relief, eyes closed, with a guttural sigh. "I thought you… ugh. It's so good to have you here."

Embarrassment floods into me as my atrophied condition is a stark contrast to Jacob's vibrant strength and vitality. His eyes are so bright, but with a twinge of pain, he grips his side.

"Are you hurt?" I ask, reaching up, but lacking the courage to touch him.

He waves one hand. "It's nothing, just a scratch."

Strange bland memories distract where I'm compressing a wound, but the blood is the only color in the gray scene. "Was I…" My eyes squint, searching. "A nurse?"

His smile is even more enthralling here. "It's weird, right? Now you know why it's hard to go back."

I rub my atrophied arms and look around. "Well, it's nice with you around."

The comment makes his expression fall, and I cover a cringe at not knowing the rules.

"For now, but you'll learn to stand on your own."

"Ha!" My honest disbelief can't be hidden.

"I felt the same way at first, but you've got to eat. Here…" He digs through a small pouch at his hip.

He holds out a small section of parchment that looks like leather, but smells amazing. It would be easier if he wasn't looking at my sunken cheeks and sallow skin, but he smiles without the repulsion I deserve.

"Thank you." I take it, making sure not to touch his fingers, so my condition won't rub off on him. The scroll is delightful, with a warm, buttery flavor, but a voice echoes from everywhere at once.

"Who said that?" I ask, looking around.

He shakes his head, and I catch myself staring at his wide neck. "It took me days to hear the scroll, and you get it on your first bite?"

The delight on his face makes him seem even more a part of this place, of the wild energy that surges here.

He traces a strange shape on the ground while I listen to the words whispering inside. The voice is gentle and strong, not mine, but familiar.

Th... Therefore if any man be in Christ... He is a new creature: old things have passed away: behold, all things are become new.

The words leap straight into the depths of my heart. *New.* My skin doesn't glow like Jacob's, but it once oozed darkness. Now, it's life pulsing there, and His light is written on every bit of code. The scroll matches it, and lends a solid sensation which radiates into every limb, chasing out weakness.

Jacob's eyes narrow, and he sniffs the air. A shadow races over the forest, leaving a blanket of icy chill behind it. He crouches, searching the sky, one hand on the jeweled hilt of his sword, but the other covers his side. In that gray world, I'd insist on checking the wound, but here? I'm not sure about much.

"Let's get moving, there's so much to see." But his gaze stays locked on the sky. What's making him so cautious? The warmth in the air returns as we step forward.

"So, did you fall out of the sky?" I ask.

He turns with that glint in his eye that I love most. "Did you?"

I squint, trying to remember. "Maybe."

"Then maybe I did too. Do you see anything glinting in the ground?" he asks, keeping his stride short to match mine.

"Like pink topaz?" A thin thread glistens, embedded in soft moss that releases the freshest scent.

"That's your path; always follow it. It's the Almighty's perfect will for you, and the best place you can ever be."

"Do you have one too?" I ask, squinting.

"Yes. It's saved my neck more times than I can count." He pushes a vine aside so I can pass under and I catch him staring. Heat flushes up my neck, feeling like a pauper next to a king, but he doesn't notice, and the pulsing, swirling life of this place *is* distracting. The flavor of blue fills my mouth and the sky above might be my favorite taste ever.

Jacob's whisper is like a wisp of wind, but the word is unfamiliar, so I swallow the sensation of inferiority. "What?"

He shrugs and glowing scars on his shoulder peek out from his shirt. A dull sort of memory surfaces: Jacobs on the exam table when his collar bone snaps, blood erupting; except here, the scars are entrancing, like the most incredible tattoo. "The name Jesus is a translation."

"What's His real name?"

Jacob smiles, trying to ease my tension. "He has *many*, but His given name is Yeshua."

I hug myself tighter as a quiver races up my spine, as if the word carries energy.

"Yeshua Hamashia, Jesus the Messiah." His words change the air, making it sweeter. He rubs his mouth, then turns away. A dark smudge on his shirt looks like blood and dirt mixed there. Maybe he'll let me check it later.

A million sensations swirl as Jacob leads us through the trees, but a twinge in the air makes my skin prick. "Wait."

Jacob stops, head cocked, then the ground trembles with a low rumble that makes sweat appear between my shoulder blades. A snarl and a scream entwine, knifing through the air. Jacob's hands clench and two long daggers snap open. The faintest wisp of green haze floats near his jaw. The growl fills the forest, bringing a shudder. *There must be someplace to hide.*

"My path runs forward," he says, eyes ablaze. "Yours takes a left, and we've got to stick to them. Stay low and quiet. I'll find you." He takes off, sprinting toward the sound. The smudge on the back of his shirt is larger. Fear clamps tight.

Alone.

There must be somewhere safe, somewhere high. The glittering pink vein cuts left, but the lions are close, and there's nothing to keep them at bay. As I slip from tree to tree, my hair sticks to my forehead at odd angles and my heart rate spikes. The forest is old, with no low branches.

I freeze at movement ahead. A flash of dull tawny fur and a massive, gaunt frame make vomit surge in my throat. Rough tree bark bites into my back. Even in its starved condition, and crisscrossed with rotting wounds, the lion's ferocity radiates outward. It stops in mid-stride with one paw suspended. Its immense head turns straight to me, black eyes locked on.

"No." I whisper.

The beast condenses, but I can't outrun him, so I spread my hands and glare back.

"I don't belong to you," I say, voice wavering. The lion's eyes flash as one ear dangles, the tip holding on by a shred.

"One more reason to hate you, then." The lion's cruel voice shivers into my bones.

Did he say hate or eat?

"No!" The command comes out strong, but what's going to stop him? His ancient, consuming power locks me in place and his bloodstained mouth opens.

"Jacob I know, and Demyen I know, but who are you to defy me?" the lion rasps, stalking forward. I brace for the charge, then his eyes widen, and he hesitates, setting his paw down. My lungs pull hard for more air, but showing weakness isn't acceptable. I lean forward, clenching my jaw to cover chattering teeth, and the lion snarls, but sinks down with long claws, impaling the forest floor.

Maybe my bluff will work. I feint forward, and the lion turns tail, disappearing past the ancient trunks. My hands hit my knees, struggling to stay upright as trembling sets in deeply. I go wide-eyed at a whisper of sound behind.

My ultra-slow turn morphs into an involuntary flinch. A man stands there, a few feet away, with piercing green eyes that see my soul. Embarrassment floods me, complete with heat flushing up my neck.

"That was smart, standing your ground." His baritone voice is soothing, putting me at ease.

"*That* was a bluff," I retort with an empty laugh.

He arches one brow, but his eyes gleam with a mischievous joy. He's a mountain of a man, his shoulders rippling with muscle as he strokes a dark, curling beard.

"I believe we've met."

I frown, wavering there as if a stiff breeze could blow me over.

"Met Jacob the same way." His mouth turns up at the memory. "I'm Demyen."

"Didn't think you knew my real name." Jacob's there with tawny fur stuck to his shirt.

"Aye, Boy," Demyen laughs.

"Mara's waiting, we'd best hurry," Jacob says. Our eyes lock, but anxiety flares, crushing me inside. What if we get separated? For the first time, the worry seems foreign, and *wrong*. It's an enemy lurking even closer than the lions.

My gaze drops to my hands that still tremble, but the soft light there sparks a new thought: What if anxiety isn't a part of me anymore? Crossing the threshold into the holy of holies destroyed the code of darkness; could anxiety disintegrate too? Freedom sends a thrill straight through me. Is it possible?

Demyen sets off through the forest, and Jacob falls into a protective position behind me. Exploring the future without the choking plague of anxiety is enthralling, a dream come true. Jacob nudges me, offering a piece of scroll.

Be... be anxious for nothing, but in everything by prayer and supplication, with thanksgiving, let your requests be made known to

God; and the p… peace of God, which surpasses all understanding, will guard your hearts and minds through Christ Jesus.

Both hands clench over my heart. It *is* possible! Tears flood my eyes but don't spill over as the knowledge settles within. Ahead, Demyen stops in a feral sort of stance. Jacob steps closer, scanning the hill. Demyen points to a snake draped over a branch. But no, it's too thin…

Pulling his long sword, Demyen eases forward, then laughs. "A belt?"

Jacob pats his sides. "It's mine, I think."

Demyen turns with a sharp scowl. "Yours, Boy?"

Jacob snatches it, coiling the soft leather around one hand as a look of consternation clouds his face. Then, from far off, a grating howl rises to a shriek of pure rage, ascending until we clutch our ears and that electric snap sends a concussion across the distance.

Jacob groans, gripping his back as he stumbles to one knee. Demyen's eyes narrow as I help Jacob up. His skin is pale, and sweat beads on his upper lip. The belt lies on the forest floor; Demyen picks it up again, brushing it off. "Ought not be without this."

"Eh." Jacob pulls his arm away, taking the belt with even more force. "It's broken, anyway."

Demyen's eyes narrow further. "Easy, Boy."

The trees press in as if watching the growing tension.

"It's not your problem, anyway." Jacob's growling comment spikes my nerves. I step between them, both hands out.

"Please, let's keep moving."

"Aye," Demyen says, eyeing Jacob with a frown before continuing.

Leaves crinkle when the belt hits the forest floor and Jacob sets off. I wipe the sweat off my palms, glance up to be sure he's not watching, then grab it. My waist is the only place to hide it, but Jacob is correct; the clasp is broken. There's enough length to tie it on and hurry forward before he turns, scanning for me. He offers a tight smile, but it doesn't cover the strange expression in his eyes.

When he starts forward again, I gasp; blood is trickling onto his pants. "Jacob, we need to clean that wound."

He doesn't turn, but waves one hand. "It's fine, a scratch is all."

"There's blood." I say, tone flat.

"It's fine."

Arguing is pointless. Maybe Demyen will side with me later.

The second I step into The Tree, all tension falls away as I follow Mara up the winding stairs. Her wizened skin and sparkling eyes set me at ease, as if we've known each other for ages.

A dark-haired woman is coming down; her face lights up with a smile upon seeing us.

"Myah!" they embrace, looking as if they could be mother and daughter. The younger woman bites her lip.

"I've something to show you." She glances around, but Jacob and Demyen are far up on the next landing, so she pulls her shirt up, revealing an intense glow near her navel.

Mara gasps. "A child! You and Ian must be thrilled."

They embrace again, and then Myah says, "Yes, I must be going, but you're the first to know."

Mara's rooms are full of interesting things; exploring them could occupy me for hours. A small glass globe full of blue liquid surges with ocean waves and sand, but a figure appears beside me out of thin air. I shriek, leaping back. He's *so* tall, and a brilliant white shirt stretches over solid muscle, though his kind brown eyes make the fright dissipate.

"Galel, welcome!" Mara's wrinkles deepen as she smiles, like nothing's unusual. Another figure appears beside the first. "And Raeual, good to see you."

My eyes flick to Jacob. He isn't surprised as he sits on a couch, seeming quite at home. The Tree has eased his mood as well, and his eyes are soft again.

"W… what?" Is all I can manage.

"Oh, Sage, have you not met your Watcher?" Mara takes my elbow. "Galel has watched over you all your life. Isn't that right?" She reaches way up to pat his giant arm.

He dips his head toward me, delight in his dark eyes. "Welcome to the light, Sage."

My mouth falls open as his words fill me to the brim with a Christmas-morning feeling. The sensation swirls higher, bursting inside. "Ha. Thank you. I guess… I guess that's a thank you for a million things I never even knew about."

Galel's mouth tips up. "Two point one."

"I'm sorry?" I ask.

"It's 2.1 million rescues."

"Oh," my brows arch. "I see. Maybe… next year will be quieter?" I shrug. Faint memories of helicopters, rifles, and running crash in. I tilt my head. "Probably not, though."

Raeual crosses his arms, eyes bright. "My last charge was a woman. I must confess, she talked so much I often plugged my ears."

The mental image makes me stifle a laugh.

"Yes," Galel nods. "Women love to talk."

That makes me scowl. "I don't think *all* women do. Sure, some of us, but not all…." I trail off as the Watchers exchange a knowing look as I prove their point.

Jacob is sitting forward without touching the back of the couch. "Do *you* think I talk too much?" I ask him.

"Oh." His brows flatten out. "I… I like the sound of your voice."

Raeual's bark of laughter fills the room, "Smooth, man. That was smooth."

Mara takes my elbow. "Come, Sage. We women have much to *talk* about."

She giggles as we turn, and I look over my shoulder at Jacob. He's leaning forward, his hands pressed together as he listens to

Raeual talk about weapons. The moment we stepped into the Tree, his bleeding stopped.

"The best ones are double-bladed," Raeual says, with both hands on an invisible hilt.

Galel adds, "With the faintest curve at the tip."

Mara draws me further into the tree. Being inside feels safe, and the peace grows. We come to an arched door with a bright green knob.

"Open it," Mara urges, as goosebumps spread up my arms.

I reach forward, hesitate, and then grip the knob. At the touch, everything is in my soul; the physical order, the spirit, and the connection between the two. Frozen, I see Paco's wound sealing up and Artan's smile as he waved goodbye.

My voice echoes from that reality, almost accusing. "So, you bent the rules?"

The word *rule* reverberates inside my head, driving me crazy. My survival depends on knowing them. Mara lays her ancient hand on top of mine on the knob. The tension lifts, but not the burning questions.

"Things have been happening that are not explainable. I don't understand this world." My voice cracks.

"Open it."

Two small words that terrify me. Whatever is beyond this door will change everything, and I'm not ready.

"No one is." Mara's whisper propels me forward and the green knob turns. We step into a room full of scrolls. They fill cubbies and shelves, and the air is laden with the most incredible scent, like warm bready notes mixed with mouthwatering beef and a faint tinge of bitter herbs. Mara sighs.

"This is my most favorite place, amongst the *Words.*"

A thrill races up my skin as my fingers run along them. At the first touch, the room transforms into a desert. Hot air buffets me as a man in a rough garment cries out to a crowd. "Repent, for the Kingdom of Heaven is at hand!"

I pull my hand back, and the room returns. "What was that?"

"The words are alive, and here, they take you into the meaning. Come this way," she says, and I follow in the reverent hush, careful to keep my hands clasped at my waist.

"Here we are." She caresses a scroll, then turns, seeing another time. "Yes, this is it. Place your hand alongside mine."

I hesitate, then my fingers brush the soft scroll. The room disappears, and the expanse of space surrounds us. We travel until a dot of light expands and details take shape. It's a glorious Kingdom, full of light, shaped like a perfect cube whose walls and citadels gleam. Its perfection and beauty fill me with a longing unlike any I've known, and my spirit whispers truth. This is the visible expression of the source code!

"If you don't understand the beginning, you'll stumble over everything else."

Closer now, we hover, watching the vast gates swing open. The King of Kings steps out, surrounded by a thick cloud of glory, and surveys the darkness. There below Him, Earth appears, both formless and void. The King steps through space to study it, and

He speaks words I don't understand, but the tone reveals His tender care and attention.

Creation issues from His Words, that ripple outward forever, taking shape before our eyes. The sun, moon, and stars appear, and far-flung galaxies spin around us. Below Earth, a burning furnace glows, so familiar that I shrink away even now. But above, descending from the celestial city, a cord of light connects the perfection of Heaven to Earth.

Mara leans close as He forms the first man.

"The Almighty made Earth for Adam and set him as ruler over it, an ambassador who would walk with the King of Kings. The lineage of Adam became the first dual citizens of both Heaven and Earth: a colony that will expand Heaven's rule—but it soon went wrong, against the will of the Master."

Nearer Earth now, a river pours into a lush garden, then splits into four strong river heads. Adam and his wife hold scepters, the symbol of rulership over Earth. But far to the west, a dark smudge hovers, seeking entry. A serpent creeps near the shadow, and the darkness enters its body.

"The only way to steal the Kingdom of Earth was through deception. After all, our enemy had already convinced a third of the angels to rebel, and the lineage of Adam proved a simple conquest. Hava, whose name translates to Eve, was the Queen of all Earth, but she gave up her heavenly citizenship and became an outlaw on Earth as well. She sold life to know evil."

Earth shudders as Adam takes the bite, and the beautiful strand of light detaches from Earth, drawing away, leaving the planet bereft of Heaven's influence.

"And know evil she did." Mara says. The serpent rears high, striking Adam's hand, and the scepter falls. Fear fills Hava's eyes, and she throws her scepter down before the viper, backing away. In that instant, a vortex of dark flame rises from the furnace under the earth, and attaches there, shaking Earth's foundations, and rippling outward, as death, decay, and sickness spread across the globe.

"The legal right to rule Earth passed to our enemy, and the Kingdom of Heaven no longer had earthly ambassadors. You see, the lineage of Adam didn't lose a religion. We lost an entire kingdom. That is why religion doesn't satisfy, only a reconnection to the King of Heaven."

Earth, now bound to those terrible flames, suffers violence and death, and sorrow twists in my gut.

"Loyal to His own rules, the Almighty could not take back what the ambassadors legally gave away, so He sought a covenant with man that would restore His right to influence the realm of Earth. The first was with Noah, the next one, far greater, was with Abraham, and it opened the way for the Redeemer to come. You see, Abraham laid his son at the altar, proving to all that a man would be obedient, even at the greatest cost. Through his actions, the Almighty gained the legal right to offer His own son as payment for sin."

From the gates of Heaven, a figure steps out, and instant recognition leaps inside. Yeshua Himself strides to Earth, and the darkness gathers into a dense cloud before Him.

"One price was required to pay for Adam's sin: blood. A perfect sacrifice alone could win the scepter back."

I cover my face as He suffers on the cross, unable to bear the sight. Mara shakes my shoulder. "See!"

Yeshua's spirit lets go of His tormented body, and the darkness rushes in, obliterating the sight of Him. The writhing mass of shadowy shapes drags Him down the vortex into the abyss. Frozen time passes, and anguish fills Earth.

Then the furnace expands with shrieks of glee that echo across space as the wicked chorus putrefies Earth. All at once the clamor falls silent, cut off, and from the depths of hell, the scepter rises, puncturing the dark, clenched in the mighty fist of The Victor. He ascends, striding out of the midnight, the essence of perfection.

He reaches Earth, and His light beats back the fingers of eternal night. Heaven's thread of connection extends, reaching Earth once more. Yeshua holds the scepter out to all, bowing the knee to Him. In that instant, the scepter multiplies, appearing in their hands. The gates of Heaven open and Yeshua ascends, with the Kingdom of Earth restored to the lineage of Adam. The thread of darkness still pumps its poison into the earth, making war against all who hold the scepter.

Many hold the scepter for a time, but the darkness pounds, until many abandon their appointment, groveling instead, where the attack lessens. Generations pass, and most can't recognize the scepter; instead, they bow before the shadow of it, never knowing the scepter is their calling.

"Oh, the tragedy," Mara whispers. "Religion takes the place of citizenship. So few realize Yeshua came to restore the kingdom, the very thing we lost."

She hands me a brilliant white section of scroll. "Hidden in plain sight, the kingdom has ever been the Almighty's plan."

The words come with the meaty flavor.

Jesus… Jesus answered, "My kingdom is not of this world. If My kingdom were of this world, My servants would fight, so that I should not be delivered to the Jews; but now My kingdom is not from here."

"His Kingdom is not a continent, or a certain government, but the right to rule. For, *the kingdom of God does not come with observation; nor will they say, 'See here!' or 'See there!' For indeed, the kingdom of God is within you.* Beginning, middle, and end, the kingdom is the message, yet without knowledge we live as slaves."

She lifts my hand, and we're back in the quiet room filled with the scent of scroll. The sense that I've wasted every moment until now grows until I curl forward, arms around my stomach.

"Here, take this." She hands me more scroll. "It's what you do now that matters."

According as His divine power has given us everything we need for life and godliness through the knowledge of Him that has called us to glory and virtue.

"I… I don't have to earn it?" I ask. Is it possible that He already gave me all I need, but I lack the knowledge to use it? Is this what Jacob meant, that he *used* a rule?

Mara turns with a smile as she opens the door. "Knowledge problems are easy to fix."

Jacob and Demyen are on Mara's couch, laughing, their hair wet as if they'd been swimming. I sigh, wondering if I'll ever be where they are, confident and strong. Relief floods that the tension

Jacob had earlier is gone. It would be like the clash of the titans if he and Demyen argued.

Jacob stops mid-sentence on seeing me in the doorway. His familiar scars glow, and I'm thankful to have a small part in their history.

Demyen's eyes shift from Jacob to me and back again. "Ah."

That one guttural syllable makes my face flame red, but a smile spreads across Jacob's. "Aye."

Flustered, I turn, desperate for a distraction. All at once, Galel, Raeual, and another Watcher appear. Shoulder to shoulder, they fill the room, but it's their vibe that knocks the breath out of me. Their faces are solemn, fathomless eyes burning.

Jacob and Demyen stand, caught by the sensation that the world is shifting.

"Word has come," Raeual says, his quiet voice like a cannon blast inside of me.

The other Watcher dips his head. "Time is coming to a close. Every second burns with purpose. A journey is before you to begin the prophecy's fulfillment."

The air in the room is kinetic, almost too heavy to breathe.

Galel nods. "Through the water and the wilderness to the mountain of the Almighty."

I inch backward toward the door. Jacob and Demyen deserve privacy. Galel's fervent gaze finds mine. The slightest shake of his head makes me freeze.

Raeual continues, "Each of you must hear and obey. The enemy's eye has turned to you. Watch, and pray."

All three of them disappear, sucking the air from the room. I sag against the doorway as the men nod at each other. Demyen draws his sword, and the ringing sound sends chills to my core as he rubs one finger along the bright blade.

"*Ne'eman baderekh histiyem.* Faithful to the end." Demyen's face is lit with complete dedication.

Mara steps into the room, handing us each a parcel. "For the days ahead. Keep to the path always."

She takes Jacob's right hand, wincing as she touches his palm. "Do not turn back; plunge forward, Jacob. Every victory must be accomplished."

I tuck the parcel in the scroll pouch at my side, knowing that the comfort of this Tree is ours no longer. Silent, the three of us file down the uneven winding stairs as a pulsing urgency pushes us forward. A chill wind rustles the leaves, and Jacob and Demyen scan the sky, hands at their swords.

"What is that smell?" I ask, trudging between Jacob and Demyen. We've traveled far and thorny scrub catches at my clothes in the arid landscape. A piece of scroll held under my nose wards off the greasy scent.

Demyen sighs. "The marsh."

The grim look on his face is far from encouraging. I squint, weaving my head, trying to see my path as far as possible. "Looks like we're heading straight for it."

"Strange that we would. It's ever been a border, uncrossable. But," Demyen pauses and I recall Raeual's words, "we must pass by the bounds of all that's known. Stay ready."

"For what?" I ask.

He glances at me with one brow arched. "For anything."

My foot sinks in soft mud as I glance at Jacob. He's been quiet since we left, traversing the miles consumed with thought. We're far from the Tree, or any pleasant forest, and the land is parched and rocky. We haven't met another soul for miles.

"Boy," Demyen calls, scowling at the path. Jacob doesn't respond. "Boy!"

"Hmm? What?" Jacob wipes one hand over his face and I frown at his odd behavior.

"What do you make of this?" Demyen points to a rock inscribed with a symbol.

Jacob kneels before it, one finger tracing the familiar rune.

"It's not of the Almighty, that's certain, but I've seen it before." He clenches his fist and his daggers unsheathe as we look at the odd pyramid inscription.

Sweat beads on my back as memories from the physical warp the air, where Jacob is tracing this ruin. A glance over my shoulder brings a gasp and the men spin, glaring at three lions stalking right behind us. A metallic taste floods my mouth and my feet sink deeper into the muck.

"Go back!" Demyen orders, "In the name of Yeshua Hamashia."

Growling, they sink to their bellies; but the gaze of the largest one, with the tattered ear, stays locked on mine.

"Aseph," Jacob warns, and the beasts slink away. That glint is back in Jacob's eyes. "Never let doubts sneak up on you. He's a nasty one."

My nod is too fast, making me dizzy since my heart is still slamming, confidence gone. Out here, there's nothing between me and the lions.

"Will they follow us?" My voice betrays the terror.

"At a distance. Never forget, lions steal everything they can. If they can catch you off guard or scare you into running, they'll do their worst," Demyen says, striding down the damp path.

"Thanks," I mutter.

Jacob chuckles. "I know the feeling, but you're more than a conqueror."

I slip on a fallen log, and his grip prevents me from a mud bath. "Thanks."

It's still hard to look him in the eye, knowing how pitiful I am. He squeezes my hand before letting it go. His voice is husky and low. "Actually, I enjoy being with you."

I huff, face hot. "Can you read *all* my thoughts?"

"No, but that one was pretty plain on your face. We all start out the same, Sage. The moment we become one with the light, we possess everything, but don't know how to use it. We have to grow in that—and I'm still learning too, always will be."

The mud sucks at our feet with every step as we duck vines and dead tree limbs. I can't stop scanning for spiders or snakes. Jacob's company is all that keeps me going. Another glance back reveals the lions, keeping pace at a respectful distance. What if I were alone?

All at once, the lions flinch, sinking low, shocking me with how fast they disappear. The next second, an awful shriek sounds, rising until I cover my ears. The sharp crackle at the end doubles me over, tasting acid. Jacob staggers next to me, his face contorted as he grips his back.

When he straightens, his mouth is turned down, and his eyes have a hard edge. The fitful breeze brings a whiff of odor that's worse than the lions' or the marsh. Jacob shakes his head, pulling in a long breath before starting off after Demyen, but his hand remains on his back, just below the stain on his shirt that's damp again.

"Anyway," he forces the words around a grimace. "Knowing about authority will change things for you. Remember what cars are?" A gruff tone replaces his amiable one.

I scowl, trying to bring up an image for the word. "Yeah, sort of."

"Could you stop a moving car with your hands?"

"No."

"And here, can you force a lion into submission by the power of your arm?"

I study my scrawny limbs. "Not a chance."

"But what if a police officer instructed traffic to stop?"

"Cars have to. It's the law." It's hard to pull up the flat memories.

"But he couldn't stop an 8,000-pound truck with a revving engine any more than anyone else. It's the *authority* behind his position that makes it happen." He groans, bending forward until I touch his shoulder.

"What's wrong?" I ask.

"Nothing." He turns to look at the lions, who are standing again, but still scanning the sky. "What's keeping Aseph from tearing us to shreds? He's no driver avoiding a ticket."

"Teach me, please," I request.

"He's under certain laws, ones he hopes you never learn. The car won't stop if the officer stands aside. Aseph won't either unless you take specific action. Light always overcomes the darkness. You can't shine darkness into a light room."

We're sinking with every step, and the murky stench is growing. Jacob winces as one foot comes up with a suction sound. "What if Aseph has you pinned? He would like you to believe that you're as powerless as you look and feel, but he can't hurt you unless you agree to it."

"*What?*"

"It's true. If you expect him to get you, he can. But if you force your mind to see the truth…." He digs in his pouch, handing me some scroll.

I chew, listening. *Behold, I saw Satan as lightning fall from heaven, and I give you authority to tread on serpents and scorpions and over all the power of the enemy: and nothing shall by any means hurt you.*

He swallows a piece, but coughs hard, holding his side. "That one changed me forever."

"So, you're saying I can tell Aseph to leave and he will?" If only I believed it.

"Almost. It's the name, *Yeshua*, where the power is. You're just the conduit."

"The what?" I rub my forehead, feeling miles behind.

"Remember electricity?"

"You're straining my brain, reaching for the physical order." It's only half in jest as we struggle through the mud. Sweat is running down his temples in the cool air.

"Let's say someone wants their lights on, so they call the power company and beg them to do it. The records are in order and everything's paid, and the building's wired to the power grid. Still, the owner begs for the lights to come on. Except nobody from the power company can legally enter their home and flip the switch. The switch is the resident's responsibility. All the power they could ever want is ready to flow, but if they don't flip that switch, they'll stay in the dark."

"Sure, but how does it connect to the lions?" I ask, leaning to peer at his back. The wet patch on his shirt is larger.

"As long as your switch is off, darkness will rule. Lions want to kill you. Most people of the light live there, at the mercy of evil, thinking they are only human, after all."

"Uh, but I am…"

He coughs, trying to get the words out. "No, Sage, one third of you is solid Holy Spirit. That's what allows you to live in the law of the spirit of life through Yeshua."

We're sinking up to our knees in the mud. Demyen is having the same struggle, his bulk forcing him even deeper as we approach the swamp.

"So, I flip this mysterious switch and Aseph can't attack me anymore?" I ask, hauling Jacob up, treasuring the touch.

"No," he grunts, "he'll still come after you."

I sigh, hands flapping at my sides. "See? This place makes no sense. I need something concrete. 2+2 = 4. The half-life of a photon is 10^34. Those are things I can count on."

"There's the illusion, Sage. What we're talking about is more solid than any fact of the physical order. It's stronger than everything in it put together. Spiritual Laws always trump physical ones."

It's like a puzzle piece that should fit, but still sits cock-eyed.

One hand covers my nose as we trudge after Demyen. The slimy water sloshes his sides, and he covers a groan.

"Ready?" Jacob asks, his chin tight.

"Nope."

He laughs, covering a grimace, then offers his hand. I take it, letting the touch distract from the repulsion of the water.

Dead trees loft sharp fingers to the sky and long strings of moss droop toward the salty liquid.

"Aseph will attack you because he's disobedient, but you'll turn him every time. It's just that you can't go by what things look like. We must *see* the Almighty's Words on the inside, because that truth doesn't change things until you believe and speak them. Those are the switch."

He gets it, but I shudder as the water climbs to my ribs; at least the mud has lessened. My path glimmers here and there, far under the tepid algae. It reminds me of...

Something brushes my leg.

Freezing, I replay the sensation, fingers clenched on Jacob's as murky water sloshes my ribs.

He turns to me, brows lowered, "What?"

The touch comes again—a long scrape that makes it impossible to move.

Jacob scans the murk, his blue eyes intense. Something strikes my waist hard from behind and I crash underwater, losing Jacob's hand.

My head smashes against a submerged tree trunk. The water churns red; there's no air. Jacob and Demyen are shouting as the water froths. Snake. I rake the scales without effect, then my face breaks the surface for a split second.

"Ye..." It wasn't enough time to call His name.

Blackness presses in, my muscles weakening as the coils tighten. The men slice through the marsh, but I'm far to the left, clamped in. It's the essence of every nightmare, my most primal fear. I can't fight this enemy in the frigid embrace of the water.

I can.

The warm voice echoes in my heart, and the words grow inside. *He* can. I believe that. The Almighty can. I reach for the switch, opening my mouth, which fills with rank saltwater that burns, but I force out one tiny bubble filled with a word.

"Yeshua."

It's ripped away in the crazed swirl.

Light explodes against my eyelids, and the beast lurches to a halt. Its weight pins me with the surface tantalizing inches above.

The pressure on my waist releases, and I claw for the surface, sucking in a desperate breath, falling over a rotting log, and the water behind explodes. Battle rages behind as I sag against the dead tree. Water sprays upward as Galel, Demyen, and Jacob chop at a viper's horned head that sinks into the shadowy swamp. Gasping, I climb the tree, watching the water.

"Whoo!" Galel pants, shedding water as he flings green slime from his sword, wading over to me. "Let's not open that door again."

"What?" I question, with the cold bringing a shiver.

"You were thinking of that dream you used to have just before it attacked you. Right? Notice it didn't go for anyone else."

"But that's not fair!"

He shrugs, "Fair or not, your expectations create the boundaries of your life, either good or bad. Life or death. What you focus on opens doors."

A sigh escapes as I force myself back into the water, determined to think of anything other than vipers or spiders.

"Might have helped if you pulled your weapon." Galel's fond look of pity makes me force a laugh.

"Yeah. What did you mean: 'opens doors'?" I draw my sword. It's short, maybe eighteen inches, but it's sharp blade is ready.

"The enemy is always seeking a way in, and people give him access, not knowing how far he'll penetrate. Your job is to keep the doors closed."

We wade closer to Jacob and Demyen, arms high out of the stinking salt water. "So, thoughts are doors?"

"Yes. Don't forget beliefs," he prompts, then disappears, leaving me to frown at the spot where the water swirls, filling the space.

"Come, we best not tarry here," Demyen warns, wading forward. A stand of dead trees is dotted with crows the color of ink, watching.

Jacob's soaked shirt clings to his skin, revealing a swollen spot on his lower back that turns my stomach sour. We hurry out of the marsh, and I take Jacob's hand. "I need to clean that *nothing-but-a-scratch.*"

He shrugs, reaching for his shirttail, but stops, eyes narrow, staring behind me. One finger moves to his lips, and I give the faintest nod, eyes flicking to Demyen, whose face is a shade paler too. Both men ease backward, silent, and careful. Nerves pricking, I set one foot down, refusing to look behind.

Jacob's cat-like movement ramps my stress higher as he lets me pass, his gaze unwavering. I dare not look, not when my nightmares brought the serpent. Three more cautious steps, and a rotting branch snaps under my foot.

We freeze, senses straining. A rustle of motion behind cuts off my air. Demyen's hand goes to his sword hilt as tense seconds build, then his free hand beckons and we start forward, testing each footfall. Demyen eases behind a massive decaying trunk, but Jacob's hand on my wrist brings a full stop. I wait, desperate not to think, forcing my mind to the room full of scrolls, until the scent fills my lungs.

His fingers loosen, and I slip behind the tree where Demyen waits with a drawn sword. Jacob steps close, and Demyen juts his chin toward the south, where my path glitters, winding behind a low hill. The men don't breathe easier until we're well past it, and hidden from… whatever that was.

"Best keep moving," Demyen says, scanning the path. "I'd hate to be here at night."

But soon, the light is waning, and the air smells worse by the moment. I squint at a shadow in the distance. "What is that?"

An enormous pyramid rises, black as sin. The terrible odor of sulfur and rot grow as a hot wind flows. With a knee in the dust, Jacob spreads his fingers on the ground. "The question is, why are we here?"

My path winds toward the imposing structure, leaving no option but forward. Demyen sheaths his sword.

"Let's take a moment to…" Demyen begins.

"Eat," Jacob interjects with a smirk as he stands, his expression falling with a wince.

"Aye," Demyen laughs, "and pray. Mayhap we will find guidance."

We settle under a tree with a few remaining leaves. The scroll fills the air with a tantalizing buttery aroma that tastes even better. Demyen has an elbow resting on one knee, closing his eyes while he chews. Peace radiates from him, and I lean into it, mimicking his focus. Inside, it's a shock to find the same sensation, growing as I focus on it, but urgency is there too; Jacob's wound can't be put off any longer.

"Let me see that cut," I say, voice low in the hush.

He sighs, turning, so the stain is visible.

"What caused it?" I ask, lifting his shirt. I don't like the strange color spreading around the wound's edge. It's darker than blood, almost like tar.

"Uh, it was… an enemy."

My eyes narrow, wondering what he's not telling me, but a chill descends as a faint noise brings Demyen's eyes open. In an instant, he's crouched with a short dagger in one hand. "We need to move, *now.*"

A long, serpentine figure creeps in the falling darkness, not thirty paces away. The sweeping horns on its head are clear cut against the last of the light. It's tracking something, snout to the ground.

Us.

It's larger than Aseph, but not by much. Is that what they saw near the marsh? The same dread spreads, tainting the atmosphere. Jacob draws me away, and for a moment, all three of our glimmering paths show, leading straight to the pyramid.

I don't let go of his hand in the heavy night as we hurry away. He uses every scrap of cover to break up our crouched silhouettes, keeping a few strides behind Demyen. The pyramid dominates the bleak landscape, and with each step my legs feel heavier.

A scuffle of rocks behind makes me flinch; the creature found our resting place. Demyen glances back, then leans into a trot. The night rushes over my hair, infusing it with the stench of death as we shelter under a rocky overhang.

"My path runs straight up the side," Jacob says, eyes glittering in the starlight. "Yours?"

"Aye," Demyen answers. But I'm too out of breath, nodding. "Make it to the base, then we'll take the next leg. How high you figuring those steps are?"

Squinting reveals what fear made me miss—it's a step pyramid, and each block is massive. My aching legs are not thrilled, but our pursuer isn't far behind.

"Objective one is staying covert. No telling how many of them there are," Jacob says.

"How many of what?" I ask.

"Dragons," Demyen answers. "Something tells me this is home base. I've never seen one in all my years. Some sort of sorcery is at work here, and they're the result."

"At least they're small," I add, trying to corral the twisting fear.

Demyen and Jacob frown at each other, turning to eye the distance.

"Fast and low," Jacob instructs. His hand engulfs mine, tugging me forward, and with each stride, the sensation of evil grows. My legs are weak as we pile up against the first obsidian stone. The instant my hands touch it, a vision flashes up, so real that pain streaks into my heart. Jacob is dead, his body strewn across dry cracked ground as a huge dragon rears high in victory over him.

"No!" I shout, and Jacob's hand covers my mouth.

"Shh." He whispers in my ear, one hand still clamped tight, the other pointing at the dragon following our trail. But the image is so real that I turn and hug him, ear pressed against the steady beat of his heart. He shifts, studying the perfect symmetry of the structure that rises past the clouds, and his hands move to my ribs, breath tickling my ear. "I'll boost you up."

Before a protest forms, he lofts me to the first level, but the smooth rock is hateful to touch, and I refuse the vision that wells up again. Jacob's right there, reaching up, not dead. Our hands connect, and I haul him up until he catches the edge. Demyen backs up, takes a running start, and scrambles next to us.

"Got to set a better pace," he says, standing on the ledge. Each level is about ten feet high, just too far for either of them to reach, and with no room for a running start, we settle into a leap frog pattern that strains every muscle I possess. Jacob boosts me up, then Demyen and I get Jacob up, next we pull Demyen.

About halfway up, a cold flush rushes up the rock and the pitch of night lowers until the reflective obsidian returns no starlight. I hold my breath, as a concussion of wind blasts us against the stone, something massive rushes past, and my legs give way. Jacob snatches my arm, pulling me away from the edge.

At the base, our pursuer shrieks, and the sound of its claws scratching stone gives way to wingbeats. The creature soars past, joining the other, which remains invisible in the gloom. They circle twice, but the wind of their passing is the only way to track them. The top of the pyramid glows red and the gale from their wings stops. We press against the rock, desperate to locate them.

"Where are they?" I whisper.

Jacob leans out so far that my heart skips a beat before he crouches next to me. "There are two more levels."

Demyen pulls tension from his shoulders. "This is where things get interesting."

"Monday," I whisper, making them both scowl. "Remember those? With a long stretch of monotony out ahead. Monday sounds better than interesting."

Demyen's mouth turns up. "Aye, but interesting is what we're in for. Boy, I'll boost you up to reconnoiter."

He hooks his hands together, and Jacob steps up, disappearing onto the next level. My heart goes with him, every sense straining. A half second later, he lands hard beside me, and I almost dive off.

"Men." He leans in, pulling us closer to the stone. "Three of them, with a baby dragon on a chain."

Demyen strokes his beard, eyes intent when Galel somersaults into visibility, rolling to a stop with his back against the black rock, panting hard. "This place is crazy."

Raeual and Jaden arrive in similar fashion. Smoke curls from one of Raeual's shoulders. Jaden smacks it out.

"Monday sounds good," Jacob quips with one brow arched.

Galel shakes his head, keeping a soft tone that the wind steals away. "Dragons can see us when we're invisible. It's disturbing."

"Yeah, they can see us too, all the time," Demyen says, positioning to move.

"Wait, there's a message," Jaden says, pulling him back.

"Well, what is it then?" Demyen asks when the Watcher stays quiet.

Jaden shakes his head, looking skyward. "The ankh rests at the top. An engraving on it will unleash chaos, but it's not time, not yet. You must cast it into the sea."

"There's no sea here," I note, proving I'm on top of the obvious.

"Correct," Jaden acknowledges.

"So, this is an extraction," Jacob adds with a nod.

"Stay together and quiet. If they detect us..." Galel frowns without finishing.

Another glance confirms my path runs straight up.

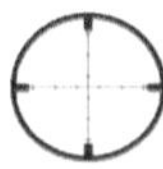

Demyen's laced fingers boost Jacob into the gloom, and I brace hard so Demyen can leapfrog off my back. The Watchers soar after them, and I'm alone in the pitch dark as chill wind rushes past. The meaty sound of concussion makes me flinch, then a reptilian screech ends in a death-like silence in which I can't breathe.

Jacob appears, reaching for me. He hauls me onto the flat top where three men with miter hats writhe on the stone, their hands tied. Raeual and Galel have the young dragon's head pinned down, but its sharp horned tail sweeps our way.

We leap over it, but Jacob's eyes lock on a golden altar covered in grotesque carvings. His hand falls from mine as he steps forward, and a smear of green haze flowing from him skyrockets my heartbeat. A wind gust disperses it and he shakes out his hands, reaching the altar. In the center is a golden cross with an arched loop on top that's covered in strange inscriptions.

A rage-filled roar and a blast of putrid wind tear the silence. The young dragon's scales flash a myriad of colors, and Galel groans.

"Incoming!" Raeual shouts, half a breath before something slams me into the altar and everything spins into chaos.

Galel yelps, tossed upward, twisting in midair to return fist-first with a roar. He slams into a massive patch that's darker than the night and sparks spew from the impact. Jacob pulls me to my feet, the ankh clutched in his other hand.

"We need an exit!" Demyen shouts just before something smashes into him, slinging him away over the edge.

"No!" Jacob shouts, hauling me behind the altar that shivers at another concussion. The three Watchers form a line before us as a roar forces us against the stone. It rises, pitching to that terrible electric snap that makes Jacob arch backward with a cry. Blood trickles from his ear as he collapses.

"Hey, Boy!" Demyen's shout just registers as Raeual's shield takes the brunt of flames that reveal the immense figure of a dragon, rearing high, just like I saw.

"Got an entrance, hurry!" Demyen must be one level down.

I drag Jacob toward the edge, leaving a dark smear on the obsidian. Movement to my right makes me twist, but Galel is there with a mighty uppercut to the young dragon's snout, inches away.

"Go!" He shouts, slammed back, then chopping with his flashing sword.

Jacob moans, eyes rolling white, as we reach the edge, and the ankh falls from his fist. Demyen's outline is hard to make out below.

"Catch him!" I shout, shoving Jacob over as a jet stream of fire slams into the altar. The ankh skitters past, and I snatch it, then roll into the night.

The air leaves me in a rush as I slam into the lower level. Demyen pulls me back from the edge. The inky dark is a terror all its own as I search for Jacob. Something huge crashes just beyond, but Demyen tows me into an arched doorway.

"Hurry!"

"Sage," Jacob's voice slurs, but it's the best sound ever. We huddle close, pressing further inside the narrow opening, away from the chaos outside. Pain streaks up my arm as Jacob holds me close, and I scowl at the ankh, glowing with a vile orange hue in my fist.

Jacob takes it, wincing. "It's hot."

It burned my palm, leaving the imprint of those vile carvings. The pain pulses harder, then Raeual slams into us, driving us into a tight tunnel that slopes downward. His luminosity reveals Jacob clutching his back. Raeual's shirt is smoldering again, polluting the close air.

Galel bursts in, driving us further with a hammerlike blow. He throws his shield down, its curve creating a saucer. "Get on!"

His huge hands clamp my arms, tossing me on, where I struggle for balance as it teeters, sliding down the tube. I screech as sparks fly, lending enough light to see Jacob kneeling on Raeual's shield behind. The speed flings my hair into a blinding mass.

The sparks cut off as the shield goes airborne, and I yelp before plummeting into a pool of sulfur water. Jacob and Demyen hit, making the water churn as I stroke upward, skin burning in the acid. The Watchers stand on the bank, illuminating a tiny portion of the immense cavern below the pyramid. It's enough to see the ankh surface in Jacob's grip before his face breaks through. He gasps, mouth filling as Demyen and I tow him to the ledge.

He lies there, struggling for breath as Galel snaps his fingers then points at the water. It churns, and his shield whips into his hand as I study the chamber, slapping Jacob's back. Immense columns wrapped in bright copper rise out of the mineral water that froths as the other Watchers' shields surface.

Demyen rubs his forearm over red-rimmed eyes. "Which way out?"

Jaden points at the smallest tunnel. "Just checked. You three go that way, and we'll take the other exits. Drawing the dragons away won't be hard, not when they want to eat Raeual so much."

He gives a cheshire grin with a shrug. "It was a good blow, admit it."

"Yes, that's why my plan will work so well," Jaden says, dipping his head, then turning to us. "Get the ankh to the sea, at all costs."

Demyen nods, pulling Jacob to his feet as I take his other arm. "Aye."

Between us, we drag Jacob into the tunnel. Behind, the Watchers nudge each other with wild grins, then, with a flash, they shoot down the far tunnel so fast it's like they were never there. It's dark without them, and an eternity passes as Jacob stumbles along, lurching with every step.

"Got to figure out where he's hurt," Demyen grunts as something soft brushes my skin.

"I'm…" Jacob grunts.

"Fine, I know, we've heard that before," Demyen says.

"What's this?" I ask, brushing plants aside. Starlight glints over an open plain, but in the west a fireball shoots skyward, and a battle cry sends shivers across my skin. "Let's go."

"I can walk," Jacob pants.

He limps along with the ankh still glowing in his hand. Demyen and I frown at each other, following a few steps behind. I lean in close, pointing to the stain that's spread across Jacob's back. "That wound doesn't look good."

"It's… fine," Jacob growls, his lungs pumping as if he's sprinting.

A brilliant flash zaps across the plain, and I throw one arm over my face. The metallic screech echoes as the terrible outline of a dragon shows against the outburst of light. I clamp my ears, knowing what's coming. The electric crack throws Jacob face-first, and the ankh skitters away.

Crying out, I run to him, but he continues to crawl. Demyen scoops up the ankh, glowering at it. A black flow is coming from Jacob's wound, plastering to his shirt.

"Give it back," Jacob says, rising to one knee.

"No, Boy, you're in no condition to deal with it; there's a strange evil in it."

Jacob growls in response, launching for him, and Demyen staggers back. "Hey, Boy!"

But Jacob hits him again, throwing one shoulder into his gut. That's enough for Demyen, and his free hand shoves Jacob away. Jacob gains his feet with a sneer. "You got no choice, anyway."

He launches a weak attack that makes me cry out, helpless to stop him. They wrestle, and Demyen takes a hard blow to the chin before his expression shifts and he spins, clamping Jacob's arms behind his back. He's facing me now, and for a split second, his expression clears and it's the real Jacob looking at me, but then the rage descends and with a wild struggle, he pulls forward.

"No!" I cry, but Jacob's eyes roll white and he falls limp. I rush forward, cradling his face, but can't rouse him. "What happened to him?"

Demyen towers over us, blinking hard, wiping a thick black smear from his arm. "Never seen the like."

Another battle clash from further across the plain makes me wince.

"We can't stay here," Demyen points out, handing the ankh to me and taking Jacob's wrist. The metal's touch flares the pain in my palm as Demyen hauls Jacob's limp form over his shoulders.

Demyen staggers forward and my tears spill over, watching Jacob's arm swing limp. Blood drips off his pants, and I trace its path to his back, where the fabric is black.

Hesitation bites deep. Between the ankh, his strange behavior, and the dragons hurtling through the night, nothing I can do could make a difference. I shake the sensation off and reach for Jacob's shirt. My gasp makes Demyen stumble.

"Is that smell coming from him?" he asks.

"Yes." The wound has overtaken his back, flayed open and oozing black, tar-like blood. The scent makes an acrid taste fill my mouth as I search the gray memories for answers. All those experiences are useless here, to fight the strange infection that's stealing him from me.

"Got to make it to the tree line. Pray, Sage. Pray hard."

A dilapidated lean-to with three decayed walls is far too little shelter, but Demyen carried Jacob so far, until he couldn't drag his feet another step, and morning light is spreading in the odd way it does here. I brush Jacob's brow, but his skin is pale. The wound has festered, looking worse by the moment, and nothing will rouse him from the comatose stillness.

Demyen paces in the small shelter, three strides, turn, three strides. One hand rubs his beard, brows knit, as he mutters. My gaze falls on the ankh with a sneer. I hate it and every cell flares with the passion. Is his condition because of it, or the wound? Maybe both. The slipperiness of not knowing makes my jaw clench. The worst part is there's nothing I can do to help him, no antibody to rescue him.

My fingers tremble as I pull up his eyelid, finding the expected. Pure white. But wait. Leaning closer, the capillaries are turning black, just like the wound. I pull back with a shudder. "We have to do something."

Demyen's tread falls silent. "My path is right here, wound like a ball of yarn in this hut. Yours?"

Extra slow, my eyes trace the traitorous pink topaz vein that runs straight into the scrawny trees. Words won't come, so I point, chin quivering. "I can't leave him."

He squats next to me and his sheer size is comforting somehow. He tosses the ankh in the dust between us and it lands with an unnatural heaviness. "This isn't helping; sucking the life out of him. Completing the mission will affect our future in ways we can't see."

"You want me to take it?" I ask. "Through dragon infested territory. Me. The one with a ten-inch sword, and no idea how to fight?"

He grimaces, emerald eyes surveying the land. "What I want is unimportant. Your path runs west, toward the sea. Mine stays here."

His correction hits hard, forcing my gaze to fall. What I want is to stay with Jacob.

"You have everything you need, as long as you eat. The safest place to be is on your path."

Both arms wrap around my waist, resisting the sour twist there. "What if we don't make it?"

He sighs, a long solid breath that takes the question in stride. "Making it depends on what you believe, and if you're willing to stand or not. There's…" Tears prick his eyes, sending a shiver through me as he rubs the loose dirt between his fingers. "A prophecy for Jacob and me to fulfill. How far would the enemy go to stop it?"

Time slips past as his strong fingers sift the dust, at war within.

He nods toward the glowing ankh, and my lip pulls back. "Somehow, this is part of it."

Spreading my hand, I examine my palm, where the hateful hieroglyph shows in a bright red welt.

"If we deviate, we fail. Don't waiver, Sage. There is always a way through." He shifts, looking down on Jacob's still form. "My brother…" His voice breaks as he places one hand on Jacob's chest. "He *will* recover. We will fulfill the call."

"How far is the sea?" I ask, throat hot as I take the ankh.

"I've never seen it, but we're deep in enemy territory already. You better eat."

The comforting aroma of buttered bread calms my gut as chewing reveals the words.

Because you have made the LORD your dwelling—my refuge, the Most High—no evil will befall you, no plague will approach your tent. For He will command His angels concerning you to guard you in all your ways. They will lift you up in their hands, so that you will not strike your foot against a stone. You will tread on the lion and cobra; you will trample the young lion and serpent. "Because he loves Me, I will deliver him; because he knows My name, I will protect him. When he calls out to Me, I will answer him; I will be with him in trouble. I will deliver him and honor him. With long life I will satisfy him and show him My salvation."

A solid sensation rises up as the Words settle inside. "I choose long life."

Jacob groans, face contorting as if my comment struck him. We frown, but the puzzle of what's ailing him remains. My fingers brush Jacob's cool brow. "It's like he fell asleep and can't wake up."

"Aye. The Almighty will reveal it." Demyen leans back, rubbing his beard. "Say that again, but include him."

Leaning in, I press a kiss to Jacob's brow, cutting off tears. This *won't* be the last time I see him. "We choose long life."

He grimaces before his brow smooths out. I stand, the ankh like a millstone in my fist, and jog out, leaving everything I love most behind, settling into a punishing pace. Dust floats upward with each footfall, and I chew scroll while panting. Heat builds, sapping my strength until my tongue feels like cotton, but the path still runs ahead, calling me onward as the day wanes.

Gnawing exhaustion tugs, but in the distance, a dune rises with sparse grass sticking up. I stagger up it on all fours in loose sand, and the sea stretches away forever under a dark, brooding sky. Waves pound the shore, but the salt scent has a bitter flavor that leans toward lion.

My lungs strain in the dank air as my feet hit wet sand. I re-grip the ankh, glaring at it. "Almighty, help me now."

Galel appears right next to me. "He already has. Let's throw it together."

I nod, turning so his powerful hand closes over mine, and we test the motion, getting in sync.

"On three," he says.

He counts down, and we wind up, but it's Galel's intense strength that forces the Ankh far, far over the writhing water. Its glowing arc ends in a massive explosion of salt water that boils long after it sinks. Maybe right then, Jacob stood up, free of the ankh's dark power.

The thought makes me lighter. Galel nods, a smile forming. "There, that's done."

He looks down at me, and one eye tightens as his smile fades. "It's a long road back. Stay sharp."

His disappearances should be commonplace by now, but I still flinch. Turning from the bitter wind, I trudge over the dune, focusing on getting back to Jacob. There wasn't a single lion on the way here, or anything worse, like the serpent. A shiver wracks my spine as old nightmares flit through my mind, so I shake out my hands and ease into a limping jog.

My route takes a fresh course back, cutting east, then diving near a stinking marsh. I stop, needing more air, and study the lay of the land. Staying higher around the rim of the marsh would avoid the mud altogether.

With a sigh, I veer up the hill, hurrying around; it won't take long to reconnect with the pink shimmer, just a few yards beyond. A narrow path winds around the first healthy vegetation in days, and it's nice to be among the green leaves again.

Their happy rustle in the wind tastes like fresh rain, and a calm green scent pervades. My fingers brush a tree trunk and the taste of maple syrup produces a brown humming sound. Needing the rest, I walk for a while, but the taste is so sweet that I rub the bark again, licking my lips. The breeze plays with my hair, filling the six-dimensional sensation to the brim. I soak it in as my mouth curves into a smile.

Wait.

What is that sound? This hum is different, with a tone that turns my muscles to ice as my eyes inch up the tree trunk. A papery cone dangles from a branch over my head, and thick, red-bodied wasps swarm around the nest.

The exit hole is straight above. The wind gusts, tugging on the thin thread that holds the nest up. An angry funnel of wasps buzzes as the breeze jars it again, fraying the connection.

"No." I whisper because the gray world is too close, where one sting could kill. The thin thread snaps with a wisp of sound that's like a gunshot. I launch forward, arms over my head, but the nest slams onto my back, and a horde of angry wasps coats my skin.

The red cloud settles like stinging dust. A scream only lets them in my mouth, injecting venom. Each one is a needle that burns with poison. My blood runs colder with every pulse. I sprint, swatting like mad, but the effort is pointless; there are thousands when one would be enough to kill me.

Terror surges, lists of symptoms binding me to the inevitable outcome; knowing makes it so much worse. Pain surges as my throat itches with an aching dryness. My legs churn, but the wasps pursue.

It's already done; their evil is spreading fast, my chest tight, skin swelling everywhere. The red cloud lifts and my knees hit the ground. A fitful breeze makes me waver there, breath whistling past the swelling in my lungs. There's one last whiff of air before my nose closes off.

It's full of a dead, rank stench.

"No," I mouth the word, lips so fat they won't move. My blurred vision reveals the blood crusted paws of a lion straight ahead. Muscles quivering, I look up.

Tattered ear.

My eyes water as they swell. I crawl away as my breath wheezes; fingers in the dry dust.

"Look at you now," Aseph creeps behind as I force one knee forward. *"Dying."*

My lungs strain; the sharp whistle of air is far too little, more terrifying than the massive teeth and claws.

"Anaphylactic shock," he growls, drawing out the words. "And there's no drug to fix it. You're not worth saving, anyway."

Empty. My chest slams into the dirt, muscles useless, but a tingle of truth zings up my spine. I never was worthy, but *He* bought me back from the dark, anyway. None of this is about me. It's all about Him, about what He said, and what He wants, but the symptoms press in with iron certainty.

Aseph's mane brushes my back. "There's nothing that can save you now. *Nothing.*"

Nothing. The word reverberates in my brain at war with the faint buoy of hope. *Nothing.* The Almighty spoke to nothing and made the world.

I open my mouth, but the words are indistinguishable with no breath, lips numb. "He... said..."

"I can't hear you, speak up," Aseph's growl holds a tenor of glee.

Nothing shall by any means harm you...

There are only two options. Believe what I feel, or what I know. I clutch dust in my fists, squirming like a worm, reaching for freedom. Can words save me now?

"He... said..." It's nothing but a pitiful squeak. One hand slithers forward, trembling like a winter leaf. If I stay here, I'll die, and never see Jacob again. My jaw clenches, lips like balloons.

I *won't* die here.

The image of Yeshua's face, tortured on the cross is forever inside me. His sacrifice isn't meaningless and I won't fall short when He's given everything. I'm going to run. I'm going to fly— if I get a hint of air, but my lungs are closed off, and the world fades to black.

"HE SAID..." the thought echoes in my soul. They are not my words, I didn't think them up, and I don't enforce them. The lawgiver gave them to me. Perfect, perfect words that whisper in my soul as the rest of me dies.

Surely, He bore your pain and carried your sickness... By His stripes, you were healed.

But I have to choose which to believe. My eyes finish swelling shut, the darkness complete, but He said I would trample lions.

"You can't run, you can't see," Aseph whispers, his tattered mane igniting pain as it brushes the stings on my neck. His heavy paw settles on my back, the touch a bolt of pain. "You can't even breathe."

His bloody claws pierce my skin as his weight crushes me. I strain for a strangled sound, but nothing comes. My right hand inches forward.

He said!

In a flash, the truth of it drops in like pure oxygen. *I need nothing else.* His Word is enough. *He* is my air. My mind screams, railing against it, but it's mine now, so far inside that no lion can steal it. I drag myself forward an inch, legs like lead weights, blind.

Aseph shifts, then his weight lifts.

"Go!" I mouth the word, lips cracked by the intense swelling. Limbs numb, one knee shifts forward.

No air.

Dead.

The thought is too loud as realities battle within.

Next leg.

Elbow scraping, I pull forward, force one blurry eye open.

There's water near. Clean water. I shudder, the blackness returning. Can't keep the eye open. It's easier to see with it shut, anyway.

HE SAID!

The shout explodes, only on the inside but full of such innate power that I stagger to my feet, swaying on zero oxygen.

Get to the water.

Expired, my heart seizes, almost gone, cold spreading to my limbs.

Aseph knocks me down. I hit the rocky ground so hard that it forces stale air out of my lungs.

Anger flares searing hot and I roll to sneer at him, swollen face resisting motion.

"You liar!" but nothing comes out.

"Were you saying something?" His paw crushes my chest.

My tingling fingers land on a rock. A brilliant sip of air caresses my lungs before Aseph's weight forces it out. Fury rages. He's the lawbreaker. How dare he?

"Leave me!" It comes out as a squeal as my lungs scream, but *I will not yield!*

My sluggish fingers curl around the stone, mouthing the name. "Yeshua."

Lunging, I smash the rock against his face, fear evaporating in my rage against him. The blow forces his head aside and I twist, squirming toward the water.

My fingertips sink into the life. There's no air, but water will do. I slither into the flow, and its cool touch against my skin surges up every vein. My feet slide under, and the pain fades, energy building inside empty cells.

I need air, but the surface is too far as the water's silvery voice fills me.

But you will receive power when the Holy Spirit has come upon you.

The current rolls me over, brilliant light filtering through the surface above.

So beautiful.

So sad that I didn't make it.

B…born… Born of the water and the spirit…

The cold water eases the swelling as I sink, watching the light glint.

I'm sorry.

My lungs pull hard; can't stop them. Water rushes past the gate of my throat, filling me.

6
JACOB

AS YE HAVE SPOKEN IN MY
EARS, SO WILL I DO TO YOU. ~
THE ALMIGHTY

The dragon's strange shadow fills me with a cold dimness. Wind rips past, so dry that it mummifies my skin, but there's a voice within it, silky smooth and wise, that goes on forever, mixing with the stripping currents.

"Leave it all in the Almighty's hands. He causes all things for your good."

Water. Just a sip would ease the burning thirst.

"He'll lead you through the valley, into desperate need, so you learn to give it all up to Him. Trust the process." On and on it answers every thought until it's pointless to resist.

Iridescence flickers to the east, so foreign that it demands attention, but a gust picks up, flinging sand into my eyes, forcing me further into comatose patience. Whatever comes is from the Almighty, no matter how bad the thirst or stabbing pain in my back is.

"Yes, every good servant will bear their burden in meekness."

Other sounds penetrate the cruel gale with a tinge of sweetness that the wind attacks and captures, then sweeps away. The chill sensation of a cocoon stirs a desire to struggle, but I'm bound too tight.

"Dare not resist the will of the Almighty when every trial shapes you into His image."

The lulling voice and desert breeze are my existence, but far to the right, the sweet sound reverberates, louder, with a clarity it lacked before.

"Is he alive?" The voice is so different from the smooth baritone that grows louder, pinching out other sounds, that make this cocoon more like a coffin.

A new voice responds, stirring strength from a forgotten place, even as a gust shreds it apart. *"Baptized, Sage?"*

The name is like a spear straight through my empty core. *Sage.* It's important, but the wind pelts sand into my face so hard the skin is disintegrating. Resistance to wisdom means failure, yet the other sounds prod me awake, wavering in the endless arid environment.

"Yes, and I got rid of the ankh, but there's no change?" the sweet voice cracks, so broken.

"Been thinking," the man's tone is familiar, but it eludes capture. *"That roar…"*

A hurricane force shoves me aside, eating up the words. Clenching my eyes, I block out the droning mutter, hunting for the frequency with the tingle of life.

"It bothered Jacob most, that electric crackle. He got worse every time."

Images rise, of falling through the sky, winged terror close behind, then searing pain stabs my back. It's real even now. The typhoon tumbles me so hard that I land face-first, unable to turn my head for breath.

The sweet tone is choppy now, as if the gust tore it apart and reassembled it. *"He's... struggling! We've... help..."*

The bitter pain in my back and need for oxygen implode until I buck like a bronco, slamming against iron restraints. Something heavy smashes my ribs, then, like pure life, soft lips press against mine and force air into my lungs.

"Jacob! Stay with me!"

The wind throws me again, each impact a paralyzing agony.

"Here now, Boy, come up from there!" The command rattles in my bones as I tumble through the endless stinging sand.

Teeth clenched against the pain, and the iron binding, I strain toward the iridescence that shimmers there, high above. The drone transforms into a roar of rage that ramps higher into a piercing snap that stuns me into dead stillness.

"No, by Yeshua, you'll not have him!" The words shake the coffin, and I kick hard with a last strength. The fetters fall away, leaving me exposed to the blasting sand. Hands grip my jaw, forcing it

open, and a soft, leathery sensation fills my senses, but my throat rejects it, retching.

"Boy, you must take it." They're closer now, the voices that tingle with life, and this command fills my mind.

Even if it kills me, I won't spit it out. It burns, but the words come, so faint at first, then rising to a cleansing power that shields me from the sand.

If… if… if you continue in My word, then you are truly disciples of Mine; and you… you will know the truth, and the truth will make you free.

Truth. Another flavor fills my mouth, this one with a pungent herbal taste.

For false messiahs and false prophets will appear and perform great signs and wonders to deceive, if possible, even the elect.

"Wake up, Jacob!"

Deception… The word lives in the wound in my back. Knowledge comes, filling in my empty past. Sage is calling me, with a desperation that stirs, but the dry gale force has already sapped every drop of vigor. More scroll is jammed into my mouth, sending a shockwave through my frame.

S… seek… seek ye first the kingdom of God, and His righteousness; and all these things shall be added unto you.

Seek. I can't seek anything while bound here. Obedience demands that I rise, and a tendril of pure life trickles onto my lips. My eyes snap open to a world full of color and sound. Sage leans close with both hands cradling my jaw.

"Jacob!"

Her warm tears splash onto my face as Demyen nods down at me. "Aye, Boy, 'bout time you came around."

"Where was I?" My voice embodies the weakness that grips like a vise.

"The Shadowlands. Tis a place from which many never return."

The agony in my back makes me arch, rolling to relieve the pressure. Sage gasps with one hand over her mouth.

"That bad?" I groan, curling forward.

Demyen grimaces, waving a hand before his face. "Leviathan's poison. Should have guessed. When did it wound you?"

It's difficult to pinpoint the answer. "The first time... it attacked."

"It didn't activate until the beast sent out that sound, searching for you. We've got to abrade it. Won't be comfortable, Boy."

An acrid taste fills my mouth. "Just be sure you get it all. I'm never going back there."

Demyen's solid hand locks with mine, and his eyes brim. "Aye, Boy, but I don't look forward to the doing."

Sage brings water that floods me with pure life and focus.

Be d... diligent to present yourself approved to God, a worker who does not need to be ashamed, rightly d.. dividing the word of truth.

Demyen's firm hand grips my ribcage, holding me down. "I'm sorry."

"Just do it," I say, as he draws a short blade.

At the first scrape, pain forces me off the ground, wild and savage. The dragons' words croak out my throat, an acid poison that taints the air. "But the Almighty is sovereign."

Demyen draws back as if I struck him. "Aye, Boy, but the question is, what do you mean by that?"

My lungs heave so hard the words grate. "He controls everything, every action is His plan, His design."

"There's the venom: truth mixed with a lie." He scrapes the knife over the wound, and a tar-like puss splats to the ground, filling the shelter with a pungent odor.

I lock a primal roar behind clenched teeth as I thrash, but the pain and the droning words mix into one, too strong to escape. "Tell me… how that's a lie."

"The Almighty is the Creator, so all things belong to Him, all three worlds." The blade scours again, and Sage backs against the crude wall, tears flowing.

"*The heaven, even the heavens, are the LORD'S: but the earth He has given to the children of men.* Earth belongs to Him, but it's on lease. He does not cause every action, because He gave dominion to Adam's race." Demyen's voice is stern, fighting to keep me still with the blade poised.

By sheer determination, I settle onto my stomach, but my jaw seems locked shut forever by the agony, slurring my words. "Make me understand."

Demyen takes out a large section of scroll and shakes his head. "Only this can."

He sets it on the wound, and I leave the ground. Sage leaps forward, sprawling over my shoulders as the scroll eats at the infection, but a sweet voice is close, flowing through my veins and chasing out the poison.

I… I call heaven and earth as witnesses today against you, that I have set before you life and death, blessing and cursing; therefore choose life, that both you and your descendants may live; that you may love the LORD your God, that you may obey His voice, and that you may cling to Him, for He is your life and the length of your days.

"Choose?" The scroll rams the poison, driving it out.

"Aye, the lineage of Adam must choose who they will serve, and what they will do." His blade is there again, but I know, *I know,* the vile dragon's serum has to go. My fingers dig deep into the dirt, every muscle straining to stay still.

"Science says actions are the sum of energy affecting matter, that every action is set in stone and unchangeable, but if there is no choice, there is no responsibility!" Demyen grunts.

I'm struggling, squirming though trying not to, and it's only my weakened state that gives Sage the ability to hold me down. A surge of bitter bile can't be contained, spewing away.

"That's right! Get it all out and let only the truth remain!" Demyen slaps another section of scroll onto the bare wound, and I arch back with a scream.

For unto us a Child is born, unto us a Son is given; and the government will be upon His shoulder. And His name will be called Wonderful, Counselor, Mighty God, Everlasting Father, Prince of Peace.

I sag, cheek in the dirt, as the fight goes out, and wonderful, fresh life washes away every molecule of contamination, and deep peaceful sleep draws me away.

I awake and eat, and sleep again until my eyelids don't feel like weights, and a fresh breeze fills the old shanty. The words haven't left me, *the government shall be upon His shoulder,* like a tide washing away the dark. Demyen crouches before me, backlit by golden light, and a question pricks me.

"Why that piece of scroll? A Christmas verse? How did that free me?" I ask.

He laughs as Sage slips next to him. Her eyes are happy again, watching me, and that alone tells me I'm better.

"The Kingdom answers all things, Boy."

Mara's words should have been enough to make me fill the knowledge gap. "How?"

Sage inspects my back and makes a cheerful sound when she pulls off the wide section of scroll. "All healed up."

"That's what the Kingdom does. It sets the right order for everything and makes poisonous beliefs turn tail and run."

"But how?" I insist, sitting up but needing to know.

"Many want to arrive at the top level without ascending the staircase. The Kingdom is the foundation, and skipping it leaves you open to all kinds of confusion." I deserve his look, but still drop my gaze.

"Everything sounded so right, though." There isn't much to gather up before we go, and Sage has already tidied up.

"Aye, that's the strongest lie, when it has a shred of truth. It sounds right that the Almighty controls all, and in many ways He does, but He won't violate our right to choose."

"Wait, what does 'the Kingdom' even mean?"

He grunts, looking out over the dry land, listening. "A kingdom is a system of government that owns all within its bounds, including the people. It is NOT a democracy, but dual citizenship makes people of the light able to do the same works as Yeshua."

"He is the Alpha and Omega, the beginning and the end. He gave the middle to us. Kingdom knowledge straightens out the crookedness that religion leans toward."

"That's what Mara meant," Sage realizes, nodding.

Demyen rubs his beard, still looking into the distance. "The Kingdom of Heaven ruling Earth through the people of the light was Yeshua's purpose and message. It also settles forever questions about sickness."

"How so?" I ask, not seeing the connection as we set off across the arid landscape.

He rummages in his scroll pouch and hands us pieces. A jolt of pure energy shoots along the second it's past my lips.

Your... your kingdom come. Your will be done on Earth as it is in Heaven.

Mischief gleams in Demyen's eyes as he stomps up a low hill. "How *is* it in Heaven?"

Sage shrugs, saving me the embarrassment. "I don't know."

"Baah!" He waves one hand. "Yes, you do, you've just never thought of it before. Is anyone sick in Heaven?"

The answer is so clear that it leaps off my tongue as I step out. "No."

"Is anyone poor and miserable?" he asks.

"No," Sage whispers.

"Yeshua Himself told us what the Almighty wants, for Earth to be like the heavens. Yet, we make it difficult, mixing half-truths, the influence of Hell on Earth, and experiences to come up with a doctrine of suffering that suits millions far better than the reign of the King of Kings."

It strikes hard, knowing the same made me comatose, and easy prey.

Demyen slaps his leg. "*For this purpose, the Son of God was manifested, that He might destroy the works of the devil.* Then this, if you dare swallow it… *as the Father has sent me, I am sending you.*"

"So, we *can* fall short of a calling, or deny it," Sage says as her fingers rub her lips.

"That's why the beast went after Jacob first." I can't hold his gaze. "To break the prophecies, but he failed, and he'll be infecting many others with his poison now."

Sage snaps her fingers, then twists her shirt, tugging a belt free.

"Is that mine?" I ask, knowing it because my heart leaped.

"Yes, I saved it when it fell in the woods." Our fingers brush as I take it, but it sends a jolt of knowledge that steals my breath. Completing my call means losing her. She must go into hiding; I couldn't bear it otherwise. It brings me to a full stop, staring at her.

"Best not be without it again," Demyen adds.

"Without her," I echo.

"I said *it*, Boy, your belt."

"Of course." I put it on and turn to tie it tight, just like the determination to save her from the end. Weakness surges, so I stuff scroll into my mouth out of habit.

And… and if it seems e… evil to you to serve the Lord, choose for yourselves this day whom you will serve, whether the gods which your fathers served that were on the other side of the River, or the gods of the Amorites, in whose land you dwell. But as for me and my house, we will serve the Lord.

The choice is mine, but that only sparks another question, one that might be an answer for my longing for Sage. "What about the calling? Do we have a choice about that, since it was prophesied?"

His eyes gleam as he turns to look at me. "Aye. That we do. If you shirk, the Almighty will find another, but consider this: The work was set out for *you*, before the foundation of the world. That would be quite a thing to miss."

We've gone far, and the desert lands are turning green, and the air has a tinge of life. Inside, I'm the same, wavering between the two things I want most: the call and Sage.

"So, the ankh is in the sea," I mutter, enjoying Sage's expressive story, and dropping behind. There's no possibility of denying the call. I *am* His witness. A surge of determination solidifies it. Whatever the cost, I'll be faithful.

"Yes, but my gut says we'll see it again," Demyen remarks as Sage drops back with me.

Her hand brushes mine as we walk, sending a shiver up my skin. I veer away to maintain the distance. She doesn't miss it, and a flicker of disappointment crosses her face, but the best thing for her is safety from me.

Galel appears. Both of us flinch.

He holds out two leather straps to Sage, and I step back, realizing what's happening.

"Well fought, Sage. Although you made me wait on the delivery, these are rightfully yours."

He straps two wide leather bracelets onto her forearms. She touches one, and a sharp-toothed metal disk, like a saw blade, snaps halfway out.

"What *exactly* did you fight to earn those?" I ask, knowing she left *something* out of her story about the ankh. What if she hadn't returned? I step back as the war between wanting her and needing to protect her pummels.

She hesitates, then plucks a disk free with a shrug. "A nightmare."

"Throw it," Galel whispers, his eyes flaring as he turns to me. "You should have seen her," he says, his tone full of delight. "It's been a long time since I saw the like."

She frowns at him. "You watched the entire thing and never showed up?"

Coiling back, she whips the disk forward, and it zings away, biting into a dead tree.

Demyen whistles, his brows raised.

"How many of these are there?" Sage asks, peering inside the leather.

Galel grins then disappears, but the heat flares inside my mouth, rolling over my tongue with an electric tang. My heart rate spikes, and I turn, shielding it from the others, trying to blow it away.

A green flicker leaps to my right hand, but I refuse to cradle it, shaking it off, keeping my mouth open against the building flames.

"Boy," Demyen's voice makes me flinch, hoping he won't see. Demyen's gaze locks on my mouth. His slow nod and lowered brow make me brace for the same repulsion as Mara.

"We'd best be off." His quiet tone leaves plenty of room to doubt his thoughts as he stares, then strides away.

Sage turns to me, eyes bright, brimming with life, and the fire dissipates.

"Sage, the long-range weapon," I tease, forcing a light tone, tilting my head toward her wrists, wishing for normal. Do I even remember what that is?

She rubs the bracelets with reverence. "I'll have to work on my aim *some.*"

The way she says it brings an honest laugh, but my heart clenches. Ignoring the truth won't change it. The death throes of this age are no place for her. Jaw tight, I turn, striding after Demyen and ignoring the ache.

We follow the stream as intense emotions batter me. It makes the heat on my tongue roil and grow again, distracting from all else. The heat was insistent before the swamp too, but it faded without swirling down to my palm like it does now. How do I force it away?

Gray memories of my last journey here surface; I see a small glass vial, filled with the spirit's water. Thinking of it ignites the flame further and I twist away, coughing into my elbow. *That was stupid.*

"You okay?" Sage asks, still behind, yanking at the disk that's buried in the wood.

"Yeah." I use the moment to clear my mind, spitting for good measure as I return to help her.

Raeual appears, his arms crossed, staring at me. *So much for privacy.*

He leans close. "I don't believe fighting it is going to help."

"What will?" I whisper with my back to Sage.

With a frown suggesting my lack of intelligence, he disappears.

Sage can't loosen the disk, so I reach up, my stomach brushing her back as the proximity spikes the urge to hold her. A half shake of my head rejects it. She'll never be mine. The disk slides free, and she takes it with a laugh.

"You must have loosened it," I offer, etching her features into a memory I can admire later as she tucks it into the leather.

Galel materializes, wavering for a moment as he watches us.

"Why are you visible?" My skin pricks, glowering at the now-suspicious path where Jaden is striding along behind Demyen near a large river.

Galel laughs. "Nice to know I can make you jumpy just by showing up."

"Yeah, are you always there, or only when I can see you?" Sage asks.

I grimace. "You'll never get that answer out of him."

"True," Galel laughs. "Though I can always see other Watchers. Take Raeual, for instance. He's looking a little unnerved right now."

Raeual appears next to me, scowling. "Listen, you would be too, if you were me."

Tension coils in my gut. "I'm sensing a story here."

"We should be quiet." Raeual's eyes stray to the river.

Sage glances at me, but a shrug is my only answer. Jaden draws his sword and the singing sound of Galel and Raeual drawing too makes my skin tingle.

"What's going on?" I whisper as we hurry forward in a tight knot.

Demyen turns as we catch up, searching for danger. "Am I missing something?"

The air is clean, without a hint of lion stench, yet Raeual shifts from foot to foot, letting out a slow breath. "Why here, out of all places?"

Demyen crouches on one knee, scowling at the water. A low moan makes us all freeze, growing in tone until Hadena snaps out.

A low metallic clink makes me flinch—the sound of heavy chains. Raeual's sword slices the air, cutting a swath around him. The sinister voice grows to a lament of pure frustration, and the chains clang, louder and faster, as the water boils before us.

"What is this place?" Demyen whispers, his sword in his hand, legs spread in battle stance.

"One I hoped to never see again," Raeual says, shoving my shoulder. "Hurry."

We move fast and low as the river beside us froths white and a huge figure rises from the depths. A wave ramps over the bank, slamming up to my knees. The surface swirls as the being rises higher until it towers above, a Watcher of immense proportion, but this one exudes darkness. I flinch as it surges forward, the water like a tidal wave that soaks us all.

"Ho!" Demyen leaps back, but the Watcher's gigantic wrists are bound, and the eerie sound of his impact against the chains reverberates across the hills.

Raeual skitters to the side, taking short, harsh breaths as he keeps himself between us and the creature, sweat shining on his brow. Another giant rises next to the first as if waking from sleep. It roars upon catching sight of Raeual, and its enormous fists clench, straining against the chains.

Jaden's sword is up. "You sure you locked them good?"

Raeual switches his sword to the other hand. *"Pretty sure."*

"Pretty sure," Galel mutters, weapon ready.

Two more similar figures rise, waist-deep in the river and towering twenty feet above, with their burning eyes locked on Raeual. We hurry away, with the Watchers guarding our six, and I urge Sage farther from them. The monsters roar as we round a distant hill.

"Never thought I'd see you nervous." I prod Raeual in the ribs, making him jump to the side.

"Never thought I'd be back at the Euphrates," he replies, shaking out his hands and pulling tension from his shoulders.

"They recognized you," Sage notes, looking over her shoulder.

"Suppose so. I'm the one that put them there."

My brows rise at his comment. Beside them, Raeual looked puny, which I didn't think possible before.

"That must've been quite a battle," I remark.

"Aye." His expression is far away, then he shakes free of the memory. "Can't blame me for being a bit on edge, can you?" Raeual asks, as one by one, he and the other Watchers disappear, leaving just the three of us again.

Night is falling but we push on, eager for more distance between us and the creatures. Demyen nods at a small valley. "This looks like a good place."

Soon, I've got a fire going, and an area scraped free of rocks and lined with soft grass.

Demyen sets another log on the fire, but Sage sighs, "I'll be right back."

Watching her fade into the dusk makes my heart twist; our paths run together, but they'll split soon. Half of me reels in the other direction; now that she has the light, there's nothing to stop us from growing closer. A silent laugh chides the idea as pure selfishness.

I turn toward the fire, where Demyen is blowing green flames from his mouth into his palm, and freeze. A shocked grunt escapes me, and he turns, looking as guilty as I feel.

"What is it?" I whisper.

He clenches his fist, crushing the ball of green flame into wisps of smoke.

"A prophecy," he says, staring at the sedate red fire before him.

"Have… have you always had it?" I ask, blinking fast.

His fathomless eyes burn into mine. "No."

"Does anybody else?" I press, desperate for answers.

"No, Boy. It's just you and me, the two olive trees, pouring out our oil."

The words strike like a shot through the heart until I grab my chest, and for a millisecond the future is clear. The world is bleak and dry, but I've given all. Then it's gone, leaving a sensation of grief inside that drives me down to a sitting position.

Thoughts fly as Sage returns and drops an armload of branches, then watches the campfire. In the silence, Raeual's voice wavers, the way it sometimes does, at the edge of detection.

"Only a fourth of them have ever gotten it."

Galel's voice is ethereal as well. "But why is believing so hard for them?"

Sage smiles as we eavesdrop, but inner paralysis from the vision clutches me.

"Consider this: They've never seen the throne room… or our kind serving at the altar… nor the crystal sea, or the *glory.*" The way he says that last word makes longing kindle. That's what awaits at the end, if I'm faithful.

"Uh… fellas? We can hear you," Demyen says.

The silence is instant, but the longing in Raeual's words mixed with the wrenching look at the future simmers, too hot to touch, but entrancing nonetheless. Was Sage beside me there? Should have looked while the glimpse lasted.

"Jacob!" Sage is staring at my stomach, where a familiar green cloud flows from my belly, pooling around my feet.

I stare at Demyen, but hear Jaden's words from so long ago, *your work, it is one.* He has the fire too and I'm not alone. He nods at me, knowing. *Brothers.* That's enough. It has to be.

Sage steps closer, leaving green footprints behind.

"You too, eh?" I ask, taking her hands, absorbing these precious minutes together, letting her touch wash away the weight.

She shudders as the snapping energy seizes us and we surge away, speed rising, but there are no dark flames trying to tear us apart, and the travel is delightful with her so close.

A shadowy scene materializes. My body is sprawled in the abandoned hangar with an antelope grazing nearby.

"Where are you?" I shout, words ripped away as Earth sucks us in.

"There!" she points, buffeted by the solar wind.

In the dirt beyond the hangar, she's crumpled, one hand under a bent piece of roofing.

I brace for the awful pinch of fitting inside my body, rolling up, bound tight as I rush towards Sage. The impala leaps away through the dry grass. She groans, jerking as I hold her, head lolling, then her brown eyes snap open, and the steady pulse in her neck makes my shoulders relax. "Hello."

She gives an exhausted laugh. "It's been two seconds, Jacob."

A shiver racks my frame and I tuck her against my chest. The memories from the spirit haven't lost their crisp edges yet, and they soothe the pain of letting her go. "I'm glad you're one with the water now."

"His life for mine. It *was* simple. He provided everything." Her lips possess the life of the spirit still, vibrant and warm, even here in the gray physical, and longing sweeps higher—if only there was a way… I lean forward and her fingers trace my face.

I grunt and sit back, breaking the connection. "Let's hope He provides a ride, too. It's one hundred and fifty miles to Durban."

"Jacob?"

"Yeah?"

"Why do you think it's us? Why can *we* jump, and no one else?"

A prophecy. I bite back Demyen's words, unwilling to crush the warm hope in her eyes. It's better if she doesn't know beforehand. The physical cloaks the spirit now, and it's easier to bear the knowledge here, where each moment distracts. "I'm just glad it is."

For now.

She crosses her arms and stares at me in the cramped concrete bunker that gathers all Africa's heat. "This is crazy."

"What else can I do? Let Tex continue his rampage? The Collective isn't interested in controlling him or producing its precious peace in the forgotten parts of Africa. They can report whatever lies best suit their rhetoric, but people are dying," I say, laying out my gear.

She sighs, glaring at the laptop. Turns out Sutton had an exact location on Tex the entire time, complete with readouts on his body temperature, heart rate, and blood pressure. Opening her personal storage was revolting. They've murdered hundreds, seeking superpowers.

The most disturbing discovery is the global surveillance system that links the electromagnetic field of each human life to the web. Most of the population has received nanobots in pandemic vaccines, and now, they're linked to the N.W.O. without knowledge of it.

Their secondary surveillance system functions off the unique frequency of individual heartbeats, allowing them to track the population with startling accuracy. A thorough search of Sutton's database revealed no location on us, though Sage found a massive document that covers our cases.

The K-60 has altered our frequency signals into a cloaked type that creates a buffer from their all-seeing eyes for now, at least. Plus, the strenuous energy spikes of jumping fried whatever nano tech we had. Turns out being degaussed has its perks.

"Nothing about this is adding up." She rubs her forehead in the blue light of the screen in the bunker near Durban. It's the perfect hole up. "How is it possible that Sutton can't bring Tex in with all of this info on him?"

"She doesn't care to," I reply, putting on body armor. "I knew Tex was playing them, letting them believe they had control until he got the upgrades he wanted."

"I don't trust Brooks, either. Why is he *helping* us?" she ponders with one hand on her neck.

I crouch before her, taking both her hands in mine. "Every battle I've stepped into as a soldier was ordered, commanded, documented, but this fight is my choice. I won't let Ash torture people. I'll bring him to his knees. Stopping Tex is step one. It's my calling."

Emotions play across her face. "What if you jump?"

I cinch a row of grenades and smoke bombs above a mag pouch, half my mouth curling. "Then you'll have to come get me." Her mouth falls open, eyes wide, the most beautiful thing on the planet. I laugh, adding, "Fast."

"Th… that's not funny," she protests.

My heart twinges. The thought of leaving her cuts deeper than I dare examine. "I wish there was another way."

Her eyes drop to the floor as I tuck a strand of hair behind her ear. She takes my hand, pressing her cheek to my palm. The touch ignites inside, with my thumb caressing her face, but it's my right hand, the same one the green fire builds in. My breath comes faster, both worlds swirling together as my mouth heats. I scowl, pulling back. *Not here, in this reality!*

She reaches out, and her fingers on my jaw calm the burn. The faintest whisper of sound at the doorway sets me off. My arm locks around Sage's ribs, sweeping her off the chair as we roll under the table, a Glock in my hand. I crouch, barrel steady on the door, holding Sage behind me.

Two taps, a pause, then two more. Margie's code. I ease to the door and nudge it open with my boot. The towering man flexes his arms, his skin matching the night. It's reassuring to know he'll protect Sage as he did on the boat.

I lower the Glock, and he steps in as Sage crawls from under the table, dusting off. "Hey, Margie."

His black hair brushes the ceiling, and a fresh burn glistens on one bicep. "Paco say you need me, *rapido.*"

Sage snorts. "You've got that right—Jacob's going after a deranged super soldier."

"Pity that man." Margie's forearms flush with goosebumps. "I know you divine. Paco be strong again."

"One third divine, same as every believer," I say, and the words fill me. My spirit is a new creation, and the threads of unease about going after Tex break away, confidence taking its place. It's not just me going after him. I jut my chin at the burn. "Pretoria was tough, huh?"

Margie tilts his head, covering a smile. "For them." He turns to Sage. "I keep you safe. Nobody touch you."

His resemblance to Galel's and Raeual's size brings her the same calm it brings me, as I push an arsenal toward him. He selects a 1911 and checks the clip, nodding as he tucks it into the small of his back.

Thanks, Paco. There's nothing like a baby brother to protect Sage.

I adjust the body armor, running over its specs. Team Three tested the upgrade a month before Project 157, and we'd been more than impressed. That Brooks has access to it gives me a pause; what else does he have up his sleeve? What other upgrades is Tex equipped with?

Pulling on a helmet, a quiet, consuming focus forces the doubt down. I visualize the hunt, the fight, the victory.

"It's time," I announce, studying the screen. A wide, lifeless circle, devoid of heat signatures, surrounds Tex in a concrete building.

Sage rushes into my arms, but heavy layers of gear make her stretch for my neck.

"Sage," I whisper into her hair. "I'll see you soon." *Unless the Almighty takes you into hiding before then.*

She leans back, one hand on my face, and her mouth opens, but only a whimper escapes. I nod, letting my confidence flow into her.

"Margie." The big man nods at me. "She's worth the entire world. Keep her safe."

"Yes, sir." His solemn expression mixes with awe as his nose flares, looking at her. There's not one shred of doubt he'd die for her.

I find her eyes, nod, then stride out. Her hand traces down my shoulder, my arm, to my fingertips. Can't look back, not when she's my burning desire.

Durban. A third world, inner-city hell on Earth. Concrete structures lean together and clogged roads snake with no particular plan, stained by bodies left to rot. It's dead quiet as a starving dog slinks through the night.

I ease between two buildings, scanning. Tex is a quarter-mile south. The unique sound of leather scraping concrete makes my rifle's muzzle tilt toward the second story in an instant.

Tex has been in Durban long enough to kill everyone in this section of 6,800 people per square mile, and the smell of death is heavy. The sound echoes again, and I stalk toward a lopsided metal staircase, creeping up.

Breathing steadily, I sweep the second floor. Near the balcony, moonlight reveals a young man on his knees, rocking, as he holds a limp body. He moans, and I brace against his anguish.

He's muttering in IsiZulu, grief flowing. A rifle lies on the floor next to him, but its magazine is missing. I step into the room, and he whirls, lofting the weapon, his chest heaving.

We stare at each other, fear shining in his face. I ease forward, kneel next to the woman and shut her eyes, then raise my hand, fingers spread wide. The woman's stomach is rounded; he's lost more than a wife.

He slumps, sweeping his hand through the room. In broken English, he says, "My family. All dead."

Tears drip onto his chest, and his clenched fist slams into his thigh. "I kill him."

"He's…" I swallow, searching for words. "A weapon."

The man shakes his useless rifle. "I fight for them."

His words hit hard. A man has the right to stand up for his family, even if it's only their memory.

"You won't live through the night if you do."

"I am already dead." His brown eyes burn into mine. "I go to them tonight." He nods. He'll go for Tex with or without me. A heavy sigh escapes as I pull a full magazine from my pack and slide it to him.

He presses both hands together, bowing. He slides the bolt; the sound makes him flinch. "For Amahle, and my little Bokang."

I nod. "Stay with me. Aim for his head."

We creep from the building, and he proves a decent partner. I force my breathing into a slow rhythm as we close in on Tex's location. The building has multiple exits and levels, impossible to control. I study it for a long time, memorizing distances and structures, then flick on the night vision.

The man eases one eye around the concrete wall. He jerks back, rifle tucked against his shoulder.

I shake my head, point to the ground. *Stay put.*

But his eyes are wild, lip pulled up in a sneer. He rolls out, lowering the rifle. A single shot rends the air, but it's not his weapon. He flies back, lifeless, rifle skittering away.

"That you, Carter?" Tex shouts, his voice making my skin crawl. "Brought a buddy along, eh?" He laughs. "Didn't do you much good."

I crouch, focusing within, waiting for that still, small voice. He's on the first floor, barricaded behind an interior wall.

"Welcome to the party. I let Ash give me one last upgrade before I split: infrared vision. I can see you now, no more playing in the dark."

Jaw clenched, I stare at the man's body. There's no point in clamping down the rage—Tex deserves every ounce. That upgrade is going to have to go, must be a contact with interior wiring. Got to flush him out first.

I stalk up a staircase, silent, keeping concrete between us. At the top, I pull a triple-phase teargas canister and pull the pin. The open windows line up floor to floor in this building, and another structure stands a few feet away.

I wait until the smoke flows, then whip it out the window. It rebounds off the other building and through the lower window, where it tings on the floor below; I surge into action, caution gone. Leaping the last five stairs, I roll, catching the man's lifeless arm to heave him onto my back. Rifle leading, I sprint into the next building. The night vision reveals an open-air balcony one floor higher. Seconds ticking, I sprint up as a shadow moves two buildings over.

Tex.

He's in full battle gear, minus that handy control pad to shut him down. Locking on his trajectory, my focus narrows further. Without a sound, Tex leaps, crouching on the concrete railing, studying the building with one eye shut. *Interesting.* Still, his position prevents a clear shot.

Everything stays quiet, as if the world is watching. Tex slips around the corner and I fire at his head. He ducks, and concrete explodes.

"Eh, did I forget to mention it's not infrared alone? I got full radar on all incoming ordinance."

I curl inside a doorway, back against the wall, take a breath, and lean out, weapon leading, and pull the trigger based on memory alone. His helmet emits a splat of magnetic energy as it repels the round. I lean down the hallway, forcing my voice to emerge far from my location.

"Got some glitches, Tex?"

"Come on, Carter, you're the most fun I've had in weeks. I'll let you in on a secret: I'll kil—you with my knife—it's so much closer, *intimate*, to watch you die that way."

Taking the dead man's wrist, his weight settling across my shoulders as if it holds every drop of innocent blood, I sprint to the far side of the building.

The body sags against the rail when I prop him with the rifle under his limp arm. I yank a laundry cord with two dangling shirts, then tie it to his ankle and back into the doorway. I sweep the counter with my forearm, sending clay dishes flying.

Waiting requires every ounce of control. Tex is impervious to pain, plus with those bone enhancements... Jaw clenched, I shut down heavy breaths, forcing calm, six senses straining. Time grinds to a halt.

His shadow is a darker midnight, wavering in the courtyard below. Seconds later he's on the roof, hunting. I flinch at the soft ting of his boots hitting the railing ten yards down.

I tug the string, the body shifts, listing toward Tex. He explodes, covering the distance in a heartbeat. His first round tells him it's a setup as the body slips over the edge.

I'm already there, too close for data to do him any good, popping off two shots with one goal: remove his weapon. His body armor flashes, emitting plasma, as I lock the trigger down until his rifle wings over the rail. He lowers his head like a bull, slamming us back against the waist-high rail. His hands clamp on my rifle as I bend back, wrenching it free. Before I can fire, he uppercuts my arm, and the weapon sails into the night. I use the motion, lurching away to land on my feet. Crouched, we face each other, launch forward, and clash together, trading blows.

I drive him back and pull the pistol. He slashes with a knife, drawing a ragged line on my body armor. His other hand clamps on the pistol; we war over it, trigger pressed tight between us, dust and concrete raining down until it's out of bullets.

I twist away, then smash the empty pistol into his face and throw it down. He rips off his puckered helmet, eyes red from the teargas.

I grin. His right eye is cloudy; my strike took out the infrared. "How's that vision now?"

He growls as he comes. I feint right, then roll left, kicking his legs out from under him. His elbow pummels my neck, stunning my back and arms, but I evade his next blow, and the knife sparks next to my face. I force the numbness away to uppercut his jaw, then kick the knife out of his hand.

His grin is a twisted smirk, savage and deranged, as he shoves a pistol into my cheek, but I saw it coming, already twisting to slam his head against the wall as his shot goes wild, deafening. I follow the blow with a knee to his gut.

Blood trickles from his brow as he freight-trains me into the wall. Breath won't come, but I fight through it, surging up to kick another pistol from his grip, then duck as his fist smashes into the wall behind me.

He roars, hand limp, already bloody from my first shots. I drive him back, raining blows. Pain surges, but I mash it down as he empties the pistol into my vest. Breathless, I keep him from raising it to my head as the vest emits a pungent electrical scent.

Lungs frozen, my arms go up too slow to prevent his punch, and my head snaps to the side, vision blurred. He leaps on me, knee driving into my spine.

One.

That quiet voice echoes inside. Tex yanks my helmet back, exposing my neck.

Two.

Blackness creeps in, my chest too battered to function. In the silence, the sound of a blade slipping free echoes so loud.

Three.

His knife falls. My hand flashes up, snatching his wrist. He rolls and the absence of his weight creates an artificial breath. With it comes the scent of diesel.

Condensing, I pull for air as Tex drags me straight through a puddle of fuel that's gushing from a hole in a truck's tank.

He's going to wing me into the wall, head-first. I twist as he tows me through a doorway, spinning hard on my back, boots taking the impact. I push off, sliding away through the diesel slick.

Tex turns, glaring. I draw the bowie knife, lungs smoother now, gaining my feet. We clash, brutal, all in. I drive the knife up under his armpit between the body armor plates. It sinks home; he arches back as I yank it out and dive for his leg, drawing another wound across it.

He staggers back through a narrow doorway as I pummel him with blows, his armor deflecting the next two strikes.

Wait.

I freeze, head cocked, because engines roar close by. I sprint for the door. *Ash.*

Tex catches my heel, and I go down hard, twisting with the motion to smash his face with my boot. There are no other exits, just solid concrete.

"Your weakness is showing, Carter. I want you conscious when I kill you!" Tex shouts.

Haze is flowing as adrenaline peaks. I claw toward the door, but Tex's knife stabs into my calf. Focus broken, I inch toward the exit, dragging him forward. Ash's forces are closing in fast, and far too close.

I roll, kicking Tex in the neck. His eyes roll back in his head for a half second, and there's a flash of fear as he shakes it off.

The virus.

Something zips through the doorway; a metallic clang is like shackles inside. A steel plate seals the door off as a gas canister rolls past me. We stare at it spinning between us, leaving a lazy circle that expands through the small room.

Tex's body slams the steel plate. It shudders, but there must be twenty soldiers holding it tight.

I suck in the last clean oxygen, yanking him back. Tex's punch whips me hard, but I come up swinging. We fight on that last breath, skin stinging in the gas.

Our motions come slower; Tex sags, then his head hits the floor, eyes rolling up in his head. His entire body flinches as the ruined infrared in his eye flares, then goes dim.

Sluggish, I hit the metal, but it doesn't give. One sniff is enough: It's Kolokol-1, a fentanyl derivative. Motion comes slower.

He was bait.

My lungs heave, suck in.

Thoughts turn to mush as a cold black cloak closes around me.

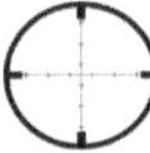

Pain pounds in the inky blackness with the same rhythm as the helicopter's thrum. Everything burns—my skin, my lungs, my eyes. Forcing them open, pitch-black greets me. Too bad I didn't jump. Sure could have used the refresher.

A swinging sensation overtakes me and cold metal greets my fingertips, each breath sending searing pain through my chest. My vest is gone, no weapons anywhere.

I groan, rising to slump against the wall. Dizziness makes my brain swirl as my calf rebels at the motion. Funneling all my focus, I concentrate on melting through the wall, but nothing happens. I can't produce a shred of haze. Plus, there's no sight like on the ship. The pain and mission failure are a 50-caliber round straight to my heart. What am I doing wrong?

When I need it most, there's nothing but a battered body to work with. My groan echoes as the dark penetrates, growing until it consumes me.

A small pack is fastened to my belt, but I fumble it, hands shaking.

"Come on," I rasp, fingering the contents. Survival kit. Thinking is like struggling through mud. The kit spills and tiny pieces ping on the metal floor. Every moment is agony as I search, then my hand closes on something. A glow stick spreads green light between my fingers. The color makes me cry out, longing to escape the pain.

Can't.

Shifting focus to study the environment is all I can do. A small aluminum box serves as my prison. It's not much larger than I am, and a pool of blood congeals under my leg. One eye is almost swollen shut, and my chest is an enormous bruise. My T-shirt's torn wide open, hanging off one shoulder.

The sickening sensation of spinning makes sense now. My best guess is, this box is hanging from a helo. Forcing my mind from the debilitating sickness, I study the contents of the med kit, clutching a small instant ice pack. The ingredients list blurs in the dim light: water, ammonium nitrate.

The white plastic covering seems made of steel as I rip it and pull out the small clear bag of water, then shove it into my mouth, biting down. It tickles down my dry throat, spreading life. And words.

Therefore take up the whole armor of God, that you may be able to withstand in the evil day, and having done all, to stand, stand firm then.

The water and the green glow are a heady mixture, an intoxicating elixir that solidifies into a burning flame within. Every sense tells me I'm done, beaten at my own game, but the words rise in shimmering waves, and I bind them to myself. *I will stand.* That's the truth.

The logical part of me laughs in derision. This failure is complete—I walked right into the trap they set, and deserve what's coming. With a growl, I fumble for a tiny pack of matches that skitter across the floor. The frustration snaps the connection to logic, and I catch the Word instead.

He gave me everything I need. It may not be the ability to melt through the wall, much preferable, but there is a way.

An idea sparks, an old memory from training. The ammonium nitrate crystals shift as the chopper takes a hard turn, and I struggle to keep the white pebbles inside the bag. Blood and diesel fuel soak my pant leg, burning the knife wound. I force my tattered body to contort in the box, but my swollen hand refuses to squeeze the fabric.

"Come on, work." Funneling every ounce of determination, I make two drops of bloody diesel fall onto the crystals.

Blackness hedges at my vision when I tug off my belt, the movement creating waves of pain. Have to do something about that before it takes me out. "Surely He bore my pain…"

My voice is ragged and the words feel so powerless, but I cradle them like an ember. "By His stripes I *was* healed. I *am* healed. Body, be well."

Convulsions of anguish ramp higher, so I set one hand on my chest, lungs shuddering. "Pain… leave me… in the name of Yeshua."

All I can do is breathe for a moment, then finish easing off my belt. The metal clasp has a dull edge, but it will have to do. My arm shakes at the effort to scrape the aluminum wall. A few tiny shreds of metal fall into the soaked nitrate.

I scrape the heads off all but one match and pile them on top, then drag myself over to the door at the end of the box. The hinges are outside, but an indented circle at the bottom of the door must be the lock.

The box tilts, then slams down on something hard, the concussion deafening. I crumple against one end, wincing at the punishment as the glow stick spins away. Outside, someone shouts as the chopper's engine strains. Escape would've been easier while airborne.

I cradle the tiny open bag against my chest, my only plan. The box rocks again and the steady beep of a backup alarm precedes another shove that makes my head slam against the side; I see stars. Then, there's a long journey. They must be on a forklift. Ear pressed to the side, I wait until the box shivers and the backup alarm sounds again, growing quieter by the moment.

My hands are steadier now, belief and words mixing to effect change. Everything's still, and there's no time like the present. The bag fits on the narrow ledge above the lock and I strike the match, setting it on the match heads and scrambling for the far end, head covered.

Seconds pass; the matches are not enough to strike off the nitrate.

"Light," I whisper.

Boom!

Ears ringing and vison blurred, I pant on hands and knees until my head clears. The glow stick reveals a tiny, blackened hole, but the door won't budge. Slamming it with my shoulder produces nothing but dicing pain. Eyes closed, I trace its edges.

It opens vertically.

The door slides up a centimeter, then jams. "Genius."

Speech reminds me how brutalized my chest is. It takes a while to work the door free of the broken lock inside, and time is not a friend. With a metallic click, the door slides, revealing a well-lit concrete room not much larger than the box. A steel door is the only exit.

Contorting out brings a convulsion of pain as I limp forward. It won't be long until they come for me, but no cameras are visible in this holding room for semi-toxic waste. Those chemical placards mean there's a massive ventilation system in here.

One large vent sits right above my box and precious seconds pass as the slick diesel ruins my first climb. The cover squeals as I rip it off, ignoring my body's demands. The tube is tight and my ribs shriek as I climb in. I leave a blood trail until a faint sound makes me freeze.

They've discovered an empty room. Shouts give way to a siren that ramps adrenaline to a dangerous level. Crawling forward, my elbow smashes another vent cover. It clangs to the floor and I follow it in like manner, legs giving way.

Movement.

I spin and launch forward, shoulder slamming into the gut of a security officer. In two moves, I relieve him of his pistol and secure him in his own cuffs, then sag against the wall with the room spinning.

Stashing him in the small room, I gather his weapons and spy four more guards trotting down a hall. They pass and I follow. A glass wall reveals the blue-tinged light of computers beyond, with no personnel in the room.

The guard's ID opens the door and I slip inside, ducking behind the farthest desk. Twisting a screen toward me, I search files, locating security. The state-of-the-art system means very low chances of escape.

A schematic reveals I'm fourteen levels underground, and the sensation of complete failure drives me to my knees. Two screens later, I request an emergency electrical shutoff and hiss when it requires a password and two-step verification. Can't stop the security feeds from here, either. A schematic of a tunnel system catches me with a tingle of the spirit. Motion outside the glass makes me drop behind the desk.

A security platoon rushes past, well-armed. I ease back to the screen, studying the tunnels that carry vast amounts of water from a central location five levels lower. The coolant runs around an immense hole, but resetting its flow rate requires a password. The cursor blinks like a heartbeat as my body responds to the words I spoke earlier, the pain lessening.

It's time to move. I memorize the tunnel access points and limp to the door. Rough concrete walls stretch in all directions, but that check within twinges, making me scan the hall. It's clear, but the sensation doesn't let go.

I slip back through the doorway and crouch there, listening. I'm missing something. My gaze lands on the computer, where that green light inside leaps, drawing me forward. I click the tunnel system, bringing up the password box.

The symbol.

I grunt, tracing the familiar shape onto the screen.

Incorrect input.

Training insists I keep moving, but that quiet knowledge holds me here. There's a picture on the desk of a child, grinning at the camera and *My Pippin!* written in gold across the bottom. I type in the name.

Incorrect input, system locked for thirty seconds.

I need to move, but it's as if my spirit weighs two tons; it's not going anywhere. Behind the child there's a birthday cake with a candle shaped like the number twelve. The box reopens and I type MyPippin!12, then click submit. It flashes green.

Clearance granted.

My forehead sinks to the desk. "Thank you."

 I drop the water flow to 10%, reading the next option.

Submit system and maintenance report?

I click no, then clear the screen. It's time to move, now free of restraint. Two turns later, I drop another solitary guard. He's about my size and his uniform fits. My chest is a well-used target, deep red and purple, but if I weren't leaving a blood trail, I'd be another officer. The crisp sounds of another platoon send a shot of adrenaline up my spine.

Manning the guard's post, I square off to them, hooking one finger in my belt, standing at the corner like I own it. In the middle, a familiar figure trots along.

Sutton.

I flinch and drop my gaze, letting the brim of the hat shield my face, cocking one hip. Nobody glances my way as I fall into step behind them, leg stinging. The team ignores the elevator, a major security risk, taking a set of stairs as the alarm pounds the air. We clip up the rectangular staircase; a glance over the rail reveals a stories-deep opening in the center.

Sutton slows to a walk on the second rise, one hand over her vile heart, her heels clicking.

Minutes later, we turn into a finished corridor; the lead guards swipe us through a double set of bulletproof doors. Safe in her lab, Sutton waves one hand, dismissing her escort.

I turn with them, veering off at the last second to duck into a restroom.

The mirror reveals soot and blood on my neck. The guards' ineptitude is my gain; all they saw was the uniform, but I've got to see further. This facility, with its massive coolant-capable level, serves some purpose.

I wash, then slide back into the hall. My new ID swipes me into the room next to the one Sutton entered. Everything is white and clean, but an exam table with shackles sends goosebumps across my skin. A search of the drawers rewards me with a digital stethoscope.

Squeezing behind a cabinet, I press it to the wall and concentrate. Sutton clears her throat, the sound muffled.

"I told you he was not containable," her voice trembles, betraying her.

She must be on the phone because she's quiet for a moment.

"We only have twenty-four hours until the window closes. That's a tight timeframe to prep him, even if we *had* him."

Something tells me I'm the subject of this conversation.

"Well, you'd better, or will have to wait six more months. This is why we pushed Project 157 so hard."

I flinch, the truth like a bowie knife in my side. The experiment. The *Olympia*. It was a single step in whatever plan Sutton and Ash are carrying out.

How could I have missed that?

What if they have Sage? She has as much K-60 as I do. I curl forward, sickened at the thought, the room spinning. How stupid to leave her. But thinking like this guarantees failure. Fingers pressed into my clenched eyes, only a dark future looms.

"Almighty, help me, please."

Sutton's quiet now, and I need to scope this level and then move. I slip out the door and stride along, refusing the limp, keeping the hat brim tilted low under the cameras. Rooms with glass viewing windows line this end of the lab.

My stride falters as I glance inside. Bodies lie in orderly rows, hairless and pale-skinned, each one on a table, eyes closed, their faces exact copies of each other. A room full of teenage males. I swallow hard, pulse spiking. The next door reads Generation Twenty.

These bodies are older and more muscular, but just as colorless and unmoving as IVs feed each one. Voices make me duck into another empty exam room.

"Lost another one this morning," a woman says. "As soon as we inject the K-60, the shell dies. But without sufficient K-60, no transfer is possible."

A man responds as they pass. "Except for the younger ones, under age five. They can handle K-60 so that's where we should concentrate our efforts."

"But they can't take the energy surge. Children don't survive within three feet of the cauldron. They're too small; we need K-60 *and* strength."

The man's voice is familiar, so I ease one eye out. Philip Rathmore. My arm pulses where he'd injected me on the *Olympia*. Knowledge is like a tidal wave destroying my calm. K-60, the epitome of Project 157. The only thing that facilitates a jump into the spiritual realm.

"Shells"?

I'm back in the hall, passing a room with ten tiny bodies that can't be over age three. Shells. *What for?* My skin crawls. What would Ash gain by accessing the spirit?

My brow knits as sweat breaks out. I'm missing something, and that means I'm losing. Swiping out of this level, my calf spasms as I climb to level eight, heart slamming. This floor is crawling with personnel, and I try to swipe into two rooms before locating a door that will open. A woman in a white lab coat scowls as I back through the doorway.

"First day," I shrug at her, reading *Raji Puti* printed in block lettering on the door. A computer displaying a Swiss flag is on at a wide desk. The icon on the screen steals my breath. It's the symbol

I've been tracing everywhere, the dragon's shadow. Clicking it opens a program called Cyclone. In the search bar, I type Sage Emerson.

A box flashes up *Classified.* I dig through the drawers, find another ID and push it under the small hand-chip reader. The light flashes green and I enter Sage's name again, almost crushing the mouse. The readout shows all her info, age, height, qualifications… Location: *unknown.*

I sag, muscles trembling. It's time to use those water tunnels. I open the door; the same woman is standing there with her arms crossed. "What were you doing in there?"

Flashing the ID with someone else's picture on it won't do.

"Dr. Sutton requested Mr. Puti's presence. Where is he?"

She squints at me, nods to the left. "He's on lunch."

With a nod, I walk off, weaving among people.

"You're bleeding," she accuses, trailing me. A quick glance reveals a retina scanner in her hand.

"And you don't want to be."

Fear flashes in her expression as I spin, pulling her free hand behind her back, stepping close to conceal the motion. "Move."

We lurch forward; she's casting wild glances all around as the pistol presses into her back. Most of the personnel are absorbed in their devices, ignoring our stilted progress. I shoulder into the men's restroom, finding it empty and cuffing her to a stall, longing for tape. A strip of my shirt is the best I can do for a gag.

She's screaming before I'm out the door, muffled, but enough to make people look up as my hand settles near my weapon, turning into the stairwell. Five guards descend with weapons drawn. She must've called before I came out of the office.

Footsteps reverberate up from another squad below. *Trapped.* My hand finds the rail, gauging the distance, then I tuck and roll over the edge, catching the next level's railing, then leap across the open space where the platoon is.

"Take him alive!" the commander shouts. "Tasers only!"

Two electrodes bite into my back as I let go. Muscles rigid, my ribcage takes the blow against the lower railing. The taser leads rip out before delivering a complete shock, but I still miss the rail.

I slither down the stairs as muscle function returns. Doors swing open and troops flood the stairwell. This will not be pretty.

I grimace, sliding downward, taking out the first three's legs with my shoulder. I snatch a taser from one and drop the next, but there are hundreds more and no way out.

Three sets of leads bite into my chest. Rigid, I fall as they force a mask over my face. Tastes like fentanyl.

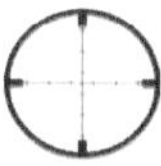

Thoughts surface like blasts from a shotgun. Brutal stiffness and a splitting headache from the drugs. Without opening my eyes, my wrists tell it all. *Shackles.*

Lying still requires sharp focus on the spirit, but there's no surge of a jump to pull my body away. Sutton's voice gives me something to direct the anger toward. "Monitor his Quisile levels;

they've got to be at twenty-seven to contain the K-60—he has abnormal amounts."

So, she's found a drug to control it with. But it's the spirit that gives life, the flesh counts for nothing, and it's not K-60 that will save me. I lie there, building an image of pain-free muscles until I can taste it, feel it inside.

Someone checks the pulse in my wrist, but my hand stays loose. Then the room goes silent, the air heavier.

"Out," Sutton orders.

A rustle of movement, then eerie silence. Soft footsteps approach as the same pinching darkness of the dragon fills the room.

"He's finally here." Admiral Ash's voice is like a fifty-caliber in my gut.

"Everything is ready. We've got five hours left in the window. His K-60 levels have increased, even higher than we could've hoped." Sutton's voice drips with fawning admiration.

My stomach rolls as Ash responds. "All we've been working toward, my entire life spent building this. Today, a new era is born. A new existence. Nothing can stop it now."

His words slice like a knife edge, but my own well up to combat it.

"I can." My eyes snap open in time to see them both flinch.

Ash recovers, laughing. "You, Jacob Carter, are powerless."

It feels that way, like Aseph's claws are pressing into my veins. The heavy atmosphere around Ash makes it so believable, but another voice whispers within.

You were made for such a time as this.

"I'm an overcomer, Ash. A *believer.*"

His jaw clenches. "Let me show you how far believing will get you."

He releases the ankle shackles and Sutton backs against the wall. "Adm...."

He gives her a harsh look, releasing my wrists. I roll off the table, fists clenching, eyes locked on Ash. An electrical jolt hits my neck and everything spasms, but I manage to stay on my feet.

Ash smiles, his heavy brows shielding a vile gleam in his eyes. "Meet the collar, designed for individuals like you with no respect for authority."

I shift, sensing the metal band around my neck, but refuse to touch it. Exhaustion tugs, like the entire world's pressing me down. I shake it off, gritting my teeth.

He leans forward. "I own you, Carter."

He meant to tear me apart, but peace rises instead, rock solid. Every molecule of me belongs to Yeshua. "I hope you kept your receipt, Ash."

He steps forward and backhands me across the mouth. I don't flinch, sucking blood from the inside of my lip to spit in front of him, lifting my chin.

"We'll see how cocky you are at the cauldron." His voice trembles with rage as I face off with him. "Since you were so kind as to disable our faulty model, I'd like to introduce you to our latest work." He sweeps his arm up, and a tall soldier steps through the door. He's so similar to my height and build that my gut churns.

Ash steps closer. "We loaded all of Tex's data into Drake. He's reviewed every fight, every move of yours, and he's beaten you in every single simulation."

I study the soldier's dark eyes, searching for the flare of rebellion Tex always had, but his gaze is clinical, as if there's no soul inside. "So, you want me to be afraid of a guy who's studied computer models?"

The collar jolts, blood flows from my tongue at the spasm, and I grab the exam table to stay on my feet. I glare at Ash, heat building until the taste of fire fills my mouth. It's a matter of time until the tables will turn. The image builds until it's my reality, and my grin makes his face go pale.

"Move," he commands, his finger hovering over the button.

I step to the door, scanning the hallway lined with troops, skin pricking as Drake falls into step behind me. "Everything's feeling homey now."

At least Sage isn't here. *Location, unknown.* Two words that mean the world to me.

They poke and prod, taking blood and testing Quisile levels. I stand like a rock, listening to the peace in my spirit. Even when they push a shell on a stretcher closer, my mind stays clear, like a boxer before a fight—loose, supple, and ready.

The shell's face is hairless with a firm jaw, sharp brow, and straight nose. It's mature, at least twenty years old, and it's the epitome of male structure, but its pale, clammy skin is devoid of life.

Do they want me to drag this thing into the spirit?

Rathmore is on the far side of the stretcher. His fingers tremble as he takes the shell's hand, then reaches for my wrist. His eyes flick to Drake, still at attention a few feet away.

"Rathmore," I glare at him until sweat pops out on his upper lip. "I owe you one."

"Ignore him," Sutton orders, sneering at me, as she spreads the shell's fingers. I lock my arm at my side when they pull my hand toward it.

Ash presses the button and the shock lurches me forward. Rathmore swears as he pushes the shell's fingers against mine. The touch is repulsive, but immediate knowledge rises. It has no soul, no spirit inside. It's a lab-grown bunch of cells kept alive by machines.

Sutton binds my fingers to the shell's one at a time with rubber bands. Tingling in my lips distracts from the creeping feeling radiating from the shell's hand, palm to palm with mine.

I focus on the throbbing power, reaching for it, willing it to grow into a rolling heat. My tongue burns, but no green smoke issues from my nose. Still, that peace is there, feeding me.

Sutton forces a webbed metal glove over our hands, now joined fast. When they step back, I exhale sharply; the air strikes my wrist, and a layer of heat builds like a shield between the shell's skin and mine. One word reverberates in my mind.

Hadena!

It sends a throb of energy down my arm, slamming into the shell. The lifeless body bucks and its blank eyes flash open. Everyone leaps back and Sutton cries out.

"What was that?"

"Check it!" Ash bellows, his face red.

Rathmore creeps forward, hesitant, running a scanner over the shell.

"E… Everything looks fine, sir."

Ash steps forward, his thumb ready. "Shells don't move, Carter. What did you do?"

I smile at him. "Wouldn't you like to know?"

The shock makes me cringe, but I don't break eye contact. He covers the fear well, but I shift forward, chest heaving, knowing I could take him. Drake steps between us, glaring.

"You gonna protect him," I ask, stepping closer, the shell's dead weight holding me back, "after all he's done to you? Not smart enough to find an override like Tex, huh?"

His dark eyes flare for a half second with the same crazy as Tex had. Maybe uploading all that data wasn't Ash's brightest idea.

"Get them in the cauldron, now!" Ash barks.

They wheel the stretcher next to me as we move into a large circular room with viewing windows set at higher levels in a huge concrete tube. This is the pit with the cooling structures from the schematic—the one with 90% less water than normal.

A quiet peace builds, keeping time with the armed escort. We step onto a shiny metal floor with a deep concrete hole. The familiar scent of rotting meat rises from the pit.

Senses on fire, I scan the room. The metal floor isn't connected to the concrete, and it rocks a hair when we step onto it. The armed guards stay behind.

Ash stands with the guards, elation on his face. Rathmore double-checks the glove's connection, movements swift, his eyes shifting. A dark sensation rises from the hole, wafting over us as Rathmore lifts the shell and Sutton pushes the stretcher away. He lays the revolting body at my feet, its muscular arm stretching up to mine. Rathmore sprints off the metal, and it's just me, the shell, and the pit.

The rattle of weapons makes me turn. A ring of soldiers takes aim at me, all of them shaking, their faces tense as a pulsing fear fills the room, seeping into every consciousness. I glance at Drake, but the robotic stance remains, the only one in the room who's unaffected.

"Stand down," Ash commands, but there's a trace of fear in his voice.

A quiet hum precedes the rise of three smooth metal walls, sealing me next to the pit. A gust of sulfuric heat rises from the pit.

"Almighty Yeshua, help me now."

The walls rise to ten feet. My heart pounds, searching for a way out, but the floor tilts toward the pit with a hydraulic moan and I flinch, rebalancing. The collar beeps, then falls off. It hits the floor, wobbles, then rolls into the pit.

I won't leap for the walls like a desperate animal; the shell's weight would prevent it anyway. I brace against the tilting floor, thoughts flying. The atmosphere is straight out of hell. More heat belches from the pit, its acrid stench searing my lungs. The floor continues its steady tilt and I backpedal, facing the pit.

The shell sags toward the hole, making me haul back. My lips sear with tingling heat that builds again, but green haze rises straight from the pit. Mesmerized, I grapple with the unknown. The floor passes a 50-degree angle and I slide forward, resistance futile.

But you have overcome them little children, for greater is He that is in you than He that is in the world.

I cradle the words closer, sliding forward as they echo as if my hands are in the spirit's water. The hot green haze thickens to a cloud. They're trying to mix the worlds, to bring something from there to Earth.

The fire builds in my mouth as I slide toward the drop-off. As I exhale, tendrils of haze flow from my nose. There are inches left until the edge.

The shell goes over first, tugging me. I balance with one arm spread, sliding over with my eyes wide open, feet first. The speed of a jump takes me, but it's in the wrong direction, like Sage's first.

I blast through the energy, sulfur burning, before landing crouched, fingers spread on the hot floor. The shell is crumpled at odd angles, limp. Darkness creeps into my lungs. I study the pit, lit with green, but there's nothing but concrete walls.

Hurry.

At the spirit's whisper, I build the fire and blow it toward my palm; green sparks crackle over the webbed glove. I roll it again and put my lips on my wrist. Green flames burst out on my breath in a ball under the glove. It cuts into my skin, searing, loosening enough to shift my fingers.

A shriek rends the air, falling to a rumble that rattles my battered body. *Dragon.* Heat builds in the pit, sucking away the air, singeing into my lungs.

A sweltering wind billows, sucking away the oxygen, and the darkness flickers. *Something's behind me.* I turn. A black gate shows through smoke that flashes with green lightning. Within is a figure, striding through the embers. It's a dark Watcher, but different somehow.

The pressure increases as he approaches, crushing me in a viselike grip. I can't swallow, can't breathe. The shell is its sole object, and its power intensifies to a nuclear level as it closes in. The energy pummels. I fight it, holding the fire long past burning.

The creature is only two steps away, its rotten stench killing the air.

Lucifer.

Everything comes together at once. He wants a body, evil incarnate, *the beast.* His final imitation of Yeshua.

Green flames explode from my mouth of their own accord, hitting my hand so hard that the shell blasts backward. The glove disintegrates in the curling heat and I rip my hand away. The shell curls into a ball, its skin blackening.

Lucifer's eyes lock on mine, his fists clench, rage flowing; his voice is hell itself. "How dare you!"

My mouth is hot as the words flow of their own accord. "Go back. In the name of Yeshua, go back!"

His lips pull up into a snarl, revealing lion's teeth. He launches toward me.

7
SAGE

FAITH PROVIDES WHAT FAITH HAS SEEN. ~ ANDREW WOMMACK

Jacob strides out of the safe house, and I stare at the laptop screen, empty. Without him, the room feels like a tomb. Margie settles next to me, the chair creaking under his bulk. I'd implode without him here. The satellite map has an infrared overlay of Durban. I zoom in on Tex's location, longing for daylight and Jacob. Counting seconds is hateful. It will be hours until I hear from him… but it could be longer. Much longer.

Hands clenched, breath wild, time feels like syrup. Margie's voice is like a rumble of a diesel engine with its thick lilt. "Firepower. It doesn't always determine the outcome."

I frown, staring at the screen, grasping the lifeline. "No?"

He shifts, the chair threatening to give way. "A warrior can change the outcome by what he believes."

My skin pricks, looking at his solid arms crisscrossed with scars in the soft blue light.

"Paco tell me. He say Carter always a fighter, the best. But now, he different. More. I feel it."

"Me too," I whisper. But Jacob's gone now, one man striding into war. What if… I cover my mouth, but a whimper escapes.

Desperate, I scroll, focusing on Tex's red dot. So many are dead because of Ash's cowardice. I wish Jacob had a tracker, or some way to see him, but the risk of a signal hijacking is too high.

Tears prick, imagining Jacob stalking through the dark. It's who he is, an operator, the very best. I wish it would ease my heart rate. Unless I escape this spiral, I'll be useless.

I turn to Margie. "So, you're Paco's baby brother?"

He laughs, the sound vibrating my chair. "Different mama, same slouch for father," he sighs. "Paco find me. Six years old, barefoot, digging lithium. He save me." Margie's eyes lose that faraway look. "Your husband, he a survivor."

"He… we're not… not married."

Margie crosses his arms, and his dark eyes make me glance at the floor. "Margie know, Margie see. You and him, inside, belong to each other."

The coil of tension cranks tighter. Could he have chosen words that meant more? I glance at the laptop.

"Oh!"

My finger presses the screen. Two heat signatures appear for a half second, between buildings within the half-mile radius of emptiness surrounding Tex.

"It's him," Margie says.

My brows knit. "Who's with him? Come on!"

I zoom in further. They're steps from Tex's location! My heart slams. *Please, please, get out of there.* They disappear under a dark square. I'm frozen, eyes glued to the screen. One thermal image sprawls into the alley, its arms spread wide. I cover my mouth, horror rising.

"Zoom out."

But I can't move, staring at the fading heat signature. A flash of white and red appears, then they're both gone, under the next building.

"Hurry!" Margie's insistence forces me to scroll. The map zooms out, encompassing the entire city.

"No!" I shout. Three convoys are converging with hundreds of heat signatures, speeding toward the city. Toward Jacob.

I stand, chair slamming back. *"No!"*

But there's no stopping the events playing out miles from here.

"Brooks!" I shout, fingers longing to throttle him.

"Helicopters." Margie's scarred finger traces two incoming birds. Tex's red dot and another hotter infrared signature flash among buildings, moving fast, locked together.

"Jacob!" It's all there in my breaking heart, and desperate need for the one man the entire world wants.

Everything converges as hundreds of operatives surround the building. Seconds tick past. Emotions congeal, everything inside blank as the helicopters lift off and the troops disperse. *That's it.* In seconds, he's gone.

Anger roils, filling my soul. There's only one way Ash could've known where Jacob was. *Brooks.*

Margie stands, cocking a lever-action rifle. "My turn."

Without Jacob, what will I do? What torture will they subject him to?

"Move out," Margie rumbles.

"Where to?" I slam the laptop shut, the empty city like death inside.

"Ten miles south. Safe house for a man named Brooks."

My eyes snap to his. "Jacob told you?"

He nods. "I take you there, if things go south."

"What if they didn't?"

"Plan B." His gaze steadies me.

Jacob's still taking care of me. Margie's right. It's *my* turn. I'll spend every breath to get him back. I jam two extra pistols into my belt and lash Jacob's knife to my thigh, caressing its hilt where his fingers had been.

"Margie?" I begin, as he straps on a pack, towering over me. "Don't let me kill Brooks. I need him alive."

He frowns. "Brooks hurt your husband. Margie help you."

I jam the laptop into a duffel and let the rage build like a shield around me. Margie's Jeep is too narrow for his broad shoulders as we jostle along the bumpy African road, and he shuts off the lights long before he stops the vehicle.

"Stay behind. I got ten guards to drop." Margie is impossible to see in the night as we step out and I draw both pistols, nodding. Jacob is my single goal.

"Go quiet. I want him alone and surprised," I instruct.

Margie's dark eyes flash in the starlight. "Yes, ma'am."

The spicy African air presses in, and I'll hate it forever. The big man is a shadow as we approach a singular building. Margie points to the ground, then eases behind a bush.

He's gone a heartbeat later. I crouch, listening to the night sounds. Then a grunt and a scuffle. To the right, footsteps approach. I ease down to one knee, dig the toe of my boot into the warm sand.

Two more crunching steps come my way. When they pause, I bolt forward, the pistol ready. A lithe figure ducks, whirling toward me. I lash out again, catching his shoulder. A kick to my ribs knocks me flat, but I scramble up as the guard leaps.

He crumples in midair as dark hands snatch him. Margie.

Chest heaving, I unsheathe the knife, its blade glinting in the starlight. Jacob's knife. I trade tears for a dangerous freedom, where nothing holds me back. Margie kneels at the door where two lock picks are tiny in his hands. He turns the knob in silence, spreading one hand and ushering me in.

Blue light shines down a short hallway, and I creep to the corner. Brooks works at a small desk with three laptops spread before him. A readout on one shows a familiar outline of Tex, revealing him sprawled, head lolling. Words scroll on the bottom showing blood pressure, heart rate, temperature. The numbers add up to one thing—drugged. My best assumption is that Jacob faces the same condition. A list of symptoms fills my mind: severe headache, muscle cramps, possible brain damage. I grip the knife and slip closer behind a pile of gear. He'll pay for this.

I rocket forward to leap on Brooks's shoulders, roaring in his ear, the blade at his neck pulling him back, my hand in his hair, exposing his neck. His hands go up as he freezes beneath me.

"Give me one reason to let you live." My hand trembles;, and keeping the knife from pressing in takes every drop of control. The scent of him turns my stomach: crisp cologne and pride.

His hand moves, one finger clicking "Enter" on the keyboard. The middle screen jumps to an interactive map where a red dot is jetting across Africa.

Brooks makes a strangled sound so I ease the knife off a hair. "That's him, right there."

"Alive?" The word comes out solid, but it screams inside.

"Yes. He's far too valuable to waste."

The knife bites harder. "You have a way with words."

Margie's hand covers my entire shoulder. He's right. I take a pistol from the holster at Brooks's waist, remove the knife and step back, needing the space, chest heaving. He spins away, crouching as his eyes widen as they travel way up to Margie's stony face.

My voice trembles, betraying me. "I knew it was a trap the second you showed up in the jungle."

His jaw flexes. "No, whatever you did to Sutton set this off. It was bad timing. If he had carried the radio I gave him, I could've pulled him out." Brooks scans me, his gaze too warm. "It's so good to see you."

I sneer at him.

"Jacob," I redirect him, pulling the pistol, aim steady on his forehead.

"You need me, Sage. I'm your only connection to him."

I've never *wanted* to shoot someone before, and my finger curls on the trigger, but he's right. Brooks straightens, and I long to wipe that confidence off his face. "Where are they taking him?"

He eases to the desk, zooming in on the border of France and Switzerland near Geneva. "Europe 12."

My heart slams, terror rising. "Switzerland?" Then my blood turns to ice. *"CERN?"*

Horror descends at the name. CERN operates a physics lab that includes a large particle accelerator.

Brooks laughs. "CERN? No. They're light years behind us. Cyclone lies beneath CERN, but it's a convenient shield from prying eyes. They'll kill him there."

Both pistols point straight at his heart. "Not if you want to keep breathing."

A cruel grin curls his mouth, the expression unsettling at a primal level. "Oh, I give you my word, they won't succeed. You and I will make a good team, you'll see."

Margie steps forward, pulling my hands down as my skin crawls, jaw clenched.

"How do... *we*..." that word burns, "get him out?"

He turns to a briefcase, flipping it open. Inside are five sets of contacts, silicone fingerprints and IDs.

"How do you feel about becoming Lya Andre?"

The plane circles, pressure building in my ears as I slide Lya's contacts in. Brooks takes my hand and my skin crawls as he glues a clear tracker onto it with tweezers. The tiny dot of glue is cold, and I yank my hand away when his thumb caresses my wrist.

I wish Margie was here, but it's just me and the knife hidden in my boot. My heartbeat ramps higher, knowing we could be anywhere. Relief floods in when the blue waters of Lake Geneva come into view and the city of Geneva spreads below us.

CERN lies at the lake's southern tip, but we land at a small private airstrip to the north. Brooks's ability to evade the Collectives' grasp is disturbing, not fitting into the puzzle. The power he's shown shifts me further off balance as he offers a hand down the narrow staircase.

I refuse it, shouldering past him to the sleek black car that's waiting. He slides behind the wheel and I let out a slow breath, hands ice-cold, hoping the false fingerprints will cling to my clammy skin. A small purse holds the one thing I never want to be without. A bottle of water. What if Jacob jumps, and there's no water for him?

The thought freezes me. He's already so far underground. I clench my eyes and pray for help.

"Relax, Sage, you're safe with me," Brooks reassures.

"You seem to have no end of resources," I respond, my tone dripping with resentment.

He raises one brow. "I come from old money and power. Ancient, in fact."

I tilt my chin as the engine roars on the deserted road toward CERN and our goal, which lies far below it. How did he keep all that wealth when the New World Order made everyone equal and powerless? But I bite back the question, focusing on what's ahead.

"Won't the facial recognition flag us?" I cross my arms. What are they doing to Jacob?

"I'm a man who can make things happen. All technology can be… manipulated. Your face and mine have merged into our new identities in every single database that exists."

He turns, pulling into an almost-full parking lot. Now that public transit is the only option for almost everyone, it tells me all these people have government clearance—the elite few who benefit while everyone else suffers. Being near Brooks will be worth it if he gets me underground.

An enormous statue of Shiva, dancing inside a circular portal of some sort, rises against the clear blue sky, and a tendril of lion scent makes me shiver. My blood runs cold as we breeze through the first stage of security, everyone obliging. That ID must pack a punch.

"See?" he whispers in my ear, sending dread slithering down my spine as we step into an elevator.

I yank my elbow from his hand, the motion small because of the cameras. We exit where a large sign announces "Edda Gschwendtner's Experiment", and a chill races over my skin. Security ushers us through a second set of retina- and hand-scanners where my knees threaten to buckle until the screen flashes green.

We step into another elevator and drop 164 feet underground. CERN. It's like a tomb, and the name alone makes me nervous. A series of thick yellow security doors close behind us one by one, sealing our fate. What are the chances of escaping with Jacob?

A few others move along the sloping tunnel, but Brooks slows, allowing them to outpace us. His sly glance behind makes sweat break out as he tows me into a deep-set doorway. There are no markings, just a solid steel door with a small screen.

He takes out a device, studying it before tracing his finger over the lock screen by the door. It flashes red, and he swears, sweat beaded on his upper lip, sending my heart rate through the roof.

He types on his device again, then traces out a different pattern. Another red flash. He hisses, jaw tight. I glare at the pad. Jacob is on the other side, somewhere.

They'll kill him there.

Endless memories of Jacob run across my mind, his finger tracing out a strange symbol so many times.

I reach for the pad. Brooks's grip is like a steel on my wrist. "We get three tries, then it locks down and the goons descend."

I sneer at him, ripping away, one hundred percent sure. He lets my arm go and I trace out the shape of an eye with a triangle laid over it. The light flashes green and the door slides open.

Brooks's eyes harden, staring at me. Ignoring him, I lift my chin and breeze past two well-armed guards. *I'm coming, Jacob.*

He takes my elbow again, guiding me through endless hallways and doors he's familiar with. He swipes through an extra-heavy door.

Icy air flows from the room, its touch making green energy leap inside. *Not now. Brooks can't know I jump, too.*

He draws me into the room. It's a morgue, the far wall lined with freezer boxes. My muscles clench, green flaring in my retinas, as Brooks opens the first one. A cloud of frozen air clears, revealing a child's hairless body. I hug my stomach, hunching forward. *A boy?* Why would they have children here? Horror descends when two more boxes contain the same face on bodies of different ages. *What is going on?*

The next box he opens makes me flinch. It's an older version of the boy, but the skin is burned like Rivera's. Brooks casts a sideways glance at me, frowning as he slams it shut.

The next one holds an older, normal-looking human with salt-and-pepper hair and a familiar face. I scowl at his features, trying to place it as the energy ramps higher. Brooks mustn't see the haze, but turning away isn't much of a shield.

He tilts the frozen body on its side, hissing when he sees an incision at the base of the cadaver's skull. He takes an extraction tool from his pocket as I clutch the empty exam table, focusing on pushing away the jump. I need to escape Brooks, but he's leaning over another body, this one with jet-black hair and the same incision. I wince, holding in a cry as my muscles go rigid. The freezer clangs shut.

"You alright?" Brooks's breath on my neck makes me shiver. "You're a nurse, figured you could handle bodies."

I stumble forward, uncaring what he thinks. "I'm going to puke."

"We don't have time for this." His fingers cut into my arm as he scans the hallway, then drags me to another door as I trip over my own feet.

Inside are shelves full of cleaning supplies. He shoves me inside. "Don't move. I'll come back for you."

I collapse into the corner as green haze flows from my body and the purse zipper refuses to slide. The door shuts, but I'm making my own light now. It's a pool by the time the bottle is crinkling in my fist.

Arms seizing, I force the lid off and dump it on my face.

Instant freedom.

The travel is like layers of chains falling away as light grows and I twist, landing feetfirst, scanning the incredible landscape, breathing in colors.

"Where am I?" Nothing about the field bordered by trees is familiar.

Galel appears, his eyes intense. "Hurry!"

He sprints forward, outpacing me. Soon I skid to a stop next to him as warm air rushes up a sheer cliff.

Far, far below, another field spreads out, set with something like chess pieces.

A wicked red dragon curls in the middle, so lifelike that I grab Galel's arm. A golden torch flares, far smaller as it inches closer to the dragon. Its flicker leaps higher, but more dark pieces move around the perimeter, shifting positions. The fate of the golden torch catches my heart. The dragon uncurls and its vile jaws open wide with a ferocious blast of breath that makes the torch waver and gutter.

The torch flickers out, shutting off my own breath until a long, keening cry of sorrow rends my throat. I cover my eyes, hating the sight.

"No!" Galel shakes my shoulder. "You must watch!"

The black pieces move fast on the outside, circling, but the dragon won't relent, leaning closer, blowing away the remaining embers. The torch's fate is killing me. I writhe, desperate to get away.

"Listen!" Galel shouts.

A female voice echoes across the field, a battle cry that rends the air: *"Magen Tsinnah!"*

The words pulse above the chessboard, like a living thing, but the torch's last embers gutter, then fall, dark and empty. Still, the voice rises, reaching farther than before, and a spark flares in the dull soot. The strange words reverberate again, and the torch rekindles, bursting into full flare. The force sends out a shockwave that crushes the dragon and the black pieces, laying them flat.

I can't see my feet in the pool of green.

Galel is in my face… both hands on my shoulders, eyes wild, "Magen Tsinnah, Sage!" Then, I'm gone, sucked away, soaring faster than ever, his voice a distant cry. "Remember!"

I slam into my body at full speed, wrestling the clamping tension and bucking energy. A shelf collapses, bottles crashing down. Chest heaving, I reach for the spirit, but it's fading, dripping away like water between my fingers. Galel's burning eyes are the last to fade.

It's just me, in a dark room, far underground, knowing that Jacob is facing death. I burst out the door, sucking in wild breaths. A woman in a lab coat gasps, leaning away, clutching a tablet.

I hold up one hand, wheezing, the other on my head. "Shelf… fell on me."

She hurries away, and I look down the long hallway. Without Brooks, I'm lost.

"Almighty, please help me," I pray, and for half an instant I see Galel's glowing outline, far down the hall.

Know ye not that angels are ministering spirits sent to minister for you?

I cling to the words, drawing in the steadiness they bring.

"Galel," I say, flinching at the oddness of it in the physical, as I hurry forward. "Where?"

At the end of the cold concrete hall, a light flares. I blink, but nothing is there.

Maybe it's enough.

I trot along, clutching my side, heart rate erratic. Another flicker at the next corner leads me forward. Gnawing weakness pursues me, but I push it down.

Run.

I trot down five sets of stairs, keeping my face averted as I pass workers. Four soldiers hold rifles across their chests at the next door. Rock-solid knowledge wells up. This is it; Jacob is somewhere beyond.

I push my chin toward the door. "Open it."

"Clearance?" one asks.

I slap my ID into his palm, annoyed at the delay. He reads it, then nods at the pad next to the door. I trace out the symbol and breeze through. The air here is malignant, making my skin crawl as tendrils of lion scent reach me. I freeze, eyes wide. *What world is this?*

A flash of light near a door pulls me forward. I scan through it and skid to a halt before a dense glass wall. Jacob's there, one story down, surrounded by Ash and Sutton. My fingers press against the window as I take in the scene.

"Hey, you can't be in here!" a man shouts, rising from the desk.

My head snaps in his direction, and his face pales. I draw the knife on him in an instant, the blunt handle chopping his neck as he scrambles back. "Learned that from Jacob."

He convulses, eyes rolling in his head. He lies still, but it won't last long. A frantic search of the drawers reveals Velcro strips used to tie wires together. I cinch his hands down and rush past state-of-the-art video equipment to the window.

Jacob stands tall, but something's clamped around his neck as Rathmore wheels a stretcher forward.

"No!"

A smudge of smoke billows from the pit.

What do I do?

I search for something, anything, to break the glass, but it's useless—it's got to be an inch thick and there's an army arrayed around Ash. Now, Jacob's on a metal floor, a hairless body dangling from his arm. The image is so sick that my head swirls.

He's sliding toward the pit! I cry, beating the glass, powerless, as haze swirls upward.

"Stop!" I scream, but the floor keeps tilting. I blink, and Galel's face is there, shouting something, desperate, but without sound!

The hairless body slides over the edge, yanking Jacob along. I scream as he disappears, green light belches from the pit, rising to coat the window, blocking everything.

I turn, rushing to the screens where one shows an x-ray view that's aimed straight down into the pit.

A dragon's shape uncurls next to Jacob and the body. The spirit has melded with this reality. No, wait, there's another figure next to Jacob. My sight shifts again to the spirit, where black cogs are racing around and the dragon closes in. What were the words? They seem as far away as the spirit.

"Almighty, help me!"

A wisp of honey-flavored breeze touches my face in the tight underground room. With eyes closed, I breathe it in, as traces of sound reach me. "Thank you."

The words echo inside, and I bellow them into the atmosphere that's clouded with a sickening stench. "Magen Tsinnah!"

The words reverberate, caught inside the room as the floor trembles. I scream it again, fighting the hopelessness that crushes in. What good are words against this power? I clutch the desk as the equipment jumps, jittering out of place.

In my heart, I see the torch going out and roar against it, pushing back with every ounce of energy. "MAGEN TSINNAH!"

A jolt of pure energy zaps through the building as the words rip past my throat, unstoppable in both realms. The lights go out, and the eerie red and green glow rising from the pit bathes everything in a vile fluorescence until the exhaust fans catch up, affording me a clear view as my hands press against the cold glass.

The pit explodes in a rippling ball of dark flame that mushrooms up as chunks of concrete vomit past the window. It implodes, shards striking my face as I fly backward, slamming against the far wall with hot rivulets of blood running down my cheek.

The room spins. My chest is constricted by the immense pressure. My ears ring as I hold my head, trying to figure out which way is up. Pain helps solidify reality where a desk pins my legs to the ground.

Jacob needs me.

I strain to rise, but only my fingers twitch, my body crumpled against the smoking wall. Everything goes black as the buzz in my head reaches a fever pitch.

Jacob.

My eyes snap open, the bright torch in the spirit blazes before me. *Jacob.* With a cry, I shove the desk away and drag myself to the broken window, one leg stinging.

Emergency lights flash, disorienting in the sulfur smoke. Palms on the hot edge, I lean out, searching. The pit's edges are blown away, ragged now; the metal floor lies in a twisted heap twenty yards farther, where Ash was. Blood trickles from my cheek as the vent system sucks away the smoke. A chunk of concrete falls from the ceiling, imploding into dust when it hits the floor. Nothing else moves. Bodies lie crumpled at the far end.

Wait.

A burned, square hand slaps onto a bent piece of rebar at the edge of the pit, blackened with soot.

"Jacob!"

I swivel out the window, fall forever, crumple hard, rolling. Body stunned, I growl, crawling toward his hand, the floor singes my knees, green haze making the worlds twist together.

I scream his name, ears ringing, then grab his wrist, grimacing in the furnace heat belching up. He's hanging over nothing, grip slipping, head lolling.

"JACOB!" I scream.

His eyes roll, neck twitching, singed, and bleeding.

His split lip moves, but no sound comes out. I jam both boots into the rubble and add my other hand to his arm, teetering over the abyss, straining back, roaring, the intense heat stealing strength.

His other hand swings up and catches a chunk of concrete. It's the most beautiful thing I've ever seen.

He groans, eyes unfocused, as I haul him out of the pit. We fall back, his tortured body on mine, uncaring of the sharp rubble beneath. His skin sears, burned and raw.

His eyes slide shut, breath ragged, pulse jumping in an erratic pattern in his neck. I push aside his torn shirt, gasping. Massive hematomas cover his chest, and blood is seeping from multiple wounds crisscrossed over older ones. Potential complications converge.

"We've…" He swallows, his voice as torn as the rest of him. "…got to get out."

Years of training flood me. He shouldn't move; he needs immediate attention.

Flashlights bounce off the far wall. There's no time. Wincing, I pull his battered arm over my shoulder, groaning to sit up. He's still limp and his weight is like two tons.

He trembles, straining now as we gain our feet on the uneven rubble, listing wildly as he sags into me. I scan the room, teeth bared as the smoke makes each breath agony.

"Left," he directs, his free hand cradling his abdomen. Left was the single spot on the chessboard free of dark shapes.

We limp around the pit, finding the air better. My legs tremble as we lean against the damaged wall. I scowl, searching my spirit, desperate for knowledge this world doesn't contain. The black cogs are behind us.

Two heartbeats later, Jacob's boots drag as I strain forward. Within, the cogs become visible as one rushes past, hidden in the lazy smoke. I stop to let it pass, but Jacob is moaning, the sound breaking me inside.

Now!

The cry inside makes me stagger down the hall through the caustic smoke, around piles of debris. Guards sprawl around a battered ATV, limbs at odd angles. *So still.* I hold Jacob, vison blurring as I avoid stepping on them.

Jacob's tortured breathing makes me wince as I ease him into the passenger seat. I haul three bodies from behind the vehicle, collecting their weapons and shoving rubble away. The familiar cold of a pistol brings comfort. I leap behind the wheel and the engine cranks on the third try. Jacob leans against my shoulder, his dull eyes unfocused. Breathing is all he can do. I caress his jaw until he looks at me.

"We're getting out of here." I just don't know how.

"Water tunnels," he rasps, with one trembling finger pointing up the tunnel.

The vehicle jerks over debris and I hold him down with one arm as the engine screams, slamming over concrete chunks. A narrow beam of light bounces in an erratic pattern through the dust. I take a left, careening away from it.

"Two... levels up..." Jacob's split lip bleeds at the motion. "Door T... 22."

There's a screen on the dash that's cracked and coated with dust, but still functioning, and a blue dot shows our location.

"There's a ramp, hold on!" I shout.

The left front wheel wobbles as we surge one level up into clearer air. This far underground, what are our chances of escape? My heart slams into my toes as three more ATVs speed toward us. I stop, shoving Jacob with a grimace until he slumps face-down.

The first one stops and I shout, "Hundreds of casualties! Medical attention is paramount! Look for pulmonary distress and lung embolism!"

My blackened face is all the convincing they need. I jam the pedal, turning out of the ramp a level higher.

Pop. Pop. Pop.

I crouch, clutching Jacob's arm, my skin crawling. His head comes up, and our eyes meet. *Knowing.*

"Tex," I whisper, tears blurring everything.

Pop. Pop.

The concrete wall chips next to my head, shrapnel biting hard as I look over my shoulder. Tex stands there with a rifle settled on one hip, grinning, with a riot shield in the other hand.

"Go," Jacob gasps, making me cry out. Not now! *Not when Jacob's like this!*

The tires squeal as I roar down the corridor, straight past the door marked T 22. I hold up the dangling rearview; Tex is sprinting, gaining as his legs pump like machines.

"No!" I scream, mashing the pedal, willing the engine forward.

Pop. Pop.

The vehicle bucks, swerving like an eel.

Pop. Pop.

The dash explodes and the steering wheel spins, loose and ineffective. I dive for Jacob, holding him down as we crash, the ceiling and floor spinning into one.

We roll to a stop upside-down, the backseat torn away, revealing a tool kit. I crawl out, the wheels spinning above. Tex is there, twenty yards away. The expression of glee on his face makes the world stop spinning.

Jacob's hands clench as he unfolds, his head turning toward Tex. "Run, Sage."

I stand and lower a rifle I pillaged. "Not without you."

I pull the trigger, the recoil bruising my shoulder.

Tex leaps to the side, crouching behind the shield. A portion of wall with yellow and black paint narrows the corridor between us.

An emergency door.

I finger the ID card from Brooks. Tex has everything else. Enhancements, training, weapons, rage. He even has *time*, but he doesn't have a tiny plastic card.

He steps out, gloating. I'm closer to the door than he is.

"Sage!" Jacob gasps.

But I sprint forward, rifle flashing. Tex tucks behind the metal shield, moving fast. *Coming for me.*

A battle cry rips my throat as the rifle runs dry. I drop it and leap for the keypad. My hand is shaking too hard to make the card swipe.

Two more strides and he'll be on me. The card slides home, and I jam the button at the bottom with flames on it. A strobe light flashes, but Tex grabs my shoulders, lifting me high, slamming me against the wall.

Pop.

His shoulder mushrooms blood, and his head turns toward Jacob, who's slouched against the concrete, pistol wavering. The hatred flowing from Tex makes my skin crawl as I dangle in his cruel grip. With a savage growl, he tosses me across the hall, where the hydraulic hum of the door resonates against my cheek on the floor.

Tex leaps high, his elbow a weapon as it falls toward Jacob. His lethargic roll can't escape it, and the hammer blow lands on his back. Time slows to a crawl as my screams echo off concrete. The door is closing as Jacob blocks another blow that pummels him into the floor.

The ruined side-by-side is my only asset now.

I limp forward, pain radiating. Tex clutches Jacob's neck, sliding him up the wall. I slam against the side-by-side, veins standing out in my neck as I take the roll bars and rock it twice while Tex hammers punches into Jacob's gut. With a metallic groan, the ATV flips over, rocking onto its wheels, two of them flat.

The engine is still purring. I get in, blocking out the sound of Tex's fists. The steering wheel flops, the pin that holds it on is shredded. The box in the back has a metal clip holding it shut. I rip it off, bruising my fingers as I force the clip straight and jam it through the shaft, then crank the wheel.

Tex is killing Jacob.

I smash the accelerator with a bellow of pure rage and hit Tex square on as we flash past Jacob. Tex folds over the hood, *right there*. He snarls, his face inches away. The doors are halfway shut. I speed through them, aiming straight into the wall, pedal to the floor. The impact crushes me against the dash as Tex roars, pinned against the unforgiving tunnel.

There's no air; my head swirls, vision blurring. Then Tex's hand grips my hair, cranking me closer to his red face, blood trickling from his mouth. I whimper as sensation returns: the cut on my cheek, the ripping sound of my hair being pulled out, and the sharp pistol cutting into my back. Sluggish, I draw it, the barrel wavering. I press it against his vest, blind as he smashes my head down. The blast throws his upper half against the wall, freeing me. I spill from the ATV and land hard on my side.

The door is almost shut.

Jacob is just beyond it. I crawl forward, lungs stunned. Tex shouts, the side-by-side resisting as he strains for freedom.

"Go," I mouth, gaining my feet, twisting through the closing gap. I turn. Tex tosses the ATV back, his eyes locked on me, teeth bared. He lurches forward, one leg dragging.

With a quiet sigh, the door shuts with Tex inches away. He slams into the other side and I flinch, turning to shoot the panel until its guts and wires lie exposed.

"That… was… a nice move." Jacob is limp against the wall, blood running from his mouth.

I skid on my knees, whispering his name.

"No time," he gasps.

The slamming on the door falls silent. Tex will find another way.

"There's… another… exit. R 81." He shifts with a groan, rolling up. He points to a rifle. "Need that."

Blood smears as I take Jacob's arm over my shoulder. We limp forward, panting, turning to a doorway. Jacob nods. I swipe in, the brilliant white hallway empty.

"Personnel… on lockdown," my voice is husky and burned. We stagger past rooms full of bodies as my skin crawls. It's the same boy from the morgue.

"What are they doing here?"

Jacob shakes his head, breath gurgling. "Lab grown. There."

He's taking more of his own weight, but I've got to check him soon, his injuries are extensive. The equipment in the empty exam rooms is tantalizing; it could save Jacob's life, but Tex is coming, hunting us down. Plus, we've no location on Ash or Brooks. A flash of anger lends heat to my icy hands. They *won't* touch Jacob again. We swipe into another bleak hallway, the ramp agonizing. A sign reads level R.

"We're here. Come on." I drag him to door 81, and swipe in, flicking on the light. Huge pipes run along the far wall.

Jacob nods. We stop in front of a large metal wheel. He sinks to his knees, curling forward in pain, hands reaching for it. I set mine next to his, grimacing as it creaks. Lights flash red above the five-foot pipe, but we keep turning, opening an access panel for the tube.

Warm water gushes over our feet, but the level inside the pipe is only a foot or two deep. I stare into the inky blackness that smells like slime, and cringe.

Jacob's hand slides into mine. "Only way out."

The image of Tex bursting through the door with Ash and Brooks is too much. I stifle a cry and help Jacob in. The rifle on my back catches in the round opening, making me contort, sliding in, clenching Jacob's hand in a death grip.

He is sitting in the flow, water rushing against his back. "This is… the fun part."

I snort, easing next to him. "This is the *terrifying* part."

His arm wraps around me, trembling. "Do it… together."

I set my hand on his chest and a faint spark leaps in his ocean-blue eyes. It's enough to face the long dark tunnel. He leans back and the current sweeps us into total darkness. *Together.*

Time blurs as we sweep around turns in the midnight pipe. The slick edges wash us along faster and higher. At regular intervals, pumps turn the current into whitewater as we surge higher through the pitch dark. The loud hum of the pumps we zip past gives me hope as the pipe grows larger, no longer curving under us, and light appears far ahead. The current sags and we moan, getting to our feet.

The gurgling water is calf deep, but its roaring voice reverberates in the twenty-foot pipe. We splash forward, unsteady, toward the light.

A hollow laugh escapes—there's blue sky beyond. "We made it."

Something slams into my back, jamming me forward, ripping me away from Jacob.

Tex.

He skis on Jacob's back through the flow. Jacob twists, forearm blocking blows, before Tex leaps off; the current sucks them both to the edge.

"No!" I scream, but Jacob goes over!

His fingers clasp the edge, the water frothing over them. The drop could be a hundred feet.

Tex strides up, a malicious grin on his face as he steps hard on Jacob's fingers.

My vision blurs red as I swing the rifle to my shoulder. My hand settles on the trigger, finger curling as I stalk forward, the barrel between his shoulder blades.

Sneering, Tex twists his boot. I pull the trigger, my foot slips on algae, and I go down hard on my back. Scrambling up, I see that the water is smooth at the edge. The pipe is empty! I catch the rim, pulse spiking because the water dives in wild abandon down to Lake Geneva.

I scream Jacob's name, but the surface far below is quiet, unruffled by a swimmer. I leap for the boulders next to the pipe, racing down at breakneck speed, counting seconds. *Too many.* The slick rock jabs my legs, churning faster, trembling in the bitter wind.

"Jacob!"

Frantic, I hit the lake's edge. The wooded slopes are so beautiful, framing the most hateful place on Earth with the water rolling under the misty fall.

There!

The curve of his back breaks the surface farther down the shore. The water is like sludge holding me back as I stroke hard, then flip him over. Glassy blue eyes are far too familiar, staring skyward, but this isn't the result of a green haze disconnecting him from his body. I surge for shore, falling on his damaged chest, clasped palms pumping his heart.

"Jacob!" I scream, lowering my lips to his, pinching his nose shut. His skin is like ice as I blow, longing for him to twitch.

I pump like mad, his bruised rib cage resisting the motion, fitting my mouth to his again when the sound of rocks tumbling further down shore freeze me. Tex hunches high on the edge of a cliff, his chest heaving, one arm hanging limp. Unsteady, he staggers forward, blood running down his face.

A savage cry rips my throat as I pull the last pistol from Jacob's side and sprint forward, firing. He reels sideways at the blow, the rocks giving way beneath him. The rounds pump out. Every second slashes the chance of Jacob living.

"Haven't I shot you enough today?"

My last bullet catches Tex on the shoulder, spinning him. His shredded armor shows bone glinting in the crisp mountain air. In slow motion, he tumbles over the cliff and I throw down the empty weapon, chest heaving. I skid back to Jacob, and tears fall on his chest, his face, as I continue CPR.

"Jacob! Come back *now!*"

His finger twitches, and my mind reels. ATP energy can cause twitching for hours after death. I push the thought away, filling his lungs, longing tearing me apart. I continue long past the time, sobs wracking my lungs. There's only darkness ahead, without him. Ash will take me, and science will kill me, but it's a single moment without him that destroys me inside.

Sorrow sweeps me back, but every effort to rouse him is useless. The world is empty, with his body so still beneath my hands. The air stirs, and with it, images of another dimension, where Jacob's skin is glowing with power, where he's an unstoppable force, where *life* is.

I clench the images in my soul while my hands hold his dead body. The world's war, this one so powerful, so real, the other a dream that slips through my fingers.

"Yeshua, help me!" The words rake the atmosphere, reverberating. The wind's chill fingers steal heat as each heartbeat takes me further from Jacob. But then, inside the cutting air, there's a whisper of the water's voice.

And I will give power to my two witnesses, and they shall prophesy a thousand two hundred and threescore days, clothed in sackcloth.

The words seep into my soul, where they solidify into rock-solid knowledge that makes my eyes snap open. That's Jacob's calling, unaccomplished, but his glassy eyes are empty. I condense, curling forward, battling reality.

"Jacob's not done yet."

The words, empty and powerless, fall flat. I press my fists against my eyes, needing true sight, but Aseph is here even now. The sensation is consuming, but the outcome was different *there*, life instead of death.

Jacob's blue lips tell an eternal story. He's gone.

"It's not about you, Sage. You can't save yourself—that's His work; all you've got to do is accept it."

Jacob's words led me to salvation once. He said we're the conduit that power flows through. Something leaps inside. It's not my job to generate the energy, all I have to do is put it where it needs to go.

My hands tremble as I hold them above Jacob's battered body. *Just the conduit.* I lower them to his chest. The prophecy pushes me, and it's a solid place to stand, on the Almighty's Word. Time is irrelevant as I crouch there, seeing it inside until I can feel him rising. Now, the words aren't a plea, they're a command. "Jacob, come back now!"

Seconds pass, but I refuse to back off, leaning in, seeing it. He coughs, and I flinch with a cry as he hauls in a ragged breath. With a grimace, his blue eyes come open. I cradle his face, heart slamming. All the worlds swirl around us, but right here, there's only us, together.

Quiet footsteps sound close by. I whirl to my feet, every nerve on fire. An old woman stands there, her ancient face wreathed by a brown shawl. She mutters in German, then switches to English. "The darkness has broken."

Her knobby fingers entwine before her. "I pray and pray that the evil go from here." She lifts watery eyes heavenward. "I see you in dreams. I help you. *Hurry!*"

I nod, tugging at Jacob's wounded shoulders, scanning for helicopters. She unwinds the long shawl, revealing snow-white hair. We spread the fabric and shift Jacob onto it. His eyes flutter open and I caress his battered face. "Stay with me, Jacob."

"Hurry," the old woman urges.

I wrap the shawl in my fists and tow him up a narrow path, every muscle screaming at the effort. The old woman is praying, and the words strengthen me until a small wooden shack emerges, perched on a rocky outcropping and well-hidden in the forest's shelter. A blond boy stands in the doorway, staring. The woman claps her hands. "Go, clear away our trail. *Sich!*"

The boy rushes past, his eyes glued on Jacob. I sway, long empty. The woman takes my elbow, steadying me. "Thank you."

Her ancient face crinkles in a smile. "The Most High keeps His servants. Now, we get him inside."

We wrestle him through the door as the boy returns, ushering us into a tiny bedroom. He and I lift Jacob to the bed, which is nothing more than ropes with a thin mattress. It looks like heaven.

Jacob is on the bed when his eyes open again.

"Tex?" he rasps, brow knit.

"Shh," I smooth his forehead. "I shot him plenty. We're safe now." Exhaustion eats at me. Ash and Sutton will have Tex back on lockdown before he recovers enough to hunt us down, a fate we must avoid.

Jacob blinks, his bleary eyes on mine, always the one to defy the odds.

"Thank you," he says, pressing my hand to his cheek. "Wouldn't have made it without you."

I kiss his palm. "You told me to come, remember? Our paths run together, Jacob Carter."

The old woman shuffles in, a pan of steaming water in her hands. Together, we wash Jacob's wounds, and I stitch up five of them, inspecting the older wound on his calf.

"Happened in Durban." He hasn't winced at my work.

I shudder, unable to resist. "Told you it was a trap."

His lip curls in that familiar smile that I love most of all. "A woman's always right."

"You are a wise man," the old woman says as she dabs a third-degree burn on my shoulder.

Jacob's eyes grow dark. "I was supposed to be here today, to stop them."

"Yes," the woman pets my hair, soothing my nerves. "I pray for many years. Jehovah shows me what they do, far under the earth. But today…" her eyes shine, "today, light has returned. You sleep now. No one finds you here, I have prayed, and Sven will keep watch."

I don't doubt her, not one bit, so I ease in next to Jacob, my head on his shoulder. Tears burn, listening to the gurgle in his lungs. He sighs as my eyes slide closed.

Disorientation fills me, staring at the log ceiling. How long have we been here? The woman shuffles past the doorway with a warm loaf of bread in her hands. I look over at Jacob, and his eyes flutter open without that terrifying cloudy look.

"Oh."

Green haze flows, mingling above us.

Jacob shivers, his eyes igniting, "Ah."

The satisfied sound makes longing sweep over me too. I stagger up, muscles in agony as the old woman returns.

"Please… shut the door. We will sleep, but you can't wake us. No doctors." I grimace, leaning most of my weight on the bed in the green pool.

She nods, eyes on the strange glow as she shuts the door. I swipe the water pitcher off the table and collapse next to Jacob, slide my fingers into his.

I pour the water out, letting it splash down on our skin.

"Oh."

We're pulled free from the searing pain, and the travel seems like a dream. We land flat out, plowing into the spirit at full speed.

Neither of us moves, just breathing, pain-free as we lie next to each other. The air tastes fantastic, with its warm tint of honey.

"This is what I needed," Jacob says, his voice like velvet. "To get out of that *body* for a while."

We stare at the sky, hearing the grass grow and a soft tread to our right.

"That was quite an entrance," Demyen quips, his mouth pulled to one side.

Jacob's laugh is the best sound I've ever heard. This glorious freedom, as we stand, is a relief from Earth's fading memories.

"We'd better move along." Demyen's gaze locks far ahead where a mountain hunches against the horizon. It's shrouded in clouds, but everything in me leaps at the sight of it. The long walk does us good, laughing, talking. There's a balance inside again. Our paths curve up foothills until we're single file, climbing a steep rocky trail that hugs a cliff.

The shale beneath me shifts, and Jacob steadies me from behind. "You good?"

I laugh at myself, continuing on. "Sure thing."

We ascend until the clouds are below us and the path is mere inches wide. A sharp gust races up the immense space to my right, shoving me forcefully.

"I should have gone first," Jacob mutters.

My hair swirls in the gale, but we can't trade places without falling.

I shrug. "Y…"

The rock beneath us explodes.

Crack!

Jacob swipes at me, but I plummet, clawing the air, a scream ripping my throat. Gray rock races past, but I only nick it with my fingertips. Something body-slams me against the granite, searing hot. The impact flips me into a wild tumble where there is no up, just a stench that's too familiar.

A metallic screech sends ice through my blood as the dragon shoves me aside. My chest slams onto a ledge, fingers catching rough rock, but I'm sliding too fast. One toe catches a hold, and I scramble up, clinging to the cliff face on a slim shelf.

A shaky glance reveals nothing but a gray cloud bank below. The replay of hot scales makes me tuck tighter to the mountain. My path glitters there, marking a trail that a mountain goat would resist.

What if it got Jacob? My teeth chatter, but the black mouth of a cave shows dark against the light stone. The scramble to reach it leaves me sweating and my skin tingles in the damp air as I duck in. The cavern widens and my outstretched hands can't span it.

Further in, a calm pool of water fills the way, but the topaz thread dives right under it. It's hard to disturb the water, which may not have seen a ripple in a hundred years. Still, there's no other way. I dip my toe in, shivering at the temperature and the voice that fills the cavern.

For the kingdom of God is not a matter of eating and drinking but of righteousness and peace and joy in the Holy Spirit.

Up to my knees now, the words wash over me.

Come, you who are blessed by My Father, inherit the kingdom prepared for you from the foundation of the world.

The cold water makes me gasp as it covers my stomach.

Unless one is born again he cannot see the kingdom of God.

Then, my tip toes leave the rock and I swim through the cold dark water.

Truly, truly, I say to you, unless one is born of water and the spirit, he cannot enter the kingdom of God.

I am one with the spirit's water, so I take a breath and dive, the temperature tickling over my scalp as all the Earthbound worry washes away. The other side arrives too soon, for the refreshing water lends pure, endless life. Dripping wet, I hug myself on the far side, my mind full of the Kingdom.

With bated breath in the sacred cave, I ease around a bend, knowing *something* lies ahead. Galel is there beside me, but his eyes focus on the way to come, and there, in the center of the cavern, lit of its own accord, is a wooden pedestal.

"Go on," Galel whispers when I hesitate.

My heart's pounding as if I ran a mile. On the pedestal sits a golden keyring with several keys on it, all inscribed with fascinating script.

"These are the keys to the Kingdom, and it is the Father's good pleasure to give them to you," Galel says.

The sensation of holiness grows heavier as I study them. "What would I do with them?"

An amused expression crosses his face. "Why, you open things, of course. They give you access to everything you need."

"Does every believer have them?"

"Interesting question. All the Almighty's children have *access* to them, but not all are using them. Some don't even know about them. Yet, these keys are crucial. They're how things work."

"So, will I know where to use them?"

"With time and study, yes. Without them, believers are at the mercy of the law of sin and death. Take them," he urges.

I reach forward my fingers hovering just above them. "What if I mess up?"

"The Almighty dwells outside of time. There is not a single thing that will surprise Him, and He is more pleased with messing up in the right direction than no growth at all. These keys unlock everything He gave you inside your covenant."

"That's like a contract?" I ask, heart leaping. Contracts are understandable, spelling out responsibilities and outcomes. They're something I can understand.

"Yes, signed in blood. It's an unbreakable agreement on the Almighty's end. Eternal. How much of it you use and experience is up to you. They do nothing lying on the shelf. Put them in the right place. What the Almighty provides is grace, and the keys that activate that grace are faith and words."

"Okay." The second my hand closes over the keys, something settles inside, as if I was off balance before without even knowing it.

"See, you were made to use them. Take hold of the first, all by itself. That's salvation. It's yours, forever. You can turn away from it, but that is not the Almighty's will." Galel's voice rumbles in the hushed cavern. "Now the next."

The inscription on this key looks like fruit and an even deeper calm overtakes me.

"That's provision. It's yours, forever. After all, the Almighty said His children would never beg bread, and that He Himself will supply all your needs according to His riches and glory."

I take the next key, hungry now for the fascinating future where He makes all things possible.

A stack of medical papers appears on the pedestal. I pick them up and scan page after page of symptoms, diagnoses, and life expectancies for every disease known to man. Then, as I flip the pages, the words disappear until every page is stark white and empty. An ember flares on the top page, streaking across to spell out the words *paid in full.*

"That's healing. It's yours, forever, for by His stripes, you were healed."

The beautiful words blur. I devoted my entire life to helping people get well, but to live free from sickness is a thought beyond me. It opens a way never seen before, even if I can't quite grasp it yet.

The next key seems heavier than the others, with a deep kind of importance.

"That's authority—the right to make the Almighty's will come to pass on Earth. It is yours, forever. You must keep this one handy, Sage. Now the last."

This key is covered in tiny, scrolling writing, with not a single part of it smooth.

"This is the key of knowledge that Yeshua spoke of. Knowledge is always the first key to use. You must know the scroll, then the others will unlock the greater mysteries of His Word."

I draw breath to speak, but he's gone in a heartbeat, leaving me alone, clutching the keyring. My path shows in the floor running straight toward a set of tall, arched doors that are thirty feet high. How did I miss them before?

Hesitant, my fingers brush the golden handle. Wonder floods in, along with knowledge. *He's* here. An all-consuming longing sweeps through my soul as I pull it open.

A throne room spreads before me; its floor is the most incredible solid blue gemstone. The full spectrum of light fills the room, both white and every color at once.

And there, in the center, is the *Lion of the Tribe of Judah*. His glorious mane surrounds the most intense green-gold eyes, and He is *everything*. Incredible power radiates from Him as I fall on my face, stripped of myself, full of Him.

"Holy, holy, holy." This word, from deep within me, deserves endless repetition. He steps closer, each paw wider than my shoulders.

"Two ways lie before you, daughter; you must choose between them." The glittering gem floor shudders at His voice. "One direction holds great cost to you. The other, great cost to Jacob." Each word is alive, filling me. "But now, ask Me what you will."

I blink, still flat on the smooth blue crystal, but the worlds collide in my soul: Our wounded bodies lie somewhere, and Jacobs is *so* battered. There is one thing in my heart. "Can… can we have a rest? Some time for him to recover."

A pleased rumble fills the air. "Time is a law that can be suspended."

Then He nudges me with His nose and eternal energy races from His touch. "I AM always with you."

I lift my head and spin around, but the smooth cavern is empty. My path leads around a bend, into the daylight. How do I figure out which way stays with Jacob?

A forested valley stretches away into the distance, its ancient trees sending out a pungent odor of life. A shadow flits overhead, blocking the light for a heartbeat, bringing a stench. It's not lion—it's worse—with the same revolting scent as the poison from Jacob's wound.

I crouch behind a wide trunk, fingers sunk in the soft forest loam, as the keys clink in my pocket. The ground trembles and something's changed. Now the air has an icy tinge.

A scan of the forest reveals nothing out of place. Galel half-appears, still translucent, then he's gone. A slow breath gathers strength for whatever comes.

Thud.

I freeze, holding my breath.

Thud.

Rough bark bites my skin as I press against a tree, recalling the pyramid and how huge the dragons were. The light dims as if night were falling, and my skin crawls.

Thud.

Breathing hard, I ease half my face out. A dragon's fiery eye glows, not three feet away, seeming to float in midair. It shifts, and its outline shows for an instant, but the scales are a perfect image of the background. It snorts, breath blasting the leaves beside me. I spin, sprinting like mad, and the trees shudder.

Leaping a fallen tree, my scream pinches off as I plummet, crashing down a steep slope. My ribs smash against a trunk near the bottom where I crumple. *Maybe it can only see motion* On the hilltop, it skids to a halt, thick hind legs plowing dirt, which reveals its location. This one knocked me off the cliff; the odor alone proves it. *Jacob!* My heart constricts. Did that thing…?

A blast of breath is paralyzing. What if…? Trembling sets in hard, but the image of Jacob and Demyen fallen won't leave my mind. Eyes clenched, I cringe as the leaves rustle above, every sound magnified. The rustle of leaves shifting means the enemy has moved without spotting me. Easing up, I back against another tree. The move failed last time, and the beast could be anywhere.

Air ripples past, filled with the metallic taste of fear, and I inhale the paralyzing gas. The trees waver, an outline appearing as the scales shift colors, matching the forest as he hunts for me.

Alone.

I shift to keep the tree between us, but a branch snaps under my foot.

Thud.

The beast has crept far too close. I focus hard on the trees, teeth chattering. A grove of younger elms grows tighter there, like a fence that might keep him out. The beast shrieks as I sprint, its hot stench on my back. I leap, stretching into a swan dive between two tightly grown trees, and crash-land as the dragon's snout jams on the trunks. Its teeth shear off long curls of green wood as I scramble away.

My arms pump, branches slicing as I race through the grove. There's a sharp click, then the roar of flames. I duck, covering my head and rolling. My shoulder digs into the warm forest loam as the heat intensifies above.

A tree shears off under the dragon's assault and smoke burns as I scramble forward. A blast of wind knocks me off my feet as leathery wings beat the air and its scales turn jet black, no longer hiding as it lands hard beyond the grove, straight ahead.

The open meadow allows him a better attack.

"No!" I collapse against another tree, longing for Jacob and Demyen. "Galel!"

He appears right next to me with his brows furrowed. "Why are we running?"

A sharp retort is on my tongue, but a stream of fire makes us duck and cover.

I fling my arm toward the singed ground as smoke stings my eyes. "That should be answer enough."

He holds out the keys. "You *dropped* these."

It won't be long until he's on me, but… why *am* I running?

That contract that's signed in blood? Either it's enough, or it isn't. The keys are cool and solid in my fist, waiting to be used. *I AM always with you.* The promise sinks down to my inmost parts. The Lion of the Tribe of Judah will never leave me, but it's so hard to see that.

The dragon's ripping out trees by the roots. A few more seconds is all he needs. I ease back, look up at Galel. "It's a law, right? One that *always* works?"

Another blast of fire makes us huddle closer.

Galel nods, shield up. "Always."

The decision comes, rolling up from my spirit, taking over my soul as the parts of me align with the Almighty's will. *To destroy the works of the devil.* The dragon flings a full-grown tree skyward; I watch it soar like a toothpick.

Could I ever destroy that monster?

But the thought is so crooked now that I've felt what straight is. His will is what matters, not mine, and not the dragon's. He gave me authority over the enemy. Doesn't *feel* like it, though, and the longer I wait, the more danger I'm in.

My path glitters twenty yards to the right, running straight for the beast. Its jaws clamp on another trunk, and while he rips it up, I sprint for the next cover.

Galel keeps pace and the topaz path is solid under my feet. The air reverberates with the reptilian shriek, but I won't cover my ears as it rises to a crescendo. At the electric snap, I grin. Jacob's not suffering from its poison anymore, and that victory pushes me forward.

A wisp of clean air gives me focus as I whisper, "I have all authority over the power of the enemy."

Galel nods, adjusting his grip on his shield, jaw tight. I lift my chin, studying the beast with narrow eyes. It's deranged as it hunts with one goal—my death.

How dare it? The question seems to echo inside forever. The Almighty's here with me. How dare that thing attack? It deserves what's coming. The anger builds until it's a seething force that pushes me past the cover of the trees. Galel stays between the beast and me.

"HEY!" I shout, unhinged.

It freezes, drops a massive tree, and its blazing eyes lock on me, out in the open. The jaws drip, shuddering as it shrieks, the sound a punishment that I roar back at.

Its long stride covers half the distance between us, but it's limping. One back leg is bloody, the claw unresponsive. It's not invincible after all. The knowledge sparks the embers within. Galel braces, shield high, sword drawn.

But I am a soul on fire.

"Leave me!"

It snarls, towering above, wings spread over the sky, blue sky showing through five long tears.

"You dare command me?" Its eyes flare and my knees threaten to buckle. I push back. *He's* here, the King of Kings, the Lord of Victory.

"I defy you in the name of Yeshua," I shout, each word creating a ripple that rolls over Galel, growing until the first one slams into the beast's chest. It convulses, shaking its head, but it takes a half step closer, its claws sunk deep in the dirt.

Its head snakes closer, lightning fast, eyes blazing. "Prove you can."

Click.

A stream of seething red fire rockets towards us, but I won't flinch. Galel's shield catches the blast, and he roars, feet skidding as the torrent pushes him back, but a sense of elation takes me, standing in the intense heat. *I believe it.* Because He's right here, nothing will harm me.

The blast runs out and I smile, head lowered, poised for battle, drawing a disk from my wrist.

8
JACOB

Black scales whip past at jet speed as Sage falls. "No!"

There's not one shred of hesitation as I dive off the cliff after her. The beast is below, wings tucked as it dives after her. Curled into a tight swan dive, I will myself downward. The wicked jaws open inches from her.

"Hadena!" The windshear tears away the war cry, but the blades are there, sparking off midnight scales. The impact is enough that it misses, its snout pounding Sage hard from the side. She slams into the cliff, and we plummet past. The dragon rolls, red lit eyes locked on me.

The tail lashes at out, but I hook it and stab with my free hand, but it's a stupid move. The beast whips me off so hard that it's impossible to orient.

Bam!

Claws wrap around my torso in a death grip, proving he was toying with me last time. At least now, my arms are free. Without the luxury of air, I stretch back and cross Hadena's dual blades behind the immense leg. Eyes shut, all that exits are the blades' keen edges seeking the scales.

Blackness presses in. They're sealed too tight. "Yeshua!"

Muscles bunching, I pull Hadena across the armor. The shanks hiss, then the sound softens, no longer fighting the bone-like scales, and I finish the stroke behind my head. The awful pressure falls away, and I fall, lungs expanding, but the only thing that matters is keeping it from Sage.

"Ha ha!" I bellow, rolling in the jet stream, blasting through cloud cover at a fantastic rate as black blood streams from Hadena's tips. "You're bleeding!"

Slam!

The universe swirls, igniting pain. Nausea heaves, but I clamp it down, spinning faster, until the beast snatches me, hind claws clamped tight on my ankle. The mountain is below, but the dragon is pumping skyward, where the air is too thin. Dangling upside down affords a clear view of the injured leg, bleeding a few feet away.

I lunge over, both blades slicing into the first wound. The creature shrieks, wheeling hard, its wicked head snaking straight for me. Hadena is there, warding off the crazed attack. The wind catches the leathery wings, flipping us hard.

I'm loose, flung higher, and spreading out, needing every speck of resistance to slow me as the dragon unfurls below. It's lost track of me and a savage grin takes hold, tucking hard, speeding down, straight for the wing with twin tatters. The upstroke comes a second before I expect it, so Hadena punches clean through. The roar dominates the air, whistling through the fresh slices.

I latch onto one wing, close to the feverish body, and reach over for another slash so the mountain shows through below. The beast rocks, adjusting to the new air flow, then tucks its head and flips.

A shout rips out of my throat as I rocket toward the unforgiving rock. The vile shadow races along the stone and everything goes black.

Opening my eyes doesn't change the darkness.

"Boy?" It's Demyen's voice, close by, as sensations register. Rocks dig into my back as an explosion rocks the narrow corridor, followed by scraping and snuffling. "He's a grumpy brute. Glad there was a cave to carry you into."

"Ouch," is all I say, finding movement less than pleasant.

"Here," Demyen offers, with a rustle in the dark.

"I know," I say, reaching out. "Eat!"

"Aye," he says with a laugh.

The scroll he stuffs into my hand is warm and savory.

Surely He has borne our griefs and carried our sorrows; yet we esteemed Him stricken, smitten by God, and afflicted. But He was wounded for our transgressions, He was bruised for our iniquities; the chastisement for our peace was upon Him, and by His stripes we are healed.

The words wash the pain away as silence fills the cave. "Thank you."

"You're heavy, I'll give you that. Hard to snatch as you plunged past," Demyen says. "We'd best be moving." What he doesn't say drives me to my feet. The beast is angry, and Sage is out there.

"The air is fresh this way." My gesture is meaningless in the inky black, but my path draws me further into the mountain. Movement comes easier as I stretch, then lean into a trot. We both breathe freer when sunlight shows in the distance, but we're slick with sweat by the time we reach the opening.

Where is Sage? I half slide down the scant trail as a shadow races overhead.

I crouch, scanning the sky. "No, no, no!"

Demyen is there, breath pumping. "Hurry."

We rush forward, the steep cliffs giving way to forests below. The dragon wheels hard, catching sight of something, and its wings tuck as it plummets into the trees.

"No!" I shout, Hadena flashing as I run, and Sage's shriek echoes across the distance.

The reptilian roar splits the air in return. Teeth bared, I fly down the narrow path. How could I miss catching her?

"Boy!" Demyen leaps a boulder, his beard whipping at the speed. "You take the right flank, and I'll take the left!"

"Aye!" But there's so much distance to cover, and the dragon soars into view with sunlight glinting through, then it disappears far below.

"I'll take its neck!" I roar as we fly forward.

The beast is attacking the trees, which means Sage is *right there.* She yelps again as a torch of flame pummels the woods.

"It's too far!" I cry at full speed, careening up an incline.

Demyen's grip on my arm tows me to a halt. "Listen, what's that?"

Head tilted, I search for the sound. "Hooves!"

Raeual and Jaden appear, riding up the rocky scree. The horses skid to a halt and Haseleph shakes his thick white mane. Raeual hops off. "He'll take you."

The horse's ears lie flat against his head, and his nostrils pinch in a nasty way.

"Um," I say, my last ride too clear.

Demyen is already astride Jaden's bay. "Not a second to lose, boy."

Shaking my head, I step close and grip Haseleph's mane. He stomps one iron-hard hoof, bobs his head, then slams the hoof down on my toes. "Gaaaa!"

"Here now!" Raeual chides, shoving the horse's shoulder. "He doesn't like you any."

I grit my teeth and swing up. "The feeling is quite mutual."

Raeual smacks Haseleph on the rear before I'm settled, and it's all I can do to hold on as the stallions race down the mountain. The foothills block our view, then, sweeping around the foot of one, we skid to a stop. Sage steps from cover. She's so small against the dragon's bulk.

"HEY!" Her shout makes my breath catch. We can't reach her in time!

"No," I whisper, blood congealing.

Demyen flinches as Galel wards off the flames. "Almighty."

The beast steps closer, and my heart pounds, but Sage draws one arm back, body twisting as she whips a disk straight for the wicked forehead. It strikes home, sparking amongst the bone and horn.

Useless.

The dragon shakes its head, its roar tearing apart the atmosphere, but lacking power to make my back twinge. Demyen takes my arm, steadying me, mouth agape as he whispers a prayer.

Sage takes another disk, whipping this one underhand. It curves at the last second, burying in about a foot below the first one. She bellows, entire body contracting, pulling her sword, pitching toward the beast. Her legs pump and I slump against Haseleph.

The dragon shudders, its long serpentine neck coiling. The disks are flashing! Electricity bolts between them and smoke rises from the creature's head, mixing with flames that belch in random bursts from its mouth.

Sage is there, striking double-handed at its rear leg, sword biting into the wound I left.

"Can she do that?" Demyen whispers.

The dragon flips over, driving its head into the dirt, clawing at the disks, which arc again and again with blue bolts. Sage leaps out of reach of the flailing limbs and tail as the beast contorts, mouth agape, eyes dulling as electricity streaks through its brain.

"She just did," I say as it drags itself across the valley. Demyen spurs the bay and we resume our crazed pace. We gallop up to her and Galel in the destroyed meadow.

Sage turns with one hand over her heart, relief plain. "You're alright! Where did you get horses? They're amazing."

I waste no time dismounting, then stare at her with too many thoughts to form words. "How… how?"

She rubs Haseleph's wide forehead, and he shuts his eyes and leans into it. "Victory is a law. I like laws. They're logical, and safe."

A high-pitched laugh escapes me and the horses bolt away. She scowls, fingering the leather at her wrists. She snatches a disk, turning to whip it at a tree with its top already sheared off. It bites the wood with a low thud.

Another follows it, burning in close to the first. The disks glow, and we leap back as a sizzle of electricity sparks, joining between them and exploding into a lightning bolt. The power jumps again and the tree groans, falling in slow motion. It crashes to the ground, and the tremor rises through my legs.

"That's neat," she says.

"Neat," I echo, eyes wide. She looks down, frowning, then her bright brown eyes find mine.

"What if I hadn't thrown the second one?" she whispers. "If I hadn't *persisted*. I'd be dead. One couldn't stop him."

I nod, turning to the meadow where mounds of dirt and broken trees prove it happened. Demyen grunts, scowling at my legs.

I look down where green haze is pooling at my feet. Sage steps closer, surveying the damage, sealing it inside. Her blazing eyes find mine, standing in her own pool of green. "It's all true, Jacob Carter, every Word is true."

One flinch of my body is enough to lie still.

Sage groans beside me. "Ow."

Looking down at her brings a grimace, but she's the most beautiful thing on earth, nestled beside me. In the quiet moments where the worlds still mix, one consuming desire fills me. "I want that 'well done,' Sage."

Her dark brown eyes pool. "Me too. No matter the cost."

Laying here, breathing is an accomplishment, but my mind runs over all that's happened. I can't see the future slowing down.

"You and me, Jacob, we'll do it together."

I wish it could be.

A voice is murmuring in a German lilt, slipping through the door. "The Lord is my shepherd. I shall fear no evil…"

The old woman's blessing seeps in, easing my cramped muscles and tender chest. How long we lay there, listening to her read, solidifying, and gaining strength from the words, I can't tell.

"I've *got* to use the restroom," Sage murmurs, easing up, every motion slow. The burn on her shoulder makes me wonder if it came from the spirit, or here.

When she opens the door, the old woman turns. An untouched tray of food lies beside her on the floor. She looks up at Sage, a warm smile lighting her face.

"Danka," Sage murmurs.

I stay flat, replaying all that's happened, pushing down the cortisol spike, and forcing my mind to handle the details without clouding up. The forest outside the small window is quiet and undisturbed. They must've collected Tex, but we'll need to move soon. If Ash and Sutton survived, they'll be searching for us.

Sage returns, hovering over me. *It's time.* Sitting up makes stars that don't exist swirl.

"Where will we go?" she asks, taking my elbow.

For a moment, all concentration goes to breathing.

"You go further in," the woman answers, leaning against the doorway. "The mountain shields you."

It's illogical to stay so close to Ground Zero, but her words settle inside with peace.

"The horses know the way," she adds, with a confident nod. "But first, you eat."

Standing is a battle I win by determination alone, but each breath comes easier as the swelling resettles. My chest is so heavy, every muscle hidden under dark bruising. I turn the thoughts like a twenty-ton ship, setting them in a new way. *Surely, He bore my pain.*

The heavy Swiss bread and golden butter lend immediate energy, and the old woman smiles, watching us eat. I stand, exhaustion tugging at me. She steps close, takes one of my hands and presses a small worn Bible into it. She stays there, both hands clasped over mine, the Word in between, praying in German.

It sends shivers of life up my arm so similar to the spirit's water that I close my eyes and focus on it, willing my body to receive.

When we step outside, the blond boy holds the bridles of two sleek horses. I frown, toes throbbing.

"Oh, they're beautiful!" Sage is there, caressing the black one's nose.

Sven's eyes light up. "I keep them hidden from the New World Order. They can't take what they can't find."

Sage smiles at him, but all I see is Artan. This boy is in danger, too, because of us.

"We should go, now," my voice rasps, still burned from the pit. I turn to the woman, her slight form strangely comforting. "Thank you."

Sage agrees, taking the reins from the boy. It takes a long time to convince my body to swing aboard. I groan, settling in the saddle, glancing at Sage. "You know how to work these things?"

She laughs, stroking the horse's neck. "You rode the last one just fine."

I grunt, and at some invisible signal, her mount turns into the forest; mine follows hers of its own accord. I watch its ears for any sign of angry flattening. She twists in the saddle, grimacing at the motion, jealousy shining in her eyes. "How did you get to ride a Watcher's horse, anyway?"

"There was mutual dissatisfaction with the situation." This horse's easy gait is loosening my tension as we cut up a faint trail.

Sage gives the horse its head, and it climbs with confidence, turning onto smaller paths at every split. The mountain's piercing beauty grows as we continue into its embrace, but it's sad not to taste the warm pine nor hear its low hum.

A small meadow opens before us and the horses whinny, calling to two more in a wooden paddock, their coats lit with the golden sunset. A tiny hut perches near the clearing, its roof made of living grass that sticks up everywhere, a decent shield from satellite images.

We dismount, and movement is easier after the ride. Sage unsaddles the horses as I step inside. A small pile of wood sits next to a brick chimney; two low pallets line the walls. The air grows cooler by the moment and shivering is a thought I can't abide.

I ease down, and the simple task of starting a fire brings a strong satisfaction, like when I was a boy alone in the woods, but I keep it small, so the smoke will dissipate faster, only risking it because so many mountain dwellings do the same. Flames are leaping when Sage steps in, and all my senses tune to her. She settles close, staring at the blaze that casts a copper glow on her skin.

"Fire… what is it?" She pokes the wood with a stick, sending a flurry of bright embers into the stone chimney. Watching her is way too enjoyable, so I turn to the poke the embers with a stick.

"It's the visible force of combustion, a chemical reaction resulting in massive releases of energy as heat, sound, and light. Sounds sort of familiar, doesn't it?" A smile grows on my face, my body relaxing in the warmth. "You're welcome for the answer."

She snorts, rolling her eyes. "That's the *result*, but what's the *cause?* Look at it… like a living thing."

We watch the light dance and crackle, the worlds mixing. It's something untouchable that could kill me. While fire's effects are measurable, the flames themselves remain uncapturable.

"It's spiritual," she whispers, making goosebumps race across my arms. "A crossover between worlds with a spiritual beginning and a physical outcome, like a description of faith."

Night falls, framing the leaping light. We sit together, feeding on the precious words from the worn Bible. Time is irrelevant as we absorb the life inside them. Then, in the quiet, feeling my way through it, I tell her what happened in the pit. One tear traces a path down the curve of her cheek as we stare at the firelight, the darkness surrounding us. I thumb to the book of Revelation and read the last chapter, seeing it inside. "We win, in the end."

A rueful smile turns one side of her mouth. "Seems a long way off."

"It's the long road that's worth traveling."

Exhaustion won't be denied any longer and I grimace, settling on a crude bed. It seems a single moment passes before the half-light of dawn punctures the dark. Sage rolls toward me in sleep, her face peaceful, and my gaze wanders over the curve of her hips.

She defies all my well-constructed goals, the careful step-by-step focus that's pulled me through battle. Thoughts of her are far from controllable, refusing to be locked down. It's dangerous ground, as the more I love her, the more I'll lose when she reaches safety.

Muscles cramping, I rise, silent and needing fresh air. The view of the mountains is stunning, with peaks cut against the purple light of dawn. The horses graze, quiet and easy, their earthy scent comforting. I sigh, stepping toward the woods. An Alpine Swift's trilling song fills the air, but there's no color to its music. My boots sink into the soft sand of a creek bed as the sun crests the horizon. The water glides by, silent, and making my skin tingle.

The first rays of sunlight pierce through the tree trunks in shafts of gold that ignite the water in thin strips of brilliance. Steam swirls up from the flow, merging with the light. The breeze makes it curl, minute twisters that evaporate into another state. Mesmerized, I study the snake-like wisps, *seeing the unseen.*

The sharp-edged strips of sunlight border dim shadows that hide the fantastic sight. There, in the darkness, I can't watch the water turning into clouds. One millimeter separates the two—the light and the veil of shadow. The physical covers the intense beauty of the spirit that way, but it's still right here, all around me.

Slight motion behind makes me tense, senses on fire, but Sage's light tread is familiar. The heightened sense doesn't diminish as she scrambles down beside me, rubbing her leg with a grimace. A bar of sunlight transforms her hair into pure gold. The urge to hold her is overwhelming, so I press my arm against my side.

She studies the stream as I tuck this moment deep inside, where I can visit it later, when the tribulation haunts the world. Her lips tense, one corner of her mouth turning up as she runs her fingers through the steam. "Same as the flames."

Her whispered conclusion to my thoughts catches in my throat. We're the only two people on the planet who get it. There's so much that binds us together, and so many reasons we have to be apart. She reaches for my hand, and the touch kindles as her fingers entwine with mine, slim and fine against my calloused strength.

My heart slams. She's never touched me like this, on purpose and personal. It's like walking on ice, knowing she's better off without me, yet needing her. Standing here, seeing invisible things *together*, is my definition of perfection. But that won't last. It can't.

Her content sigh makes it impossible to pull away. Why not give her this moment? We wander toward the hut and find a basket full of vegetables and a jar of broth sitting in the doorway.

"I'm going to make you soup," I say without thinking.

"You cook?"

"I do today." Reaching for the basket produces a groan as muscles refuse the stretch.

"Sounds great, I'm starving," she says, caressing a horse's outstretched nose.

There's a small pot and knife in a cupboard, and the simple motion of chopping brings satisfaction, as if normal life still exists here. The incredible view doesn't hurt either, with the mountain's purple tint pouring through the door.

The horses surround Sage, sniffing her hair, nuzzling her shoulder. Her laugh makes me look up, entranced. The knife slides on the slick layer of an onion, and my thumb pumps blood. With a disgusted sigh, I wrap it, then finish the veggies. By the time Sage steps in, the tantalizing scent of broth fills the tiny room.

"What did you do?" she asks, pointing to my thumb.

"Eh…" I grunt, still sliding on the slippery emotions surrounding her.

"So, you can dodge bullets and survive destroying advanced scientific facilities, but you cut yourself making soup?" She leans over the pot, stirring it with one delicate brow arching.

My eyes narrow and I'm slipping further. "It was your fault."

Both her brows rise, and a smile plays on her mouth. "Oh really? How is that possible?"

"You distracted me."

She freezes, happy gaze locked on mine, telling me one thing for sure—I shouldn't have said it. My pulse spikes at her warm grin. "Well, I'd better take care of it then, and your fifty other wounds."

She rummages in the basket, pulling out thin strips of cloth and finding a small jar of fragrant salve wrapped inside. Pulling off my shirt uses far too many painful motions. I poke my chest with a frown. "I'm fat."

Her laugh fills the room and my soul. "Not for long. These injuries are already sixty percent better. It would take a normal person weeks to recover, but the swelling is going down by the minute. You can't beat that K-60."

I shrug and regret the motion. "It's faith-filled words that make it work."

She's behind me, dabbing on salve, and her finger runs along my shoulder, tracing the old lion scars. "Remember when you got these? I was so far past okay. You were on the table, unconscious, spewing blood from wounds that appeared with no cause," she sighs. "Remember how you howled, touching those scars after you woke up?"

"Yeah, must've sounded crazy, sorry." I reach across my chest, my traitorous hand covering hers. "You're trembling."

"The lion almost killed you."

"You should've seen how close I was to killing him."

"Ugh!" she laughs, then grows thoughtful. "I didn't get it then. It wasn't the *scars* you were excited about, it was the *victory.* It wasn't the *fight*, it was the *finish.* It wasn't the *facts,* it was the *truth.* "

I nod, with her hand under mine, and the day stretches long, eating soup, resting up, enjoying the light. It's so long, in fact, that the swelling is almost gone and I'm feeling loose and supple as evening inches closer.

"Does... does it seem like this day went on forever to you?" she asks.

"Yeah, it did. We needed it to."

She nods, brow pinched. "That's what I asked Him for. Time for you to heal."

"You're always watching out for me, aren't you?" Soon, I'll do the same by ensuring she makes it to the hiding place.

She fingers my shirt, hesitant. "Remember the first time I saw you?"

"Across the deck on the *Engage*."

Her lips tilt at my immediate answer. "Right then, I knew…"

"Knew what?"

Her soft brown eyes flick to mine. "That we…"

I hold my breath, but all the horses' heads come up, looking in one direction. In a flash, I pull Sage out of the cabin and into the far woods. We slip under its shelter like shadows, turning to watch. The black horse knickers as the boy slips into the meadow. He turns, watching the trail behind him for many minutes, so long that the horses return to grazing.

"He's good," I whisper as the boy turns to the hut, searching for us. What *did* she know? I push it down, stepping forward. Relief shows on Sven's face.

"My Oma says you must go, men are coming. She is sorry for rushing you."

"You've seen them?" Distance, speed, and intel fill my mind, along with a shot of adrenaline.

He hesitates. "She…" he squints, "she sees it in the future."

I nod, letting out a breath, not doubting the warning. His nose wrinkles as he stares at my neck. "What happened to your bruises?"

I pat my chest. "Had plenty of time to heal up."

He cocks his head. "Overnight?"

Sage and I glance at each other, and she smiles.

I turn to the boy and set a hand on his shoulder. "Hide the horses and stay out of sight."

He nods. "I know this mountain. They won't find me." He holds out a small cloth bag with the outline of a pistol showing. "I found these by the lake."

Sage shifts, scowling at the trees. "We should go, now."

"Wait!" The boy takes a phone from his back pocket with tape over all the cameras. We watch as the screen shows the N.W.O. flag, switching to clips of rioting crowds, people shouting, and officers pushing back. The narrator's voice is silky smooth and sickening. "Consistent unrest and violence from those in the Christian sect will not be ignored."

Sage gasps, gripping my hand.

"The Collective has issued a warning to all religious activists; gatherings of any type are prohibited. Punishment for disobedience will be permanent." Then the screen flicks, the news rolling along as if everything is normal. "The Collective will celebrate the release of its new global currency this week at Château de Chillon."

Sage's fingers dig into my arm, but a harsh sigh escapes me. The Collective must go down.

"Ready for another op? Chillon castle is only six miles from here, and I think we should pay them a visit."

"Jacob, we need to get to safety."

"Playing it safe is like dying slow, Sage. I'm not wired that way."

Her mouth falls open, but I turn to the boy. "Pitch that phone over a cliff, far from here. Be a shadow of the mountain."

"There's one more thing," the boy says with a nod. "Take this. My Oma says you'll need it, and it will be useless next week when cash is outlawed." He hands me a few folded bills.

"Thank you."

He nods as we slip toward the woods, my thoughts heavy. What chance will believers have under the Collective's hand?

Two days later, I crouch on the shore of Lake Geneva, a half mile from Château de Chillon. Moonlight reflects off moderate waves as I check my gear. A tiny corner store had everything—one of the few that took cash. I tuck the items into Ziploc bags: soft bulb syringe, a can of clear spray paint and a roll of duct tape.

Their "celebration" at the ancient castle proves that their grip on the world is a chokehold. Everything is traceable, with perks given only to those who score high in complete obedience. Sighing, I seal the pistol and taser into three layers of bags, longing for a dry bag.

"You got the syringe loaded with powder?" I turn to Sage, who's crouched at the water's edge.

"Yeah... beware, world! Jacob Carter has baby powder *and* duct tape."

I laugh, but her chin is tight as I wrap the supplies and tuck them into a pack.

"I'll be back in an hour."

She bites her lip, dipping her fingers in the inky lake. "It's so cold."

"A balmy sixty degrees is like bathwater. It'll bring back good memories." I shoulder into the backpack and slide into Lake Geneva. This is my forte, covert water entry. It's homey, the dark water and the dangerous path.

My silent strokes aim for the stone castle's rocky foot, nestled on an outcropping a quarter mile out. It's one of the oldest in the world and the stone construction is impressive. The cool water loosens my muscles and the jagged rocks of Chillon's base draw closer. Twenty yards out, I tread water and pre-breathe, loading every cell with oxygen.

Focus builds as I dive, holding a northeast line five feet below the dark surface, and long before I need a breath, my stroke grazes algae-covered rock. Tilting my head, I ease one eye to the surface. Moonlight glints off the casing of PIR security cameras that monitor the castle base. The twin devices scan the castle itself, since the lake's unruly waves would cause too much confusion.

Adjusting my position, I slide from the water, staying against the rocks. I freeze against the sheer cliff face as lights bounce from a third-story window where interior guards patrol. Two breaths after their light blinks out, I pull the syringe and acrylic paint from my bag.

From the side, I mist the camera lens with clear acrylic, then puff a fine layer of powder down onto the wet sensor with the bulb syringe. I repeat the procedure until a thick film of powder coats the sensor, mimicking heavy fog. I pack up and swim past the far sensor. Soon it's shrouded as well, and I crawl between them to the castle wall. Metal grates block off small, deep-set stone windows.

The holes in the grate are just large enough to jam a fist through, but it takes a considerable amount of effort to get the pistol through.

I tape it to the inside wall, adding a taser as well. I risk a little light, blocking off most of the penlight's beam with my fingers. A cut rock tunnel descends to the wine cellars, far below.

I slip back into the water, leaving Chillon quiet and none the wiser.

I lounge inside a parking garage, using the pillars as cover. A delivery van stops behind Hôtel Des Trois Couronnes, where the parking garage is perfect cover. The driver opens one rear door and disappears inside.

He's alone. In three long strides, I step into the vehicle. It rocks, taking my weight, and I spin the man around. The van is full of fresh pressed uniforms. I chop his throat, reaching back to shut the door. He clutches his neck, eyes bulging, hitting the floor. I let him gasp as I relieve him of his button-down uniform, then force him over, wrapping his wrists with duct tape behind his back.

He's getting enough air to make noise as I tape his ankles, so another strip covers his mouth. His shirt fits me tight, and the risk of ripping the chest buttons out is high.

His back pocket shows the outline of a wallet, and I study the IDs inside. His name is Luca Nichola, but it's the N.W.O. logo in the top corner that gives me a jolt. It's a video that loops the logo and the smiling faces of the Collective, then an image of the globe. The card must use ether energy, another golden child of the N.W.O., since it doesn't have a charging port.

A second digital display in another corner shows his citizen points. It flashes red for a moment, with a vector image of a van, and the number drops. I guess he's left it running too long. I take a device from the shelf over the uniforms, keeping its camera pointed away. Looks like a big delivery today. I grab uniforms off the rack, putting the stack over my shoulder to shield part of my face.

I squeeze out the door and slam it shut behind me. The device beeps near the hotel's back entrance, then the security light blinks green as I keep the uniforms near the building's cameras. I push through, nodding at a woman with a cleaning cart, and follow my nose toward the crisp scent of bleach, then dump the delivery on top of a rocking set of washers, keeping one male uniform, and backing into an employee restroom.

I emerge as part of housekeeping and snatch an abandoned cleaning cart from the hallway, pushing it into the elevator. Three other employees stand blank-eyed as we go up. I exit behind them, pausing when a voice with a strident accent echoes from the next doorway.

"Everything must be perfect!" A sharp handclap punctuates the demand. "Ensure that tonight's guests have every luxury. Fresh flowers in every room."

I rummage in the cart as two maids pass, their high heels clicking.

"Especially room 445. I want no fewer than five of you waiting for any call from the Stantons."

A rustle of movement means the meeting is over and a trio of maids exits the room, their arms loaded with flowers, and I catch the door before it shuts. A red-faced woman points at me. "Hurry! They forgot these."

I take the armload and set them on my cart. A bellboy leans on the wall, looking at a phone. He's got a set of key cards clipped to his pocket, dangling like ripe fruit. I swerve the cart on passing him, one wheel running over his foot. The cart rocks and I fake a stumble, slamming into his ribs.

I apologize in German as he shouts at me. I hurry away, tucking the cards under the flowers and take an elevator to the fourth floor, then knock on 445. "Housekeeping."

"Entrez," a female voice says from inside.

Ready or not, here I come.

I swipe the card, the flowers in my left arm. The suite is large; with at least four rooms branch off the center hub. A slim, middle-aged woman points to the long dining table. There's a vase already full, but I add these to the arrangement, ruining its symmetry. A rustle from a doorway behind reveals the location of another guest.

I round the table, moving fast. Her eyes widen, but she doesn't get time to whimper before my hand is over her mouth and I drag her to the sitting room and tape her mouth. Her wrists are bound when a metallic click behind makes me freeze.

The reflection in a silver urn on the end table reveals a man with a pistol leveled at my back. Everything condenses into one smooth motion. I haul the woman around, keeping her between us, then drive her into her husband. He plays into the motion, swinging the pistol away as I slam him into the doorjamb. I drop the woman and kick the pistol, one knee on Stanton's back as he goes down.

So, Mr. Stanton feels none too safe while attending the opulent Collective gathering.

Soon, they're bound, gagged, and tucked in the closet, and their invitation to the gala at Chillon is velvet-soft under my fingers. His suit is loose around my middle and too tight around the shoulders, but the crisp tie is the most hateful.

"I need a car, now," I say into the intercom.

"Certainly. Come to the lobby, Mr. Stanton."

The posh driver bows as he opens the sedan's door.

"Route de Sonchaux." I give him the destination as I slide in, looking out the window as if he's already late.

The driver's eyes study the rearview, proving he might be more trouble than expected. It doesn't take long to exit the city, cutting into the old-growth forest near Château de Chillon.

"Pull over," I say as we curve up the deserted mountain road.

"Here?" he questions, eyeing the small dirt logging road.

I glare at him in the rearview—a powerful man like Mr. Stanton takes no questions from underlings. The driver drops his gaze and pulls over.

"Wait for me." I step out, adjusting the suit and striding around the bend past a gate that leads into the mountains. Five strides later, with the dirt road empty in both directions, the slick-soled dress shoes slip on the forest loam as I whistle, waiting and sensing. She's there, just beyond in the trees.

A long sigh escapes, watching Sage come to me. She stretches tension from her shoulders as she scans the suit, then pats her tattered clothes with a frown. Soon we're in the car, but the driver's eyes flick toward Sage far too often. He's earned a trip into the van.

"Pull behind the hotel."

"Yes, sir." The hard edge in his voice makes me certain he'll file a report on my strange requests in order to earn bonus citizen points.

"My company sent out an alert on that vehicle." I point to the uniform van still parked outside the hotel as our car stops next to it. "Go see if anyone is inside."

The driver balks, then reaches for his phone. I clap my hands. Mr. Stanton waits for no one. "Now!"

Sage glances at me, covering a smile. The driver shakes his head but gets out, striding to the van.

"Follow me in ten seconds," I say, slipping out. The driver peers into the back and sees the delivery guy tied up, but I'm already shoving him inside. He puts up a pretty good fight as I leap in and shut the door, the van still rocking when Sage comes in. The driver's eyes spit fire as he is bound and gagged next to the other man.

"Busy place," she says.

It takes a few tries to find a uniform in her size. Should've thought of leaving one of the hotel's for her before.

"Want to work for Saffron Catering?"

"Taste-testing sounds good."

Both fugitives watch us wide-eyed from the floor as I slide into the driver's seat and tuck the van into a dark corner space in the garage. Soon, we've got the valet car backed in its row as well.

"Oh, no," Sage whispers.

Two other valets hurry our way, their faces horrified as we exit the vehicle.

"Mr. Stanton! Where is your driver?" The man's face is pale as I get out of the driver's seat.

I flap my arms in disgust. "He's gone! I had to drive myself back! File a complaint *now.*"

I turn to Sage, covering a half grin.

Later that evening, I step out of the dressing room in 445 and loosen the bowtie a little. The suit could fit better, but it will do.

The look Sage gives me starts a slow burn inside. She's in an elegant black dress that's tight in all the right places. She licks her lips as she approaches, stopping with inches between us. Watching her in the soft light is like heaven.

"You're beautiful."

She looks down, a pretty flush on her cheeks as she fingers my lapel. Her warm brown eyes shine as she traces my jaw. "You're the soul of my soul, Jacob Carter."

I lean my forehead against hers, breathing her scent, memorizing how she feels in my arms, knowing I should step back.

"And you look superb in a tux," she whispers against my neck.

The future pierces me, but I force a smile. "Sadly, its rightful owner is locked in a closet. How many more will end up like that before morning?"

"There's no telling. This time you'll have a gun *and* a taser."

My heart gets two tons heavier as I step back. "We'd better hurry. The Stantons can't be late."

She sighs, taking a set of long gloves from the table, checking the chip glued to the back of her hand before putting them on.

"Let me see yours." She inspects the back of my hand, where we'd gotten creative with Mrs. Stanton's makeup. "Looks pretty good."

"Let's move."

The drive to Chillon is short, and Sage lets out a wavering breath as the valet stops and we get out. The lake glitters around the singular entrance to the castle, a narrow walkway leading to the bulwarks. *A fatal funnel where the guards hold the high ground.* I push the nerves away as we join the crowd gathering at the security checkpoint. She takes "our" invitation from a small purse.

Something glitters on the ground, but the milling crowd of high-class attendees obscure it. It flashes in the soft light, making my breath catch.

"Do you see that?" I whisper into Sage's hair.

Her eyes dart side to side, fingers like steel on my arm. "What?"

"Your path? Can you see it?" My breath comes hard as the golden line glimmers. *Here? In the physical?* She lays one hand on her stomach, searching for haze at my feet.

"No, I'm not..." my voice catches, "jumping. Can you see yours?"

She searches the ground. "No."

I squint, senses on fire. There are four stations of guards admitting people into the castle, but the spirit's thread winds over the cobblestones toward the set on the far right.

Taking Sage's elbow and easing through the crush of people, I'm soon solid on my path, which sends a note of exhilaration up my spine. One more blink and it's gone.

"What does it mean that you can see it?" She's clutching the purse, pressed against my side.

"It means we're right where we're supposed to be." The tension drains away as I say it.

The guards motion us forward through the metal detector. Sage hands over the invite and they scan our hands, then smile. "Welcome to the gala. Enjoy the evening, Mr. and Mrs. Stanton."

Nice that these two guards trust the chip so much, they skipped scanning the photo ID. We stride into the lion's den, Sage's hand laid on my arm as if we belong there. The great room teems with the N.W.O.'s elite. An elevated dais at the far end holds the ten Collective members who rule the world. Such a small group to decide who should live or die, who should eat, or have toilet paper, and who should go lacking.

A woman works the crowd. She's gorgeous, but the low-cut dress reveals a bit too much. She knows everyone's name, from guests to servers. We'd best keep our distance from that one.

Sage's fingers bite into my arm, with her gaze locked on the dais, breath coming faster. I guide her into a quiet corner.

"What is it?" I ask, shielding her from the crowd.

"I… two…" Her brows knit as she stares at my chest. "I knew I recognized them!"

"Who?" I ask, holding her arms, senses straining.

"Two of the Collective! *They're dead.* Brooks and I were in the morgue at Cyclone…. Two of them had toe tags. He collected something from their cerebra, but it's hard to recall since I was jumping."

"You jumped at Cyclone?" I lean closer, voice gruff.

She nods, too fast. "That's why I didn't remember until now."

I turn, scanning. "There are ten living people up there, Sage."

"That's a problem."

"One with a hundred possibilities. They could be doubles on stage or in the morgue."

A server steps close with a smile, offering a plate of hors d'oeuvres, but I wave her off, pulse jumping. Ash is across the room, his arm cradled in a sling. Sage sucks in another breath, turning from him.

"There's a familiar face," I say, watching as he strides onto the dais to greet the Collective like old friends. "We need to gather our *items.*"

A hallway winds into a narrow wooden stairway leading down to a wine cellar. Stone pillars branch into multiple arches in the vaulted ceiling of the ancient room below the castle; wooden barrels of wine line one wall.

"You know, this used to be a prison," a woman in a sequined dress says, sipping wine as she nudges her escort.

Sage shivers. The idea is chilling; there's only a single exit, so every second here is a risk, but weapons are priority one.

"We'll need a distraction," I murmur.

"Oh, no."

"Come on, it'll be fun."

"Is this the same sort of *fun* like in the water tunnel?" She shakes her head as we stop next to a tall stack of barrels. Hands behind my back, I locate the plug in the middle barrel, but working it loose takes longer than I like. It wiggles, and my fingertips grow damp. We stride away, arm in arm, toward the third window from the end. Seconds pass as the milling crowd stops at elegant tables, each offering an exotic wine. A cry rises behind us, and I nod, pushing forward. More voices join the first as the scent of wine fills the cellar.

Near the narrow window opening, I glance over my shoulder, where an expanding puddle of wine catches all attention. I shimmy up the long stone tube leading to the grate-covered window, contorting in the space, brushing through spiderwebs. A solid feeling fills me as soon as my hand closes over the pistol. I snatch the taser, then slide down. Sage brushes my tux, smoothing it over the weapons as the crowd backs away, keeping their shoes clean.

"I bet Ash is lonely," I say, taking her arm.

Sage lets out a tight sigh. "I can't believe we're doing this."

"You're stunning in that dress, by the way." My voice is husky, knowing the distraction will keep her from the tight grip of fear. Her eyes flick to mine, and her chin comes up a little.

We skirt the crowd as music starts, and we clip up the stairs, then stop inside the great hall. Everything looks perfect, like the world is right, and that's the illusion the Collective loves most. Ash strides toward a far exit, so we turn through a doorway on the same side.

The hall is lit with electric torches that look medieval, and I pull Sage into an alcove as the woman steps out just ahead. She scans the hall, then strides toward Ash, her hips swinging as her stilettos click along.

A sour flavor in the air tells me to pay attention. "Let's see what she's up to."

At the T, we peer around to find Ash stepping from a restroom door, smoothing his tux and adjusting the sling.

The woman is between Ash and us, but she averts her face and slips behind a potted plant. Ash sniffs, adjusting his bow tie, his heavy brow lowered. After another careful scan, he moves to a door covered in ornate carvings as the woman watches through the foliage.

"Something's not right about this," Sage murmurs, echoing my own senses.

Ash scans through the doorway. A few seconds later, the woman does as well.

Sage shies from the carving of a gargoyle that cringes at us, its fangs wreathing a long, lolling tongue. Everything would feel better if I knew the specs on the interior of this room.

"I see it!" She points to the floor.

"Your path?"

A nod is all I need. "Mr. Stanton" scans in, and I peer through the slim opening. The large room is empty. Frowning, I risk pulling the door open further. Grotesque statues line the walls, adding sharp memories of the pit to my pulsing thoughts.

No one is inside, and there are no exits. "You still see it?"

Sage nods, pointing inside, but whispering, "I don't want to go in there."

The air is heavy inside the room, and the same angled tubes rise to iron-grated windows, high above. Sage stays a step behind as I draw the pistol, stalking forward.

Something crashes beyond the far wall and we freeze. I study the wide fireplace, but it's solid rock. Another crash makes Sage gasp.

"Jacob." She points to the wall past a gargoyle statue far larger than me. "My path leads into that window."

I nod, hurrying her forward with the pistol level. "Get in."

She grunts, the dress and heels hampering her. I pick her up and toss her into the tube as my skin pricks. She slides down, arms out to slow her descent. I block her with one forearm and leap in, straining to pull us both further up.

A rush of air fills the narrow tunnel; something's changed in the room. We go still, desperate not to slip, listening hard. The soft tread of heels… I lean forward, cramped, glimpsing the woman's legs as she strides from the room.

The main door sighs shut and I slide out of the window, catching Sage as she searches the floor. "It's gone."

Pistol leading, I step to the corner the woman appeared from. My gaze locks on a familiar symbol carved into the stone—an eye overlaid with a triangle. I push it with my knuckles.

Air flows as the panel slides open. I clear the room, the familiar search pattern revealing Ash sprawled on the floor, the sling ripped away.

Sage gasps, moving to kneel at his side, pressing two fingers against his neck. She shakes her head, stepping back in revulsion.

I step to his side, an old enemy, an evil force, now so powerless. Who would want him dead?

Sage points to a puddle under his head. I roll him, finding a narrow incision in his skull.

"Just like at Cyclone," Sage says. "What is going on?"

I let Ash down, studying the bruises over his mouth and nose. "How did a woman her size strangle him so fast?"

"There are no other visible injuries. She made the incision after he died, or there'd be a lot more blood." Sage swallows hard, staring at the door.

"We need to track her *now.*"

Back in the grand hall, the woman is smiling and shaking hands. *If only they knew.* I nod to the far exit as she works her way across the room in that direction. Sage and I are in the hallway when she breezes through a door, snapping at an employee. He cowers with a reverent tone. "Yes, Mrs. Chen?"

"Guests are sweating. Turn the air down."

She strides through another doorway, and we follow until an employee stops us near the kitchens.

"Can I help you, sir?"

"We have a meeting with Mrs. Chen."

Her brows go up as she extends one arm. "Ah, have a good evening, sir."

I push open the stainless-steel kitchen door in time to see her slip through the far exit. White-coated cooks stare as we hustle past.

"There," Sage says as we enter another hall. A door clicks shut and I hand Sage the pistol, pulling out the taser as we step into the room. It's an opulent office space with an executive desk in the center, and Chen is leaning over a laptop.

Double-fisting the taser, I center it on her chest. "Busy evening, huh?"

Her sculpted face remains expressionless as she turns, launching a full-out attack in the blink of an eye. Chen ducks when I pop off the first two taser leads, twisting down, but the first prong catches her in the eye, and the other bites her neck.

She'll lose that eye, but she twitches, head slamming hard to one side, remaining crouched instead of seizing. Sweat breaks out as she stands and pulls the leads out with a disturbing calm. Sage cries out. Chen's eye is a dark hole with a wisp of smoke leaving a hot electric scent.

Her next leap is lightning fast, one leg sweeping at my stomach. The taser flings away as I grab her ankle and time slows down, condensing into one long moment. There are no tendons beneath her supple skin. Everything slams together: her electronic eye and the odd structure of her leg.

Her fist rockets into my jaw with a force far greater than Tex could deliver. Her remaining eye twitches as she glares at me. I lock her ankle down and snatch her neck with the other hand, mind racing. Her neck's not human, either. She's robotic, so a chokehold is useless.

Chen flinches. Sage is on the far side, unloading all twelve remaining leads from the taser into Chen's back. She twitches , and I jam a knuckle into her good eye, cringing at the dirty move. Then again, a robot has no rights, but the foreign sensation of glass crushing under my knuckle is sickening.

Chen goes still, adjusting to the blindness. She strikes out, but I duck it, rolling to come up behind her and sweep the leads off her skin and slam her against the wall. She pushes off with the force of a car, but an indent in the small of her back gives me a plan. We skitter across the floor, and my fist closes on an iron poker next to a fireplace. I push Sage to safety, taking two hammer blows, then grip Chen around the waist, skin crawling at her disturbing sensual form.

Twisting out of her classic jujitsu move, I spin-kick her back. Her skin tears, dripping an odd blueish substance and revealing a panel. I drive the poker into the spot. She shudders, standing at attention, the ruined black holes marring her face.

Sage crouches, her chest heaving. I place a finger to my lips, nodding to the door. Sage locks it and I move behind the bot, staring at the fantastic array of AI guts in her back. Sage steps to my side, covering her mouth. My finger runs over black boxes, landing on one marked *Main.* I push it, and its top corner tilts out.

"Certified technicians should remove circuit boards in a clean room. Risk of neuromorphic failure 95%." Chen's sultry voice is devoid of emotion as I pull the board loose. She slumps, head hanging, unresponsive.

The circuit board is black, about a half-inch thick with blue lights that race through a mass of wet, living matter sealed within glass.

"Neurons and glial cells?" Sage gasps. "Human brain cells," Sage says, her eyes distant. "That's what Brooks was after at Cyclone—the Collective's neurons, but they were already removed," her gaze snaps to mine. "Chen made the same incision in Ash."

Sage hurries to a small purse next to the laptop and unzips it, pulling out a stainless-steel syringe with a glass tube full of gray matter.

"There's no way to tell who's human, and who isn't," I murmur, fingering the board still flashing in my hand. I gaze into Chen's perfect face with the horrifying holes. "They're cyborgs."

Sage crosses her arms, shivering. "They outlawed robots that look like humans, what, thirty years ago? So no one would suspect."

"What if the entire Collective are cyborgs?" The slow thought slams into my gut. "Who's controlling them?"

Sage rubs her brow. "This is worse than Ash and Sutton put together."

"Way worse," I agree. "Someone's been planning this for decades. Tactical maneuvers executed for world dominion. Why would Chen kill Ash and extract cells unless they have a robot lined up for him as well?"

Sage's face goes pale. "What's our plan, Jacob?"

"Set the boat on fire, Sage. See who jumps ship. Without proper cooling, there's no chance that this… sample will survive." I nod, thoughts flying. "Ash failed them at Cyclone, and this was the price he paid."

"Why would cyborgs want to bring Lucifer here?" Sage asks, her face pale. "Why not put him in a body like this, a robotic one?"

My thoughts swirl around Genesis, seeing Lucifer's blazing lust as he strode toward the shell. "He'd never settle for that. Only a flesh and blood body will do for the anti-Christ. He always has. We've only slowed them down by destroying the pit. Whatever goal they're driving for is far larger than I imagined. We're missing something."

"We're missing lots of things," she says, staring at the syringe. "They're taking cells from the cerebellum, one of the major players in memory. It's possible that these cyborgs possess the memories of the person they… replace. Or maybe their soul remains, too?"

"That's a question to ask in the spirit, where all the answers are." A harsh breath escapes as I take the syringe and crack the glass against the desk's mahogany edge. It splinters, and I toss it away. "We need to move."

I pull the other boards from Chen, stuffing them in my inner coat pocket. As Sage walks past the desk, her face goes pale. *"Oh."*

She clicks on a small square of closed-circuit security cameras. The expanded view reveals a figure writhing on an ornate Chinese carpet. It's Sutton, movements erratic, her evening dress twisting around her legs as she claws at the carpet.

"She's here, Jacob, in the castle."

Stone walls and a magnificent suit of armor in the corner surround Sutton. I click the picture, accessing a map of the castle. "She's two flights higher. We better hurry."

I scoop up the laptop, and we move past the busy kitchens, locating the stone stairway. A heavy door at the next level is locked.

Entering the tight confines of the stairwell goes against every ounce of training, but I force down the stress. The door has a small keypad that I run my fingers over. They couldn't run wires through the solid stone.

"Stand back."

I reach for the taser. This type of lock uses a small electrical current to open. The right code produces the current, but so can I. Ripping off two rubber number buttons, I jam two taser leads into the guts beneath and pull the trigger.

The leads buck off the box, smoking, but the handle turns. We enter a hushed hallway with a musty scent in the stale air. I lead with the pistol. The next person we meet is going down. The eerie silence makes Sage inch closer. On the next level, multiple doorways fill a long hall.

"Second left."

Sage nods, her hand on the wrought-iron knob. She flings it open and I burst through, sweeping the room. There's only Sutton, twitching on the floor, an awful stench filling the room as her eyes bulge.

Sage puts one hand over her nose. "She smells like Rivera."

Her skin reddens, blistering in the furnace heat her body is building. Tears shimmer over Sage's fingers. "The flames, Jacob. She sees them."

Dread fills the room as Sutton jerks hard, gasping, while a patch of black skin appears on her neck, right next to an angry red welt. Sage drops to her knees, taking Sutton's hand. Her agonized eyes flicker, focusing on Sage's face.

"You're *all* here…" the words gurgle from her ruined lungs.

Sage glances at me, then focuses on Sutton. "Listen to me, Yeshua is your only hope. Cry out to Him, Sutton!"

I kneel at her other side. "Who did this to you?"

She twists, attempting to crawl away, her legs unresponsive. "Ash…" she gurgles. Sage and I share a sharp glance, but she continues, words a rasping groan. "He'll… rule the world…. you can't stop him. He'll save me…."

She's delirious, but I need info. I flip her over, her skin burning against my fingers.

"Sutton! Who injected you with K-60?"

She shakes her head, terror in her eyes as she focuses somewhere beyond us. "No, get away!"

"It's the Lions. Take Yeshua as Lord, Sutton. Do it now!" Sage cries.

I push down the memories of Sage there, in the abyss, unable to wish that on anyone. Sutton clenches her eyes. When they snap open, they lock on mine, dull and dark. She gasps, clinging to life. "You can't beat him… Ash is… he's…"

"Ash is dead."

She crumples in agony, then she hisses, "Liar."

"Sage, we're getting nowhere," I whisper.

She takes Sutton's hand. "You don't have time. Sutton, turn now! Yeshua is Lord."

"No!" The name is painful to her, and her eyes glaze over as she gasps, hovering between worlds. She scrambles back, crying out as she looks at her feet. "Get away!"

This is her forever. Every choice she's ever made is solidifying into this moment, this decision. More of her skin blackens as the stench grows. She searches the room as if she's never seen it, pulling Sage closer, choking, "Don't let them… please!"

She's breaking, struggling as her tortured eyes flick to mine, her free hand covering the injection site on her neck.

"Brooks…" Then she sucks in a ragged breath and goes limp, eyes fixing on the ceiling.

Sage turns away, one arm wrapped around herself, a broken sob escaping.

"Brooks?" I say, the name like a sucker-punch that takes my breath. "He's here?"

Sage whips around, eyes wild. "Jacob. All the chess pieces are falling down, and there's only one left standing. *Brooks.*"

From under the desk, Sutton's phone chirps and a notification shows at the top.

Threat level severe. Take all security precautions.

"They found Ash. Or Chen. We get out, *now,*" I say.

An alarm sounds inside the castle, and I move to the window where red strobe lights punctuate the night. The single exit crawls with guards; and further out on the road, blockade vehicles swing into view, converging from both directions.

"This is bad." Sage's eyes are full of dread. "Ash, Sutton, even Chen, they're all puppets." She leans over, looking out the window with me. "Does this mean we're swimming?"

"Yes, ma'am."

She shivers and I wish there was a wetsuit for her. The laptop and phone won't survive the dip we're heading for, but that's just as well. The three-story drop to the jagged rocks below isn't pretty.

"Hurry," I tow Sage by the hand past Sutton's body. "There's a turret on this level."

The musty hallway is clear and we move fast, the pistol ready.

A smaller door at the other end of the hall has no lock. I shoulder it open, the ancient wood giving way with an ominous creak.

Five lopsided wooden stairs tilt as they take my weight. The small round room leads to a single-pane window. I chop it with the butt of the pistol, clearing away the shards.

A heavy thrum rattles the atmosphere. *Helicopters.* With a hiss, I haul my upper half out the window to inspect the sharp angle of the roof, bitter wind cutting through the tux. Sliding back, I crouch, eye-level with Sage.

"The roof is steep. We've got to climb to the east point."

She bends, unstrapping the heels. "We're jumping from the roof?"

"There's a one-and-a-quarter-mile swim after that. Water is sixty degrees." The chopper is growing louder with every heartbeat. "When you hit the surface, the cold will make you want to gasp. Don't."

She cringes. "This didn't work out so well last time."

"I'll climb out and pull you up."

I curl around the window frame, the roof overhang affording no good handholds. By the time we're both teetering on the shingles, the helicopter's lights are visible, far over the lake. Sage is shivering hard as we poise at the edge, the water far below. I point to a long section of dark shore in the distance where no lights shine.

"That's where we're heading."

Hand in hand, we leap out, as long seconds of nothing but air stretch out beneath us.

I stroke onto the rocky shore, branches pricking. Sage's hand is icy as I tow her forward. The water's lit beneath her, a perfect bubble of green light that's attracting hundreds of fish. I haul her out as the energy leaps into me and force a path into the brush. She moans behind me.

I scan the sky through the filtering leaves. Three helicopters still hover over Chillon, it's lit up like a maximum-security prison.

I turn back to Sage. "Ready?"

A wild light flares in her eyes. "Oh, yes."

The jump is smooth, until the end, when my grip on her hand gets slippery.

"Sage!" I call, but the intense speed tears us apart. Still, there's peace inside—she'll be all right. She proved that last time.

I land with a thud, right next to Demyen. He tugs me to my feet, then points in silence, his expression enough to put me on guard. We're at the foot of the mountain whose top is blackened. A profound sense of awe prevents words. The mountain looms, and my heart strains forward. The air grows heavy as we crest the last foothill.

A dead lion lies on the rocks. We study the anomaly in silence. The wounded carcass is an impossibility because lions don't die. My thoughts race, ancient stories welling up along with knowledge. This is Mount Sinai, a holy place where no evil can tread.

The next step is terrifying as I look up at the cloud forming over the singed rock high above. I make sure my heart is clean to avoid the lion's fate.

Together, Demyen and I step forward into the glory. True silence grows inside, empty of myself. Mara's words echo true: "You can receive as much as you will give."

The atmosphere grows heavier until standing becomes impossible. Now, near the top, we fall to our knees, where thick clouds obscure the burned rock. An image forms in the mist. A Man with a crown on his head, but it's His eyes. *Oh, His eyes!* Everything good is there. He spreads His hands, and seven bright stars hover above them.

"Behold, the last oil. It is yours to pour out upon the earth."

The sword-like words strike and I fall to my face. Demyen hits the ground beside me.

"You shall prophesy one thousand two hundred threescore days, clothed in sackcloth. If any man will hurt you, fire will proceed from your mouth to devour your enemies; they must in this manner be killed.

"I give you power to shut Heaven, that it rain not in the days of your prophecy. I give you power over waters to turn them to blood and to smite the earth with plagues as often as you will." His next words pierce me through with a sorrow deeper than the sea. The call, and the cost, are so great, requiring all, both sacred and intense.

"When you finish your testimony, the beast that ascends out of the bottomless pit will make war against you, overcome you, and kill you. Your bodies will lie in the street of the great city for three-and-a-half days. Those who dwell on Earth will rejoice over you, make merry, and send gifts to one another, because of My two prophets who tormented those who dwell on Earth."

Demyen and I fall face-first as my heart breaks. The weight of His command is too great to carry, crushing me inside.

His nail-scarred feet are before us, and His breath of life bathes my neck. The warm flow imbues me with a strength I've never known, filling each cell, allowing me to fulfill the call to its bitter end.

When I open my eyes, Demyen and I alone face the path back to the flatlands. He's different somehow. Intense brilliance shines from his skin, but he's more noble, greater somehow, as well.

He grips my hand. "I'm glad to stand here with you, *brother*, at the end of all things."

"Aye." I dip my head as we embrace, knowing I'll need him. We stride down the path, seeing the future as the darkness gathers to make war with the light.

"I have to protect Sage, and that means she must be far from me," I say.

"She won't go, boy. I've seen the look in her eye toward you, and she's a feisty one."

"Then I'll have to force her." Some part of me kept toying with the thought of staying together, but the way is shut now. Her face is all I see inside, my longing, a burning flame within, but I bite back the hot flush. *She's the one thing I can never have.*

The price eats at me, but I'll never go back from the call, though it closes like a steel door around my heart.

PURSUED

I never expected to be what I need to protect her from.

9
SAGE

I'm in another cave. This one has two long tunnels stretching in opposite directions. Galel appears before me, but his mouth is tense.

"What?" I whisper.

"It's time. You must choose." He sweeps an arm toward the tunnels. My path glitters in *both* of them.

He points to the left. "This way leads to protection, a hiding place to shelter you from the coming trials."

"Jacob won't be there," I say, but it's not a question.

Galel nods. "That's true, but you'll… survive."

I flinch, swallowing hard at his words.

He shifts to the right. "This way is hard, filled with *great* suffering."

Galel's eyes burn with sorrow as he watches me.

I cross my arms. "But I'll be with Jacob if I take the right?"

"For a while, yes."

"A while?"

He nods, face solemn.

"And both ways are the Almighty's will?"

He dips his head. "Aye."

I lift my chin with zero hesitation. "Jacob."

"But…" he sputters, "the way…. It is *very* hard."

"Choose myself over him? *Never.* Whatever the cost to me, *Jacob.* Always and forever, *Jacob.* A million times, *Jacob.*"

Galel's brows arch.

"What? You thought it would be a hard choice?" I dash tears from my face.

"Well…" he shrugs, covering his shock. He squints, now suppressing a smile. "He's a blessed man, to have you at his side. Here." He lofts a round loaf of bread. "Eat this. You'll need the strength."

It's warm in my hands, sent straight from Heaven, and it melts like butter in my mouth.

"We should hurry, if you're sure," Galel says, stepping into the long tunnel on the right. He flexes, making the light leap higher in his skin. I look down the path and set one foot on it, then the next, until I'm sprinting forward, heart and soul committed, energy building as I move.

We run and run. It might be days, since there's only the light Galel exudes, revealing the constant gray of the tunnel. Then, far beyond, a dot of light appears. I fly toward it, faster yet, the bread still fueling me, and break into a narrow meadow at the foot of a mountain. I skid to a halt, scanning, not even out of breath. Jacob and Demyen are there, far off but striding toward us. I laugh, heart leaping at the sight of him.

Galel turns to me. "He won't want you to stay. He loves you too much."

"Well, I'm plenty stubborn. Besides, I've decided." The other way is forever closed, but my confidence wavers; Galel is right. Jacob will be determined to see me safe. I turn, eyeing Galel.

"So…"

He turns to me, folding his arms and narrowing his eyes. "Why am I suddenly uncomfortable?"

"Galel, I'm going to need your help to convince Jacob to let me stay with him."

He sighs, rubbing his forehead. "Anything you could've asked would be easier than that."

I shrug, giving him no way out, then watch Jacob come, his wide shoulders swinging.

"Thank you," I whisper to the Almighty, hands held over my heart. "For the choice."

Green builds before they reach us, but I'll be in his arms there, right where I want to be.

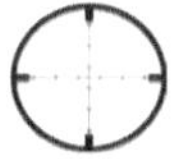

I twitch, branches poking everywhere, cold and soaked, right against Jacob, and wrap my arms around him. Day is dawning and a cold mist snakes over the lake.

His eyes slide open, finding me studying him. He sighs, the broken sound piercing. I lay my hand on his chest, and the words I long to say close off at a checkpoint inside. The right time will come. He studies my face as if memorizing it for the last time.

My fingers smooth his knit brow. "There's hope yet, Jacob."

His sad smile only makes me more determined. I'm staying with him. It's intimidating, planning to beat Jacob Carter, but as the seconds pass and the spirit becomes veiled, the weight eases.

"At least we aren't beaten to a pulp this time," he says, but his shoulders are slumped, his voice hollow.

Sand, algae, and leaves plaster the ruined black dress, and I grunt. "Somehow, you still make the tux look good."

He doesn't respond with lighthearted banter, striding away, but I put my chin in the air, determination rising. I'm staying, and that's final. Soon, we find a deer path and follow it, ducking branches. A mansion sprawls in an emerald yard with a smaller cottage near the woods.

"Looks empty. Stay here while I check it out." Jacob slips like a shadow into the cottage. I crouch, smelling the forest and the fast-warming air as he disappears.

"Eh!" I stifle a cry, slapping my rear end. Something stung me! I'm up, twisting to look, frozen in horror. The red fluff of a dart is far too bright against the black dress.

"No…" I whisper, pulling out a needle with a bright feathered tuft, then crash forward into the brush. Everything's spinning, and my hands don't catch me.

My eyes are full of sand. Swallowing is agony, and every nerve pulses pain into my brain. My hand tremors, covering my eyes to stop the spinning sensation. My free hand slides on silk. With a groan, I force my eyes open. My stomach heaves and I bite back vomit, sitting up on an opulent bed, the gray silk sheets falling away.

I've left a print of sand and dirt on the pristine surface. The marble floor reflects soft lighting that's too much for my watering eyes. I stumble into a luxurious bathroom and lean on the ornate doorframe, staring at a set of clean clothes folded into a perfect square.

The alabaster shower washes away the sick feeling as I finger a minor cut on my shoulder that stings. Where am I? My hands are scrubbing the last of the sand from my hair when everything comes back with a jolt.

Jacob! The cottage!

I scramble from the shower, slamming the door shut, getting dressed with my nerves on fire. Hyperventilating, I stare at myself in the mirror. The clothes are a perfect fit; someone planned for my presence. There are a hundred drugs that could've been in that dart, and there's more where that came from. Getting out is paramount. With a snarl, I force my trembling fingers to the cold knob and pull.

Brooks is standing there, eyes sliding down my figure. The clothes are far too thin a veil.

"Welcome home, Sage."

Vomit hits the back of my throat. I take a step back, shaking my head, paying for it when the room spins.

"Come. I've so much to show you." He reaches out a hand and I bump into the far wall. His face darkens, eyes cold. "I said," he snatches my hand and tugs me through the doorway, "come here."

My heart hammers as he stops beside the main door. A light above it flashes, the door swings open, and he forces me into a long marble hallway lined with statues. Soon we're at the top of a curved stairway where a crystal chandelier casts a million rainbows across the vast atrium below.

"It's beautiful, isn't it?" His lips, so close to my ear, make me shy away. "Not impressed? Well, it's a small taste of what I own."

Legs stiff from the drugs, I stumble as Brooks forces me forward, taking my arm as if we're a couple. I jerk, but he won't release my hand.

He leads me through a labyrinth of hallways until we arrive in a control room. The system comes to life as he steps in. Soft blue light fills a u-shaped desk that's full of security screens monitoring the extensive property.

"He'll come for me," I say, chin in the air.

"Oh, I'm planning on it." His calm makes cortisol spike.

Don't come, Jacob.

He types and screens flash past, ending on a familiar one—the outline of a warrior standing at attention.

Tex.

I stop breathing. Brooks said all technology could be manipulated. Truth crashes in. I backpedal in time, landing on the moment Jacob and I were racing for the *Olympia*'s rail in the pouring rain, and Brooks lowered the gun, letting us go. *Why?*

"Is it all coming together for you now?" He turns, studying me as I ram my spine straighter.

Wait. If he's controlling Tex… then the genocide was Brooks, using him as a lure. *The same lure I am right now.* He's put Jacob where he wants him every time.

"Why, Brooks?" I whisper, the screen with Tex's outline burning into my soul.

"'Brooks,'" he laughs. "That's not my *real* name. Maybe someday I'll tell it to you. The blood of kings runs in my veins."

I scowl at him, ensuring every drop of disdain is visible.

"My family's been ruling continents, banks, and governments for thousands of years, but *I* will be the first to rule the world." The uncanny gleam in his eyes leaves no room for doubt. "We've become… superb… at ruling in complete secrecy. Governments are simple puppets, and the world is a beast I intend to tame.”

“Then why kill Ash?”

He sneers. “Ash was a complete imbecile. If I hadn't gotten Jacob to Cyclone at that exact moment, Ash would've unleashed hell on Earth.”

He's been using us since day one. *Our true enemy.* He knew Jacob was the only one who could stop them in the pit with enough K-60 and determination to force them to fail.

He gives a merciless laugh. “To be honest, I was counting on Jacob killing Sutton right off, but it goes to show: You can't count on anyone.”

“But you're part of the program, trying to give Lucifer a body.”

“Part of? It's my heart and soul, my passion project. My family has gained the world through him, including every bit of technology. It's made us trillions and trillions, and given us power beyond reckoning. But Ash worshiped him; that was his weakness. He thought he'd be Lucifer's pet if he were the one to facilitate his inception. *Fool.* Then he'd have zero control. Do you know what would've happened if I hadn't stepped in?”

Lucifer would've used his brand-new body to kill you. But I dare not let the words out.

“Control is important. Tex was my testing ground,” he says.

A snort of disgust escapes. “I'd say your tech isn't ready yet.”

He slaps me across the face so hard that the room spins. “*Never* speak to me that way.” He glowers at me, terrifying on a subconscious level with that odd gleam in his eye, before turning back to the computers. "Still, Jacob's destroying Cyclone was a terrible setback. One he'll pay for."

"Why bring Lucifer here at all if he's so dangerous?" I ask, wiping my mouth and refusing to cower.

Brooks simmers, studying screens, his jaw clenching. "He has one last piece of knowledge that I need. He won't give it up until he's here. But then, my cyborgs will be perfect, unbeatable, even by him. Complete power at my fingertips." His fists clench. "Jacob will pay for ruining Chen, too. She was a masterpiece. Even though her files are in the cloud, those boards were irreplaceable."

Because you had to steal brain cells to build her. I cross my arms and glare at the back of his head, wondering what sort of relationship they had. A red light flashes on screens further down. Brooks rolls his chair over to it. "Ah, look how far he got before tipping off security."

Ice spreads through my veins. The screen shows Jacob crouched inside the courtyard wall in full battle gear.

"An impressive show, as always." Brooks's fond tone chills me to the core. "But the brightest talent is always bent toward freedom."

He's happy, entering codes before sliding over to the controls for Tex. His complete confidence crushes mine. "Time to let the big boys play."

His singsong words echo as the outline of Tex morphs to a real-time image. The cameras pick up his fresh scars, stretched over uneven muscle on his back. He flexes after standing still for so long, and his wicked eyes are bloodshot. Tex turns toward the doorway, affording me a view of his back. The wounds are healed there, too.

Brooks turns to me. "Impressed? It was you that shot him in the tunnel, wasn't it? You're a very brave woman, and beautiful. The moment I saw your file before Project 157, I knew there was something special about you. Pairing you with Jacob proved it. I could give you the world."

My lip curls in a silent snarl.

"That expression is why I brought you here, so you could watch Jacob die. You'll need the closure before you can move forward in the program. It may take you some time."

His words explode in my brain. I grit my teeth, longing to leap on him, but forcing truth to come instead.

Whosoever would say to this mountain…

That voice within gives me life and a plan. Words protected Jacob in the pit, and they can do it now.

"He'll defeat Tex and come for you."

"Your devotion is moving."

I lock my eyes on his. "Jacob will win. You'll see. I already do."

Tex's screen flashes. His body temp rises a degree as he leans into a sprint, working his way toward Jacob. He must have a direct link to the security cameras. Jacob eases through a side door.

I don't have long.

"The Almighty always gives Jacob all victory through Yeshua."

"Shut up!" His sharp tone makes me brace for another slap.

"The Lord God is his shield and strength. Jehovah *always* causes Jacob to triumph."

Brooks is on me in a heartbeat with one revolting hand over my mouth, clamping both wrists behind my back. I refuse to give him the satisfaction of a whimper. On-screen, Jacob turns as if he hears Tex coming, even though he's two floors away.

"That right there—I would love to know how he does that," Brooks growls in my ear.

I blow a laugh through my nose. It's that still, small voice, the one that knows everything in three worlds and beyond. It's as simple as listening. Something Brooks can never know.

Jacob sprints off-camera, popping up on another. Tex is homing in, seconds are left before they meet. My heartbeat ramps up, breath dragging past Brooks's fingers. Jacob leaps into a narrow alcove, pressing his back against one side and his boots against the other, he shimmies up toward a window, high above, waiting as Tex barrels toward him.

A short rifle is tucked tight to Tex's shoulder. He twists at full speed, spraying the alcove. Jacob leaps out above the pattern, curling in midair. He tucks up, leading with one elbow to hammer Tex in the shoulder. They both go down, and the rifle spins away. In a burst of speed, Jacob's boot connects hard with Tex's ribs. Tex grabs Jacob's ankle, but Jacob uses it, dropping to one knee in a strike to Tex's sternum. He chops at Tex's exposed throat.

"Come on!" Brooks hisses in my ear, dragging me forward, typing with one hand, freeing my mouth.

"He'll win, you'll see."

"Shut up!"

Tex surges up and they grapple, lightning-fast moves blurring together, but Jacob's a half step ahead, as if he's a millisecond in the future.

Tex takes the battering like a machine, rage growing. Jacob's disarming him at a steady rate, weapons flying aside as they battle down the hallway. The cameras switch views as the pair slams into the atrium. Tex roars, rushing forward, head down. Jacob slips from his grip and Tex crashes into a marble statue. It tilts, shattering across the floor.

"That's it," Brooks snarls.

My arms are numb in his iron grip as he reaches for the mouse. A box pops up on Tex's screen. Brooks types *"no parameters."* He hesitates, hovering over the "Accept" button.

"You sure you want to do that?" I ask, looking at his face an inch away. "Ever seen a lion turn on its trainer?"

His eyes flicker, but he opens another box, this one rimmed in red. *Release anthrax 6.9* is at its center. He clicks the first box, accepting the "no parameters" command, but leaving the second open.

Tex twitches, a crazed grin on his face as Jacob's fist rockets into his jaw. The expression grows as Tex doubles his pace, but Jacob's focused and Tex hasn't landed a blow yet. Tex fights like a freight train barreling forward as he takes the beating.

"Getting nervous?" I say, earning another tear in my shoulder.

They crash through double doors, tearing them off their hinges. The cameras struggle to keep up as Jacob drives Tex into an immense kitchen. I imagine the fantastic clang as they sweep a display of utensils to the floor. Jacob's shoulder slams Tex in the gut, driving him into a stainless-steel sink and ripping it from the wall. Water sprays everywhere as they grapple. The momentum forces Jacob to slide on his back across a huge wooden-topped prep area.

There's a knife in Tex's hands! I grimace as he whips it, pegging Jacob's arm, biting through his bicep and penetrating deep into the wood below, pinning him there.

Brooks barks a laugh. "How fitting, on a butcher block."

Tex leaps onto the table, his boot on Jacob's other wrist. The sigh of satisfaction that Brooks breathes on my neck is like a serpent's tongue. It spins in my mind as Tex gloats over Jacob. I moan, fighting back inside, refusing the doubt, seeing victory instead.

It isn't just blood oozing from the long blade buried in Jacob's arm—green haze is also flowing from the wound.

Tex grins. He's saying something, spewing words, but Jacob's eyes are clear, one side of his mouth tipping up. His nose flares as he forces his elbow to move below the knife. Blood gushes as his fingers grip Tex's leg, ignoring the pain.

Jacob's I've-got-you-now grin grows until Brooks swears. "Take him Tex! *Now.*"

But Tex is gloating, leaning closer, enjoying the win. The green spreads, curling around Jacob's arm and up Tex's leg.

"Oh, look, he's finally going to fall limp at the right moment," Brooks says, letting me go, confident.

The haze is still spreading.

"Oh," I breathe, knowing. Brooks's sharp gaze turns to me, but I nod. "Do it, Jacob."

Tex twitches, his expression changing, his bloodshot eyes unfocused, now staring at the wall.

"What's happening?" Brooks types fast with one hand, entering command after command. Tex doesn't respond. His muscles go rigid. Water is dripping from clenched fists. Brooks doesn't know that I've jumped, that Jacob and I jump together.

"You lose," I whisper.

Tex convulses, muscles hammering as the haze surrounds him, and his eyes roll pure white.

"I'm sorry for him, for what he's going to face," I whisper as Tex sinks through the wood.

"NO!" Brooks shouts.

I nod. *It's done.*

They both go limp, Tex, with his legs halfway through the table, slumped to the side.

We stare at the screen, heartbeats like centuries. Tex's screen to the left releases a hair-raising, flatline beep as his vitals fall to zero. Jacob's eyes snap open, and he rolls off the table, his free arm snatching the knife. He's staring straight at the camera, glaring.

"He's coming. *For you,*" I say, straight into Brooks' ear. A sheen of sweat coats his pale upper lip in the dim blue light.

He slams the desk, sending the keyboard skittering. Then he turns to a far screen and mashes a red button. Sirens wail, and Brooks steps back.

"I *never* lose," he says, turning to sprint for a narrow doorway.

Arm limp, I bend over the screens, swallowing hard. Zooming out shows we're surrounded, N.W.O. agents closing in from every direction. I rush to the door Brooks went through, but it's sealed tight, with no key panels.

The screens show Jacob running straight for me. Skidding into the hallway, I run right into his arms, hot blood flowing as he grabs me. I lay my forehead against his chest, breathing in his scent.

"Brooks escaped," I tell him, eyes on his.

He shrugs. "You're what I came for."

My fingers spread against his chest. "Well, you've got me now."

Sorrow leaps into his eyes, but a window explodes a few feet away. A metallic canister rolls across the hall, ejecting a cloud of smoke.

"Run!"

We sprint down the long hall, windows crashing in behind us.

Jacob puts a small radio to his mouth. "Paco. Extraction, *stat!*"

We careen up the grand staircase, slipping on marble shards. The heavy beat of helicopters makes me cringe.

"I really hate those things," I shout as we crouch against the wall.

"One of them is our ride, so…" He eases under a shattered window, one eye scanning the lawn. "It's a good thing he's coming."

A massive explosion rocks the chandelier and concusses my ears.

"That would be Paco," Jacob says with a grin.

The radio crackles with a Hispanic accent. "East rooftop, fifty-five seconds!"

Jacob nods once, pulling me up and sprinting as the windows explode and the far wall disintegrates, puckered by bullets. Marble shrapnel stings, drawing red down our left sides until we hit the floor. Jacob rolls to his back, pulling two grenades from his vest. He yanks the pins, fingers held tight.

"Clearing a path in three seconds!"

I'm all in, planking an inch off the floor, focused on the door.

Jacob soars past a window headfirst, lobbing both grenades. "Now!"

Dual explosions flare outside, peppering the building as I sprint forward. A savage growl carries me past the shattered glass, and I turn into a room to the left. We sprint up another staircase, this one dark, shielded, near the heart of the mansion.

Two more blasts make Jacob cover my head. He flicks a radio at his chest. "Paco! We're still in here!"

We burst out a door onto a large rooftop veranda. It's a paradise with a central fire pit surrounded by a ring of couches and a garden all around. A helicopter rises, the prop wash forcing the cushions to skitter aside.

The pilot is white-skinned.

Jacob knocks me down as rounds smash over us, the roof behind pulverizing. My ears buzz, reeling from the blasts. As the tail of the chopper explodes, the bird tilts hard, whipping toward us. It spins faster, careening inches above, until it crashes into the mansion, driving deep, sending wood shards into the sky.

The explosion rolls me hard, and I yelp as embers rain down. Jacob lifts me up, one hand locked around my ribs, skin slick from his wound, the other catching a rope dangling from a second helicopter. I'm slipping away in the slick of blood.

Paco's firing at the lawn, front guns pumping out ordnance.

I snatch the rope, desperate. We dangle in the punishing wind, but I can't make the climb on the thin rope. A shadow makes me look up. Margie is there, his wide hands hauling until we crumple on the tilting floor.

Paco shouts, the sound morphing into a wild laugh. The bird swings as he fires, his voice eerie with its Hispanic lilt as he sings at the top of his lungs.

"I, I, I, I, I am the *Frito bandito*." Rounds slam into the forces below. "I love Fritos corn chips, I love them, I dooo." We slide as the chopper lurches, and Paco rains rounds, a garage blowing to bits as his voice ramps higher. "I love Fritos corn chips, and I'll *take them* from youuuu!"

I lie against Jacob's chest, the rotors' thrum vibrating straight through us. The mansion swings out of view, and a wild jungle sweeps away as Margie blocks the doorway.

"Where are we?" I shout, watching Jacob's lips for a response.

He throws back his head in a laugh I can't hear. "Central America. Again."

I look out the window, watching the rainforest race away beneath us, knowing Brooks is out there, his desire for power as dark as ever.

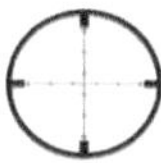

Paco has proved his worth, again. Our long run from the mansion included smaller vehicles until the men agree that the jungle has swallowed us. Paco gets out of an old Jeep, stretching in the humid embrace, wandering into the brush. Jacob's next to me, his good arm over my shoulder. I lift my face to his.

"Sage," he says, but there's torture in his eyes when they find mine. "We… we can't be together." He grimaces. "It's not…" His eyes slide closed. "It's not a happy ending."

I spread my fingers against his chest, trying not to tremble. "I'm not leaving you."

His hand cups my chin. "There's… a place where you can hide from all the hell that's coming. The Almighty will feed you there, provide for you." A single tear falls. "He'll walk with you, Sage, and you'll be safe. I need to know you're safe."

Galel must be around here somewhere, rooting for me. I swallow. It was easy to convince myself this would work when I wasn't staring at the firm set of his chin, recalling how he doesn't give in. Ever. "Yeshua is right here with us now."

"Sage!" he cries, sorrow spilling over. "I *die* at the end of this. Its prophesied. Unchangeable."

Time grinds to a halt.

His words are a knife in my heart. *One way will have great cost to you.* Could there be a heavier price? I open my mouth as searing pain pinches off the words, but it will never change my choice.

Tears fall between us, mingling.

"And you'll be alone after that." His voice wavers in agony.

I nod, blinking until my eyes are clear, and press against him, gazes locked, pouring myself into the words. "Then I want *every... single... second* with you."

His chin tenses, wrinkling. "I can't let you do that."

Come on, Galel. My gaze is steady as I play my trump card, heart fluttering. "It's too late. I already decided. *There.*"

His eyes widen. "But..."

I lean closer, lips almost on his. "It can't be undone. The Almighty gave me a choice, and I chose you *forever.*"

His eyes slide closed, our foreheads together, breathing as one. Relief floods my being, along with searing pain that I shove down, refusing to dwell on sorrow as he draws me closer.

"Soul of my soul," he whispers.

I shut my eyes, pushing away the tears to tilt my face and cover his lips with mine. His hand cradles my neck, drawing me closer.

A branch snaps. We spin toward the sound, reality descending. The giant ferns shift beyond the narrow muddy path. A figure steps out, bearded and so... *familiar.* I cock my head, scowling, skin pricking.

Emerald green eyes stare at us. He's not as muscular, and his curling brown beard is shot through with silver; but I *know* this man.

"Demyen?" Jacob and I whisper together. I lean forward, a shiver racing up my arms.

That grin splits his beard, teeth brilliant. "Aye, Boy."

Jacob laughs as I glance back and forth between them. The two anointed ones, the olive trees that stand before the Almighty. I slide my fingers into Jacob's. He grips them back as we step from the jeep — together.

"So, you jump like we do?" I ask, trying to wrap my head around seeing him *here.*

"No, but, as… a wise man once said, I was in the spirit, on the Lord's Day. I just don't use green haze to get there." His warm voice seems like part of us.

"That might be easier," I say, making them both laugh.

Demyen's face grows serious. "There's not much time until they try the portal again. We've got to be there to stop them."

I touch Jacob's good arm. "Adam Brooks is not an easy man to hunt down."

I tell them everything Brooks said, making the clear jungle air feel greasy.

Demyen sighs. "I should have guessed. Brooks. Of course, they would use that name. Since the dawn of sin, Lucifer has wanted to exceed the Almighty." Demyen clenches his right hand, and Jacob does the same.

I stare at him, brows knit. "Jacob. Your… There's…"

Green haze flows from his nose. I glance at Demyen, but he has the same tendrils twisting toward his right hand.

A helicopter's heavy chop chills my blood. "No."

I reach back and finger the scab on my shoulder. *A tracking chip*. Missing that is inexcusable. I grimace as three sleek black helos appear above the trees. Jacob and Demyen don't flinch as the green fire swirls in their palms. I stare, entranced, as it builds into a brilliant sphere in Jacob's right fist.

They stand, shoulder to shoulder as the copters nose in. In unison, their voices roar over the rotors. Jacob coils back, whipping the fire, and the first bird explodes in midair. The second dives to the side, taking Demyen's fire at the base of its rotors, careening into the jungle.

The jungle all around shudders as the third opens fire—trees snap in half, sending wooden shrapnel skyward. Jacob breathes into his palm, eyes reflecting the leaping flames. His wounded arm hangs at his side, but his right throws true. The chopper goes down like a rocket, sending a mushroom of smoke into the sky.

"And if any man would hurt them, fire proceeds out of their mouth, and devours their enemies: and if any man will hurt them, he must in this manner be killed," Demyen says, staring at the destruction.

Fire *is* spiritual.

Jacob turns to me, searching my face as if he expects revulsion. He reaches out, hesitates, then wipes a tear from my cheek. I step forward, pressing against him. "The safest place for me is right here with you."

His shoulders loosen, that half smile appearing. "I must be slipping. Figured we were way out of range."

"That's my fault." I pull my shirt down over my shoulder. "Care to do the honors?" I ask, pointing to the cut.

"Ah, Brooks." He winces as he digs the chip free.

"And us with no toilet to flush it down."

Everything that's happened since the *Olympia* combines as he shifts closer. My heart pounds as I tilt my head up.

"Kiss the woman," Paco smiles, stepping out from behind a tree.

Jacob draws me closer, running a hand through my hair.

"Thank you," he whispers, blue eyes spanning realms. "I need you here with me."

"Our paths run together," I breathe, pressing in.

Then he kisses me with a passion that makes me forget the jungle, the fight, the calling. In this second, he and I are all that exist.

He leans back. "Sage, I'm gonna rock the boat."

The worlds are mixing, and prophecies long dormant are coming to life.

"I captain, you know?" Paco says, eyeing us. "I can do a… service."

Demyen rubs a hand over his beard. "I'll be your witness."

Jacob laughs. "In more ways than one."

Demyen tilts his head as a grin splits his beard.

My universe is Jacob, right here, holding me close. I tilt my chin, lips brushing his.

"I've got your six, Jacob Carter."

Got Dragons?

Jesus said, "These things I have spoken to you, that in Me you may have peace. In the world you will have tribulation; but be of good cheer, I have overcome the world."

If you've got dragons in your life, then you have a choice to make... what half of that verse will you focus on? If all you see is the tribulation, then that's as far as you'll get, but if you can catch the vision of Jesus the Lord of Victory, then you'll see mountains move, strongholds conquered, and the dragons fallen. Press in, believer!

Go to shilocreed.com to learn more, and don't forget your copy of the Pursued Study Guide! Sign up for the newsletter to stay up to date, and keep an eye out for book 3!

Would you consider leaving a review? I would love to hear your thoughts!

Author Bio

Shilo Creed is a follower of Christ Jesus, with a passion to
share faith with others. After being healed from
a heart condition, seeking the kingdom first became a lifetime
goal. The gospel is the power of God
unto salvation, believe what it says, and you
will find all things are possible.

9 781966 601535